JAGUAR RISING

NOCTURNAL DAWN #1

AMANDA S. GREEN

To Mrs. Winslow, who recognized a young girl's desire to write and encouraged it.

An enemy from her past returns to threaten everything Mac holds dear. Will she be able to protect those she loves and prevent a war between paranormals and humans?

_____

"Ten minutes, ma'am," Marie Duncan said from across the office.

Captain Mackenzie Santos nodded without turning. Instead, she studied her reflection in the mirror over the sink in the small bathroom adjoining her office and carefully adjusted her tie. As she did, her mind wandered. For more than ten years, this office had been her second home. For even longer, the officers of the Dallas Police Department had been her second family. After today, that relationship would change—again—and she didn't know if she was ready for it

And you're dithering—not to mention delaying.

Mac reached for her jacket where it hung on the back of the door and shrugged into it. Her fingers moved almost on their own as she buttoned the jacket and settled it in place. Then she turned a critical eye to the placement of her medals and badge. Over the years, the number of medals had grown. They didn't matter. Not in the grand scheme of things. The badge did. She had worked hard to earn it and she was just as proud of it today as she had been when she first received it what seemed a lifetime ago.

Her phone vibrated, interrupting her thoughts. She pulled it from the inside breast pocket of her jacket and smiled to see the text.

Mom, we're here. You coming?

Her fingers flew across the virtual keyboard of the cellphone as she typed in her response. **On my way. Remember, I'll be sitting onstage.**

Mom, twelve-year-old Cami texted back. Mac didn't need to be there to know her daughter rolled her eyes. **I know. But you aren't here now and you're going to be late.**

Implied was the "again" and a pang of guilt stabbed Mac's heart. Because the job was 24/7, she'd been late or had missed too many important times in her children's lives. That was one of the reasons why she wore her dress blues today.

On my way.

She returned the cellphone to her pocket and once again smoothed her jacket. God, she didn't remember the last time she wore her blues. No, that wasn't right. She did remember. She simply preferred not to. Two years ago, Dallas was hit by one of the worst ice storms in its history. In its wake, a massive multi-car pile-up tangled traffic on one of the main freeways leading into downtown. With more than fifty vehicles involved and who knew how many people trapped, it was all hands on deck for both DPD and Dallas Fire and Rescue. Detectives and uniformed officers worked side-by-side with firefighters to clear the vehicles before more lives were lost.

Among the uniforms assisting at the scene was Officer Karla Benton. For a little more than a year, Benton had been assigned to Sex Crimes, part of Mac's command. Like the exceptional officer she was, Benton accepted the assignment to help direct traffic off the freeway and onto the side streets without complaint.

Less than half an hour later, an approaching car lost control and hit her. The only good to come from the accident was that Benton had been dead before she hit the ground—and before several other cars struck her. They buried her with honors and Mac still mourned her, just as she mourned every cop under her command who fell in the line of duty.

Thankfully, this time was different. She wasn't saying goodbye to anyone.

Instead, she was saying goodbye to a job she loved.

Quit it, Mac. You know this is the right choice, the only choice considering everything.

She straightened her shoulders and nodded once. She could do this.

She needed to do this.

"Ready, ma'am?" Marie stepped forward and Mac stood still as her admin checked her appearance, flicking away a lone piece of lint Mac missed.

"I think so."

"Then quit looking like you're walking to your firing squad. You'll scare the new rookies." Marie smiled, reminding Mac she would help greet the newest class of police academy graduates to the Dallas Police Department.

"Thanks." Mac grinned and slid an arm around the woman's shoulders, giving her a quick hug. "Guess I'm not as sure about all this as I thought."

"All this" was the reason, or at least one of them, for her wearing her dress blues. For the last ten-plus years, she commanded the Crimes Against Persons Division. During that time, the division had changed, mainly because the "persons" in the description of the division took on a whole new meaning. It now included not only humans but shapeshifters and witches. A number of people now l waited for more paranormals to reveal themselves. Mac wasn't one of them. She had her hands more than full dealing with those already out of the proverbial closet.

Especially since she was one of them.

"Mac." Marie cocked her head to one side, her expression concerned. "You don't have to take the job. No one will blame you if you change your mind."

Thinking of her daughter's text and the implied "again", Mac shook her head. No one else might blame her, but she would blame herself. Besides, she'd made the commitment. What kind of example would she set for her children or the cops under her command if she backed out now?

"I have to, Marie. It's time."

In more ways than one.

Together, they left the office. Cops and their families crowded the elevator car, almost all of them heading downstairs to the auditorium where the ceremony would take place. People moved closer together to make room, a few greeting Mac by name and others by rank. As the doors slid shut with a groan, she offered up a silent prayer to the elevator gods to get them to the ground floor safely. When the doors slowly opened a short time later, Mac elbowed her way off, apologizing as she did. All she wanted was to get out of there before the doors closed again, sealing them inside the all-too-often temperamental elevator car.

While Marie joined the crush of others moving inside the auditorium, Mac made her way down the corridor toward the stage entrance. As she did, she texted Cami, letting the girl know she was there. Then she put on her game face. She would not, could not let anyone see her doubts.

Stop it! It's not like you're leaving the force. It's just a new command. That's all. So quit acting like the world's about to end.

Unfortunately, that was easier said than done.

But, if she was honest with herself, she felt the same way when she was promoted to captain and took over command of the CaP Division. The circumstances had been different. Dear God, how they'd been different. The assassination of her captain and two other good cops led to her promotion. Even though she'd dreamed of one day commanding the division, she never dreamed it would happen like that.

She certainly hadn't wanted it to be at the cost of Michael King's life. He'd been more than her captain. He had been friend, mentor and pride leader. Hell, he had been one of the three who kept her sane when she started turning furry.

She shook herself. Now wasn't the time to get lost in those memories. Mike wouldn't thank her for it. He might even come back and haunt her for being such an idiot. Chuckling softly at the thought, she pushed open the door leading to backstage and stepped inside.

Show time, whether she liked it or not.

Damn, but life had been so much easier before she started turning furry.

"Ladies and gentlemen, please join me in welcoming the newest members of the Dallas Police Department," Chief of Police Darnell Culver said half an hour later.

As he spoke, the thirty-five new officers stood. At the same time, every cop in the room rose and saluted them. Civilians clapped and cheered. Culver stepped away from the podium. When he did, one of DPD's training sergeants called the rookies to attention. Culver returned their salutes and then motioned for everyone to return to their seats. As they did, Mac smiled slightly, proud to be part of this family of blue.

A family Culver headed. He might have aged since he took over as chief, but he hadn't changed. Not where it counted. He was the first in a very long time to work his way up to the Chief's office from within the ranks. That was one reason the rank and file respected him as much as they did. Another reason was because they knew he had their backs. Oh, he had no use for cops who didn't follow the rules and had made that clear over the years, but he also didn't back down when anyone, no matter who, tried to take pot shots—literal and figurative —at his cops. That was something this new crop of cops would soon learn. . . and something every cop would miss when Culver retired.

The thought brought with it another memory. Not that long ago, both she and Culver tendered their resignations to the then-mayor, Carter Z. Humbolt, when he demanded they misrepresent evidence in a murder investigation. Culver convinced her to hold onto hers until after the election. After all, the mayor faced stiff competition for the office and it might be he would lose. If he did, the new mayor was a strong supporter of the force and wouldn't try to put them into the position the then-mayor did. She'd agreed, albeit reluctantly. Fortunately for them, and even more so for the city, they soon had a new mayor. In his time in office, he'd proven not only to be a solid friend of the force but of the paranormals in town as well. Because of that, Mac had few regrets about her decision to keep her badge.

"Ladies and gentlemen, today is very special for the DPD," Culver continued once everyone returned to their seats. "Not only are we welcoming these thirty-five new officers to our ranks, but we have several well-deserved promotions to announce as well."

Mac looked out at the audience from where she sat at one side of the stage. She smiled slightly to see her family. Jackson, her husband and mate, sat between their children, twelve-year-old Cami and five-year-old Xander. Mac's mother, Elizabeth, sat next to Xander. Her dark hair, now threaded with silver, and the few wrinkles at the corners of her eyes the only things betraying her age. For a moment, Mac's heart hurt. Her mother was a normal with a normal human's lifespan. That meant she would die too soon, much too soon. Especially since they'd been estranged for so long until they finally patched things up between them. So Mac relished all the time they spent together and pride filled her to have Liz there, especially since her mother had refused to come when she was first sworn in as an officer.

Sitting next to Cami was Mac's grandmother. Like Mac, Ellen Santos was a shifter. She was, in fact, one of the most powerful shifters alive. And, because of what she was, she enjoyed a longer life and didn't look as old as her daughter. However, Ellen learned long ago the need to hide what she was and had mastered makeup techniques. Now she looked like an eighty-something year old blessed with good genes and probably some careful plastic surgery. Without the makeup, she looked maybe sixty.

Cami caught her mother's eye and grinned, waving. Mac nodded once, a smile lifting the corners of her mouth. Then she turned her attention back to Culver.

"Lt. Patricia Collins King."

Pride and affection filled Mac as Culver called her former partner forward. The blonde stood and marched smartly across the stage. When she stopped in front of the chief, she braced to attention. As she did, only those who knew her well realized how nervous and how proud the woman was.

Or how hard she fought to hold back her emotions.

"Approximately fifteen years ago," Culver continued, "one of the best police officers I knew was killed in an ambush that cost not only him but two other excellent cops their lives. That officer was Captain Michael King. It is only fitting that today, when she is promoted to captain and begins her new assignment as commanding officer of the Crimes Against Persons Division, his widow is presented with his captain's bars." Culver looked to his left, to where Mac and the other officers receiving promotions or new assignments sat.

As Mac stood to join them, memories washed over her. She and Pat had been thrown together as partners by Michael King. At the time, Mac never guessed the changes that seemingly simple action would bring to her life. Pat had been there when Mac started shifting. She helped Mac accept what she'd become and, with help from King and Jackson, kept her from eating her gun. Soon, she and Mac were more than partners. They became friends, even family. There was no one Mac could see taking over CaP from her except Pat.

"Attention!" Mac said once she stood next to Culver.

Pat braced to attention. She swallowed hard as Culver held out his left hand. Mac pulled a jeweler's box from her pocket. Seeing the tears suddenly pooling in Pat's eyes, she smiled slightly and nodded in understanding. The blonde knew the box and what it represented. She'd treasured both since shortly after her husband's death.

"I believe this honor should fall to you, Captain Santos," Culver said softly.

"Thank you, sir."

Now it was Mac's turn to swallow hard against the lump of emotion in her throat. She glanced down and opened the box, removing its contents. Then she placed the box in the Chief's extended hand. Once she had, she stepped forward, holding Pat's gaze.

Very carefully, she pinned King's captain's bars, the ones he'd worn the day of the ambush, to Pat's collar. Then she stepped back, watching as Culver handed Pat her new badge. Once he had, the two of them braced to attention, accepting Pat's salute and returning it. As they did, Mac chuckled softly to hear not only the applause that welcomed Pat's promotion but the cheers of Pat's son, fourteen-year-old Mike, as well as her own children.

"Dismissed, Captain King," Culver said with a smile. Pat executed a perfect about-face and walked back to her seat at the side of the stage.

"Remain where you are, Captain Santos. You're next."

The gleam in Culver's eyes warned her he was about to go off-script. Swallowing even harder than Pat had earlier, Mac waited, wondering if it was too late to make a break for it.

"Ladies and gentlemen, from the moment she joined the Dallas Police Department, Mackenzie Santos promised to be one of our best. I've had the pleasure of watching her grow from a raw rookie patrol officer into a seasoned detective and gifted commanding officer. She has always put her duty above her own interests, often placing herself in danger to protect the citizens of this great city of ours.

"She has accepted every challenge we've presented her. That includes being instrumental in helping the Department adapt to the changing needs of our community as the world around us has changed. She's been our point of contact when we've worked with federal authorities on matters concerning many of those changes. If that's not enough, she is also a loving wife and mother."

Mac felt her face heat. Couldn't he just get on with it?

"It is no secret here at Headquarters that Captain Santos has refused promotion several times now."

Mac couldn't help it. She ground her teeth, fighting the urge to snarl as Culver very carefully avoided looking at her.

"Like any good CO, she didn't want to leave her command to just any person. That's something I reminded her when she recommended Captain King be on today's promotion list." Now he grinned like a kid who scored unexpectedly in some playground game. "Not only did Captain King deserve her promotion, but it gave me the leverage I needed to ask Captain Santos to once again step up and answer the call."

He turned his attention to Mac. As he did, the chief of detectives moved to his side. Waiting, Mac reminded herself she couldn't turn and run, no matter how tempting it might be.

"But that left me with a quandary. I already knew what her new command would be. The only question was her rank."

Mac's eyes went wide, and she didn't attempt to hold back her growl. He was most definitely up to something and she did not like it one bit.

"By rights, she should already hold the rank of assistant chief. However, she's been a bit stubborn." He grinned and she bared her teeth. "So I consulted DPD and Texas law enforcement history. After that, I made the decision to follow the example of several of other agencies here in the state."

As he spoke, he removed Mac's captain's bars, replacing them with her new rank insignia, something he very carefully kept hidden from her. Then he once again looked out over the audience.

"It is my extreme pleasure to present to you Colonel Mackenzie Santos, the new commanding officer of the Special Crimes Bureau. Congratulations, Colonel."

"Thank you, sir." She shook his extended hand and then narrowed her eyes when he glanced to the far side of the stage.

"You aren't dismissed quite yet, Colonel," he said softly as he released her hand and stepped back.

Mac frowned. Culver was up to something. She knew it just as she knew she probably wasn't going to like whatever it was. Unfortunately, he had her right where he wanted her—onstage in front of everyone where she couldn't beat a hasty retreat.

Or so he thought.

Mac inhaled sharply, the color draining from her face as she recognized the man in Marine mass dress uniform who stepped out from the shadows. General Gerald Flynn shouldn't be there. He certainly shouldn't be there in uniform.

Damn it, what were he and Culver up to?

She waited, muscles tensing, as the general neared.

As he approached, Mac carefully considered her options. She was fast, especially with her adrenaline spiking. She could outrun pretty much everyone without having to shift. Of course, it wouldn't change things, only postpone them. Besides, she might be borrowing trouble that wasn't there.

Riiiight.

And she might start turning into a cute little bunny instead of a jaguar.

At that thought, her jaguar-self, Cait, rose up in the back of her mind, wanting to know if she got to eat the little bunny. Cait sent Mac an image of them hunting little bunny foo-foo that had Mac forcing herself not to smile, much less laugh.

"Ladies and gentlemen, General Gerald Flynn, United States Marine Corps," Culver said and stepped aside.

"Thank you, Chief Culver." Flynn glanced at Mac, amusement dancing in his eyes. Then he turned his attention to those gathered. "As Chief Culver said, Mackenzie Santos has dedicated her professional life to protecting the citizens of this wonderful city. What you might not know is she also answered the call of our country to help protect it as well."

A murmur ran through the crowd that had Mac once again considering making a run for it.

"Before joining the Dallas Police Department, Mackenzie Santos served as a member of the United States Marine Corps."

Someone near the rear of the auditorium gave a shout of "ooh-rah!" and Mac closed her eyes before counting to ten. This was most definitely not going the way she expected.

"Ooh-rah, indeed," Flynn said with a grin. "She served with distinction. Despite her dedication to country and Corps, her heart belonged here. She left active duty and entered the police academy. Even so, she didn't hesitate when called back to duty to help deal with a dangerous situation with implications that went far beyond the Dallas city limits. She proved then, as she has so many times before and since, that she is the embodiment of the motto 'to serve and protect'.

"When Former-President Montford revealed the existence of shapeshifters to the world, Colonel Santos and others like her helped form special taskforces to aide local law enforcement when it came to crimes committed by or against paranormals. She's been key in helping the police and military adapt to this new normal."

He moved to stand in front of her and Mac once again braced to attention. Moving only her eyes, she watched as he pulled something from his pocket. As he did, Culver moved to his side.

"In the Marine Reserves, Mackenzie Santos holds the rank of colonel. However, she is much more than a typical reserve officer. Because of that, President Micah Duscayne and the Congress of the United States wanted to reward her for her service. There was serious discussion about promoting her to the rank of brigadier general."

Mac's eyes went wide. Without realizing it, she took an involuntary step back. No. This couldn't be happening. Flynn knew better than to try this. She didn't care if there were others present. Insubordination didn't come close to covering what she was about to do. Then Flynn chuckled softly. Mac glared at him, daring him to continue.

"As you can see, Colonel Santos is more than a bit averse to receiving another promotion, just as Chief Culver said."

Mac growled deep in her throat before returning to her place in front of the general. He would pay for this. She wasn't sure how, but he would. She'd make sure of it.

"So let me reassure her that I'm not going to risk her making a run for it."

Now the audience joined in his laughter. If she hadn't been close to doing exactly that, she might have resented it. Instead, she waited, eyes narrowed as he opened the small box he held and withdrew something before handing the box to Culver. Mac swallowed hard as he cocked his head and studied her.

"You are technically out of uniform, Colonel, but I'll forgive it this time." Flynn smiled at her, his eyes dancing with devilment. "Colonel Mackenzie Santos, it is my extreme pleasure to present you with the Liberty Cross." He glanced at the audience before continuing. "Until this year, only five others had received this award. It recognizes a member of the Armed Forces, one who is a paranormal and who has gone beyond all expectations to preserve and protect the very foundations of our nation. I can think of no one who deserves this recognition more than Mackenzie Santos who has, time and again, put her personal welfare behind her determination to protect this nation and those who live here. Congratulations, Colonel." He paused, pitching his voice for her ears only. "This is only because we know you'd resign and hide from us for the next decade or two if we tried for more."

He stepped back and saluted. Instinct alone had Mac returning his salute. She certainly couldn't have figured out what to do otherwise. Not with her brain babbling incoherently.

"Colonel Santos will continue to command the reserve division code named Ghostwalkers. Their mission will continue to be working with local and state law enforcement agencies in matters concerning paranormals," Flynn said as he stepped back and Culver once again took his place.

"Colonel Santos." Culver grinned and looked out at the audience. "I charge you to continue doing as you have for so long: keep our city and its citizens safe." He leaned in a bit closer. "And don't try to run, Mac. We will find you." He chuckled softly as she once again growled deep in her throat.

"You can try, sir," she replied just as softly.

"Dismissed, Colonel."

Mac returned to her seat, barely hearing the cheers from her children, the Marines under her command who had someone managed to get in without her knowing it and the others in the crowd.

Damn it, all she wanted was to be the best detective she could be. When and how had she become the brass?

2

Mac carefully closed her office door and leaned against it. As she did, she closed her eyes and inhaled, striving for calm. Somehow, she managed to hold her temper in check for the past hour. She didn't even go running to the hills. Instead, she smiled, shook hands and made small talk with other cops, their families and even a few politicians and members of the press.

Dear God, the press. Whose brilliant idea was it to let them attend the ceremony?

Unfortunately, she knew the answer. Chief Culver. Like most of the police chiefs before him, he wanted media coverage of events like this to show the human side of the DPD. It was a PR event as much as anything. That wasn't necessarily bad, but did she have to be part of it?

Damn it, why the hell had she gotten out of bed that morning?

"Cami, Xander, I need to talk to Gran and Grandma for a minute. You two wait here. I promise we won't be long."

Please let them agree without argument. She didn't need any more stress just then.

Her daughter's brow furrowed, but it was five-year-old Xander who protested. "Mom, you said we could go." He didn't stomp his foot, but it was a close call.

"We will soon."

"Mom, I'm hungry. I wanna go now."

This time he did stomp his foot. Jackson started to say something, but Mac shook her head.

"Xander, there's no way you can be hungry. I know you had at least two pieces of cake." And that despite her telling him one piece only.

After the swearing in of the new rookies and the promotion ceremony, Mac and the others stayed for the official pictures and for the first hour of the reception. No matter how much she wanted to escape, Mac knew she couldn't. Seeing how proud her family was of her, not to mention wanting to be there for Pat and all the others, she accepted a cup of coffee and a slice of cake—which had been surprisingly good—and contented herself with the knowledge that they'd soon be able to slip away. Later, they would stop by the Irish Rose Pub for dinner and a drink or three. Then it would be home where she could finally relax with the people who mattered—her family.

First, however, she needed to deal with her son and get a few answers from her grandmother.

"Xander, I promise we will leave just as soon as I change clothes and have a quick talk with your grandmother and great-grandmother." When he opened his mouth to say something, Mac tilted her head and arched one brow, unconsciously mirroring her grandmother's expression when Mac or one of her cousins did or said something they shouldn't.

"Yes, ma'am," he drawled and scrubbed his toe against the floor.

Cami looked at her mother for a long moment and then grabbed her brother's hand. "C'mon, Xan. I bet Aunt Jael has some candy in her office. How 'bout we check it out?"

Mac stepped away from the door and watched as they moved into the corridor. A moment later, they turned into the next office. Making sure they didn't turn right back around, Mac waited. Then she once again closed the door. As she did, Jackson moved to her side. His hand reached for hers and their fingers twined. That was enough to remind her she wasn't alone in this. Not now and not ever.

"Gran." She pinned her grandmother with a look that would have sent her kids running for cover. Ellen, however, simply stood there, one silver brow arched. "Did you know?"

"Did I know what?"

"Flynn's little surprise."

Ellen shook her head. When she did, Mac frowned slightly. Her grandmother would never lie to her, so that meant Flynn hadn't told her. But that didn't make any sense. Flynn worked closely with Ellen in her role as head of the Tribunal. Taking part in Mac's promotion and bringing public attention to her unit was most definitely one of those things he should have discussed with her. More than that, the two were old friends. So why hadn't he told her?

Or had Mac not been specific enough with her question?

"Gran, I don't mean being here for the ceremony. I meant the medal and his talk about promoting me."

And thank God, that hadn't happened.

Now Ellen had the grace to smile slightly and shrug.

"He didn't say anything to me beyond how he wished he could be here for the ceremony," she said. "But I knew there were changes coming to his command. Your cousin called yesterday to let me know he's been promoted to brigadier general and given command over all the units in the Western US. I also knew the president and others in Congress were making noise about promoting you. When Ger talked to me about it, I told him you'd turn the promotion down and warned there would be members of the Tribunal who would look at the promotion with suspicion." Now she held up a hand, stopping anything Mac or the others might have said. "Not because any of us doubt your qualifications or that you deserve it. Call it a suspicion that certain politicians were using it to gain influence with you and, by extension, the rest of the Tribunal."

Mac nodded, understanding. That was one thing she'd worried about since they made their existence public. Politicians were politicians and they would use anything to their advantage if it would score them political points.

"I didn't know about the medal." Now Ellen smiled proudly at her granddaughter. "But it is something I wholeheartedly agree with." She lightly cupped Mac's cheek with one hand. "You are the second member of the family to earn that medal. Your grandfather received the very first one handed out."

Mac blinked, surprised. "Really?"

Ellen nodded. "I still have it. I'll show it to you when we get home."

"I'd like that." And she'd like to hear how her grandfather earned it. But that was for later.

"Mac, I know Ger and Culver ambushed you with all this. I wish they hadn't, but I understand. The world has changed. I think for the better because now, with our kind and the witches public, we don't need to worry as much about keeping news of crimes involving us secret."

Now it was Mac's turn to nod.

"And you, better than the rest of us, know most of the crimes involving our kind or the witches are crimes committed against us. There are groups who still believe we should be killed or locked up and dissected. That makes what you do so very important. Just as it is important those who want to harm us know someone will stand up to them."

Mac couldn't argue, not that she wanted to. She'd dealt with people like those her grandmother mentioned. They made her life "interesting" all too often. Fortunately, they were the minority and laws had been put in place to protect the paranormals before they made their existence known to the public. That was due, in large part, to the efforts of her grandmother and General Flynn and others like them.

"And the medal?"

"I suspected he had something planned, especially after he finally admitted promoting you right now would not be the best thing."

Mac nodded, glad her grandmother had been able to head that complication off.

"And?" Mac relaxed enough to lean against the wall. As she did, she motioned for the others to have a seat.

"As I said, Mateo called yesterday. To say he was stunned is putting it mildly. It seems Gerald showed up unannounced and promoted him to brigadier general and put him in command of all your units west of the Mississippi." She smiled at the memory before sobering. "And, before you ask, I didn't know about that either until your cousin called."

"Mom, I don't understand," Elizabeth admitted as she looked from her daughter to her mother.

"I think I do." Jackson slid an arm across Mac's shoulders and pulled her close. "I think Flynn let Ellen know changes were afoot. But, when she and others quashed his idea to promote Mac, he came up with something different. Something he didn't tell Ellen about."

Ellen nodded.

"Okay." Mac sighed and pushed away from the wall. "But tell your buddy the general that I really don't like surprises and I owe him for this one." Not to mention for everything he said.

Ellen smiled and Mac groaned, recognizing the amusement in her grandmother's expression.

"What?" she drawled, sounding very much like her daughter at that moment.

"I reminded him of just that during the reception?"

"And?"

And did she really want to know?

"He told me the President still wants to promote you to brigadier general. Something about recognizing and rewarding service to the country."

Mac's eyes went wide, and she shook her head. Nope. That wasn't going to happen. Not now and not ever. Nope, nope and hell nope.

"Don't worry. Even though Ger agrees, he knows you. He told the President you'd run for the hills. But you need to understand the plan is in motion, Mac. The day will come when they consider it again."

Then she'd have to make it very clear to the general and everyone else that she didn't want the promotion and wouldn't accept it. She had more than enough on her plate as it was between her duties with the DPD, the Tribunal, Flynn and her family. At least her grand-mother seemed to understand.

Before she could say anything else, the door opened. Cami and Xander entered and Mac chuckled softly. Judging by the paper plate with the remnants of yet another piece of cake on it, "Aunt Jael" had more than candy in her office. But at least the boy seemed happy if messy, with cake crumbs and icing ringing his mouth and dribbling down the front of his shirt.

"Let me change and we'll get out of here," she said as she ruffled Xander's hair. Then she mouthed a silent *thank you* over his head to Cami.

"Mom?"

"C'mon, Cam. You can help me." She draped an arm across Cami's shoulders and led her through back to the small bathroom. "What's up?" she asked once they were alone.

"Are you going to keep this office?"

Mac glanced through the door to her private office and shook her head. Maintenance was packing up the last of her personal and professional belongings in preparation for moving them upstairs. By Monday, this would no longer be her office.

"No, sweets. Aunt Pat's going to get this office. She needs it so she's close to her command."

"But it's your command, too. Isn't it?"

Mac finished unbuttoning her shirt and slipped out of it. As she reached for a DPD polo, she nodded.

"It is, but it isn't the only division under my command now." She pulled on the polo and kicked out of her shoes. "Besides, it's only right Aunt Pat gets this office now. It used to be her husband's office before it was mine."

Cami thought for a moment. She'd been born after Michael King's death in that thrice-damned ambush. But she'd grown up with stories about the man. She knew how important he'd been to her parents and now, showing a maturity that always impressed her mother, she nodded in understanding.

"What about Marie? She used to work for him. Is she going to stay here and work for Aunt Pat?"

"That's up to her."

What Mac didn't say was how much she hoped Marie stayed with her. In her time as captain, she'd come to rely on the woman, not just as an admin but as friend and confidante. Still, she knew Marie was devoted to Pat, as she had been to King. Because of that, she'd forced herself to leave the decision to Marie and, now that Cami brought it up, she worried about what that decision might be.

But Marie wasn't the only one of her inner circle Mac was leaving the decision to when it came to what to do now that Mac was assuming a new command. Jael Lindsay had been offered a promotion to captain. With the promotion would come command of the Central Patrol Division. Even though Jael hadn't talked about it, Mac knew her mentor was torn. Jael was a patrol officer at heart. She'd been Mac's first training officer. Hell, she was one of the best training officers in the history of the Department. But, when Mac needed her when Pat and others had been kidnapped by renegade Pures and lycans, Jael left her beloved patrol assignment. She did so again when it became clear new dangers were being presented that could expose the existence of shifters. For most of the last five years, she'd been Mac's aide and partner.

There was another reason Mac wanted Jael to remain on her staff. Jael might be human, but she had known about shifters long before they made their existence known to the world at-large. In fact, she'd know about them before Mac did. She understood the politics of the current situation, especially those between pures and lycans, much better than Mac did, although Mac was getting better. She also knew how to keep Mac from taking the heads off idiot politicians who thought they knew what was best for everyone when the opposite was true. Even so, Mac would not stand in her way if she wanted the new assignment. If a miracle happened and Jael turned down the transfer, Mac planned to make sure she still received the promotion to captain.

If for no other reason than to see the woman who still considered herself nothing more than a Marine gunny try to wrap her mind around the fact she was now brass.

"All right. Let's get the others and I'll take you upstairs to see my new office. Then we can get out of here." Mac buckled her belt and checked her appearance in the mirror. Better. She much preferred the golf shirt and jeans to her dress blues.

Cami grinned and raced out in front of her. As they entered the outer office, the others turned to look at them. Mac grinned, love filling her at the sight of her family. Jackson had loosened his tie and now held Xander at his hip. Fortunately, someone had tried to clean the little boy up after his last piece of cake. Elizabeth and Ellen stood nearby, smiling indulgently at the boy. As she watched Cami hurry to stand between her grandmother and great-grandmother, Mac knew this was what was important, what she fought for. Now all she wanted was to get out of there and spend some time with the most important people in her life.

"Mom's going to take us to see her new office."

"Cool!" Xander wriggled out of his father's arms and raced to his sister, grabbing her hand and tugging her out of the office. "C'mon. I wanna see it," he called over his shoulder.

Laughing, Mac reached for Jackson's hand and brought it to her lips. Then she shook her head as the sounds of the two racing to the elevators reached her. "I guess we ought to catch up."

"Or we could let them wait for us," Elizabeth said with a smile. Then she turned serious. "Are you all right, Mac?"

She nodded. "I am. Flynn just caught me off-guard." Not to mention Culver and his announcement of her new rank. Something else she needed to discuss with the man at the first opportunity. "Sorry about earlier."

"Don't apologize, child." Ellen moved to stand in front of her and lightly cupped Mac's cheek with one hand. "You were blindsided, we all were. But look at it this way. All that really changed is that more people know about your other *job*." Mac couldn't help it. She snickered when her grandmother used air quotes around the last word. "You've been using your military team to help other law enforcement agencies for years now. It's become more and more rare for you to have to act without bringing them in. It's time the public knew that as well. It may actually help quell some of the animosity toward us."

Mac nodded. That was one thing about being out of the closet. There were still times when an accused wasn't turned over to local authorities but that was usually because they didn't have facilities set up to hold a paranormal for more than a few hours. Even so, there were still some offenses that went straight to the Tribunal for disposition instead of state or federal court.

"Mom!"

Xander's voice echoed up and down the hall and Mac shook her head. She really did need to have a talk with him. Then she grinned and led the others out, closing the door after them. Come Monday, this would no longer be her office and it was more than a little bittersweet.

"Auntie Marie!"

Xander ran across the outer office and all but launched himself at the older woman as they entered Mac's new office suite. Marie braced herself, well used to the boy's exuberant greetings. Hugging him, she looked up at the others, grinning to see Mac's stunned expression as she looked around.

Mac couldn't believe it. She'd checked the office not twenty-four hours earlier. Now it boasted a new coat of paint, a light cream that was much better than the putty gray it had been. A new, if somewhat utilitarian, desk sat to one side of the door in the far wall. Someone from Tech Services worked behind it, setting up the new computer and comms system. From the inner office came the sounds of more people busy at work. Miracle or dream, Mac didn't care—especially if this meant Marie was making the transfer with her.

"Marie?"

"I wanted to make a quick check before leaving for the day, Colonel." The woman grinned as she used Mac's new rank in the Department for the first time. "And don't worry. I'll be in bright and early Monday to make sure everything's been done to your satisfaction."

"She's a taskmaster, Colonel," the tech said with a grin as he briefly looked up from his work. "Congrats on the promotions, ma'am."

Mac laughed and thanked him before turning her attention back to Marie. "Does this mean?" She couldn't quite finish the question. She didn't dare in case she was wrong.

Marie motioned for Mac and the others to join her at the far side of the office. Worried, Mac followed. She did her best not to drag her feet, but it was difficult. If Marie wasn't coming with her, she didn't want to hear it. Not now.

Hell, not ever.

"First of all, I want to thank you for not pressuring me one way or the other, Mac." She smiled and rested a light hand on Mac's arm. "And I'll admit it wasn't as easy a decision as I thought it would be. Pat deserves the promotion but it's going to be difficult for her, at least in the beginning. She's moving into the position Captain King held for so long and into his office. That's going to bring back memories."

Mac nodded. She'd had to deal with her own memories and doubts when she took over the office.

"I won't lie, Mac. She and I did have a long discussion about it. Several of them, in fact."

Mac's eyebrows winged up. It didn't surprise her, but she thought one of them would have said something about it before now.

"And?" She held her breath and then smiled as Cami slipped her hand into hers.

"She's sworn she's going to poach me from you if you ever give her the chance." Marie grinned as Mac growled and shook her head. "Seriously, we decided it would be best for her to have a clean start. I've already lined up several interviews with people I think will be excellent as her admin." Now Marie's expression softened, and she reached for Mac's free hand.

"Mac, I know you worried, but I never planned on leaving your staff. I enjoy working for and with you. The fact you didn't try to pressure me or pester me to finding out what I planned on doing is just one reason why. You're the best boss I've ever had and that includes Captain King. Besides, I'm not about to let you start on this new journey without me."

Mac dropped her daughter's hand and pulled Marie into a hug. "Thank you. I couldn't do this without you."

"You could and you would, but I'm not going to let you."

"What about me?"

At the sound of her former mentor's voice, Mac turned and grinned like a kid with a pocket full of change in a candy store. Jael Lindsay stood in the doorway of Mac's private office. The lieutenant still wore her dress blues. In one hand, she held a clipboard and Mac had no doubt she'd been checking off a list of things needing to be done before Mac officially took possession of the office.

"I thought you'd jump at the chance to take over Central."

Jael shook her head. "I considered it, but I had to admit soft clothes are much more comfortable than our blues."

Mac grinned and waited as Jael joined them. Then she turned serious. She didn't want Jael turning down a promotion.

"Don't," Jael said. "I had a long talk with both Assistant Chief Montenegro and Chief Culver. They understand my decision and I gave them several names to consider instead."

"But your promotion, Aunt Jael," Cami said.

"It will come, kiddo. Besides, I don't need it. That's something your mom and Chief Culver seem to forget. I'm not an officer. Not really. I'm just a non-com masquerading as one."

"And that is the best sort of officer," Mac laughed. Then she looked down and smiled as Xander tugged at her hand. She lifted him and settled him at her hip before continuing. "I really do appreciate it and I hope you both know how much I appreciate you. I can't tell you how much it means that you're sticking with me."

"Someone's got to keep you in line, kid." Jael's eyes sparkled in amusement.

Mac had the good grace to nod as everyone else laughed in agreement.

"Let's get out of here. All of us." Mac handed Xander to his father. "Join us at the Irish Rose?"

"Sounds good," Jael said, and Marie nodded in agreement. "We'll meet you there. I want to get out of my blues first."

"We'll see you soon then." Mac hugged Marie and lightly punched Jael's shoulder. Then she led her family out of the office.

"We going now, Mom?" Xander asked as they entered the elevator.

"We are." The doors slid shut as she programmed the car. "Mom, Gran, why don't you take them on ahead? I need to stop by the office and pick up a couple of things. Jack and I will meet you at the pub."

"You take your own advice and don't be long," Elizabeth said. "How about it, kids? Shall we head on out?"

Five minutes later, Mac stood in the middle of what would soon be Pat's office and looked around. Most of her personal things had already been packed. Some would be taken upstairs to her new office. Others she'd take home. This was an end of one part of her life, an important one. Hopefully, the next would be better.

"You okay?" Jackson asked as he picked up a banker's box Marie had carefully packed and labelled earlier.

"Just feeling a little nostalgic." She smiled and shrugged. "So much happened in this office. This is where I first confronted Mike about what we are and if he assigned Pat as my partner because he was worried I'd been turned by the lycan that attacked me. I didn't know it for a long time, but this is where he told Marie about our kind and she swore to do all she could to protect him and us. It's going to be strange not coming here every day."

He nodded and moved to her side. "I know, love. But you earned the promotion and Mike would be the first one to tell you to take it. You know that."

She did.

She even knew she deserved the promotion. But this was so far from what she envisioned her career with the Department being when she first joined. The promotion also meant her time in the field would be severely curtailed. That's what she really wasn't ready for. As captain, she didn't get into the field nearly as much as she wanted. As colonel and bureau chief it would be even less.

Unless. . . .

She grinned, realizing Culver had given her an out. The Special Crimes Bureau was hers. It was unlike any other bureau in the Department. That meant she could make her own rules, up to a point. Perhaps she could still get out into the field once in a while.

"Mac?" Jackson looked at her in concern.

"I'm okay." And she was. "Just thinking about some of the new challenges in front of me." She reached for the box resting on the corner of her desk and lifted it, settling it on her hip much as she had settled their son not that long ago. "Let's go."

"Where are you parked?" Jackson asked as they stepped onto the elevator for the parking garage a short time later."

"I got lucky and found a space on the first level this morning." She pressed the button, surprised they had the car to themselves. Apparently, many of those in attendance left as soon as they could after the ceremony. Everyone else would wait until shift change.

"Good. I wondered since you left your space open for us."

She lifted one shoulder in a half-shrug and stepped off the elevator as the doors opened. "I knew it would be a madhouse by the time you could get here."

They loaded the boxes in the back of Mac's SUV. Jackson chuckled softly as his wife moved to the driver's door and slid in behind the wheel. Normally, she let him drive. But this was her department issued vehicle. Even if regulations allowed him to drive, she wouldn't. Not that he blamed her. Still, he had one thing he wanted to do before they drove off.

"Come here." He took her chin between his thumb and two fingers and turned her face toward him. She gave a cocky grin as she realized what he wanted. One finger lightly traced her lips and he leaned in. "I'm proud of you, Mac. Why don't we see if your mother won't take the kids home with her tonight so we can celebrate?"

She sighed against his mouth and kissed him again. "I think that sounds like a wonderful idea."

Mac felt more than heard a low rumble as she turned the key in the ignition. Frowning, she sat there, hand on the gear stick. Her heart beat quicker as the concrete beneath the tires began a slow vibration.

No. Oh hell, no!

Without warning, she slammed the transmission into reverse. Tires squealed as she ordered Jackson to hold on. A moment later, she slammed on the brakes. The SUV rocked back and forth for a split-second. Then she threw the transmission into drive.

Get out. Get out. Get out.

The SUV shot up the drive, tire screeching as she took first one and then another curve. As they neared the exit, the rumbling grew louder. The pavement bucked and rolled. Mac cursed, fighting to keep control of the vehicle. Dust fell like rain from the ceiling, followed by pieces of concrete that pounded against the roof of the SUV like hail.

"Mac!" Jackson pointed to the parking arm blocking the exit.

"Hold on!"

She floored the accelerator and said a silent prayer. The fiberglass arm broke under the force of the speeding SUV, flying up, hitting the windshield. Mac cursed as the windshield spiderwebbed, making it difficult to see. Then the SUV seemed to take flight. It hit the pavement a moment later, throwing them forward. Sparks flew as the undercarriage dragged impacted the concrete. Mac spun the steering wheel, fighting for control. She cursed again as she clipped a car parked across the street from the parking garage exit.

A moment that felt like a lifetime later, she slammed on the brakes. The rear of the SUV slewed this way and that. The dark vehicle rocked dangerously, threatening to tip over. None of that mattered as the rumble grew louder and Mac recognized it for what it was.

"NO!"

3

Mac twisted in her seat, staring out the rear window. Smoke and dust billowed from the parking garage. The earth trembled beneath them. Earthquake? Possible, but training told her no. Explosion. At the moment, it didn't matter if it was accidental or intentional. People were in danger and she had to do something.

Her kids!

Her heart clinched at the thought of her children, mother and grandmother. Surely, they left the garage before the explosion. They left before she and Jackson. They might even be at the pub by now.

Please, let them be safe.

The building shook and she once again slammed the transmission into gear. "Call my mom!" she yelled as she sped down the street. The last thing she wanted was to be caught in the fallout if the building should collapse.

"I'm trying," he ground out.

She nodded and contacted Dispatch. Cursing as she waited to get through, she pulled the car across the road, blocking traffic. With Jackson still desperately trying number after number, she climbed out, telling him to stay there. She needed him to find their family. She'd take care of the rest.

"Dispatch, Colonel Mackenzie King. I'm on scene outside of HQ. Roll EMTs, Fire, EOD. Hell, roll everyone to this location. There's been an explosion of some sort in the main parking garage. I've blocked traffic to the east with my department vehicle. Tell sector command to set up a perimeter of—" She thought for a moment. – "Four blocks in all directions. We need to evac surrounding buildings, begin SAR and contain the scene."

"Roger that, Colonel. You are senior officer to report in so far."

"Any word on Chief Culver?"

"Negative, Colonel."

She nodded grimly. God, how she prayed someone higher up the chain of command showed up soon.

"Contact Assistant Chief Dolan. Request he get down here soonest." Dolan was Culver's second-in-command. Until they located Culver, he'd be in charge, assuming he wasn't trapped in the garage. "Keep me informed as the brass reports in."

For a moment, she looked around. God, this was a nightmare. People were pouring out of police headquarters and the nearby buildings. Seeing cops she knew, and uniforms she didn't, she called to them, issuing orders. They needed to get the scene under control before anything else happened.

"Ramirez!" she shouted as the tall, muscular detective currently assigned to the Domestic Violence unit reached down and helped someone up after they'd fallen in their mad dash outside.

"Colonel, what's our status?"

"I wish I knew." She shook her head before he could say anything else. "Grab up every uniform you can. We need to block the street and get this mess." She indicated the mass of people, some running for safety and others just standing there, phones in hand as they videoed the smoke rising from the parking garage. "Under control. Move the looky-loos back at least two blocks. And, for all our sakes, keep the media out."

"Roger than, ma'am." The detective looked around and started ordering cops into position.

Mac cursed as another rumble rose up from below them. A split second later, a blast of hot air hit her, knocking her from her feet. Windows shattered. Glass rained down on the street. Screams of fear and pain filled the air as a thick wall of dust and smoke billowed toward them.

"Move them back!" she ordered as she climbed to her feet. She looked for her husband, almost sagging in relief to see Jackson safe behind the SUV, his phone to his ear. "Jack?"

He didn't need to answer. His expression said it all. No answer from their daughter or her mother or grandmother.

Damn it. Please, don't let them be in the garage.

"Ma'am, what can we do?"

Mac nodded to see members of her Marine command moving in her direction. They might be dressed in business casual, but they each carried a backpack. That reminded her of her own pack and emergency equipment in the back of her SUV.

"Help evac the HQ. Tran, set up a triage area behind my SUV." She motioned to the vehicle almost a block away. Then she tossed the corpsman her keys. "Madison, go with him. In the hatch is my pack and some more emergency equipment. Grab it and bring it back here."

"On it, ma'am." The two men raced off.

"Lee, you're in charge of our team. I'm senior on site until they either find Chief Culver or one of the deputy chiefs get here. First priority is to clear the HQ. If the parking garage goes, it will take some if not all of HQ." That was the problem with adjoining buildings. "Once that's done, focus on the surrounding buildings. Hopefully by then we'll have a plan for SAR. Grab any help you need as long as it doesn't impact other operations."

"On it." He ducked as the ground shook again. Then he took off at a run, calling to other members of the team to follow.

Mac tapped her earbud and once again contacted Dispatch. "Make sure the gas company knows to cut all service to the block. The last thing we need is a secondary explosion because a gas line broke. And what's the status on Fire and EMTs?"

As she spoke, sirens filled the air. That answered one question.

29

She raced back to the SUV. As she slid to a stop, Madison tossed her the backpack he'd retrieved from the back of the vehicle. Then he followed Tran to help set up the triage area. Mac looked back, barely daring to breathe, as smoke continued to rise from the parking garage.

"Jackson?"

He shook his head. "Nothing."

"We'll find them." Hopefully, alive. *Please let them be alive.* "I promise. Just as soon as I can hand this off to someone, I'll go look for them."

If someone didn't relieve her soon, she'd do it anyway.

"We will go."

Now she shook her head. "Jack, we can't both of us go. You know that."

"And you know we don't have time to argue. Just tell me what I can do to help right now."

She smiled and gave his hand a quick squeeze. "Can you help Tran?"

"Yes. You go. I'll be here."

She kissed him. Then she pelted back down the street.

"Colonel Santos!"

She turned, looking to see who called to her. A uniformed officer she recognized ran toward her. He held a radio in one hand, holding it out to her. "Ma'am, Dispatch is relaying a message to you from Chief Culver."

She almost sagged in relief. Culver was alive. Thank God. But where was he?

"Santos," she said as she took the radio from the young man.

"Status?"

"Still working to get a handle on things, sir. Your situation?"

"Working our way down from the top floor."

"Is the general with you?"

"Yes."

"Are you injured, sir?"

She heard the pain in his voice. No doubt about it, he was injured.

The only question was how badly.

"Nothing serious, Colonel. Are you in command?"

"For the moment, sir, at least until someone senior gets here."

"Status?" he asked again.

"Still trying to get a handle on it, sir. Best guess is one or more explosions in the parking garage. The last one was strong enough to break out nearby windows and knock folks from their feet. I have teams working to secure a perimeter and clear the buildings in the area, including the HQ. Fire and EMS are arriving on scene now."

She lifted a hand, signaling Lee. The master sergeant nodded and jogged in her direction, easily dodging cops and other first responders now making their way inside the building to start the evac.

"Sir, I'm sending a team up to escort you and the general to safety. I'm going to turn you over to Master Sergeant Lee. Please give him your location and current status. I'll check in shortly. I need to coordinate with DFD right now." She pressed the radio into Lee's hands. "Culver and General Flynn are inside. I want a team dispatched to locate and extract. If anyone objects, send them to me."

"Right away, ma'am."

Leaving him to coordinate with the Chief, Mac strode over to where several DFD trucks parked. Firefighters grabbed equipment and moved with well-rehearsed precision toward the different buildings. As they did,

"Colonel Mackenzie Santos." She extended her hand as a man about her age in full fire response gear approached.

"Colonel, Assistant Chief Zachary Danvers. What can you tell me?"

"Not much. There have been two, maybe three blasts that seem to have originated in the parking garage next to HQ. At least that's what it felt like. I was inside the garage, ground level, when the first hit." She checked her watch. Had it only been eight or nine minutes ago? It felt like a lifetime ago. "That was less than ten minutes ago. Since then, there have been two more blasts. The last was strong enough to blow out nearby windows. I have teams working to secure a perimeter and help evac HQ and the nearby buildings. I just got off the radio from Chief Culver. He's trapped inside HQ. I have a team on the way to extract him and General Gerald Flynn."

"Status of the garage?" Danvers asked.

"Unknown, sir. I felt it better to get as many people to safety than risk sending untrained officers into the garage."

He reached out and rested a hand on her shoulder. "You made the right decision, Colonel. I'll get teams in there shortly. Is your EOD squad on the way?"

"Yes, sir. EOD, more unis to help out, everyone in my command. Hell, sir, I told Dispatch to basically send for everyone."

He nodded and then listened as someone reported in over his comms. Then he turned his attention back to Mac. "Right now, get that perimeter set up. I see you've got a triage area already going. We'll keep it there. EMTs are here and more are on the way. Now tell me about these Marines you sent into HQ. Are the qualified for this sort of operation?"

"They are, sir."

"All right. Keep me informed." He shouted out a series of orders before turning his attention back to her. "Any chance you have a copy of the plans for the garage and HQ?"

"Sorry, sir, not yet."

"No problem. You've done a damned good job in such a short period, Colonel. If you don't mind, I'll take over the fire control and SAR aspects now."

"Yes, sir."

Leaving him to talk with his own people and put a plan into action, Mac looked around. As she did, her stomach pitched. The parking garage still stood, but for how long? More importantly, how badly was it damaged below the surface? God, don't let her loved ones still be inside.

The thought of her family brought others to mind. She once again tapped her earbud, waiting impatiently for someone, anyone to pick up.

"Colonel!"

Mac turned. Relief filled her to see several detectives from Homicide hurrying across the street in her direction. Watching them, she remembered images from 9/11. Men and women moving through the streets near the Twin Towers, clothes and skin coated with soot until they looked like the walking dead. The detectives, her detectives, looked much the same. But they were alive.

"Tim, report," she said as they joined her.

Sergeant Timothy Nguyen motioned four others over. They nodded grimly to Mac as they neared. Anger and concern burned in their eyes. She had a feeling it did in hers as well.

"Ma'am, we were in the bullpen when the first blast happened. We weren't sure what it was, but Captain King ordered us out. Then the second blast hit. She repeated the order, telling us to clear the building on our way down."

That sounded like Pat.

"The rest of the squad?"

Nguyen shook his head. "We lost contact after the third blast. Last we heard, everyone was working their way down."

"Pat?"

"Nothing, ma'am. She had her son with her and said they'd meet us down here."

Damn it!

"All right. DFD is running SAR, but they're going to need help. Get some water and then report to Master Sergeant Lee for an assignment. He's coordinating the evac of the surrounding buildings. Tim, think you can pull up plans for the garage and HQ?"

Nguyen nodded and told the others to do as Mac said. Then he pulled out his phone and began typing away. A moment later, he looked up, frowning.

"You got a laptop, Colonel?"

She nodded and led him back to where Danvers and his team worked. "Assistant Chief Danvers, Sgt. Tim Nguyen. Sir, Tim's a bit of a tech guru and he can pull up the plans you were asking for. He just needs a laptop or tablet."

She left Nguyen with the firefighters and turned back to the main entrance of the HQ. Nothing she could do there or the parking garage. Not yet. So she did what she could. She put cops to work. None protested as she gave them orders. Instead, they nodded and hurried off to report to team leaders. Slowly, some semblance of organization was happening. It wasn't much, but it was better than nothing.

She started when her cellphone rang. She reached up and touched her earbud, praying it was Cami or one of the others. Instead, Master Sergeant Lee responded to her simple greeting of, "Santos".

"We're on our way down, Colonel," he said. "I've got Culver and the general. We picked up Lindsay and several others on our way. Tell the medics to meet us."

"What will they be looking at?" She prayed it wasn't too bad.

"The chief has a broken arm and probably a couple of broken ribs. A bookshelf fell on him. Flynn's battered and bruised but otherwise appears all right. Lindsay has a head lac that needs some stitches." He paused and she waited, worry building. "Ma'am, we have Mrs. Duncan with us. Her leg's broken and she's got a possible head injury. From what the LT told us, one of the ladders in your new office fell and caught her. The LT had her splinted up and was helping her out when we found them."

"Do I need to send help up?"

"Negative, ma'am. We're picking up folks along the way. It looks like most of the building has already evacced. But if you can have transport and medics standing by."

"Consider it done." She ended the call and alerted the EMTs to be ready.

The next ten minutes were a blur. Assistant Chief Dolan arrived and wanted a brief. Then he moved to where Danvers had set up a command tent. Helicopters, some law enforcement and others from the media, circled the area, scanning for anyone who might be trapped on the upper floor and broadcasting video to the local TV stations. Reporters pushed at the cordon Mac ordered set up, shouting questions at anyone close enough to hear.

God, why hadn't they heard from her family?

"Medics!" she yelled as the doors opened and people once again stumbled out.

First through were several detectives and uniformed officers. Lee followed, supporting Chief Culver. General Flynn was on the chief's other side. Next came Jael. Two men Mac recognized as part of the maintenance team working on her new office carried Marie in a modified fireman's carry between them.

Racing forward, Mac checked her admin, relieved to see her eyes open and aware. Then she checked Jael. Without a word, she motioned for two of the responding medics to take the women. Then she turned her attention to Culver and Flynn.

"Chief, you need to come with us," the final medic said.

Culver shook his head. "Not yet." He looked behind him and then moved further away from the building. "Report, Colonel."

"Danvers from DFD and Dolan are coordinating our efforts now, sir. We're still focusing on securing the area and making sure the buildings are evacced. I think DFD is about to start checking the garage, but Dolan can tell you more about that than I can."

He started to say something and then stopped. Mac waited, hoping he was all right. Then Flynn stepped forward, his eyes flashing dangerously. His coyote was so close to the surface, Mac was surprised he hadn't already shifted.

"Mac, your family?" he asked, his voice surprisingly gentle.

She shook her head, not sure she could say anything. Then she cleared her throat. "Jackson's over there." She pointed to where her SUV still blocked off the street. "The kids are with Mom and Gran. We haven't heard from them."

He rested a hand on her arm for a moment and then glanced at Master Sergeant Lee. Before he could say anything, Mac stopped him. "Let Lee help you and Chief Culver to the triage area. Chief, I'll let Dolan know you're on scene. I'll be there in a few minutes to check on you."

With that, she turned, motioning to several others of her Marine team as she did. Instantly, they fell into step around her as she moved away.

"Listen up, it looks like the evac of HQ and the other buildings is in hand now. Gather your gear and head into the garage. If anyone tries to stop you, send them to me. I'm officially activating the unit. You know the drill. If you come across survivors you can help out, do so. But we need to make sure there are no more explosions waiting to happen." She rubbed a hand over her face, wincing slightly as she did. She'd forgotten she'd been cut by flying glass earlier.

"We still don't know what we're up against. This could have been a natural gas line break or a fuel leak in a car or truck that caught and then touched off other explosions. Or it could be an IED of some sort. So keep your eyes and ears open. Body cams on and recording from the moment you make entry."

"Understood, ma'am."

She didn't tell them to find her family, but she knew they'd look. She only hoped she could handle what they found.

The next half hour dragged for Mac as she did her best to keep busy so she didn't obsess about her family. Culver finally broke away from the medics, ignoring their suggestion he go to the hospital to get his broken arm treated. Telling him they couldn't guarantee he wouldn't suffer complications from delaying treatment, they splinted him up and settled his arm in a sling. He assured them he understood, but he had more important things to deal with just then. He had cops, not to mention civilians, still missing, perhaps injured and trapped.

Mac needs to shift. We need to hunt our loved ones, Cait said, pressing against Mac's control once again.

I want to, Cait, but we can't. We'd just be in the way right now.

Or would they?

She stepped away from where Culver looked over the blueprints of the building with others of his makeshift command staff as well as Danvers and others from DFD. As she did, she looked around. Here and there, she saw those she was looking for. Five minutes later, she stood in a tight circle with Detectives Loquita Murray and Nate Norwood, Jael, and several others. All but Jael were paras and all were members of her Marine unit as well. Hopefully, once they heard what she had in mind, they'd be willing to help.

"Any word on Pat and Mike?" she asked.

Murray shook her head. "Nothing yet. The last we heard, they were on the north side of the building, clearing the sixth floor. DFD has a crew working their way there."

Mac's hand fisted at her side. So many of their friends and fellow cops, too many, were unaccounted for. That needed to change and she was tired of standing on the sidelines.

She might not be able to get inside—yet—but she could start the investigation. While the other cops interviewed everyone, she wanted her people to start pulling video not only from witnesses but from every business, every traffic cam, every ATM in the area. If this was anything other than an unfortunate accident, she wanted to know and she wanted to know who was involved.

They promised to get right on it, using all their abilities—*all* of them—to do as she said. She nodded and started back to the command tent. As she did, her cellphone vibrated in her pocket. When she pulled it out and saw the display, the world stopped. Then she heard Jackson yelling for her. Spinning, she tried to find him. He struggled against two uniformed officers who tried to hold him back.

"Let him go!" she ordered as she took off running, Jael and Murray on her heels.

The officers obeyed. A moment later, Jackson sprinted toward them. Mac stopped, her phone still gripped in her right hand. Then Jackson was there, fear and hope shining from his eyes. He glanced at her phone and then pulled her close. She wrapped her arms around him, holding him tightly as tremors racked them both.

"Mac?" Jael spoke softly, fearfully.

Mac reached back, letting Jael take the phone. Jael gasped and then called in the rest of their team. She'd seen the same thing Mac had.

Mommy, Cami says you need to come help us.

That simple text sent from her daughter's cellphone was enough to cause any mother's blood to run cold. But it was the time stamp that Mac held onto with all her heart. It had just been sent. That meant there was hope.

And she was damned if she would sit still and wait for DFD to find her babies and her mother and grandmother.

"Get a location. See if Xander can tell you if they're still in my parking space or if they'd started out of the garage," she said, turning to face them. She rubbed her eyes, knowing they wouldn't condemn her for a moment of weakness.

Jael nodded and quickly texted Xander back.

"I'm going in. I need two volunteers." She shook her head before Jael could say anything. "Not you. You're already injured. You get to stay up here and keep the brass off my back." Now she gave a wicked smile. "That's the price of being my partner."

"I'll get payback," Jael countered with an equally wicked grin.

"I'll go," Norwood and Murray said at the same time.

Mac nodded, relieved. Two shifters and a witch should be able to handle just about anything they came across.

She hoped.

"Nate, get us masks and tanks. Hard hats too. Lolo, first aide bag and tac lights. Jael, ropes and at least one Halligan tool." She watched as they hurried to gather what she wanted. As they did, she turned back to her husband. "We'll find them, Jack. I promise. I'm going to bring our babies and the others out."

He rested his forehead against hers. Then he straightened. As he did, he growled deep in his throat. Hearing it, Mac stiffened. She had a feeling she wasn't going to like whatever he saw over her shoulder.

"Planning on going somewhere, Colonel?" Chief Culver asked as he and General Flynn neared.

"Sir, just doing my duty." Surely, he wasn't going to try to stop her.

Culver glanced at the parking garage and back before shaking his head. "Mac, I understand, but I can't let you go."

She pulled herself up to her full height and her eyes narrowed. "I beg your pardon, sir." She drawled it out, every syllable a warning not to push her.

"Stand down, Mac. He understands. We both do," Flynn told her firmly. "But you're needed here to help coordinate our operations. However, if DFD agrees, the others can go do some SAR."

The slight emphasis he placed on SAR told her all she needed to know. The team's orders would be to find her family and bring them out. If they found others along the way, all the better.

"The medics cleared me, General," Jael said before Mac could protest. "I'll bring them back to you, Mac. I promise."

"We promise," Murray said as she joined them.

Not liking it one bit but knowing better than to argue, Mac handed her backpack off to Jael. The woman gave a single nod, one that spoke volumes. Then she led the others toward the parking garage. Mac watched as human, coyote shifter and witch simply pushed past the firefighter who tried to stop them. A moment later, they disappeared inside the garage, their progression obscured by the smoke and dust still billowing out from inside.

Dear God, please let them find my family.

4

Mac looked at her phone again, praying for word about her family. As she did, she fought the fear forming a cold, hard fist around her heart. More than an hour had passed since Jael and the others entered the parking garage. They reported in regularly, detailing what they found, none of which reassured the woman.

And they had yet to find her family.

Damn it, she shouldn't have let them park in her space! They'd have been safely out otherwise.

When the phone vibrated, dancing on the top of the folding table in front of her a few minutes later, she grabbed for it. She prayed for another message from her son. Instead, the display had her frowning slightly. It didn't make any sense. Then she looked around, seeing the familiar van bearing the logo of the Irish Rose Pub. Telling Culver and Flynn she'd be back, she trotted down the street in its direction. As she did, Jackson joined her.

"Mac?"

She shook her head.

By the time they reached the intersection where sawhorses had been set up to keep traffic out, Moira and John O'Hara stood in front of the van. Two officers stood on the opposite side of the barricade, making sure the pub owners didn't try to get through. Instead of arguing, Moira waited for Mac to join them.

"Moira, John." Mac said, motioning the two uniforms back.

"We thought your people could use some food and drink, Mac. We've got soup, sandwiches, coffee, tea, water and soft drinks." Moira's Irish accent was thicker than Mac had heard in a very long time, a sure sign of the woman's worry.

"Thanks. That helps."

More than Moira knew. Jobs like this one were thankless under any circumstances. Knowing you were looking for friends and family, be they blood or because of the uniform, made it so much worse. The fact someone thought about them and cared enough to bring food and drink proved the world hadn't turned its back on them.

Mac nodded to the two patrol officers. As she reached for one of the sawhorses to move it to the side so John could drive through, the uniforms hurried to help.

"Jackson, take them down by triage. They can set up there."

He nodded and moved toward the van. As he passed her, he reached out and gripped her hand briefly.

"Let me get you and these two officers coffee first, Mac." John moved to the rear of the van. When he returned a few moments later, he carried to-go cups for the men. "We've talked with some of the other restaurants and bars. They'll be sending down food and drinks shortly."

"Thank you."

Tears stung her eyes again. Moira and John were more than friends. Moira acted as the de facto leader of the area's lone shifters, those who didn't officially belong to the pride. Under her guidance, many of the loners long ago started looking to the pride for friendship and protection. John, like Jael, came from a long line of humans who knew about the Pures and did everything they could to protect their secrets.

"We'll set up and then John's going back to the pub to pick up some more food. The girls will come back with him to help hand it out," Moira said as she handed Mac a tall to-go cup of coffee. "Can we bring you anything else? Blankets, other supplies? Anything at all, we'll get for you."

"Food's good. But what about the pub?"

"You don't worry about it, Mac. We've got it covered." John motioned for Moira and Jackson to get in the van.

Mac stepped aside and watched as they drove slowly down the street. Then she turned and helped the officers reset the barricades. Once she had, she turned back and studied the scene down the street. The smoke coming from the parking garage had lessened. Fortunately, there hadn't been another blast. She kept telling herself that was a good sign. But with each passing minute, her fear for her family grew. So did the need to tell Culver and Flynn to screw it and go search for them herself.

Police, some in uniform and others wearing DPD windbreakers or tee shirts, moved from building to building. Firefighters and EMTs continued searching HQ. More people were being brought out but too many of them were injured, a number of them badly. Worse, there were still too many missing.

God, please let her wake up from this nightmare.

"Anything new?" she asked as she returned to the command tent. As she did, she handed cups of coffee to Flynn and Culver.

"DFD's confirmed the three buildings across the street are cleared. Injuries from there are minimal. Mainly from flying glass or from people panicking and doing something stupid. Our crews are clearing the last few floors of HQ but it's slow going."

"And the garage?" she asked hesitantly.

"EOD teams are going through it now but that is even more slow going. "Flynn paused as their radios crackled and came to life with yet another report. More injured found and on the way out. Ambulances were to stand by. "The mayor is holding a press conference in an hour." When she bit back a curse, he gave her a sympathetic nod. "He has to, Mac. The press is demanding an update and we have a lot of folks who are worried about their loved ones."

And she was one of them. Not that the brass seemed to care.

"Sir," she started, ready to plead her case one more time. Then her cellphone vibrated in her pocket. She grabbed for it, turning away from the others in case it was bad news. "Santos."

"It's me, boss." The sound of Tim Nguyen's voice had her turning back toward HQ.

"Talk to me, Tim."

"We've cleared through to Burglary. I'm sending video now."

Mac waited, aware of others gathering around her. A moment later, her screen showed what could be a scene from a disaster movie. The ceiling had partially collapsed. So had the far wall. Light fixtures dangled precariously from wires overhead. Dust hung thick in the air. Worse, she saw bodies, some covered by debris. Alive or dead, she couldn't tell. It didn't matter. They had cops down.

Damn it!

"I'm sending help, Tim. Tell me what you need."

He looked around, his expression grim. "Muscle, ma'am. We need to clear away the debris and we're hearing sounds from survivors in the next sector. We need at least eight stretchers and that's just for here."

"I'm sending teams to you now," Danvers told Nguyen from over Mac's shoulder.

"Thanks." He turned away for a moment and told someone out of the picture to start down with the survivors. "I'm sending some people down. Injuries range from cuts and bruises to broken bones. Have ambulances and EMTs standing by."

"They're waiting for you, Tim," Mac assured him.

"Colonel, if we could speak privately for a moment."

Mac's stomach pitched dangerously. Then she nodded, trying not to show her concern. Without a word to those around her, she stepped out of the command tent. As she did, she tried not to jump to any conclusions about why Nguyen wanted to speak privately. None of the possible explanations were good and she didn't want to borrow trouble if she didn't need to.

God, what now?

"Go, Tim. I've stepped away."

"Mac, we found Pat and young Mike."

Her breath hitched. His expression was serious enough to scare her.

"And?"

"Mac, you saw the squad room. It looks like it might have been near the center of the blast. Pat and Mike were down here."

"How bad?"

"Pat's unconscious. Looks like she took a blow to the head. Probable internal injuries. Mike was conscious but in a lot of pain and worried about his mother. My guess is his shoulder is dislocated, that arm broken. Both were trapped under some debris from the wall collapse. They may both have internal injuries. Wouldn't surprise me if they have broken ribs and more."

"Where are they?"

And did she need to get a team in to bring them out?

"They're on their way out. I put two teams of two on carrying them out." He gave a humorless laugh. "We're using fucking doors as stretchers, boss. Figured it was best to keep them flat in case they have neck or back injuries."

"Understood." She pushed down her fear. "Good work, Tim. I'll make sure the medics are ready for them. You watch yourself and your team. I don't want you taking unnecessary risks."

"Same goes, boss." The look he gave her spoke volumes.

She promised once again to get him some help and ended the call. For a moment, she allowed herself to sag against the side of one of the ambulances waiting to transport the injured. Then she went returned to the command tent. There was still so very much to do.

"Chief Danvers, we have injured being brought out by Sgt. Nguyen's team. I don't know the total count yet, but two are seriously injured and are being transported on doors to keep them flat. They'll need to be assessed and transported right away," she reported. As she did, she sent a message to Pat's doctor, telling him to meet her at the hospital and have a team ready for both Pat and young Mike.

"Mac?" Culver asked, his worry obvious.

"Captain King and her son."

Culver closed his eyes and drew a deep breath. When he opened his eyes a moment later, he simply looked at her and then nodded. He'd come to a decision about something, but what?

"Colonel Santos."

"Sir?"

"You need to update General Flynn. He's down at the triage area checking the status of things there. Once you do, deal with whatever else you need to. Then consider your earlier request granted."

For a moment, she stood rooted in place, unsure she'd heard correctly. Then she nodded before bracing to attention. Before he could change his mind, she turned and jogged out of the tent, looking for first Flynn and then Jackson.

She was going to find her family and bring them out safely.

Nothing else was acceptable.

"Do you have an update?" Flynn asked as she neared. He stood at the edge of the triage area, watching as another two injured officers were loaded onto an ambulance.

She nodded and motioned for Jackson to join them. He crouched next to a young uniformed officer, assuring her she was going to be all right. Then he stood and, after wiping his palms against his slacks, hurried to where they stood. As he did, concern and hope flickered across his expression. How she wished she could reassure him, but she wouldn't lie. Not to him and not about this.

"There's no news, Jack," she said softly and reached for his hand. "But Tim and his team found Pat and Mike. They're injured, possibly badly. He's got teams bringing them out now. I want medical teams and an ambulance waiting to transport them. I've already called Dr. Nicholls. He'll be waiting for them at the hospital."

Jackson nodded, his expression grim. Then he pulled out his phone and stepped away. As he did, Mac caught Moira's eye where she stood serving several officers a few yards away. The redhead nodded, said something to Annie, her eldest daughter, and then hurried to where Mac and General Flynn waited.

"Mac?"

"They're bringing Pat and young Mike out, Moira. They're hurt.

Dr. Nicholls has already been notified. Will you go with them, make sure everything is taken care of?"

The Irishwoman didn't hesitate. She simply nodded once, gave Mac's had a reassuring squeeze and then hurried back to her husband and daughter. Relieved, knowing she could trust Moira to make sure nothing else happened to Mike or Pat, she turned her attention to Flynn.

"Sir, once they're on their way, I'm going after my family. Culver knows and approves." Probably because he knew she wouldn't be put off for much longer. "I'm going to gear up and I'll keep in contact, but I'm not needed out here any longer. I can do more good in the parking garage."

"Has there been any word from the team you sent in?"

She shook her head, not attempting to hide her concern. "Not in the last ten minutes, sir."

As if that was a signal, Mac's cellphone buzzed. She answered it, putting it on speaker and calling Jackson over. "Talk to me," she said as her husband slid to a halt at her side.

"We finally made it to the SUV. There's a path cleared. We need another team." Strain roughened Jael's voice, worrying Mac.

"Are they?" She couldn't finish the question.

"We're still trying to finish getting to them, Mac." A pause and Mac waited, not breathing, afraid she might miss the answer if she did.

"Jael?" Jackson leaned in and Mac knew he wished the woman was sending live video as much as she did.

"Mac, you need to get down here. There's a." Another pause and she cleared her throat. "There's a situation that needs your touch."

"Details?"

"When you get here."

Mac's fists clinched at her side and she fought for calm. "Jael, details."

"We have a situation, Striker, one that needs your attention."

That brought Mac up short. The members of her Marine command never used her call sign during a police operation. So what the hell was going on?

"Understood, Valkyrie." Not really but discussing it in the open or over a cell call wasn't something she was willing to do. "I'm gearing up and heading in." She ended the call and shoved the phone into her hip pocket. "General?"

"Go, Colonel. Keep me updated."

She nodded and looked around, considering. Then Jackson's hand closed around her upper arm, turning her to face him.

"You're not going without me."

As much as she wanted to argue, she didn't. She had a feeling she'd need him before this, whatever the hell this might be, was over. Instead, she nodded once.

"You'll have to do what I say, when I say it."

She led him back to her SUV and opened the rear hatch. Without waiting for his response, she dug through the contents in the back. A moment later, she tossed him the spare Kevlar vest she kept there. After pulling hers on and securing it in place, she turned to help him. As she did, she thought hard, trying to figure out what else they might need.

One of the uniformed officers currently assigned to Homicide slid to a halt a few feet away. "Chief Culver sent me to see if I can be of any help, Colonel."

"I need two hard hats, bunker jackets and Halligan tools. Grab two first aid bags and four tac lights. A couple of spare radios. Run. Meet us at the entry to the parking garage." As she spoke, she tested her department issued radio before sliding it into place on her belt.

"Jackson, I don't know what we're going to find. So you have to promise you'll do what I tell you, even if it's telling you to leave. No arguments. Understand?"

He nodded and took the tac light she handed him. "Why the four extras?"

"We don't want to get caught down there without light." She looked up as Flynn and Lee joined them. Then she turned her attention back to the contents in the rear of the SUV, choosing several knives and even a coach's whistle. "Lee, you're my eyes and ears up here. General, next time you decide to surprise me, buy me a drink instead. I can live without this sort of excitement." She tried to smile but failed.

"Trust me, Mac. We all could." He rested a reassuring hand on her shoulder, his expression softening. "You be careful."

She nodded and, with a look at Jackson, turned and started down the street toward the parking garage.

Finally.

5

Mac crawled over the hood of what had once been a Ford F150, wincing as glass and rock bit through her jeans. Once on the other side, she turned and waited for Jackson to follow. When Jael said they'd made a path, Mac knew she should have asked for clarification. Path was overstating it, at least in some areas. They'd been inside the garage for almost twenty minutes and had only just now managed to move below the first level.

Two more levels to go.

"Take a breather," she said as she pulled one of the radios at her waist.

Jackson nodded and drew a drink from his hydration pack. He waited as she radioed in their position. Then she pulled her cellphone and took a video of the area before shoving the phone back into the protective pocket on her vest.

"You okay?" she asked after sipping from her own hydration pack.

"I am." He brushed a lock of hair from her face. "We're going to get to them."

"I know." She smiled slightly. Then she studied the path ahead of them. "The next few yards look easier, but I don't know what's ahead of us. I want you to stay behind me. Let me clear the way if necessary."

"I don't like this," he growled and his eyes glowed as his jaguar made its presence known.

She chuckled softly. "I know, love. I'm not too thrilled about it myself."

And that was putting it mildly.

Mac adjusted her hard hat and shone her tac light on the area before them. As she did, she marveled that they had not come across any injured or dead. This side of the parking garage had been badly damaged by the blast. Fortunately, most of the support columns stood, although more than a few looked like it wouldn't take much to bring them down. If that happened, they would be shit out of luck.

Not wanting to waste any time, Mac climbed over two vehicles caught in the middle of the drive, A third had been trying to pull out when it was sandwiched between the two. She paused long enough to shine her light inside the three. She saw blood, but it looked as if everyone involved managed to get out.

Please let her family be so lucky.

At the end of the aisle, Mac paused. She inhaled deeply and frowned as she caught the scent of gasoline. That only added to the danger. Still, it had to be a minor miracle more cars hadn't suffered ruptured fuel lines or gas tanks.

"I smell it," Jackson said before she could warn him.

"Make sure your Halligan doesn't strike anything and cause a spark."

Ten excruciating minutes later, Mac once again lifted her right hand, signaling Jackson to stop. She stood a yard ahead of him, her head turning this way and that as she scanned the area. Worried, Jackson moved to her side. He waited in silence as she assessed their situation. Then her head snapped to the right. Drawing on the enhanced senses of her jaguar, she held her breath, listening.

"There!" She turned and started back up the aisle. "Jackson!"

Cursing softly, she studied the red Toyota Prius. A large chuck of what had once been part of the ceiling rested on the car's roof, collapsing it inward. The rear window was smashed, the safety glass pebbled in piles across the trunk. No doubt about it, the car frame was bent. Worse, a young woman sat trapped inside, her upper body bent forward over the steering wheel, the roof a mere inch or two from her head.

Mac pulled her Halligan from where it hung across her back and shoved it into the narrow space between the Prius' driver's door and the frame. A moment later, Jackson joined her, adding his weight. The metal groaned against as they tried to force the door open. Cursing, Mac shook her head. Even with their enhanced strength, it wasn't enough.

She pulled out the radio and sent for an SAR team.

"Hey, I need you to listen up." She waited until the young woman trapped inside the car looked at her. From the blood dried down the side of her face to her wide pupils, Mac guessed she suffered either a head injury, shock or both. "I've called for SAR. They'll be here soon. Can you hang on?"

"D-don't leave me." Tears streaked her cheeks as she pressed one palm against the window.

"Are you hurt?" Jackson asked.

"M-my leg. It's caught. I can't get it loose."

Mac turned away from the car, her expression grim. One of them needed to stay and it wasn't going to be her. Hopefully, Jackson understood.

"Jack."

He nodded, his expression as grim as hers. "Go. I'll stay here until someone comes. Then I'll find you."

"I love you." She touched his hand and then turned back to the car. "What's your name?"

"Gina."

"Okay, Gina. Here's what we're going to do. This is Jackson. He's going to stay with you. But first we're going to get this window open. Can you roll it down?"

She shook her head. "Controls don't work."

"Probably shorted out," Jackson commented as he cleared some of the debris from the roof of the car.

"Listen up, Gina. I need you to turn your head away from the

53

window. If you can, cover your head with your arms. I'm going to break out the backdoor window. Then I'll reach through and break your window out from the inside. Okay."

She sniffled and nodded.

"Turn your head."

Mac watched as she shifted positions enough to turn her head away from the driver's window. Then Gina covered her head with arms crisscrossed with cuts, blood drying into a macabre pattern. Before Mac could act, Jackson turned away from the car. He made a fist with his right hand and grabbed it with his left. The sound of glass shattering filled the air as he forced his elbow through the window. Mac winced as he did, glad she'd made him wear the bunker jacket. That kept the glass from cutting him, which even safety glass would have done.

"My turn," she said and nudged him out of the way. As she did, she pulled a tactical baton. With a snap of her wrist, she expanded it. Then she carefully reached through the passenger window and smashed the driver's window. "Okay, Gina, you can look this way." She reached inside and helped the young woman. As she did, Mac frowned to see Gina's foot trapped beneath the brake pedal.

"Jack, here's a radio and an extra tac light. Let me know when the others get here."

"You be careful."

She smiled, gave Gina a reassuring nod and started off. As she did, she prayed nothing else delayed her. She had a feeling there was no time to waste.

Her tac light cut a narrow and much too short path through the darkness. Every sound seemed magnified in the darkness. A falling pebble reminded her of a stone dropping from a great height. A drop of water made her wonder if a pipe was about to break and flood the area. It made her edgy and her jaguar even more so. If she never saw this much darkness again, it would be too soon.

"Valkyrie, Striker," she radioed as she neared the next intersection the garage. She shone her light, looking for a site marker. Once this was over, she'd pay for surface parking. She didn't care how much it cost. No more parking garages. "I'm at Level 2, elevator 2B."

"Roger that, Striker."

Mac breathed a sigh of relief to hear Jael's voice.

"Take the branch to your right. It's longer but easier to get through. At the mid-point, you'll need to climb up half a level, transverse to the other side of Level 2 and then head up. The SUV is midway between there and the next turn."

She nodded, not liking it. "Condition of the other route?"

"Mostly blocked. Trust me, the other way is longer but won't take as much time and time is one thing I don't think we have."

"All right." She took another sip from her hydration pack. Usually, the parking garage was cool but now, with the darkness closing in and dust and debris still hanging in the air, it was hot, especially wearing the bunker coat. For the first time in a very long time, she felt the stirrings of claustrophobia.

Don't think about that. Think about your kids, your family.

Mac should shift. Faster as jaguar.

Not now, Cait. We need the light and we might need the tools.

Moving carefully, Mac once again took off. As she did, she wondered how Jackson was doing. She hated leaving him but knew they had no choice. She could no more leave the young cop alone in the dark than she could stay outside any longer. And for every Gina they found, how many others were still trapped, still praying someone found them before it was too late?

Step by step, she picked her way through the abandoned cars. Some simply left where they stood, doors left open as their occupants fled. Others trapped by falling debris or by other cars. Her muscles ached and sweat stung the cuts to her face and neck. Her hair felt plastered to her head. Memory of late night patrols in the desert, wondering if an insurgent would pop out of the shadows returned and she swallowed hard.

"Shit," she muttered as she slithered through the wire barrier designed to keep people from climbing between sub-levels of the parking garage and a partially collapsed column. Concrete scraped her spine and she hissed in pain. Even with the bunker jacket, she knew she'd be bruised and battered. But she was closer to her family.

She kept that thought in mind as she climbed to her feet. Hands on knees, bent at the waist, she gasped for breath. As she did, she had a quick mental vision of Cait hunched down, her ear tabs plastered to her head, panting.

Almost there, Cait.

She hoped.

"Jael!" she called, her voice echoing in the distance.

"Mama! Mama, you gotta help them!"

Xander's cry tore through her. Her son lived. Instinct took over and she started running. Somehow, she managed to stay on her feet. In the distance, she saw the glow from several tac lights. The cars and trucks between her and them didn't matter. She drew on all the strength Cait could give her and picked up speed, leaping onto the hood of what had been another department issued vehicle before a chunk of concrete fell through its roof.

She slid off the other side of the hood, stumbling as her feet hit the ground. One step and then two and she righted herself. She sobbed, a mixture of fear and relief, to see Jael and Murray. Beyond them was her mother's SUV. Debris covered the hood. The windshield spider-webbed toward a hole in the passenger side Mac didn't want to consider just yet. Behind the SUV, barely visible, was another vehicle. From the angle the SUV rested at, the sedan had driven up under it.

Swallowing hard, Mac inched forward, moving carefully. What would she find when she got there? Had she lost her mother?

Her grandmother?

Cami?

All she knew for certain was Xander lived.

She pulled the radio and let first Jackson and then topside know she'd found them. Then she slid the radio back into place on her belt before anyone asked any of the questions she didn't have answers for.

She whimpered in fear to catch the scent of blood in the air. Close. Too close to be from anywhere but the SUV or one of the cars near it.

Praying harder than she had in a very long while, she moved forward on unsteady legs.

Five yards from the SUV, she came up short. Face lifted, she inhaled sharply. There! Just a hint of a scent that shouldn't be there.

Lycan, Cait growled as she once again pushed for release.

Mac's growl matched her jaguar's. Her hand dropped to the gun at her waist and she looked around, shining her light into the shadows. Was that the situation Jael said she needed to deal with?

Dear God, this was the one complication they didn't need.

Mate comes! Cait said as the sounds of someone crawling over cars below them reached Mac.

She hesitated. Part of her wanted to wait until he was there. That was the smart thing to do with a lycan possibly lurking in the shadows. But the other part knew she couldn't. If anything had happened to their daughter or the others, she didn't want him finding out the hard way.

Swallowing hard, she forced herself forward. As she neared the SUV, she lifted one gloved hand to her mouth, fighting to keep from crying out. Elizabeth sat behind the steering wheel. Her head rested at an angle against the headrest that worried Mac almost as much as the blood covering her face. Then she saw her mother's chest rise in a shallow breath. Too shallow, but it meant she lived. Now to keep her that way.

Dashing away the tears threatening to spill down her face, she walked carefully around the SUV to the passenger side. Nothing could have kept back her cry at the sight that greeted her. That door was partially open. Her grandmother lay half in-half out of the SUV. It looked as if she might have been getting back in when part of the ceiling above them collapsed. Debris covered Ellen from the knees down but that was nothing compared the rebar piercing her thigh or the blood still seeping through the bandages, slowed only by the tourniquet Norwood placed above the wound.

Thank God, they'd gotten there when they did.

"Mama!" Xander's cry broke through her shock. Mac looked around trying to find her son.

"It's okay, Xan baby. I'm here." She did her best to sound reassuring, reaching back with her left hand to signal Jackson to move forward slowly. Even as she did, she cast a wary eye to the damaged ceiling above them.

"Stay where you are, son. We'll get you out soon," Jackson added.

"Xan baby, is your sister with you?"

And why hadn't one of the others said something?

Mac glanced over at Jael and Murray. For the first time, she realized they stood stiffly, warily. Jael's hand rested on the butt of the gun at her waist. More concerning were the flames dancing around Murray's hands where she held them defensively in front of her.

Dear God, what was going on? Was the lycan closer than she thought?

"Mama, she didn't mean it. She was only trying to protect us."

"Easy, Mac," Jael said softly. "Look to your left."

Mac slowly turned. As she did, a young panther stepped out of the shadows. Teeth bared, growling softly, she padded closer to Ellen. Mac watched, confusion filling her even as she scented the air. This was no lycan. More importantly, there was something familiar to its scent. But how or why, Mac couldn't tell.

Where had the panther come from? Mac knew all the shifters in the area and this wasn't one of them. More concerning was Cait's response—or lack of one. Any other time, the jaguar would be pushing for release, demanding they protect the elder. But not now.

Why?

Mackenzie being silly, her jaguar-self chided with a very feline chuckle. *Cami's only protecting our family.*

Cami? Mac's eyes went wide and she shook her head, denying what her jaguar said even as she looked closer at the panther now sitting next to Ellen's unconscious form, mewling softly.

It couldn't be. Cami was too young to shift. Her parents were jaguar shifters. So were her paternal grandparents, not to mention Ellen. Cami couldn't be a panther any more than Mac could turn into little bunny foo-foo.

What the fuck was going on?

6

"Mama, you gotta help them. Please."

Xander's cries broke through Mac's mental and physical paralysis. She shoved aside all her questions, all the jabbering going on in her brain and shook herself. Dear God, how were they going to get everyone out of there safely?

"Nate, any other surprises I need to know about?" She once again looked all around them, wary after catching the lycan's scent.

"Negative, ma'am." He glanced up from where he worked to stem the flow of blood from Ellen's wound. "I caught the scent, but the lycan was gone by the time we got here."

"Good." That at least was one good thing going their way. "Stay with her," she added. Mac didn't need a doctor to tell her how badly injured her grandmother was.

"Cami." Mac swallowed hard against the tumult of emotions rising once again from deep inside her. Then she gave a weak laugh as the panther dipped its head once as if to confirm her identity. "Cam's not going to interfere. Right?" It felt strange pinning the panther with what Cami would call her mother look, especially when the panther did the feline version of rolling her eyes.

Norwood didn't look up, simply nodded once.

"Jackson, you and Murray see if you can get Mom out of the van. We need to assess her injuries before figuring what our next move should be."

As she spoke, she carefully picked her way along the far side of the SUV. Much as she wanted to get to Xander, there was something she needed to do first. Drawing a deep, bracing breath, she bent and looked under the rear of the SUV. She'd been right. A car had somehow managed to drive up under it. The car, a Chevy Spark, was wedged far enough under the SUV that the rear axle rested more than a foot above the pavement. Seeing the way the roof of the Spark had peeled back, Mac doubted anyone could have survived, but she had to be sure.

No one. The car was empty. It would take the accident reconstruction experts to be sure, but her guess was whoever drove the small car bailed before hitting the SUV. Bastards. If they'd stayed behind the wheel, they might have managed to avoid hitting her mother's car and her family might now be safe.

Forcing down her anger, she straightened and brushed her gloved hands on her jeans. Then she moved back along the SUV. As she did, she studied the once gleaming black SUV. It now looked more grey than black. The roof was covered with debris, large and small. Her heart hitched a beat or two at the sight of the deep dent in the roof and the way the door braces bowed outward. Then she said a silent prayer of thanks that her mother listened to her when she bought the vehicle six months earlier. The extra roll bars and other "special additions" did what they were supposed to be. Otherwise, none of them would have survived.

And, seeing Xander sitting in his booster seat, tugging at the safety belt, nothing else mattered.

Then a quick, almost bitter, laugh escaped Mac's lips. For the first time ever, the damned belt worked. Any other time, her son, who proved early on to be an accomplished escape artist, would be out of the seat and probably out of the van. But not now. Whether the impact with the Spark hitting the SUV did something to the mechanism or the bending of the SUV's frame, she didn't know and didn't care. All that mattered in that moment was her son was alive and relatively unhurt. Now to get the rest of her family out of there before she lost them.

Don't think about that.

"Xander, look at me." She waited until he turned a tear-streaked face to her. "I'm going to get you out of there. Okay?"

He nodded and rubbed one very grubby fist under his nose.

"I'm going to have to break the window. So I want you to turn the other way. Don't look at me, baby. Cover your head with your arms." She nodded in appreciation as Jael moved to stand opposite her, drawing Xander's attention. "That's it, baby. Now cover your head."

Jael lifted her arms, showing Xander what he should do.

"I'm going to count to three, baby. Okay?"

"O-okay, Mama."

She waited until he ducked down and covered his head. Then she looked through the SUV to where Jael stood. The woman nodded, her expression serious. Once again, Mac snapped open her tactical baton. She took a step back, inhaled and pulled the baton back.

"One... Two... Three."

The word still hung on her tongue when she struck the window. The safety glass spider-webbed and then pebbled. The protective film held and she cursed softly before striking it again. Well, Elizabeth paid good money to make sure she had the best protection available on the vehicle. After everything Mac and the rest of the family had been through the since Mac started shifting, it only made sense. But right now, Mac didn't appreciate the extra resistance the window put up.

Not that the glass stood a chance against a mother determined to get to her youngest child. Within seconds, Mac ran the baton along the edges of the window, clearing away any sharp shards that might remain. Then, before Xander sat up, she was through the window, a knife replacing the baton. But first, she needed to touch him, hold him, make sure he was all right.

"Mama!"

He threw his arms around her neck and clung to her like she was a life preserver in the middle of a storm-tossed sea. Her hands patted his head, neck and back. Then she gently pulled away, checking him for injuries. Her lips peeled back to see the discoloration at his collar bone from the seatbelt. But that was all she could see and if that was the worst he suffered, they were lucky.

"Okay, Xan, I want you to listen to me." She flicked open her knife and made quick work of the seat belt and then the safety belt around his waist. Instantly, he was out of his booster and in her lap, arms and legs wrapping around her. "It's okay, baby. I've got you."

She held him for a moment, breathing in the scent of sweaty, scared little boy and reveling in the ability to do so. She'd been as scared as him. But now she needed to get them all out of there without anything else happening.

"I need you to go to Auntie Jael right now, Xander. Can you do that for me?"

He buried his face in the crook of her neck and tightened his hold on her.

Heart breaking because she wanted nothing more than to hold him, she cleared her throat.

"Xander, I need you to be my brave little man right now and go to Auntie Jael. I need to check on grandma. Okay?"

He held her tightly for a moment longer and then nodded. Slowly, so very slowly, he eased his death grip on her and sat up. Smiling in reassurance, Mac framed his small face with her hands and kissed his cheeks.

"I'm so proud of you, son. You've been so brave."

"So scared, Mama. Not Cami. She was brave. She shifted and protected us."

And that, along with how and why her daughter was now a panther, was something they'd need to talk about. But later. After everyone was out of this tomb just waiting to happen.

"You were both very brave." She kissed him again and shifted to hand him through the window to Jael. "Get him out of here," she said softly as the little boy wrapped himself around the woman.

Jael nodded and stepped around the SUV to let Jackson see his son was all right. Mac watched as her husband straightened and shrugged out of his bunker coat, wrapping it around Xander. Then he settled his hard hat on the boy's head.

"There's a rescue team up a level. They're probably working their way down here by now. Go. Get him out of here. Take Cami with you."

The very feline twelve-year-old flattened her ear tabs against her skull and bared her teeth, shaking her head. Well, that answered that question. The girl was just as stubborn in her shifted form as she was as a human. Mac didn't know whether to laugh or cry.

"Jael, just go. We'll bring Cami with the others," Mac said, silencing Jackson's protest with a look.

Jackson ran a loving hand over Xander's head and nodded. Jael promised to get the boy to safety. Mac took one last look before turning her attention to figuring out how to free her mother and grandmother.

"Nate, report," she said as she cut her mother's seatbelt.

With Jackson stabilizing Elizabeth's head and neck, she lowered the back of the driver's seat several inches, all it would move. It wasn't much but it would help keep Elizabeth in a better position until they could get her out.

Knowing it wasn't enough, Mac climbed to her knees and carefully reached into the rear of the SUV. As she did, she blew out a breath. Even with the additional roll bars, the roof of the vehicle bent inward. One of the kids might have been able to climb into the back, but she couldn't. All she could do was blindly go by feel, hoping her mother hadn't taken the first aid kit out for some reason.

"Here."

She thrust a cervical collar at Jackson and watched as he carefully fitted it in place around her mother's neck. They didn't have a back-board, not that they'd be able to use it right now. That meant she either needed to find something to use as one or get one brought to them. But first, free her mother from the SUV.

"Jack, can you see if she's stuck?"

"Steering wheel's all I can see."

She bit her lower lip. Then she levered around and climbed out the side window. Once outside, she pulled off her bunker coat. It was too hot and not of any real help right then. Besides, she'd need it to protect her mother as they tried to extract her from the vehicle.

But first things first.

She pulled her radio and stepped a few feet away, watching as Murray took Norwood's place at Ellen's side. Once she had, the coyote shifter worked to clear as much debris as he could from the older woman's legs. Mac turned away, closing her mind to the amount of blood her grandmother had lost.

"This is Santos. I have two heading up from Level 3. Victim is a five-year-old male. He'd been trapped inside an SUV. Minimal visible injuries. Have medics waiting."

"Colonel, your status?" Culver asked.

She blinked as tears burned her eyes. She knew what he was doing. By using her rank, he forced her to think like a cop. At least he wanted to. But it was hard when her mother and grandmother were hurt and still trapped and her daughter had turned furry much sooner than she should have been able to.

"Two trapped, one serious, one critical. We're working to free them but would appreciate help in plowing a better egress."

"And the third?"

She glanced at her daughter and huffed out a breath. "Undetermined."

What else could she say? She certainly wasn't going to broadcast the fact Cami had shifted.

"We've got teams working their way to you. Hang tight, Colonel."

"Roger that, sir." She slid the radio back onto her belt before gathering her thoughts. "Lolo, how is she?"

The witch looked over her shoulder and shook her head. "It's bad. She'd already be dead if she were human."

"Do what you can for her."

Dear God, don't let my gran die.

"Nate, change places with me. You and Jackson work on getting the driver's door open. If you can't, try the passenger door. If we have to, we'll break the seat back and pull her out that way."

The younger man nodded once and straightened before hurrying around the SUV.

Mac drew a deep breath, steeled herself and took Norwood's place. As she bent to move the first chunk of concrete, one about the size of her head, she glanced at the young panther. She sat as close to Ellen as she could without touching the woman. Worry and fear filled her eyes, Cami's eyes. Mac reached over and scratched between her ears.

"We definitely need to have a talk, kiddo."

She shifted another chunk of concrete, knowing it was still too little. The jaguar *prrrowed* and moved to her side. It rubbed against her shoulder before using its front paws to try to move some of the debris. Hearing it whimper in pain, Mac looked at her, loving her for trying to help but not wanting her to hurt herself.

"No, baby. You can't help in that form. Paws are great for a lot of things, grabbing rocks and moving them isn't one of them."

The panther gave another *prrow*, this one definitely not amused.

"Cami, I need you to listen to me." Mac paused and grunted with effort as she tried to roll away yet another piece of concrete. "I need you to shift back. Can you do that for me?"

The panther shook its head. Mac bit back a curse. Did that mean she couldn't or she wouldn't?

Hell, how had she done it in the first place?

"Cami, please. Concentrate on your human form. Close your eyes and do it. Ask you panther to help you. You've done so good shifting and protecting your baby brother and the others. But now I need you to help me and you need to be human to do it. Okay?"

She cast a quick glance over the hood of the SUV to where Jackson worked. He looked at her, as worried as she was.

"Your mom's right, Cami. You can do this," he said before once again bending into the Halligan tool wedged into the all too small space between the driver's door and frame.

"Please, baby. I need you to do this," Mac said, tears burning her eyes.

The panther tilted its head to one side, almost as if it was focusing on what Mac said. Then it nodded. Mac heaved a sigh of relief as it almost gently crawled through the window and into the backseat of the SUV. The last thing she wanted—well, almost the last thing—was for an SAR team to come upon them as Cami was mid-shift.

"Lolo?"

"She's fading. We need to get her out of here."

Mac dared a quick look and gasped softly. Just a few minutes earlier, fired had danced around the witch's hands. Now a soft glow, now white, perhaps a pale blue, surrounded them as she held them around the rebar piercing Ellen's thigh. A sheen of sweat covered Murray's face, making her look like she'd been running a marathon. Worried, Mac turned her attention back to the debris covering her grandmother, looking up only when a screech of metal against metal filled the air.

"It's open," Jackson said, panting heavily.

"Can you get her out?"

When Jackson didn't reply, Mac paused long enough to look across the hood. He and Norwood stood, heads together, as they examined Elizabeth and her side of the SUV. A moment only may have passed but it felt like a lifetime. It wasn't helped by the sounds of Cami groaning and moaning in the backseat as she tried to shift back to human.

Dear God, please let me wake from this nightmare.

"We need a strap or something, Mac," Jackson said.

Mac closed her eyes, thinking hard, trying to remember everything she'd stocked the back of the SUV with when her mother bought it less than six months earlier.

Please let her have kept everything back there.

"Cami?" Mac prayed she'd finished shifting. It only took her a minute or two to shift, but she'd been doing it much longer than her daughter. Add in Cami's fear and Mac hoped all this wasn't too much for the girl.

"M-mom."

"Cam sweetie, I know you're scared. But I need your help. Can you crawl into the back of the car and find the yellow straps back there? There should be two."

"I-I don't know. I can't see anything back there."

Mac gritted her teeth, cursing her own stupidity. Carefully, she moved around the SUV, watching where she stepped. Once at the shattered window, she looked inside. Relief filled her to see Cami quickly pulling on her slacks. Then, seeing the girl looking at her tattered blouse in horror, Mac reached for the bunker coat she'd discarded earlier. Without a word, she passed it through, watching as Cami quickly pulled it on. It was much to big for the girl but it covered her and that was what mattered.

"Here you go, sweetie."

She held out one of the spare tac lights. When Cami took it from her, Mac shone her light inside the SUV, waiting for her daughter to familiarize herself the flashlight. She watched as Cami leaned over the backseat, squirming around the dip in the roof as she tried to find the tie-down straps.

A few moments later, Cami was back. With the tac light in one hand and the straps in another, she all but launched herself through the backdoor window and into her mother's arms. Mac held her close for a moment and then took the straps from her, passing them on to Jackson.

"Get her out of here, Mac," Jackson ordered as Norwood went to work securing the end of one of the straps around the steering wheel.

"I'm not leaving, Dad." Cami planted her feet, crossed her arms and glared at her father.

Under any other circumstances, it would have been funny. In that one moment, Mac saw herself in her daughter. That determination not to be kept safe when someone she loved was in danger. The outrage that someone thought she wasn't capable of handling something. But now? She needed the girl out of there before anything else happened.

Before Jackson could respond, Mac's radio came to life. She listened as SAR teams reported in. Her mouth tightened to hear Assistant Chief Danvers sending the order for all teams to evacuate the garage. Before she could demand an explanation, someone broke in, telling her to go to a different frequency.

"Boss, we're almost to you," Tim Nguyen said, his breathing a bit labored. "DFD is pulling everyone out. Several of their teams came across gas pockets from broken lines and EOD found a suspicious object in HQ. They want to clear the buildings until both situations are dealt with."

"Then get out of here, Tim." She couldn't let anyone else put their lives in danger.

"Sorry, ma'am. I didn't hear that." He even made the sound of the signal breaking up before continuing. "Lee, Tanaka, Ramirez and Harris are with me."

Even though she wanted her people to get to safety, Mac heaved a sigh of relief. Between them, they'd be able to get everyone out.

She hoped.

"Mac, please. Take Cami and go. They're almost here. We'll bring Liz and Ellen out. I promise." Jackson looked from her to their daughter, his message clear. He didn't want to risk anything else happening to either of them.

"Mom," Cami drawled, anguished.

"He's right, Cam." Mac knelt in front of her, resting her hands on the girl's shoulders. "I don't want to go either but look around. There's not a lot of room around us. They're going to need every bit of it to get Grandma out of the SUV and then to help Gran. We'll just be in the way."

Tears ran down Cami's cheeks but she nodded. Mac stood. As she did, Cami reached through the now open driver's door and lightly clasped her grandmother's limp hand. Then she leaned in, kissing the woman's cheek. Mac watched, her heart breaking, as Cami moved around the SUV and knelt next to her great-grandmother. The girl's hands shook as they lightly touched Ellen's chest, her cheek.

"You're going to be okay, Gran. I promise." She bent and kissed the woman's too pale cheek and then raced back to where Mac waited.

"We cleared an easier path, ma'am," Lee said as he appeared out of the darkness. "DFD may have pulled everyone back, but our people are waiting along the way to help." He stepped forward and rested a reassuring hand on Mac's shoulder before dropping to one knee in front of Cami. "Your brother's worried about you, little ma'am. He's also really proud of the way you protected everyone. Don't you think it's time you let him know you're okay?"

Cami swallowed hard and nodded.

Lee took a look at Mac's tac light before handing her a new one. "Respectfully, ma'am, get your ass moving. We'll be right behind you."

"No unnecessary risks," she ordered as she slipped an arm around her daughter's shoulders.

"Same goes, Mac," Lt. Shelly Tanaka told her. "Now get out of here so we can get to work."

Mac checked to make sure Cami was ready. Then, with one last look at their family and friends, she led the girl off into the darkness. It took almost twenty minutes of climbing over cars and through—or under—fallen debris, but they finally saw light coming from the main entrance.

"Come here, baby."

Mac smiled down at Cami and held out her arms. Without hesitation, Cami dove into them, all but burying herself against her mother. Mac allowed a moment for them to cling to one another, reveling in the ability to hold her daughter close. Then she lifted the twelve-year-old and eased her to the side, settling her at her hip. It didn't matter that Cami was tall for her age. She simply let the girl wrap her legs around her waist. The last few hours—God, was that all? It felt like days—had taken a toll on all of them. Now all they could do was wait until the others came out with Elizabeth and Ellen.

Mac blinked against the sun and lift a hand to shield her eyes as she stepped out into the daylight. Immediately, several EMTs ran forward. Beating them was Xander who broke away from Moira and Jael. The women ran after him, pushing past the EMTs.

"Cami!" Xander threw himself at his sister the moment Mac put her down.

An EMT draped a blanket around both kids and led them off. The second EMT draped a blanket around Mac's shoulders and urged her to come with him. She shook her head, telling him to look after her daughter. She'd be there soon. But she needed to take care of something first.

She looked around, shaking her head as reality once again sank in.

"Jael, you've got command of the unit for now. I don't give a damn if DFD wants to work with us or not. I want to know what happened and why. Coordinate with General Flynn and Chief Culver. Are DPS and ATF on site?"

Jael nodded.

"I want their reports ASAP. Call in the rest of the Ghostwalkers. This is all hands on deck."

"What can I do, Mackenzie?" Moira asked, her brogue thick, as she slid a supporting arm around Mac's waist.

Mac frowned, surprised to see her there. Before she could ask, Moira explained that John had called another of their daughters, freeing Annie to go to the hospital with Pat and Mike.

Mac nodded. As long as someone was at the hospital with them, she didn't care.

"I need you to stick close to the kids for me. My brother and sister will probably be heading here when they find out about Mom and Gran. If you can make sure they're met at the airport, I'd appreciate it. Contact the pride. Let them know Jackson and I are all right. We'll update everyone as soon as we can. But tell them I want each of them to take precautions until we know for sure what happened and why."

"Mac, what aren't you saying?"

Mac heard Moira's concern. She didn't answer right away. Part of her knew she probably imagined it. However, it was the only thing that made sense, at least when it came to Cami so suddenly shifting. If she was wrong, she'd gladly admit it later. But, if she was right, they had trouble ahead and she was afraid this was nothing compared to what might happen next.

"Moira, I caught scent of a lycan near my mother's SUV. There's more. I'll explain later." She accepted a bottle of water from a passing uniform and nodded in appreciation. "Once the EMTs clear my kids, will you take them away from here? Maybe to the pub. Just get them away and make sure they're okay?"

"Of course, lass." The redhead looked back at the parking garage. "Your mother and grandmother?"

"Badly injured, especially Gran." The words tasted bitter on her tongue.

"Go reassure your son and then I'll take them to the pub. My Saoirse and I will look after them."

"Thanks." Mac leaned her head against Moira's shoulder for a moment and then straightened as Culver and Flynn hurried across the street in her direction. "Let me brief them and then I'll check on the kids."

It didn't take long. A report that basically consists of "they're badly hurt" and "I don't know anything else" never does. Mac left the men and slowly made her way toward the triage area where the EMTs were checking Cami. Each step hurt as every muscle ached. Her back burned where she'd scraped it who knew how many times crawling through the rubble. Her head pounded and her sinuses were clogged. Not that she'd complain. She'd never again complain about hurting after seeing her mother and grandmother.

God, they had to be all right.

"Mama!"

That was all the warning Mac got before Cami and Xander ran to her, leaping into her waiting arms. She held them close, murmuring softly as she reassured them everything was going to be all right. When she looked up and saw one of the EMTs standing behind them, she mouthed a silent *thank you*. He nodded and then looked at her, motioning that he wanted to check her injuries.

"In a minute." She leaned back, resting on her heels as she looked at her kids. "Moira's going to take the two of you to the pub now. Your dad and I will come get you just as soon as we can."

"Mom, I don't wanna go," Cami said fiercely.

"Me too!" Xander mirrored his big sister's crossed arms and stern expression.

"Kids, please." Mac tilted her head back and stared at the sky. She

71

understood why they wanted to stay. But she needed to know they were away from here and safe. "I promise we will be there just as soon as we can. I'll let you know how your gran and grandma are doing. But it's not safe here. I can't help the others if I'm worrying about you."

"Cami, Xander, your mama's right." Moira knelt next to Mac. "She needs to stay here and do her job as a police officer and as a member of the Tribunal. Right now, she's so worried about the two of you. That makes it harder for her to do her job."

Cami looked at her brother and nodded. She didn't like it. Everything from her expression to the way she stood to her scent told Mac she didn't. But she was mature enough to do as the adults asked. Not that it would keep her from letting Mac know about it later.

"All right." She hugged her mother and then stepped back. "Don't forget. You promised to tell us know how they are."

"And I'll keep my promise."

As Mac hugged them both, she hoped she would have good news for them. Then she stood and helped Moira to her feet.

"Officer Holzer!" she called to a nearby patrol officer she recognized. Less than a month ago, Jael told her they needed to keep an eye on and possibly pull into the division.

The young man, a former pro football player who decided he'd rather catch crooks than a pigskin, hurried toward her. "Ma'am?"

"Kids, Moira, this is Officer Marty Holzer. Officer, my children, Xander and Cami, and this is Moira O'Hara."

Holzer touched a finger to his forehead and nodded in greeting.

"Will you take them to the Irish Rose Pub and make sure they get in all right?" Mac asked.

"Of course, Colonel." He looked down at Xander, a smile on his lips. "You're about my little brother's age. Bet you'd like to play with the siren on my squad car."

Xander's eyes went wide and he looked up at his mother with a huge grin. "Can I?"

Mac chuckled, not about to deny him anything after the last few hours. "Sure." Then she turned to Holzer. "No running hot once you pull out."

"Of course not, Colonel." The twinkle in his eye had her wondering if he'd obey.

She watched as the officer led them off, Xander's hand in his. Moira bent and said something to Cami, who nodded in response. Knowing she had done all she could to protect her children, Mac turned to the EMT who had been waiting with growing impatience. She'd let him check her, but only if she got an update from the others. Shouldn't they be about out of the garage by now?

7

———

Twelve hours later, Mac finally made it to the hospital, Jael with her. Much as she wanted to be there sooner, she couldn't. not until every effort had been made to clear both police headquarters and the parking garage. Certainly not when she had to deal with political pissing contests between various agencies upset because she'd activated the Ghostwalkers and brought them in to not only help with the evac but with the investigation. Thank God, Culver had her back, telling each agency she had done so with his full support and appreciation.

All but dragging as she stepped out of the SUV Jael commandeered for them, Mac straightened her shoulders. A uniformed officer hurried forward, telling her not to worry. He and the other cops standing guard would make sure no one touched it. She thanked him and entered the lobby. As the all too familiar hospital scents assailed her, she checked her phone.

No new messages from Jackson.

God. Let that be a good sign.

As they crossed the lobby to the elevator, Mac paused. From somewhere down the corridor came the sounds of reporters shouting questions to Culver and others. Mac blew out a breath, more than thankful she didn't have to take part in the press conference. Tired as she was, she'd be too tempted to tell the media exactly what she thought of it.

Not that she'd mind, but it wasn't exactly the image the DPD tried to cultivate in the press. The moment the elevator doors opened, Mac stepped inside, Jael on her heels. She didn't need to say anything. Jael moved to stand between her and the doors. As she did, she jabbed at the controls, programming in the correct floor and then hitting the close door button. The doors slide shut and Mac sagged against the back wall, out of energy and ready to collapse.

It didn't take long before the elevator gave a slight lurch. A moment later, the doors slid open. Mac pushed away from the wall and stepped off, Jael at her side. The moment she did, the sounds of someone running in her direction reached her. Turning, Mac barely had time to brace herself before Cami threw herself in her arms. Worried, Mac lifted her, groaning slightly as every muscle screamed in pain and exhaustion. Cami held her tightly for a moment before slipping down to the ground. The moment her feet touched the tile floor, the girl wrapped her in a tight hug, one that felt like she might never let go.

"Cami?"

Worry warred with curiosity. Worry for her mother and grand-mother and curiosity about how Cami knew she was on that particular elevator at that particular time. Of course, Cami possessed some sort of sixth sense where her mother was concerned. No matter what the circumstances, the girl always seemed to know when Mac shifted. Since it reminded her very much of the way Ellen always knew if she was trying to hide something, Mac usually shrugged it off. But not now. Not when so much hung in the balance.

Cami didn't say anything, just clung to her all the harder. Worry spiking, Mac looked up and, with a jerk of her head, motioned for Jael to check on the others. She'd find out what bothered her daughter and then check on her mother and grandmother.

"Sweetheart, tell me what's wrong." Mac gently eased the girl's death grip around her waist and dropped to one knee in front of her.

"I was so scared, Mom." The twelve-year-old sounded both much younger and much older than her years as she buried her face in the crook of Mac's neck.

Mac patted her back and then sat back on her heels. "You want to know something?"

Cami nodded.

"So was I." She wouldn't lie about that. "Know something else?"

Cami shook her head. When Mac didn't answer right away, she pulled back so she could look at her mother. "What?"

"I'm so very proud of you, kiddo." She smiled at Cami and lightly brushed a lock of dark hair from the girl's brow. "You stayed strong and brave and you protected your little brother and the others. I couldn't have done any better if I'd been there."

But there was still the question of what Cami had protected them from.

"I knew I had to take care of them, Mom. It's what you would have done." Cami wiped her eyes, blinking against the tears shimmering in them.

"I know we need to talk about what happened, Cami, and we will. I promise." Even if she wasn't ready for *that* particular discussion. Mac grimaced slightly. Not that long ago, she dreaded have the sex talk with her daughter. But this? This made that particular discussion look like child's play. "But let me check on Grandma and Gran first."

Cami nodded and stood, waiting for Mac to join her. "Can we go see Aunt Pat, Mike and Aunt Marie then?"

Mac hesitated for a moment and then nodded. If her daughter was old enough to shift so she could protect her little brother and the others, she was old enough for the rest of it.

She hoped.

"Of course." She slipped an arm around her daughter's shoulders and let Cami lead her down the corridor to the suite that had been set aside for Ellen and Elizabeth and the family.

"Mac."

Jackson crossed to her and held her close. For a long moment, she held onto him much the same as Cami had her. As she eased her hold on him, he stepped back. She stood still as he looked at her, checking her for injury. Normally, she'd object, but she couldn't now. Not when she was doing the same where he was concerned.

"I'm okay, love. Just tired." And then some, but he didn't need to know. He had enough to worry about just then.

She glanced across the room. Two hospital beds rested against the far wall. Elizabeth lay on one and Ellen the other. Machines monitored their conditions, their beeping sensors silenced. Even so, Mac had no doubt alarms would sound if anything went wrong.

Dear God, don't let anything go wrong.

Pushing down her fear, she smiled a little sadly to see her younger brother and sister sitting between the two. Abby and Danny were almost ten years her junior, the product of their mother's second marriage. Once, the age difference and the fact they had different fathers—not to mention the fact Elizabeth clearly preferred them over her eldest daughter—created a chasm between them, but no more.

Mac looked from them to their injured kinswomen and wished she had better news for them—or them for her.

"I'm glad you're here." She hugged them both before checking on their mother and grandmother. The women lay motionlessly on their beds save for the shallow rise and fall of their chests.

"We wouldn't be anywhere else, Mac." Abby cocked her head to one side and studied her older sister. "Are you all right?"

"I'm fine. Just tired and sore." Not to mention worried and mad. "What have the doctors said?"

Abigail took her arm and led her across the room to where Jackson stood with the kids. At her look, their brother took Xander from Jackson and suggested he and the little boy go find Mac something to eat.

"They're both injured badly. The doctor said if you and the others hadn't gotten to them when you had we'd have lost them," she said once her twin and her nephew left the room.

"Specifics?"

"Mom's got a nasty concussion. Her liver was lacerated, and her right kidney bruised. She also has several broken ribs and they are monitoring her for additional internal bleeding.

"But she's going to be all right?" She glanced at their mother.

"If she doesn't suffer any complications, she should."

"Abby, I know you've got your own practice and you need to get back to it, but can you stay. At least for a few days?" She prayed Abbie said yes.

It still amazed Mac that her headstrong and sometimes flighty little sister grew up to be a doctor. She worked in a family practice near Austin. From everything Mac heard, Abby was well-respected and her patients loved her. That meant a great deal to Mac. But she needed her sister now and hoped Abby understood.

"I'm here for the duration, Mac." Abby rested a hand on her sister's arm before smiling down at her niece who stood with an arm around her mother's waist. "The partners know and will cover for me."

"What about Danny?" Jackson asked.

"He took vacation time. Said he'd take a leave of absence from the university if necessary."

Mac nodded, unsurprised. But she didn't want her brother getting in trouble with his dean. Her brother taught business courses at the University of Texas at Austin. This year, he was up for tenure. She didn't want him to jeopardize his chances and knew their mother and grandmother wouldn't either.

"Now, have you let anyone take a look at you?" Abby pinned her with a serious look that was a perfect imitation of one of their mother's.

"I did." Not that she'd let the EMTs treat her. There'd been too much to do. Now she looked down at their daughter, letting her see just how tired she was. "Sweetie, I'll take you to see Pat and the others if you want, but it's going to have to be after I get some rest. If you want to go now, your dad will take you."

Cami looked between them and then nodded. "Aunt Abby, will you look after her?" She sounded much older than her twelve years that it broke Mac's heart. Her little girl shouldn't have to grow up so quickly and certainly not under these circumstances.

"Of course I will, Cami. You two run on. You might stop by the cafeteria and make sure the guys are getting your mom something more than coffee and a sweet of some sort. She needs real food." The look she sent Jackson spoke volumes and Mac wasn't about to argue. Just then, she felt like she could eat a cow.

"Get some rest, love." Jackson brushed his lips against hers and led Cami from the room.

"All right, big sister, strip and let me take a look at you. If you're hurting badly enough for me to see, I know it's bad."

Mac nodded in appreciation as Abby helped her to the far end of the room where a sofa and several recliners sat. Instead of going to one of them, Mac dropped onto the low coffee table in front of the sofa. Wincing, she tugged her polo shirt up and off. As she did, she felt more than saw Abby wince. Then Abby's fingers gently traced down the skin of Mac's back before she unhooked Mac's bra and eased the straps from her shoulders.

"Remind me to give you a lecture later about waiting to get treated, Mackenzie."

Now Mac did wince. She knew that tone of voice all too well. She'd heard it often enough from their mother growing up.

"How bad is it?"

"You need a couple of stitches and it's going to hurt like a bitch when I clean it up, but it could be worse." Abby moved back around the table and squatted so she could look Mac in the eyes. "I'll deal with this and then I want to see the rest of it, Mac. You'll be fine once you shift a time or two, but you're going to hurt in the meantime."

Suddenly, she threw her arms around Mac and held her close. Gone was the extremely confident doctor. In her place was the worried little sister.

"Hey, it's okay, Abby." She stroked her sister's back much as she had her daughter's not that long ago. "Mom's going to be all right. You said so yourself. And Gran's tough, you know that. She's not going to give up."

"You're right. Sorry."

Abby leaned back and wiped her face with both hands. As she did,

Mac smiled gently. She didn't doubt her sister had played the strong one for the family because she knew just how badly their mother and grandmother were hurt.

"Don't hedge now, Abby. How bad are they?" Mac nodded toward the two beds.

"I didn't lie about Mom. It's bad but she should be all right." She managed a soft chuckle. "Thank God, she takes such good care of herself."

"And Gran?" Mac swallowed hard and reached for her sister's hand. She wanted to see Abby's face as she answered.

"It's bad, sis. Really bad." Abby dropped to sit on the floor at Mac's feet. "I've reviewed her records. She would have died if Jael and the others hadn't found her when they did. Hell, Mac, I don't know how she's still alive. It's more than being stubborn as hell and being a Pure."

Mac nodded, thinking about the energies she saw glowing out from Murray's hands as the younger woman tried to staunch the flow of blood from the wound in Ellen's thigh.

"And?" she prompted.

"Her organs were shutting down by the time she got here. Only time's going to tell. Even if she makes it, she'll have a very long road ahead of her as she recovers."

Mac blew out a shaky breath and nodded. "What can I do?"

"Make sure nothing else happens to her or Mom."

"I'm on it." In fact, she'd already ordered security for the two. "What else?"

"Let me fix you up. Then you need to contact the Tribunal. I don't know everything about it, but I do know they need to hear what happened. Gran's not going to be able to perform her duties on the Tribunal for potentially a very long time. You and they need to prepare for that."

And that was another headache, one Mac most definitely did not want to deal with. Not that she had any choice.

"C'mon, big sister. Let's get you cleaned up now. I brought you a change of clothes when I stopped by the house earlier."

"Thanks, kid." She smiled and painfully climbed to her feet.

Half an hour later, Mac sat on the sofa, Xander in her lap. Cami sat next to her, her head resting on Mac's shoulder. Jackson sat on the recliner to their right. Abby and Danny had returned to their chairs between the beds, giving the family a bit of privacy. Mac looked up and smiled at her sister. Somewhere along the line Abby had become a very thoughtful and intuitive young woman. Mac kind of missed the headstrong girl she'd been but, for the moment, knew they needed this Abby more than the other just then.

"Mama." Xander looked up at her, his expression screwed up in confusion.

"What is it, sweetheart?

"Why can Cami turn furry and I can't?" His lower lip protruded in a pout. "I've been trying and trying, but I can't make it happen. It's not fair."

Mac hid her laugh behind a cough and then sobered. Leave it to the five-year-old to broach one of the subjections they'd been dancing around since her arrival.

"Xander, I kind of want to know how she did it too," Mac said, hugging him before handing him off to his father. "Cami, can you tell us what happened?"

The girl glanced at her hands where they rested in her lap. When she looked up, Mac sighed softly. Then she took Cami's hands in hers and held them.

"Sweetheart, you aren't in trouble. I meant it earlier when I said I'm so very proud of you. You need to believe me."

Please let her believe me.

"I was so scared, Mom." If possible, she burrowed even closer to Mac's side. Understanding, Mac pulled her onto her lap, much as she had Xander earlier. "We didn't know what happened, but I could tell Gran and Grandma were worried. Grandma told me to make sure Xander was buckled in. She said she was trusting me to take care of him. Then she told us all to hold on and she sped up."

Xander nodded from where he sat in Jackson's lap. The little boy's eyes were wide as his listened to his sister recount the way a loud boom seemed to roll through the parking garage. A moment later, a dust cloud blew through. Elizabeth sped up even more as she raced through the garage toward the exit.

"I could see stuff falling from the ceiling, Mom. Gran yelled for Grandma to watch out. Grandma hit the brakes. The SUV skidded and I remember Grandma reaching out to hold Gran in place like you do to us when you have to slam on the brakes." She looked up and gave Mac a shaky smile.

"Where do you think I learned it?" Mac nuzzled her daughter's hair. "What next?"

"Then something hit us. The airbags went off and it felt like the back wheels went up off the ground. Like maybe something drove up under us. Once the SUV stopped and the airbags went down, Gran opened the door to get out and see what happened even though Grandma told her not to.

"Suddenly, Gran yelled for Grandma to get us out of there. But she couldn't. Whatever hit us hurt her. Then there was a rumble and part of the ceiling fell. I heard Gran cry out. Then something hit the top of the SUV."

"What happened then?"

Mac looked at her husband and had a feeling her expression was just as haunted as his.

"It got really quiet and the lights went out. The only lights were from our headlights. All I could hear was the engine and Grandma trying to breathe. I tried to get her to answer me but she wouldn't. Neither would Gran." She sniffled and ran a hand under her nose.

"I knew I had to do something, Mom. Grandma told me to take care of Xander. That meant I couldn't just sit there. So I got out of my seatbelt and climbed into the front seat." Tears ran down her cheeks and she scrubbed at them. "I knew Grandma was hurt. She wasn't moving. I remembered Dad saying once that it was bad to let a car run in a garage, so I turned off the engine. I tried to call you, but I couldn't get it to go through."

"That's okay, love. You did everything right. What happened next?"

"I didn't know what to do." She sniffled again and Mac wished they didn't have to make her relive it. "Grandma was hurt. I leaned her back from the steering wheel so I could check her. When she wouldn't wake up, I tried told Xander to stay where he was. Then I crawled over to check on Gran." Her sniffles turned into a sob. "She was bleeding so bad. I started to get out to see if I could help her. That's when I saw them."

Mac swallowed hard. Then she reminded herself not to overreact. The kids didn't need that.

Hell, she didn't need that.

"Saw who, Cam?"

"Them. A man and a dog. But it wasn't a dog."

Mac stomach dropped and her arms tightened around her daughter until Cami looked up at her in concern. It was all she could do to ease her grip. When she looked at Jackson, his eyes burned with an intensity she recognized. He understood what their daughter hadn't said. Had he scented the lycan as well?

More importantly, how had Cami?

"How did you know it wasn't a dog?"

Cami rolled her eyes and Mac relaxed a little at the display of pre-teen attitude.

"You and Dad taught me what to look for."

"What else?" Mac had a feeling there was more. That *more* was the only thing that made sense of the rest that happened.

"Mom, they didn't smell right. I know it doesn't sound right, but they didn't. I don't know how I could smell them over all the dust and stuff, but I could."

"I know, baby." She brushed her lips against the top of Cami's head. As she did, she looked at Jackson, worried and yet relieved. If their daughter hadn't realized something was wrong, who knows what would have happened. "What then?"

"I didn't mean to, Mama, Daddy. Really. But I didn't know what else to do." Once again, Cami buried her head against Mac's chest.

"Sweetheart, just tell us. You aren't in trouble. I promise."

The rest of them might be because they hadn't planned on her being able to shift so soon, if ever. Then there was Xander, who was really perturbed that his big sister could do something he couldn't.

"I knew I had to protect Gran and the others. I couldn't let the man and the wolf get any closer. All I wanted was to be able to shift like you and Dad. Shifted I could protect them better than like this." She waved a hand at herself.

"She told me to keep really still and be quiet." Xander took up. "Then she changed. It was just like you, Mama. Except it hurt her bad. She cried and I got scared again."

Jackson bent his head and brushed his lips against the boy's cheek. "Shifting hurts, Xander. As you get older and get used to it, it doesn't hurt as badly, but it still hurts."

"And once you shifted?" Mac reached down and tilted Cami's face so she could look in her daughter's eyes.

"I climbed out of the car and stood between Gran and the others. I roared." Now Cami grinned and her eyes sparkled. "That was pretty cool." She sobered a moment later. "The man reached inside his jacket. That's when Auntie Jael called out and said they were coming. The man cursed and ran away, calling for the wolf to go with him. I wanted to go back to Xander but I didn't want to leave Gran until Auntie Jael were there to help her."

"Oh, baby, you did exactly right." Mac hugged her tightly. She was so damned proud of her daughter. She still didn't understand how Cami managed to shift, but she was glad she had. Things would have been so much worse if she hadn't. "I'm very proud of you."

"We both are," Jackson said.

"Mom?"

"Yes, baby?"

"Why was I different from you and Dad when I shifted?"

That was the second million dollar question to come out of all this. And one Mac didn't have the answer to.

"Because jaguars and panthers related. They come from the same family, just like us," Jackson said. "When all this is over, your mom and I will go over our family histories with you and you'll see that we have jaguars, panthers and even a few cougars like Aunt Pat in our family."

Mac arched one brow over their daughter's head and Jackson gave a quick dip of his head.

"But why can't I shift?" Xander demanded.

"Xander," Jackson warned. Then he relented. "You're too young, son. Besides, it looks like your sister is more like your mother than we thought. Mom started shifting when she thought she was in danger. Cami did when she thought you and Gran and Grandma were. Our girls are protectors."

The little boy cocked his head to one side and studied his mother and sister and then nodded. A moment later, he slid off his father's lap and ran to them, throwing his arms around them. Mac chuckled and lifted him onto the sofa to sit next to her.

"C'mon, little man. Let's go see if we can't find you some ice cream. I bet Uncle Danny and Aunt Abby will come with us." Jackson glanced at his wife's siblings and they nodded in agreement. As he bent to pick up Xander, he whispered in Mac's ear. "I think you two need a few minutes alone. We'll be back soon. Then you're going to get some rest."

"Mom," Cami said once the others left the room.

"Yes?"

"You were kind of freaked when you saw me."

That was putting it mildly.

"I was." She'd never lie to her daughter. "I've been hoping you'd be a shifter like your dad and me. But you're only twelve. Our kind don't usually start shifting until they're at least thirteen or fourteen. Your dad and I have kept an eye out for signs you might be about to start, but we hadn't seen any and neither had Gran. So, yeah, it did kind of freak me out to find you furry. Sorry."

Cami grinned and shook her head. "Don't be. It kind of freaked me too." She grinned up at her mother and then slid off her lap. "Know something else?"

Mac looked at her in question, not sure she was ready for any more surprises. "What?"

"I like it when you call me Cam instead of Cami. It sounds more grown-up."

Mac smiled, understanding. She'd felt the same way when she was around Cami's—no, she corrected mentally—Cam's age. That's when she put her foot down and told everyone her name was Mac or Mackenzie, not Kenzie.

"I think after today you can decide what we call you. If you want to be called Cam, Cam it is." Mac grinned then and gave her a wink. "I might forget from time to time because you're still my little girl."

"Mooom," she drawled.

"Caaaam."

The two burst out laughing, only sobering when a soft knock sounded. A moment later, the door opened and a nurse stepped inside. She checked her patients and then smiled at Mac and Cam.

"Moira and John are in the waiting room. They brought dinner for you."

"Thanks, Paige." Mac stood and crossed to where the young woman stood. She'd known the nurse since joining the pride so long ago. "Cam, why don't you go let them know how your grandma and great-grandma are? Tell them I'll be there in a minute. I need to make a phone call first."

"And I'll stay with Ellen and Liz," Paige said before the girl could protest.

"Okay." She hugged her mother and left the room.

"Mac, you need to get some rest."

"I will soon. If you don't mind sitting with them until one of us gets back, I'd appreciate it. I need to call the Tribunal and let them know how Gran is."

And that was one conversation she did not want to have. If her grandmother died—God, don't let it come to that—it would shake the Tribunal and leave a hole in their leadership. A hole certain folks would be more than glad to try to take advantage of.

That was something she would not, could not allow to happen. Too much rested on the Tribunal holding its present course.

8

The clock on the far wall of the conference room read 0530 when Mac pushed open the doors. As she stepped inside, she stopped and looked around. It felt surreal to report to Central Division instead of police headquarters. She hadn't worked out of this house since her rookie year. But, with the damage to headquarters, Central, as well as the other divisions, was taking up the slack. Until Culver and his staff figured out where to put everyone while the building was repaired or the city decided it was cheaper to build a new one, her command would be split between Central and the Northwest Division.

And wouldn't it be fun trying to keep track of everyone? But that was a worry for another day. Until the investigation into the bombing was closed, the Central would be home to the taskforce she now commanded.

Early as it was, half a dozen detectives and uniformed officers were already hard at work. Tim Nguyen and Shelly Tanaka stood near one of the white boards, their heads together as they conferred. Loquita Murray transcribed notes onto another whiteboard. Already displayed were still photos of the inside of the parking garage and the HQ building. Captain Nico "Nick" Deluca, EOD, sat at one of the long tables set up in front of the whiteboards, speaking with Lt. Megan Halstead from Cyber. The last was Culver himself.

Culver looked as exhausted as Mac felt. In fact, most everyone there looked as if they'd gotten little, if any, rest since the bombing. Understanding, Mac moved to where Culver stood next to yet another table. Someone, bless them, had brought in several thermal coffee pots as well as three large boxes of donuts from a nearby shop. He nodded as she poured a cup before checking the top box and grabbing a mini-cinnamon roll.

"How are they?" he asked softly. He didn't need to specify who he meant.

"Pat and young Mike should be discharged tomorrow or the next day. The only reason they're keeping Mike is so he can be with his mother. The doctors want to keep an eye on he for another day or so." She bit into the roll and then took a sip of coffee, needing both the caffeine and sugar to jumpstart her system. "Mom regained consciousness a couple of hours ago. The doctor thinks she's got a week or so before she can be released. He hasn't upgraded her condition yet, so she's still listed as critical. But he said if she doesn't spike a fever and no complications arise, he'll upgrade her later today."

"Your grandmother?"

Mac shook her head, emotion closing her throat. Ellen should be dead. They all knew it. Not even her shapeshifter physiology was enough to have kept her alive. The fact she was, Mac knew, was solely because of Murray. The younger woman did something arcane that kept her grandmother alive and she'd never be able to thank her enough for it. If Ellen had a chance, it was because of her.

And, looking at Murray, it was clear from the shadows under her eyes, so dark they looked like bruises, not to mention the exhaustion etched in her face, that it had cost her.

"Is there anything I can do?"

"Give me five minutes alone with the bastards responsible for what happened?"

Culver gave her a small smile that told her he'd like nothing more and then took a moment to refill his mug. "You're in charge of the investigation, Mac. So far, no one's taken credit for the attack. But it was an attack. EOD found the remains of two IEDs, one in the garage and one in the main building. Capt. Deluca can give you more detail. But they also found several other unexploded devices. Someone wanted to make a much bigger statement than they did."

She frowned, thinking back to what her daughter said. Had the blast been an attack against the cops or against paras or both?

And why hadn't anyone taken credit for it? Usually, fringe groups couldn't wait to get their names in the paper. The fact no one had worried her.

"Understood, sir." She thought for a moment as she studied Murray's carefully written notes on the board. "Pat hasn't had a chance to put her staff together. With your permission, I'm going to have Tanaka take over as temporary head of CaP. I know there are unit commanders who have more rank and seniority, but she has an eye for detail and she knows how both Pat and I work."

"Consider it done. What about Homicide?"

"Nguyen. It will be a good test to see if he's ready for command."

"It's your bureau and your investigation, Mac. Just let me know if you're bringing in anyone from the outside to assist with the investigation."

"Understood." She paused before continuing. "Sir, I brought in the Ghostwalkers yesterday and I planned to keep them on the case."

He looked at her in concern but said nothing.

"Sir, I don't want to get into all the details, not yet. I promise to fill you in as soon as I can. But my daughter saw a man and a shifted lycan approaching the SUV before Jael and the others arrived. She knew the 'dog' was a lycan because her father and I taught her what to look for. But she said something else that has me worried about what the real motivations behind the blasts might be. She *smelled* something about the two that wasn't right. It scared her and she knew she had to protect Xander and the others. As I reported yesterday, I scented at least one lycan in the area and Jackson confirmed he did as well. I doubt I need to tell you what that means.""

"Are you sure?" He looked as stunned as she felt when she scented the lycan the day before.

"As sure as I can be without having been there myself. I know I scented a lycan when I neared Mom's SUV. As I said earlier, Jackson did as well. Cam confirmed that's why she got scared enough to shift." She gave a small, almost sad, smile. Her daughter had grown up a great deal in the last twenty-four hours. "Damn it, Cam saw them, sir! She sensed they meant trouble and knew she needed to find a way to protect the others. The last thing my mother told her was to protect her brother. It seems my little girl took that order to heart and figured out how to shift."

Now Culver's eyes widened almost comically. "She's too young," he all but hissed.

"Tell me about it. But she shifted and was still shifted, not only when Jael and the others arrived on-scene but when I got there afterwards."

"Dear God." He ran the fingers of one hand through his hair. "All right. Then this most definitely falls under your new command, Colonel. I'll leave you to it. What time is your briefing?"

"In an hour, sir. I wanted to be here early to review the reports that came in after I left for the hospital last night."

"I want an update as soon as you're done."

With that, he turned and left the room, closing the door behind him.

Three hours later, Mac leaned back and rubbed her eyes. The few minutes of sleep she managed to get at the hospital hadn't been close to enough. She should have gone home. She should have demanded her husband and children go home and get some sleep. But she hadn't. She couldn't. Not until they knew if their loved ones would survive. In the meantime, she'd just have to mainline coffee and not sit still for long.

"Ma'am?"

She looked up and nodded to see Tanaka, Nguyen, Megan Halstead and Nick Deluca standing across the table from her. Motioning for them to sit, she reached for the coffee pot in front of her. A frown pulled at the corners of her mouth to find it empty. Before she could go in search of more, Murray was there, pot in hand. Mac thanked her and motioned for the detective to join them.

"Tim, Megan, I want the two of you working together as much as you can. I know you've got more than enough on your plates right now, between the investigation and trying to salvage what you can from HQ and getting things moved over here. But I want you two doing a dive into the Dark Web. To say I'm bothered by the fact no one's taken credit for what happened yesterday is putting it mildly."

"We've already started, ma'am." Halstead pulled a small notebook from her jacket pocket and flipped through the pages before continuing. "I've also got several teams ready to enter the garage as soon as EOD clears it. I want them to check every vehicle for cameras, don't care if they are phones or dash mounted. We might get lucky and find something that way."

"Very good." Even if it was a longshot. "I want to know the minute you find anything."

"As soon as I know, you will," the lieutenant assured her.

"Tim, we both know everyone in Homicide's going to want to help with this investigation. We've been in similar situations before." Too many times for her peace of mind. "But we can't shirk the other cases. If a detective or uniform has the free time, they can help. But it has to be coordinated with the lead detective.

"In the meantime, the squad isn't to accept any new cases the ME hasn't specifically ruled a homicide. Send all other cases back to the referring squads."

She paused, doing her best to remember court and vacation schedules.

"Ask Patrol for additional uniforms if you need them. I'll approve anything within reason."

"Understood. Am I authorized to cancel all vacations?"

She nodded. She doubted anyone would bitch, not when someone dared attack HQ. Still, people were people.

"If anyone complains, let Jael know. If she can't handle it, I'll step in."

At the mention of the woman, Tanaka asked the question Mac figured they all wanted an answer to. "Where is Jael?"

For the first time since the briefing started two hours earlier, Mac chuckled. "Probably in the Chief's office pounding her head—or his—against the wall about now."

Nguyen's eyes narrowed. "Mac, what did you do?"

She grinned and Tanaka arched a brow in question.

"Jael gave up a promotion and transfer to stay on my staff. I made sure she got the promotion anyway. Chief Culver should be breaking the news to her about now."

And, in about five minutes—ten max—Mac figured Jael would be there to remind her she did not like surprises, she wasn't an officer, and she did not want or need the promotion.

Deluca whistled softly and shook his head. "Colonel, you do love to live dangerously."

"Life's never boring that way." She gathered up her notes and slid them into a folder before standing. "This will be the op center for the taskforce. Computers, desks and other equipment we'll be needing will be moved in this morning. Once it has been, I want entry only by authorization. Until then, lock the boards up and get your teams to work. Then figure out what you need to get your squads up and running and let me know."

"Your office?"

"Just one of about a million things on my very long to-do list." She placed her now empty mug on the table and turned to Murray and Tanaka. "Shelly, I know you'd prefer to head the investigation and you will, as acting head of the division. But you need boots on the ground when you can't be there." She tilted her head in Murray's direction, her unasked question clear.

Tanaka nodded once and then turned to her partner. "Lolo, you're team lead. I'll be as active as I can but the colonel's right. I'm going to have my hands full trying to get the division set up here, making sure our other cases are covered and everyone makes it to court when they should."

"That includes making sure the DA's Office knows if any of those injured yesterday were scheduled to testify in the upcoming future. They may need to file for continuances," Mac said.

Tanaka wasn't the only one to grimace.

"I'll send a reminder to all the CaP squads," she said, making a note to do just that.

"Good." Mac smiled at the four, knowing they made a good team. "I want hourly updates. Next briefing at 1300 hours."

Half an hour later, Mac slid into the front passenger seat of a newly issued SUV. Her department issued vehicle was still parked down the street from headquarters, part of the ongoing investigation. According to the evidence tech she spoke with earlier, they might be able to release it to her in another day or two. But, until then, she needed another vehicle, like it or not.

And she did not like it. She had too many bad memories associated with Michael King's death and how he had been assigned a new vehicle the morning he died.

"Would you care to tell me why you didn't at least give me a head's up?" Jael asked as she slid in behind the steering wheel.

Mac didn't ask what she meant. Not when the woman made her displeasure, thankfully only temporary, known the moment she tracked Mac down near the conference room.

"I believe what you said to me the last time I asked you a similar question was, 'suck it up, kid. You deserve this.'" Mac waited until Jael blew out a breath before sliding the key into the ignition and starting the engine. "And you do, Jael. While I appreciate you choosing to stay on my staff, especially after what happened yesterday, I don't like the fact you gave up a promotion you more than deserve. Then there's the little fact that you turned down your own command, something you've wanted as long as I've known you. I owe you and I called in a favor or two. Sue me."

"You're just as stubborn now as you were as a rookie." Jael pulled away from the curb. "I guess all I have to say is thanks."

Mac nodded, relieved.

"Where to?"

"Let's head to the Wind Dancer. I need some decent coffee and something to eat and I'd like to see if Drea or Aya have heard anything that might help us."

Jael didn't say anything. She didn't need to. Mac knew she had questions and it was best to answer them now, rather than later, especially since the Wind Dancer Café was owned by Murray's aunt and cousin, both powerful witches and, thankfully, close allies of the pride.

"Mac?"

"I had a very interesting discussion with my daughter last night."

Well, that was one way of putting it. Judging by the way Jael barked out a laugh, she knew exactly what Mac meant.

"I bet," the woman chuckled.

"You have no idea." Mac rubbed the bridge of her nose, willing the headache building between her eyes to dissipate. "It seems she had a damned good reason for shifting, one I certainly didn't anticipate."

"I don't like the sound of that, Mac."

"You'll like it even less when I tell you."

"Just say it, kid."

"She shifted because she knew she needed to protect the others."

Jael's hands tightened around the steering wheel. Other than that, she showed no reaction Not that it fooled Mac. She knew the woman as well as she knew herself. Jael understood exactly what that bit of news meant.

"You're sure?"

Mac nodded. "You know that both Jackson and I scented at least one lycan as we neared Mom's SUV."

"And?" Jael prompted.

"That's why Cami shifted."

Jael looked at her quickly before turning her attention back to the road. "Why and how?"

"Seems she takes after me more than we realized. She shifted because the last thing Mom told her before losing consciousness was to protect her brother. After the SUV was damaged and Mom and Gran hurt, Cam tried calling me. It didn't go through. Then she saw a man and what she first thought was a dog approaching. She said she knew it wasn't because of everything Jackson and I taught her. She also said they didn't smell right. Already scared and worried, her need to protect the others kicked into high gear and she shifted. She was trying to scare them off when you and the others arrived."

"Mac, are you sure?"

Mac nodded. She knew Jael meant no insult to either her and Jackson or to Cami. Under Tribunal law, there shouldn't be any lycans in the state, much less in town. There were no packs in the area, and none had been given permission to pass through the territory, much less set up residence here. So what the hell was happening?

And did their appearance have anything to do with the bombing?

"What's the plan?"

Thank God, Jael didn't try to argue or convince her she had to be wrong. Instead, she went right to the chase.

"Like I said, coffee and food and maybe some information from Drea and Aya. Then I want to have another look at HQ and the parking garage."

Well, more than a look but she doubted she'd get the chance to shift and search the two buildings. Still, looking around in her human form was better than nothing.

Who knows? She might get lucky and actually find something to help them figure out who was responsible for the blasts and why.

9

Mac walked down the street, badging her way through the security points. Expression thoughtful, she sipped coffee from a go-cup and considered what Adrienne told her. Neither she nor her daughter, Aya, knew anything about lycans being in the area or who might be responsible for the bombing. A couple of local witches had reported being harassed by normals who viewed their kind with fear, but that was nothing new. Dallas was in the middle of the Bible Belt and many still viewed witchcraft as Satan's work.

One possible lead chased and ruled out, not that she'd held out any real hope for it.

A few minutes later, she stood across the street from the main entrance to the parking garage. A frown pulled at the corners of her mouth. If she ignored the damaged HQ building and the boarded-up windows in buildings on either side of the street, it almost looked like any normal day. Police cars, marked and unmarked, were parked outside HQ. People, some in uniforms and others in soft clothes, moved between buildings. But she couldn't ignore the damage or the barricades closing off the street or the yellow tape and evidence markers that decorated the street and sidewalks.

With Cait looking out of her eyes, Mac knew what she needed to do. As much as she never wanted to enter another underground parking garage again, she needed to. She needed to see the scene and its attendant destruction without the panic that drove her the day before. Her family was safe. Her children basically unharmed, her mother recovering. She owed it to them and to her grandmother who might still die from her injuries to be the cop they all thought her to be.

Squaring her shoulders, she crossed the street. Like the day before, she wore a hard hat and carried her tac light. Unlike the day before, several patrol officers stood guard in front of the drive leading inside the garage. Both looked too young to have graduated from the Academy. She didn't recognize them and wondered if they'd been brought in from one of the other divisions to help. Not that it mattered. Nothing was going to stop her from going inside.

Unfortunately, one of the uniforms hadn't gotten the memo. As she neared, he stepped forward until he stood directly in her path. Mac stopped and looked up at him, not quite believing he was foolish enough to try to stop her. She glanced down, making sure her ID hung around her neck. It did and not only should he have recognized what it was but he should have taken time to check it. Even if he didn't recognize her, he would have been briefed on who headed the investigation—her.

"You'll have to stay back, ma'am. DFD's said no one in except them and EOD."

Mac blinked one. When he inhaled sharply, she had a feeling her eyes had gone the darker green they were when Cait let her presence be known. Good. Maybe he'd think twice and step aside.

"I beg your pardon, Officer." She made a point of letting him see her look at his nameplate. "Lagina."

"Sorry, ma'am. But I have my orders. The scene's not yet secured."

Mac bared her teeth, her jaguar so close to the surface it surprised her she didn't growl.

"And what are your orders, Officer?" She ground it out, making his partner look over and pale.

"Lagina, let her through," the woman hissed as she hurried to where they stood. "My pardons, Colonel. He's a little on edge like we all are."

"Morales, you know no one's supposed to go inside!"

Mac had enough. Even as Jael hurried toward them to diffuse the situation, she did something she'd never done before. She grabbed Lagina by the upper arms and bodily moved him to the side. His momentary surprised at being manhandled by a woman a good eight inches shorter and fifty or more pounds lighter gave her the time she needed to duck under the yellow crime scene tape.

"Get back here!" Lagina ordered.

"You idiot!" Morales said at the same time. "You're lucky she didn't put you on report. That's Colonel Santos. She is in charge of this fucking investigation."

Mac switched on her tac light and shut out the sounds of the more experienced Morales giving her rookie a lecture he'd better not ever forget. She hadn't gotten more than ten yards inside when Jael caught up to her. The woman looked at her but didn't say anything right away. Not that it fooled Mac. She knew her former training officer was waiting until they were not only out of sight but out of earshot.

They moment they climbed down to the next level, Jael grabbed her arm and pulled her to the side. Even in the deepening shadows of the garage, Jael's eyes sparked.

"What the hell, Mac? Have you lost your mind? He's the kind to file a grievance against you."

"Let him!" She didn't care and the sooner Jael and everyone else realized it, the better. Then she rubbed a hand over her face. "Sorry."

"Mac, what is it?" Concern roughened Jael's voice. "This isn't like you."

Mac looked around, using her tac light to illuminate the area. With a jerk of her head, she led Jael to the three steps leading down to the next half level. On either side, stood metal guard rails. Mac tested one, making sure it was still solid. Satisfied, she leaned against it.

"I spoke with the other members of the Tribunal again this morning."

"Ah, shit, kid. No wonder you're on edge." Jael rested a hand on her shoulder. "They know your grandmother's still alive, don't they?"

Mac nodded, her expression grim. "They also know how badly she's hurt."

"And?"

"And I told them everything. The extent of her injuries. Cam's shifting and seeing the man and wolf coming toward them just before you and the others arrived. Jackson and me scenting a lycan. All of it."

Jael swallowed hard, her expression letting Mac know she had a pretty good idea how the conversation went.

"I take it they told you what they expect you to do."

Mac nodded again. "I'm to confirm whether or not lycans have returned to the area and, if they have, make sure the Tribunal's judgment is carried out. I am also to step up and fill Gran's spot until she recovers."

Left unsaid was "if she recovers."

"Damn, kid. Have you talked to Flynn and Culver about this?"

"Yeah. Culver reminded me my first duty is to find out who set the blast. Then we can worry about who has jurisdiction. Flynn simply said to put our team to work and let him know if we need more manpower or anything else."

"And Jackson?"

Mac pushed away from the low barrier and took several steps before turning back to face Jael. "The only thing keeping him from trying to find the lycan on his own is that our kids need him right now. I can't be with them. Even though Abby and Danny are here, they aren't parents. Cam and Xander need him and will until Mom's better and we know how Gran's going to be."

"What can I do?"

"Exactly what you have been. Watch my back. Let me know if I'm about to cross the line and keep your eyes and ears open. If the lycans have returned, even if it is just one, we need to find them before they hurt anyone else."

"You know you can count on me."

102

Mac nodded and blew out a breath. "I'll apologize to Lagina when we're done here," she promised.

Now it was Jael's turn to shake her head. "I'll deal with it. You shouldn't have manhandled him, but he handled the situation all wrong. He didn't ask for your ID. He didn't check to see if you'd been cleared for entry. He just assumed and you were right to bring him up short for it."

"I'll leave it to you then, Captain." For the first time in what seemed forever, she grinned and meant it.

"I am going to get you back for this, Mac. I am *not* an officer."

"Look at it this way, Jael. You get to show all the rest of us just how good of a non-com you are as you masquerade as an officer."

Grinning at Jael's disgruntled look, Mac started off, feeling a bit better for talking. But there was still a great deal to do and she couldn't shake the feeling time was running out. With that thought in mind, she pulled her radio.

"Murray here, Colonel," came the response a few seconds later.

"What's your 20?"

"Level 2-B by the staircase."

"On my way."

"Negative on that, ma'am. We've found what may be another unexploded device and are on our way out."

Damn it!

Mac hissed out a breath.

"All right. Meet me outside." She beat a fist against her thigh. Then she turned to Jael. "I don't buy whoever caused all this." She waved a hand down the drive and then in the direction of HQ.

"You're bothered by more than not being able to go deeper," Jael said. "What?"

Mac nodded and stalked back up the drive, her tac light illuminating the path before them. "Something isn't right about all this." Another wave of her free arm to the scene around them. "Someone knew enough to place a couple of IEDs in such a way they caused a great deal of damage to both buildings without bringing the buildings down. They knew to do so when more people, more cops and other law enforcement personnel, than usual would be in the area. More paranormals too. Yet they were careless enough to leave how many unexploded devices?

"Add to that the fact there was no chatter beforehand to indicate there might be an attack planned and no one has come forward since to claim responsibility. It just doesn't make any sense."

She climbed over the short railing between levels and turned toward the entrance. As she did, an EOD team hurried past them.

"Now, throw in a lycan and we have too many possibilities and no solid leads."

"Agreed, but the evidence is there. We just have to figure out what strings to pull."

Mac nodded but they both knew that was easier said than done. "Do me a favor and deal with the uniforms. I'll see what Murray can tell me."

Jael nodded and, as they stepped out into the sun, broke off, moving in the direction of the two uniformed officers from earlier. Mac crossed the street. She leaned against the fender of her SUV and waited for Murray to join her. As she did, she checked her email, reading a short report from Tanaka about a plan to transition CaP to Central. It wasn't optimal, but it would work. She sent him back the go-ahead to send it to Culver for his approval.

"Colonel," Murray said as she and Officer Cena approached.

Mac nodded, noting that Cena's usually perfectly pressed and spotless uniform was anything but. Clearly the uniformed officer had been crawling around in the parking garage right along with Murray who looked like she'd been playing in a dirt pile.

"Cena, you see anything that caught your eye?"

The officer, new to the division but a seasoned officer, nodded grimly. "Yes, ma'am." He turned his head and coughed before trying to clear his throat. "Sorry, ma'am. Dust's not much better down there today than it was yesterday."

Mac nodded, not doubting it one bit. "Go on."

"I had a look at some of the fragments of the device the bomb squad has recovered so far., ma'am. I can tell you this much so far. The device that went off in headquarters, Colonel. It wasn't all that sophis-ticated. But it was designed with efficiency and destruction in mind. From the images I saw of the parking garage and the remnants of the device that detonated down there, the two were more than likely built by the same bomber. What I saw just now wasn't. I'd bet my life on it."

"Explain."

"It was sloppy. The EOD guys can tell you more but I wouldn't bet money on the guy who built it expecting it to even go off."

"Thanks."

Well, that confirmed what she'd been thinking. Since learning of the unexploded devices, they'd bothered her. the only thing that made sense was they were intentional attempts by the bomber to confuse the investigators and send them chasing leads that would take them nowhere.

Not that it helped narrow down the search for suspects. Not yet at least. But maybe it was enough to help EOD get an ID based on the bomb designs. Deluca told her during the briefing, as had his prede-cessor during another case, that every bombmaker had his own signa-ture, for lack of a better word. So who knows? Maybe they'd get lucky.

"All right." She thought for a moment. "Check with the teams in HQ. If they've cleared the area up to the blast zone there, I want you and Murray to go have a look."

"On it." He dipped his chin in Murray's direction and trotted off in the direction of the building's main entrance.

"Let's take this inside, Lolo." Mac walked around to the driver's door and climbed in the SUV. She waited until Murray joined her. Then she slid the key into the ignition and started the engine, sighing in relief as the air conditioner started cooling the interior. "Did you see anything to indicate anyone but a human was involved in what happened?"

The detective blew out a breath. "You mean other than your daughter turning furry a good two years before she should?"

Mac nodded.

"Nothing that stands out."

"I hear a *but* in there."

"Yes, ma'am." Murray turned in the passenger seat so she looked directly at Mac. "I know you and your husband wouldn't say a lycan was in the area if there wasn't. So I have to take that into consideration."

Mac leaned back. Something about Murray's tone told her there was more to it. But what?

"There's something else, ma'am—Mac."

Oh-oh. It was never a good sign when Murray called her by her first name at a crime scene.

"Just say it, Lolo. There are already so many things about this I don't like that one more won't matter."

She hoped.

"Actually, two things. One a request that will probably need you stepping in and running interference with DFD. The other is, well, I'm not sure."

Mac waited, giving the younger woman time to figure out how to say what she needed to.

"Start with the request," she suggested a few moments later.

Murray nodded. "I know this is unorthodox, but after what you told us this morning about scenting a lycan, I'd like Norwood or one of the other canine Pures to shift and do a walkthrough of the garage and of HQ with me. I know it's a long shot, between the blast and all the people who have been in and out since, but they might pick something up."

Mac smiled, nodding. That was exactly what she'd considered doing. She might not be a canine shifter, but her sense of smell in her jaguar form was much better than as a human. The fact Murray wanted to do basically the same thing told her she'd been right to bring the woman into her Marine team. Not only was she a good cop but she thought like one of Mac's team—in other words, she wasn't afraid to think outside the box.

"What else?"

"I'm going to discuss it with Tanaka when I get back to Central, but I want to bring in Officer Tangie Robinson for the team. She was in one of the classes I taught at the Academy a year or two ago for witches who wanted to join the Department. I've kept my eye on her since then. Not only is she a good cop, but she's got a touch of foresight. She called me this morning out of the blue, asking if we could meet."

Mac had a feeling she was going to regret asking, but she had to.

"What did she have to say?"

"First, she assured me she didn't get any warning about the blast and I believe her. Foresight isn't her main gift and it's an inconsistent one. But, when it hits her, it is always right."

Mac chewed her lower lip and nodded for her to continue.

"She said this isn't an isolated incident. Said we need to warn other departments and agencies that openly recruit paras."

Mac closed her eyes and counted to ten. If this was the start of an open war against paras and those who accepted them, things were going to get very bad, very quick.

"Did she give you anything to help us ID those responsible?"

Murray nodded. "Lycans and one or two renegade witches."

Mac felt like she'd been hit. She'd expected lycans after scenting the one yesterday. But the addition of witches complicated matters.

"Anything more specific?"

Murray shook her head.

"First, tell Robinson good job. Assure her she did right by reaching out to you." She thought for a moment. "What's her current assignment?"

"Traffic out of the Northeast Division."

Mac took out her cellphone and made a quick note. "Talk to Tanaka. If she approves adding Robinson to the team, pull her in. She'll be your responsibility, Lolo. Put her to work just like you would any other uniform on an investigation. But use the time to evaluate her. When the case is closed, you and I will talk and see if she would be a good permanent fit in the bureau or if she should return to Patrol."

"Understood, ma'am." She relaxed and Mac smiled slightly in reassurance. "About the other?"

"Not Norwood." Mac held up a hand before Murray could protest. "Lolo, he's more than capable of doing what you ask. Hell, we both know he'd volunteer given the option. But I don't want other cops to start looking at him and our other canine shifters as nothing more than police dogs they can use as they want."

Murray's eyes widened and her mouth opened in an "O" of surprise. Then she snapped her mouth shut before nodding.

"I'll send orders to Lee to get two or three of our team over here, shifted before they arrive. Get with Lee to see who he's going to send and then set up teams that consist of one detective or other member of the investigative team, one Marine and a shifter. I will make sure there are no problems with EOD or DFD."

"Thank you, ma'am." She sat back and, for one brief moment, rested her head against the headrest and closed her eyes. As she did, Mac wondered if she'd gotten any sleep the night before. "May I ask why you were about to crawl through the debris again?"

"I wanted a look for myself. I was so focused on getting to my family yesterday, I didn't pay as much attention to the scene as I should have." And if that caused others to be hurt or killed, she'd never forgive herself.

Murray didn't say anything. Instead, she looked out the windshield, watching as members of the EOD squad exited the parking garage. Without a word, she opened her door and stepped out. Then she leaned back inside the SUV, grinning.

"Coming, Colonel?"

Mac laughed and nodded. Then she lifted one hand, signaling for Murray to wait. "Give me a couple of minutes. Make sure no one approaches the SUV except Jael. Use the time to touch base with Tanaka and Lee. Tell Lee what we talked about. If he has any questions, tell him I'll be in touch as soon as I can. If Jael returns, brief her."

"Yes, ma'am.

Mac watched as she closed the door. Then she maneuvered until she crouched in the rear of the vehicle. Doing her best not to make it rock back and forth as though two teens were getting hot and heavy inside, she slid out of her DPD windbreaker. By the time she began undressing, the first wave of pain of a shift washed over her. Gritting her teeth, she pulled off her DPD tee shirt. Her Kevlar vest followed. Scooting around until she sat on her butt, she toed off her boots and shimmied out of her slacks and underwear. Then she rolled onto all fours and gave in to the shift.

Now, Cait!

10

The jaguar shook itself and carefully climbed over the seat. As it did, it looked through the windows. Too much sun. Too many people. Mackenzie foolish to shift here. It would be much better to do so where they could hunt and run for a while.

Soon, Cait, Mackenzie promised. *And we are hunting now. Just a different type of prey.*

Cait sat in the front seat without the strange wheel in front of it and thought. There was much about this part of Mackenzie's life she didn't understand. But she understood hunt.

Hunt humans?

They'd done that before. But not hunt to eat. Hunt to find and arrest. She hadn't understood arrest then. Mackenzie explained it meant finding someone and putting them where they couldn't hurt innocents anymore. Was that the kind of hunt she meant?

Maybe.

Mackenzie could be confusing, like now.

We hunt lycans, Cait. One may have tried to hurt our family yesterday. It may have been responsible for the explosions.

The jaguar's lips pulled back, revealing very sharp and dangerous teeth. Her growl filled the inside of the SUV. She hated lycans.

Me too, Mackenzie agreed.

The jaguar growled again, unable to get out of the SUV. Angry, she slapped a paw against the window. She chuffed as Murray jumped back. Then the woman shook her head. A moment later, she opened the door and Cait jumped down to the pavement.

"Are you sure about this?" she asked as Jael joined them.

Cait nodded. Then she sat still, her tail wrapped around her paws, as Jael fastened a leather collar around her neck. She hated the collar and the leash Jael held, but Mackenzie told her they were necessary sometimes to make the humans feel safe.

"All right, EOD has cleared—again—the site and said we can go in. But they aren't happy about it," Jael said as she fastened the leash to the collar.

"And Lee is sending six of our team over. They'll be here as soon as he briefs them," Murray added.

Cait stood and waited patiently for Jael to give her the signal to cross the street. It was an act. She was alpha. She didn't need permission from them to do anything. But she wouldn't scare the humans around them, one of whom nervously fingered the gun at his waist.

They know we are alpha, Mac said. *But they don't understand what that means. They don't know we will protect them.*

Silly humans.

And Cait knew how to deal with them.

Chuffing softly, she rubbed her head against Jael's thigh. When the woman reached down to scratch between her ears, Cait rolled onto her back, exposing her stomach. Murray chuckled softly as the jaguar gave her best innocent little kitten imitation, batting at Jael's hands and demanding attention.

Kneeling to rub Cait's belly, Murray smiled in approval. "Nice, ma'am. They're relaxing. Ready to go?"

Cait batted at Murray's hand and rolled over. Once on her feet, the jaguar wound around Jael's legs and walked to the curb, sitting down and waiting for her human "handlers" to join her.

"Let's go before someone decides to call Animal Control," Jael joked.

Ten minutes later, Cait stopped. Jael and Murray waited as she opened her mouth and breathed in. There were so many competing scents, too many of them, to sort through. Cait wrinkled her nose and then sneezed as the dust that still hung in the air, kicked up by those working nearby, tickled and irritated in equal part.

Are you all right? Mac asked, her mental voice concerned.

Cait sent her an image of the jaguar rubbing her nose on her paws and the green grass, trying to get rid of the irritants. Mac gave her a mental caress, assuring her it wouldn't be much longer before they could leave. Then the woman retreated, letting Cait continue the search.

Something. There was something she couldn't quite recognize. She knew it. Growling, she tugged against the leash, straining to go deeper into the parking garage. Needed to go deeper.

She whimpered softly in pain as broken glass cut one pad. Shaking that paw, she lifted it and then bent her head, carefully licking the wound. Before Jael or Murray could check it, she took a slow step forward, trying to pick a spot without anything else that might hurt her.

Easy, Cait.

Now understand why Mackenzie wears shoes.

Senses on alert, she climbed over one car, then another, before dropping back to the concrete. Then she tugged against the leash, wanting to move faster. She scented the young one. It was faint, but it was enough to tell her they were close.

Jael cursed as Cait pulled the leash from her hand. Finally free, the jaguar moved agilely through the debris. Metal groaned as she leapt from one car to another, avoiding the pavement as much as she could. Behind her, the woman did their best to keep up. They either did or didn't. She needed to move, to hunt.

The scent of blood, old but familiar, hit her as she dropped to the ground near the SUV. She growled angrily as she recognized the scents. Elder and elder's daughter.

Easy, Cait. They live, Mac reassured her.

She growled again. Then she slowly paced forward, moving

around the vehicle, nose close to the ground. As she did, she scented the young ones. She chuffed softly, pride filling her, to scent the young panther.

Strong cub. Make good alpha later.

Wait! What?

Mac's disbelief had Cait chuffing in amusement.

Mackenzie is alpha and so is mate. So is elder. Cub will be alpha too.

There!

Another scent, one she recognized.

One that had her baring her teeth. She padded away from the SUV and further down the drive. Two scents now, both lycan. But one shifted, the other not.

Where, Cait? Where did they come from?

Cait threw her head back and screamed, the sound echoing off the walls. She didn't know. Too many scents. Too much time since they were here. Mackenzie should have brought her sooner.

"Mac?" Jael carefully approached, her hands out to show she presented no danger.

Cait shook her head. Didn't mean to frighten friends. But angry. So angry. Stupid to have waited so long.

She turned and raced back up the drive. At the SUV, she stopped and sniffed the ground all around it. She had the scents. She wouldn't forget. The lycans came too close to her family. They would pay. She would see to it.

We *will see to it*, Mac corrected.

Leaving Jael and Murray to follow, she ran into the darkness. She wanted out of there. Needed out of there.

Needed to shift to tell the others what she found.

"Mac, stop!" Jael yelled. Then she cursed as she and Murray were slowed by debris.

Couldn't stop. Needed to shift. Meant getting back to daylight and clothes. Mackenzie would not be happy if she shifted without clothes nearby.

Didn't understand clothes.

Didn't like clothes.

Don't you dare shift until we're back inside the SUV, Mac warned.

Cait chuffed but, much to Mac's relief, kept moving upward. Luck was with them because the trailing leash didn't get caught on debris or anything else. Soon, the jaguar leapt into the bright sun.

Wait for Jael, Mac ordered.

"Stop!" a man yelled at the same time.

Cait ignored them both. Instead, she slowed, remembering not to scare the humans, and trotted across the street in the direction of the SUV.

"Lagina, don't!"

"Mac, down!"

Pain lanced across Cait's shoulder a split second before she heard the shot. She roared and turned, ready to meet the challenge. Before she could, Murray threw herself on her, telling her to stand down. Across the street and down maybe five yards, two cops were wrestling. But it was the sight of Jael running full-out toward them that stopped Cait. The woman shoved the cops apart and ripped the man's gun out of his grip. A moment later, she had him face down on the pavement, his hands cuffed behind him.

"Get in the SUV and shift, goddammit!" Jael ordered as she stood, hauling Lagina to his feet. She pointed toward the SUV. "Now, Colonel!"

Mac stood at attention in front of Chief Culver's desk. To her left stood both Murray and Jael. To her right, the two uniformed officers from earlier that morning. No one said anything. No one dared, not if they had an ounce of sense and looked closely at Culver's face. To say he was pissed was putting it mildly.

Mac had no doubt at least one of them would not be walking out of the office with their badge and gun. It wouldn't surprise her if it happened to be her. Putting hands on the uniform had been one of the more foolish things she'd done in a long while. All she hoped was Culver understood. Maybe she'd get lucky and he would feel getting shot was punishment enough. Even so, the rip would still be on her record and that was on her.

Culver pushed away from the desk and stood. In that moment, he was no longer a "suit". He was the dedicated and well-respected top cop who earned his reputation as one of the best on the streets.

"No one is to say anything unless I direct a question to you. Understood?"

"Yes, sir!" they answered in as close to unison as possible.

"Then I'll start with the easy questions. Colonel Santos, are you all right?"

"Yes, sir."

"Do you feel you are able to return to duty?"

"Yes, sir."

Fortunately, the bullet had only grazed her and shifting back to human helped speed its healing.

"Did you at least have an EMT look at it?"

"I did, sir."

"Very well." He glanced up and down the row of police officers and frowned. "Captain Lindsay, what the hell happened and why shouldn't I toss all of you out on your asses and let IAB deal with this?"

Mac heard Jael swallow hard and scented her worry. But she knew if she were to look, none of the woman's uncertainty would show on her expression.

"Sir, Colonel Santos wanted to do a walkthrough of the scene. She had not been able to do more than a cursory one yesterday. Because of information that came into her possession since then, she felt she needed to do a more careful inspection this morning."

Culver indicated she should continue.

"When we attempted to enter the parking garage, Officer Lagina here stopped us. He told the colonel she wasn't allowed inside. He said it was by DFD order."

"Did he check her ID or make any attempt to verify she was included in that order?"

"Negative, Chief."

Culver glanced at the uniformed officer and frowned. "Is that correct, Officer Lagina?"

The officer swallowed hard enough Mac heard. But he said nothing.

"Officer Lagina, I need you to answer aloud," Culver said.

"Yes, sir." Frustration and resentment thickened his voice. "If I can say something, sir?"

Culver nodded.

"Sir, when I came on duty, I was told DFD had limited admittance to the parking garage to their personnel and EOD. I was simply carrying out those orders."

"I see."

Mac didn't wince but she wanted to. She knew that almost lazy tone of voice. When Culver sounded like that he was pissed. The only question was at whom.

"Officer, were you given a list of authorized personnel at the time?"

"No, sir."

Judging from the way Officer Morales stiffened where she stood next to her, Mac had a feeling Lagina had not told Culver the whole truth.

"Officer Morales?" Culver turned his attention to the senior of the two patrol officers.

"I'm sure my partner didn't mean to misspeak, sir."

Oh, she was not happy with Lagina, not that Mac blamed her.

"I think you'd best explain, Officer."

"Chief Culver, while we were instructed to keep all but authorized personnel out, we were also given a printout with a list of investigators from both DPD and DFD who were allowed inside one or both buildings."

"And was Colonel Santos' name on that list?"

"Affirmative, sir, along with Captain Lindsay's."

"I see." Culver turned, looking once again at Lagina. "Officer Lagina, was the colonel's ID visible when she tried to enter the parking garage?"

"Yeah."

Now Mac did wince. One simply did not "yeah" the Chief when he was in this mood. What surprised her was how Culver seemed to ignore it.

"Colonel, I understand you put hands on the officer and physically moved him away from the garage entry. Is that correct?"

"It is. I was wrong to do so and there is no excuse for my behavior. I'll accept any punishment you feel appropriate." Unlike Lagina, she wouldn't try to hide her role in what happened.

"I believe you had more than enough provocation, Colonel, but I would prefer it not happen again."

"Chief Culver!" Lagina actually took a step forward.

"Step back, Officer Lagina!" he snapped. "Detective Murray, I haven't heard from you."

"Sir, I met up with Colonel Santos outside the parking garage after my team found what looked to be another unexploded device. We contacted EOD and then vacated the premises. Once I joined up with the colonel, I briefed her on what we'd found so far and made several requests that would, in my opinion, assist with the investigation. One of those was to have an officer or a member of Ghostwalkers who is also a shapeshifter go through the two buildings in their animal form. Our dogs are good, but a shifter would know more what we are looking for and would then be able to discuss what they found once they shifted back to human.

"She agreed and admitted that was one reason she'd returned to the site. We discussed our options, and it was decided she would shift and take a look once EOD cleared out again."

Not exactly true, but close enough Mac decided not to correct her.

"I see. Once the colonel shifted, did you or Captain Lindsay take any steps that would indicate to onlookers that the colonel was anything but a loose wild animal?"

Murray laughed softly. Then she apologized before describing how Jael placed the collar on the jaguar and attached a leash to it. She also described how they took time to pet the jungle cat, something the jaguar instigated.

"And were Officers Lagina and Morales present at the time?"

"Yes, sir. In fact, now that I think back on it, the colonel made sure to do her innocent little kitten act after I saw Lagina looking at us and fingering his weapon."

"Officer Lagina, did you see the colonel in her shifted form before they entered the parking garage?"

"Yes, sir." He said it so grudgingly, Mac wondered how he didn't choke on the words.

"So seeing a jaguar coming out of the parking garage shouldn't have been a surprise. Isn't that right?"

"It was running loose! It could have killed someone."

Mac pursed her lips, fighting the urge to retort.

"Officer Morales, did you feel the jaguar presented danger to anyone?"

"Negative, sir. There were no others close to the garage or near the SUV where it was clearly heading."

"What did you see, Morales?"

"I saw Colonel Santos in her jaguar form running across the street toward the SUV. I noted her collar and the leash trailing behind her. Captain Lindsay and Detective Murray exited the garage a few seconds after her. When I heard my partner." Disdain dripped from her voice. "When I heard him yell for the jaguar to stop, I turned and saw him drawing his weapon. I ordered him to stop but it was too late. He'd already fired."

"I understand you disarmed and cuffed him, Captain."

"I did, sir," Jael confirmed. "He discharged his weapon against one of our own. He did so in an unsafe manner and in such a way that he put others in danger, and he did so against the orders of his partner, who outranks him."

"All right." Culver frowned and returned to his chair. "Morales, I want a full report on the incident and on any other calls you and your partner have responded to where he has shown what might generously be called a lapse in judgment. Have it on my desk by end of day."

"Yes, sir."

"Lagina, I am referring this incident to IAB. In the meantime, you have earned yourself a two-week rip. Leave your gun and badge on my desk before you leave."

"You can't be serious!" Lagina leaned forward, hands on the edge of the desk. "You can't be taking *her* side."

"And what side would that be, Officer?" Culver asked, his eyes flashing.

"She's one of *them*, sir. She's not human."

Mac stiffened, but she didn't otherwise react. She knew some people harbored a prejudice against the paras. People were people, whether they were human witch or shifter. That meant there were those who were scared of or resented or simply hated those who weren't like them. She simply hadn't run up against it to this degree in the Department. Culver and his staff had done an exceptional job fighting against those attitudes and she'd done all she could to support him. But this? Damn it, she wanted to reach over and beat some sense into Lagina.

"That is enough, officer." Culver once again climbed to his feet. "Departmental rules are clear. I will tolerate no such attitudes in the DPD. We do not discriminate against anyone based on race, creed, sexual orientation, political beliefs or whether they are human or paranormal. When you return from your suspension—if you do after IAB finishes its investigation—you will be assigned to a desk until you prove to your commanding officer and to me that you will not let your prejudices influence you again. Now hand over your badge and gun and get out of my office.

"Officer Morales, you are to escort him to his locker, let him clear out anything that is not DPD property and then escort him out. And get me that report by end of shift."

The two saluted. No one said anything as Lagina slapped his badge and gun on the desktop. Once the door closed behind the two, Culver turned his attention back to the three women standing before his desk.

"For God's sake, relax." He waved for them to find seats. "For the record, consider yourself counseled, Mac. Try not to put your hands on an officer again."

"Yes, sir." She relaxed a little. "May I explain?"

"No need. I have a pretty good idea what happened and why . But you're brass now, Mac. If something like that needs to be done again, let Jael do it."

She nodded, knowing he was right.

"I doubt you're going to have to worry about running into Lagina again, at least not with him wearing the uniform. I won't have one of my officers acting as he had. My only question for you is if you want to file charges."

Now she shook her head. Filing charges would solve nothing. Worse, it would cement his prejudice against paranormals in his mind and, quite possibly, make other cops think twice before trusting her or any other para on the force.

"I don't like letting him off that particular hook, but I agree it's the right move, at least for now," Culver said. "So two questions. Are you really all right and did you find anything?"

Mac leaned back and gathered her thoughts. "To answer your first question, I'm fine. It wasn't a bad wound and shifting helped." Although she knew her husband would not be pleased when he found out what happened. But that was a battle she'd fight later.

"As for what I found, I'm going to have to brief General Flynn and the Tribunal. I caught the scent of not one but two lycans. It was strongest near my mother's SUV, but I caught the scent again one level up. My guess is that's the way they escaped."

Culver cursed softly. Then he reached for his cellphone. They watched as he sent a text. A few moment later, he tossed the phone onto his desktop.

"I'll talk to Flynn. He'll be in contact for your report."

He scrubbed his hands over his face. Hearing the sound of skin scraping over whiskers, she realized for the first time that he hadn't shaved that morning. Looking closer, she doubted he'd gone home.

"Thank you, sir. Once you've talked to the general, I'd appreciate you making sure the orders concerning entry into the two buildings are expanded to include the Ghostwalkers. I want them able to access the buildings without having to get involved in any jurisdictional pissing matches."

He nodded. "Do we know yet how the explosives were smuggled into the HQ?"

"Not yet, Chief. Tech teams are pulling all security cam footage for the last week for both the garage and HQ. It's going to take time to cull through it all."

"Do you need more personnel?"

"Not at the moment, sir. I'll put some of the Ghostwalkers on the videos. We have certain equipment the Department doesn't."

"Let me know if you change your mind." His phone pinged and he glanced at the incoming message. "I need to take this. Detective Murray, I'll let you get back to work."

"Thank you, sir." She stood and glanced down at Mac,

"Update me in an hour. I'll be in the field."

"Roger that, Colonel. Chief, Captain." She waited until Culver indicated she was dismissed before leaving the office.

"As for you, Mac. You need to let the departmental doctor see your injury and you need to let Jackson know before someone else does. I want your report by two. There's a press conference at three you're to be at unless you need to be in the field."

Somehow, she would make sure she needed to be in the field.

"Yes, sir."

"Jael, make sure she does as I said."

"I'll try, sir."

He chuckled softly as Mac glared at her. "Dismissed."

The two women stood and briefly braced to attention before leaving the office. Neither said anything until they stood in the elevator and the doors closed behind them. Mac sagged against the back wall and blew out a breath. Then she lifted her hand to her injured shoulder, lightly fingering the thick bandage under her shirt.

"Don't say it."

Jael didn't, but her look spoke volumes.

"I was an idiot, but I had good reason. There was something I didn't tell Culver. Something I won't tell him until I've had a chance to talk with my cousin and we've checked a couple of things."

"You'd better be willing to tell me," Jael said simply.

"Once we're in the car."

Jael nodded and programmed the elevator to take them to the ground floor.

12

An hour later, Mac stalked inside the non-descript building little more than a mile from police headquarters. Outside, the building looked like so many in this part of town: an old warehouse that had yet to be reclaimed and repurposed for an art gallery with lofts or trendy shops. A little rundown, undergoing yet another round of renovations that were taking so long it didn't look good for the building's continued existence. But on the inside, it was a high-tech center Mac's Marine command worked out of. Her goal just then was below ground and shielded so no one could pick up their conversations or intercept their comms.

And it was probably for the best as angry as she was just then.

Frankly, it was a minor miracle she hadn't started sprouting fur and fangs.

"Colonel." Lieutenant Jon Houston, one of three tech specialists assigned to her command, stood and braced to attention as she entered.

"At ease." She waved him back to his seat. Then she glanced at the various monitors in front of him. "Anything?"

"Not yet, ma'am. It's slow going. We're working our way backwards, starting with the time of the blast. But the cams that would tell us the most were damaged or destroyed by the blasts."

"And?" She heard his unsaid "but" and that worried her.

"We haven't yet received the video from yesterday that had already been dumped on the off-site servers."

Mac didn't growl or curse but it was only because she was currently trying to grind her teeth to pebbles. Damn it! Well, at least that was something she had control over. Telling him he'd have the video feeds shortly, she pulled her phone and moved through to her small office. If she discovered someone was stalling handing over the videos—or anything else—heads would roll.

"Tech Services, Officer Villareal," a young sounding man said a short time later.

"Colonel Santos here, Officer. Put me through to your day shift supervisor." For the life of her, she couldn't remember who that might be.

As she waited, she put the phone on speaker and settled behind the battered desk. Several reports awaited her review. Messages from General Flynn and her cousin Mateo rested on top of the reports. They had to wait. When she finished with Tech Services, there was another call she needed to make before dealing with anything else.

"Good morning, Colonel Santos. Lt. Andrew Abbott here. What can I do for you?"

"Lt. Abbott, I find myself with a problem. Are you aware that I am also the Department's liaison with the Feds?"

"Yes, ma'am."

Good. Hopefully, that would make this easier.

"And are you aware that I called them in to assist with the investigation into yesterday's attack on our HQ?"

"Y-yes, ma'am."

"It is my understanding that there has been a request filed with your office for copies of security cam footage from both the parking garage and the main HQ building, said footage to cover the twenty-four hours prior to the explosions. Am I understanding that correctly?"

He didn't answer right away. Instead, she heard the clicking of a keyboard as he quickly typed in a series of commands. Interesting. Either he didn't know about the request or he did and he thought the files had already been sent over. Of course, there was one other possibility, one she didn't want to consider: someone had purposefully ignored the request. If that was the case, there'd be hell to pay.

"My apologies, Colonel," he said a few moments later. "I see the request was filed yesterday evening. I assume my people are working on pulling the files together for you but everything's a mess right now. Half my command is relocated to Central and the rest are spread among the other Divisions."

"As is my own, lieutenant. But those files are stored off-site according to my information." Mac waited a beat, letting him consider his options. "I suggest you make sure the requested videos are transmitted as requested within the next two hours. Otherwise, I will be forced to take this up with Chief Culver. I assure you he will not be as understanding as I am."

She ended the call before he could respond. Then she stood and moved to the office door. Houston glanced up and shook his head. With the door open, he'd heard enough of her conversation with Abbott to figure out what was going on.

"If you don't have the files in two hours, let me know."

"Yes, ma'am."

"In the meantime, check traffic cams in the area. Maybe they can tell us something."

"Already on it, ma'am. I may have something for you in a couple of hours."

Nodding, knowing it was the best she could hope for just then, Mac returned to the office. She didn't spend much time there, leaving the day-to-day running of the unit to Lee. Even so, there were a few personal touches like the family picture on the corner of the desk. She picked it up and smiled at the memory. She had taken the picture last Christmas. Elizabeth, Jackson and Ellen sat on the floor in front of the Christmas tree, Cami and Xander in front of them. They'd been so happy that morning.

God, was that going to be their last Christmas together?

Mac shook my head. She couldn't, wouldn't consider anything but Ellen recovering from her injuries. They would have more birthdays and Christmases together. She wouldn't accept anything better.

Pushing aside her fear, she crossed the office and closed the door. It didn't take long to strip out of the clothes she'd been wearing. She tossed her bloodstained shirt into the trashcan next to her desk. Then she moved to the small closet, barely more than a slim opening in the wall, and pulled out clean clothes. A few minutes later, she wore black cargo pants, black tee shirt and black boots. she flexed my arm and rotated her shoulders, wincing slightly.

She'd been stupid reacting to Lagina like she did. Now she needed to look into him to make sure he wasn't involved in the bombing.

As if she didn't already have enough to run down.

But that had to wait until she called the other members of the Tribunal and updated them.

And wasn't that going to be a lot of fun?

Not.

Ten minutes later, Mac sat at her desk—this time with the doors closed—and watched as the other members of the Tribunal appeared on her laptop screen. Two faces were missing: Ellen's and Pat's, who sat on the Tribunal for her son until he was old enough to assume the chair his father would have held had he not been murdered. In Ellen's absence, Malachi Levison called this impromptu meeting to order.

"Mackenzie, do you have an update for us?" he asked.

She nodded.

"Dr. Patek sent word earlier that Pat and young Mike should be able to be discharged tomorrow or the next day. He's keeping Mike mainly so he can stay with his mother. Pat was more seriously injured. From what Mike told Jackson, his mother did everything she could to protect him." Mac smiled slightly, remembering Jackson's description of what the teen had to say then. Mike was not happy that his mother was injured trying to protect him. "I'm making arrangements for them to be taken to a safehouse when they're discharged."

"Do you believe that's necessary, Mac?" Adrienne Campbell asked.

Murray's aunt, the unofficial leader of the witches in this part of the country and the first non-shifter on the Tribunal—although she'd been joined by two others in the last year—looked at her video feed in concern.

"As Lolo will tell you, Drea, I tend to plan for the worst, especially when lycans are involved."

"Then you confirmed their involvement?" Shepherd Haskins asked.

"I did. Jackson and I both scented them immediately after the blast. When I returned earlier today, the scents were still there. Fainter, of course, but unmistakable."

She paused. Here came one of the more difficult parts of her report and the mother in her wished she didn't have to make it. Not yet, at any rate.

"There's something else. I told Malachi when I spoke with him yesterday that we had one other shock yesterday after the blast." Seeing how the man's dark blue eyes danced in humor, she fought the urge to groan. He might see the humor in all this, but she certainly didn't. "After my mother's SUV was trapped, my daughter tried to help her grandmother and great-grandmother. Both were injured and unconscious. That's when she saw a man and what she first thought was a dog wolf nearing the car. She knew something was wrong about them. When I asked her about it, she said she knew it wasn't a dog or wolf because of things her father and I taught her. She also said they didn't smell right."

The witches didn't seem to understand, but the Pures on the Tribunal did.

"The last thing Mom told her before everything went to hell was to take care of her brother. Scared, Cam didn't know what she could do. She's just a kid, but she was going to do whatever it took to protect not only Xander but Mom and Gran." Mac licked her lips as she tried to figure out how to say it. "She shifted and left the SUV to confront them. Fortunately, Jael and several others arrived about that then."

And Mac's insides still turned to water thinking about what could have happened if Cam had been forced to fight the two.

"She is too young," Deanna Psaki said.

"Apparently, she takes after me and her abilities were awakened by feeling endangered. Trust me, when I finally got to the car, she was there in all her shifted glory, trying to protect our family and scared because she didn't know how to shift back."

"You do live an interesting life, Mackenzie." Malachi smiled and then sobered. "How is your grandmother?"

Mac shook her head. "It's not good. She hasn't regained consciousness and the doctors, including my sister who flew in along with my brother, say she's lucky to be alive. I know Lolo is the only reason she is. She was doing some sort of *something*." She wasn't sure what and didn't know if she wanted to. "It helped keep Gran alive until she could reach the hospital. The medicals don't know if she will recover."

For a long moment, no one said anything. Then Drea leaned forward, her expression concerned.

"Mac, would it be all right if I visited your grandmother?"

"I'd appreciate it."

If Murray could keep Ellen alive immediately after the bombing, maybe her aunt could help her recover.

"Consider it done. I will head over as soon as Aya can take over for me here at the café."

"What about the investigation into what happened?" Malachi asked.

"Chief Culver put me in charge, and I've called in the Ghostwalkers. Between the DPD and the Walkers, we have things well in hand."

That was a lie, of course, but they didn't need to know exactly where the investigation stood—yet. Besides, Mac had every intention of having things in hand soon. Then she would make it clear to the damned lycans that the Tribunal's laws were to be obeyed or the offending parties would pay the price.

"What do you want from the rest of us?" Malachi asked.

"I want your authorization to deal with any para—lycan, Pure or witch—who took part in the bombing. If they did so in violation of the Tribunal's laws, I want your approval to deal with them instead of handing them over to local authorities." Not because she didn't trust the locals but because she was all too aware they weren't prepared to deal long term with paras.

Malachi nodded as did several others on the screen. "Mackenzie, the rest of us discussed this earlier. But, before we answer your question, we need to ask something of you."

She frowned, unsure what he meant. "Of course." She inclined her head respectfully.

"Mackenzie, you have been a valued and important member of this body since our founding upon the dissolution of the Conclave," Malachi began. "You have represented the Mackenzie bloodline with honor, and you have helped guide our kind through one of our most difficult times. You helped us understand how important it was to bring in new members." Now he nodded on the screen to Drea and the other two witches who now sat on the Tribunal.

"There has been one role, one seat if you will, on the Tribunal that has been left unfilled since our formation." He paused, his expression thoughtful. "Or perhaps I should say it has been officially empty. Unofficially, you have served in that role and you have done so without question and with a loyalty each of us appreciates more than you will ever know."

"I don't understand."

And that was putting it mildly.

"What we would like you to do is take up the same role for the Tribunal that you hold in your pride. You are an alpha. None of us doubts that. In fact, you are an extremely strong alpha, one who represents her bloodline with honor. But you are also the enforcer. You make sure your pride leader's orders are carried out and you ensure the safety of your pride leader and the pride members. Will you accept the title of Tribunal Enforcer and become our official liaison with the human government?"

She closed her eyes, fighting the urge to close her laptop and run for the hills. Wasn't it enough that she was cop and Marine, the official liaison between General Flynn's special command and law enforcement? She accepted the promotion with DPD to give her more time with my family. If she accepted this, how much freedom to just be herself would she be giving up?

Still, Malachi was right. She had been doing what they were asking since the Tribunal's formation. This just made it official. She lifted a finger, indicating she needed a moment and stepped away from the desk. Any other time, she would step out to call Ellen to see what she thought. But this time she couldn't.

Even so, she knew what her grandmother would say.

Do what you feel is best in your heart, child.

She returned to her chair, sighing heavily.

"All right."

"Thank you, Mackenzie." Malachi smiled, understanding reflected in his eyes. "We will send word to the President, as well as to the local authorities down there letting them know you speak for the Tribunal. This should give you the authority you need on all fronts. Let us know what we can do to help and please keep us informed about how the injured are doing."

"I will." She glanced at her watch and grimaced. "My apologies, but I need to report in to Flynn and then check in with the different investigative teams."

"We'll let you go then. Be careful and find those responsible. If lycans or other paras are involved, we will deal with them."

"Thank you." She nodded to each of them and watched as their images disappeared from her screen. Then she smiled to see Drea remain online. "Lolo's fine."

"I know. She stopped by earlier to pick up something to eat." She smiled at the thought of the niece she raised after Murray's mother died. "But I am worried about you."

Mac smiled slightly. She was a little worried about herself too. "I'm fine. Just tired."

The look Drea gave her spoke volumes and Mac wondered if she and Ellen went to school somewhere to master it. Instead of pressing, however, Drea changed the topic.

"I'll head over to the hospital in an hour or so. I texted Aya asking her to come straight here from the Farmer's Market. I'll let Jackson know I'm bringing lunch for everyone."

"Thanks." They chatted for another minute before Mac ended the call.

She leaned back and rubbed her hands over her face. As she did, she winced slightly as pain pulled at her injured shoulder. Damn Lagina. How in the hell was she going to explain getting shot—and by another cop no less—to Jackson?

A soft tap at the door interrupted her thoughts. A moment later, Houston looked inside.

"Sorry, ma'am, but General Flynn is on the line for you."

She nodded and motioned for him to close the door behind him. Then she reached for the phone on the corner of her desk. "Santos."

"I hear you're having a rather interesting day, Mac," the general said, humor and something else in his voice.

"That's one way to put it, sir." Not the way she would. "I take it you've spoken with Culver."

"I have." An undercurrent of anger roughened his voice. "Are you all right?"

"I am." She leaned back and lifted her booted feet onto the corner of the desk. "What happened points out that we have a problem I hadn't anticipated. The question is if Lagina is an isolated case or if Culver needs to take a closer look at the rank and file."

"There's another question you need to look into as well," Flynn said.

"Yes, sir. We need to know if he might have been involved with what happened." She went on to explain her latest orders to Jael who was currently accessing Lagina's records with the DPD.

"It sounds like you have things in hand, Mac. What can I do to help?"

"I may be overreacting, sir, but I think it would be wise to put the entire division on alert. I've already issued orders for Second Regiment to stand by and be ready to ship out with little to no notice. I have also sent word to the other alphas in the region to be on the lookout for possible incursions by lycans."

"Very good. I'll pass the word on to Mateo and Barrett."

"Thank you, sir."

"How are your mother and grandmother?"

"Mom's going to be all right." Knock on wood. "The doctors aren't very optimistic about Gran."

"I assume you've issued orders for extra security on them."

"On them and on Pat and young Mike." Now she smiled. She hadn't told the other members of the Tribunal one thing. "I've also ordered security for the Tribunal members. If this is another attempt by the lycans to cause trouble or if Reed has finally decided to show his hand, I don't want to run any unnecessary risks."

"I'll confirm I ordered it if anyone asks." He continued before she could protest. "Mac, I was going to tell you to do just that. The fact you anticipated me shows I was right in *encouraging* you to accept your command."

"Encourage?" She couldn't help laughing. "You and my grand-mother, not to mention my cousin, did all but tie me down and twist my arm."

"Like I said, *encouraged*."

She pictured him grinning like the proverbial cat with the canary.

"Then I guess I ought to tell you about the latest bit of *encourage-ment*." Except there had been no arm twisting this time. "The other members of the Tribunal have asked me to formally accept the role of Enforcer. I accepted." At least for the length of the investigation.

"I knew they were considering it and I'm glad you did."

"Sir?" That surprised her.

"Mac, you've been doing the job from the beginning. You may has well have the title and the authority behind it. Besides, it will make it easier for you to deal with the local authorities. You won't have to wait for me to chime in or the Tribunal as a whole." He paused and she waited, wondering when her life had gotten so complicated. "I'm going to talk with Malachi. Between us, we'll figure out some sort of letter of office and identification you can carry. That will help cut through the red tape."

"Thank you, sir."

"Now, before I let you go, do you need anything else?"

She thought about how someone at DPD seemed to be dragging their feet about turning over the video files she had requested and mentioned them.

"I'll talk to Culver. Expect the files shortly."

"Thank you, sir. I'd best get back to it."

"Keep me informed, Mac."

Half an hour later, Mac stood in the nearby briefing room. Looking out over the members of the Ghostwalkers not currently in the field, she could almost swear she was briefing her DPD command. More than half of those present were members of the Department. Several others she had tagged as liaisons, able to work between the DPD and the Ghostwalkers when she wasn't available.

"Murray and Norwood?" she asked, noting their absence.

"At the scene, Colonel," Lee answered as he entered the briefing room. "Norwood said they'd check in as soon as they finished."

"All right." She moved to the center whiteboard at the front of the room. In one hand, she held a photo downloaded from the DPD database. Using a couple of magnets to hold it in place, she rapped her knuckles on the board, calling everyone's attention to it.

"This bastard." She didn't try to hide her anger. "Not only shot me earlier today while I was shifted but, in an interview with Chief Culver, he revealed he has a hard-on for paras. I want a deep dive into him. His financials, his history, his phone records and emails. Everything. I doubt he's involved in the bombing, but let's be sure."

"On it, ma'am." Houston said. "Give me a couple of hours. You have his identifiers, I assume."

She nodded, promising to give them to him once they finished the briefing.

"Why don't we just bring the cop in, Colonel?" Richie "Stogie" Vincent asked.

"Because he is a cop and because if he is involved, I don't want to tip our hand before we're ready to move in."

"Some of you already know this next bit, but you all need to be aware. After the bombing, I scented at least one lycan in the parking garage. Last night, my daughter confirmed she saw the lycan and either a human working with him or another lycan in human form when they neared my family's vehicle after it was incapacitated. Whether that means the lycans were involved with the bombing or just trying to take advantage of an unexpected situation, I don't know. But their presence here is a violation of Tribunal law. We have been ordered to locate and apprehend.

"Houston, General Flynn is going to add his weight to getting us the video from both HQ and the parking garage. When you get it, check the feeds from level three near the elevators to see if we get lucky and get a picture of them."

"Consider it done," Houston said.

"Lee, I want round-the-clock guards on my family and on Pat and young Mike." She paused, considering their next move. "I want someone on Marie as well." She might not be family by blood, but she was by choice.

"Yes, ma'am."

"Lee, this time we're going to play it different. I don't want our people to blend in. I want it obvious they are being guarded. I also want electronic eyes and ears on them."

Whoever was crazy enough to bomb police headquarters was crazy enough to try to get to them in the hospital, no matter what sort of security they had. She wasn't going to let that happen.

"Next up. Pat and Mike will be released in a day or two. Before that happens, I want one of the new safehouses prepared for them. When she's released, Marie will join them there. Standard protection detail will go with them."

"Alpha site is on standby, Colonel," Lt. Jim Younger said.

"Excellent. Thank you, LT." Mac gave him a nod. She still wasn't sure about him. He hadn't been with the Ghostwalkers for long. But, so far, he seemed to be fitting in.

Thankfully.

"One last item. Officially, we are working with DPD on this. However, because of the probability lycans are involved, the actual hunt is ours. We can't risk a normal being attacked and possibly turned. The Tribunal has been informed, as has General Flynn. Our orders are simple. We are to take any paras involved in the bombing into custody. We have received permission to use lethal force if necessary.

"Remember, this was an attack on humans, potentially by paras. More specifically, an attack possibly launched by lycans. It is possible my family, perhaps even me, was the target but that seems unlikely. It would have been much easier to try for any of us individually and away from the fucking headquarters for DPD. Such an attack will not be allowed to go unanswered or unpunished."

Everyone nodded in agreement, their expressions grim.

"Lee, Younger, set the initial guard rotation for the injured. I want additional teams sent to the scene to assist with the search there. The rest of you know your assignments. They haven't changed." She thought for a moment, trying to make sure she didn't forget anything. "Houston, let me know if you don't get the data from DPD by the deadline I set."

"Yes, ma'am."

"Then let's get moving. I'll be in the field if you need me."

13

At least outwardly, the building hadn't changed much since her last visit. A new coat of paint, new signage, but not much else. Some of the surrounding businesses had changed, as had the name of this one. Hell, today there was actually a business name displayed on the door. Perhaps they thought that it was all right to do a bit of advertising since the pack was no longer officially tied to the business. But that begged the real question. Were there still lycans involved behind the scene?

Mac planned on finding out before leaving.

The minimal changes to the exterior didn't quite tell the tale. A check of construction permits and licenses attached to the address confirmed major upgrades had been made to the security system. It now sported a state-of-the-art system with motion detectors and cameras inside and out. New windows designed to be "energy efficient" and tinted to make it more difficult to see what might be happening inside replaced the original safety windows. Those changes were minor compared to the other changes Mac assumed had been made inside. The fact she didn't know the extent of the changes bothered her, but not enough to stop her from going inside.

"What did you find out about the new management?"

Mac glanced at Jael where she sat in the front passenger seat. Murray sat behind her. Gone were the slacks and DPD tee shirts they had worn earlier. Now they wore black boots, cargo pants, tee-shirts and tac vests. They were also weaponed up for the zombie apocalypse. Around their necks hung not only their DPD IDs but their military IDs as well. From their attire to their expressions, they looked ready to follow Mac into Hell and back. She only hoped it wouldn't come to that.

"Wolf Properties, the rather unimaginatively named company Connor Ferguson set up when he took over as alpha of the Dallas pack, was deeded over to Davis Phelan before the Tribunal acted after you were shot." Jael checked her notes. "He brought in a 'partner' a year later, one Suzanne Oakley. On paper, they look completely legit. Pay their taxes, get all the proper city and county permits, donate to local charities, etc."

"And not on paper?"

"My sources tell me they are as dirty as Ferguson and Branson were, if not more so. But they are definitely more careful. They learned from what happened to the lycans and have managed to stay under the official radar."

"What do we know about the two of them? Specifically, what was Phelan's connection with Ferguson?"

"Phelan's smart, Mac. He managed to cover his tracks where Ferguson and the pack are concerned. But he's not as good as Cloud."

Mac smiled slightly. Very few were as good as the Ghostwalkers' senior tech specialist.

"Seems Phelan and Ferguson went to school together. Cloud found an online yearbook for their senior year. They played football together and there were enough photos of the two of them in social situations to make it clear they were good friends. They left to go to college together but Ferguson dropped out mid-way through their first year. Our records indicate that's when he was turned.

"Phelan stayed in college and graduated with a degree in finance. He started off in Houston with a small investment firm. He moved to Dallas around the same time Ferguson took over the pack up here.

Even though there's no evidence he took part in pack activities, he clearly maintained his connection with Ferguson. Cloud assured me there's more than enough there, if you know where to look, to prove he not only knew what Ferguson was but that he helped cover it up. He was also the financial brain behind the business and other less legal activities the pack took part in."

"Tell Cloud to make sure DPD and the Feds get copies but with the proviso that no one moves on him until I give the okay. It's to go out over my signature as CO of the regiment." It still felt strange calling her Marine command a regiment. The Ghostwalkers didn't have enough manpower to form a traditional company, much less a regiment. But no one asked her opinion and politics won out when it was decided to no longer hide Flynn's command behind the auspices of Homeland. "Tell him to add I am also ordering it in my role as the Tribunal's enforcer."

"Consider it done."

"What about the woman?"

"I have her." Murray leaned forward, making it easier for the three of them to talk. "Suzanne Oakley, thirty-nine, divorce, no kids. No known employment record except for her work first for Wolf Properties and later for Phelan Property Management, now Phelan/Oakley. She listed her position with Wolf for tax purposes as office administrator. She rose from that role to co-owner after the Tribunal dealt with Ferguson and the others.

"What the public records don't say is that she was associated with the pack since she was in high school. I dug up information, mainly photos, about her ties with the pack in Tribunal archives."

Mac frowned until she remembered the Tribunal had taken possessions of the pack's records. "And?"

"And she was in the back of the pack, pardon the pun, when you fought Wilcox in the Circle. She was also present, again staying in the back, at other times when the pack met with the pride or with the Council. But, from their own records, she was in training to be one of their human enforcers. My guess is she completed that training under Branson before he was killed and the pack was disbanded."

Mac frowned and then nodded. Unfortunately, the Tribunal had been unable to do anything with regard to the humans who looked to the pack unless it had evidence they violated state laws. Those they turned over to the police, along with evidence of their crimes. Obviously the Tribunal hadn't found anything on Oakley and now it might be coming back to bite them on the collective ass.

"Then we do this smart, and we stay safe."

Mac studied the building's entrance for another few moments. Then she sent word to Lee that she wanted backup, as well as eyes and ears, on the building. With that done, she radioed Dispatch, giving their location and ordering all marked units to steer clear of the area until further notice, explaining they had an op in play and she didn't want the parties to rabbit.

"We are waiting until the team's in place, right?"

Jael pinned her with a firm look and Mac nodded. She'd learned her lessons, often the hard way, over the years. Now she knew better than to take unnecessary risks, especially with others. Of course, there'd still be a risk. There always was when dealing with the lycans or their allies. But Mac planned on stacking the deck in her favor.

"I've done my best to get up to speed on Ferguson and the others, but I still feel like I'm missing a lot," Murray said, looking between her companions.

"Long story short, Connor Ferguson was the last alpha of the Dallas pack. Michael King, and then Jackson, worked hard to keep the peace between pack and pride. Mike made it clear to Ferguson he wouldn't put up with the lycans hunting humans. What none of us knew was that members of the Council, including the Speaker, Cassandra Wilkinson, were working against all of us. They didn't like the fact we'd come to a tentative peace. Cassandra didn't like the fact Mike refused to bow completely to her will. So she ordered her enforcer, a lycan on the Council by the name of Bahram Yazhari, to deal with the problem. And she had a very special way she dealt with those she saw as problems or threats to her rule."

While they waited for backup, Mac and Jael took turns explaining the events leading up to the Tribunal's formation and ultimate dissolution of the Dallas pack. They may have glossed over certain things for the sake of saving time, but they left nothing out. Murray learned how Cassandra ordered Wilcox to attack Mac. The former Speaker wanted Mac to turn because she knew the blow that would be to her grandmother, who still presented a challenge to her even though Ellen no longer sat on the Council.

When that didn't work and when King, as pride alpha, began standing up to her in a more public way, she ordered Yazhari to act. That led to the kidnappings of Pat and two others from the pride along with Ferguson and several lycans. The move had been aimed at not only forcing Mike to stay in line but to cause trouble between pack and pride. Cassandra wanted war as much as most lycans did. Except her plan backfired. Yazhari ordered each of those taken to be tortured. That came close to breaking Ferguson and he was never the same afterward.

But it also gave the pride and its allies access to the drugs Cassandra developed to use as part of the torture. The original drug forced a shift on whichever shapeshifter it was administered to. Worse, they couldn't shift back. The danger that presented was that the shifter would lose their humanity, something lycans already risked.

When they raided the warehouse where Pat and the others had been held, Mac and her team discovered not only the kidnappers—who were very dead, thanks to Yazhari—but also a supply of the drug. Experts reverse-engineered it and developed the inhibitor. That was the only good to come out of what happened.

But the bad had been so much worse than the good. Broken by the torture he'd endured, Ferguson never fully healed. Oh, physically he seemed fine. The damage was emotional. Jacob Branson, his second in the pack, quickly tired of watching Ferguson giving in, as he saw it, to the pride. But instead of challenging Ferguson for pack leadership, the two of them worked out some sort of deal. Ferguson would remain the titular alpha but Branson could do what he wanted. That included getting into the local drug trade and making a move against the pride.

Mac absently rubbed the side of her neck where she'd been shot that terrible morning. Ambushed in her own home, Jackson upstairs. That act led to the final destruction of the pack. Branson was killed. Ferguson was taken into custody and later executed for violating Tribunal laws. Others in the pack met the same fate. More found themselves locked up at the Black Crow facility, the black site the government and the Tribunal used to hold paras who violated the law. The few remaining were given the choice of facing Tribunal judgment or moving out of the area, forbidden to ever return.

Now they needed to clean up the last of the mess the pack left: the humans connected to the pack. If they got lucky, they would be able to do so today, before anyone else was injured—or worse.

"How do you want to handle this?" Murray asked.

Good question, one Mac wished she had an answer for. At least an answer that didn't put her companions in potential danger if the lycans she'd scented earlier happened to be inside.

"We go in letting them know exactly who and what we are and who we represent." She stared out the windshield and focused on their target for a few moments. "The last time I was here, we hadn't gone public. Our connection with the government and military wasn't known. Those were secrets we knew the lycans would use against us if they found out. That's no longer something we need fear. So we use it to put the fear of God into anyone on the inside."

"How far do you want us to go?" Jael asked.

"We keep within the law—Tribunal law—but we get answers."

For whatever reason and against the laws laid out by the Tribunal and formalized by Congress, at least two weres had entered the Dallas territory. Mac knew, even though she had no direct proof, that they were involved in what happened the day before. While she needed to find them, the more immediate question was if the humans who once proclaimed loyalty to the pack were involved or knew anything about what happened.

That was a question she intended to answer before leaving the building.

Now it was time to see if Phelan and Oakley had truly gone legit or if they were merely fronting for the lycans.

And the sooner they knew, the better.

Without a word, Mac opened the car door and stepped out. While the others joined her, she checked her weapons. Satisfied, she lifted her face and inhaled, tasting the various scents in the air. When she did, she recognized all the usual smells—oil, gasoline, stale food, body odors, too many different colognes and perfumes to name. Nothing out of the ordinary.

"We've got an audience," Jael said softly.

Mac nodded. It wasn't every day this part of town saw armed and armored women dressed in black, badges visible, walking down the street. Well, they were about to give everyone some excitement. With one corner of her mouth crooking up in a slight smile, Mac checked for traffic and then jogged across the street.

Showtime!

The moment her foot hit the far curb, Mac growled softly. Cait shoved her way to the front of Mac's consciousness. There! She caught the scent of both lycans from the parking garage. Worse, there was a third, one she didn't recognize. The possibility this was nothing more than a coincidence was slimmer than slim to none.

The only questions Mac had were who were they, why had they come here and where could she find them. If the humans inside had any hope to continue living a free life, they'd better answer her questions without delay.

"Stay sharp." She sent a quick text to both Lee and Culver updating them. "Three lycans were here and not long ago."

And that left the question of whether they might still be inside unanswered.

"I enter first. Murray, you're next. Jael, you bring up the rear." Mac shook her head before Jael could argue. "If they are inside, you're the weak point, Jael. So you will do as I say or wait outside."

She wasn't in the mood for arguments. Fortunately, Jael understood.

Satisfied, Mac reached for the door. It surprised her when the door swung open. Either they weren't monitoring their security cameras, or they didn't realize just how much trouble they were in. Either way, it made Mac's job easier, at least initially. Not that she held any illusions it would continue that way.

"Murray."

Without a word, Murray crossed to where the receptionist sat behind a modern-style desk of glass and steel. Her mouth formed an "O" of surprise. But the look of calculation in her eyes belied that. Even as her right hand reached for something under the desk, Murray had her by the shoulder. In one smooth move, Murray forced the woman out of the chair and against the wall. A moment later, the blonde's wrists were secured behind her back. While that was happening, Jael locked the main entrance so they wouldn't be disturbed.

Mac took a moment to look around. If she didn't know better, she would have sworn nothing had changed since her last time there. The furniture, with the exception of the receptionist's desk, was just as utilitarian as it had been under Ferguson. The scent inside might not scream "lycan!", not that it reassured her.

The blonde receptionist, unmistakably human, drew Mac's attention as she finished her examination of the waiting room. Unlike most people who suddenly found themselves confronted by heavily armed people she didn't know, the blonde wasn't afraid. Her scent told Mac all she needed to know. The blonde was angry. More than that, she wanted to fight. That realization brought back the memory of the first time Mac came there to confront Ferguson. Jael had been with her. When they left, Jael ripped Mac a new one for underestimating the bubble bum chomping, bimbo-esque receptionist. Until then, Mac didn't know lycans had their own humans who not only knew of their existence but helped them just as Jael and John O'Hara and those like them helped the Pures.

This blonde, who was no bubble-gum chomping bimbo, opened her mouth. Before she could say anything, Murray simply lifted a finger to her own lips, signaling for her to be silent. The blonde must have seen something in Murray's expression because she complied, but not without giving Murray a look that promised dire consequences should she manage to get free.

"Buzzer under the desk. Probably sends a warning to the back office," Murray said after taking a look at the desk and its contents.

"Keep her company. We'll go introduce ourselves to the others."

"Murray, if she so much as looks at you wrong, put her down," Jael said and the younger woman nodded.

Trusting Murray to control the waiting area—and the blonde—Mac crossed to the inner door. Unlike the outside door, this one was locked. For a moment, Mac considered her options. There was probably a button or controller or some sort at the blonde's desk that would buzz them through. But where's the fun with that? Mac wanted to make a statement and what better way than by showing whoever hid behind the door that they weren't going to be able to keep her out?

All right, Cait. Let's show them how foolish it is to try to lock us out.

Mac drew on her jaguar's strength and took a step back. Grinning at Jael, she inhaled, focused and kicked out. The door flew open, the knob burying itself in the wall. Phelan and Oakley stood behind the desk opposite the door. Phelan, a small, wiry man with greying hair and a weasel face, lunged toward the desk, reaching for something. The sound of guns clearing holsters filled the air and she and Jael drew down on them. Oakley pursed her lips, her eyes flashing angrily, as Phelan dropped onto the chair behind the desk.

"Make sure there's no one else around." Mac motioned for the two to move around the desk. She didn't want either of them near whatever Phelan had been reaching for.

"What the hell do you want?" Phelan demanded.

Mac chuckled softly and grinned at Jael. Most people would demand who had the temerity to break into their private office. He didn't. He wanted to know what they wanted. Interesting. Mac's money was on him already knowing who we were. But she wanted to be sure.

"Davis Phelan, Suzanne Oakley, the name's Mackenzie Santos Caine. Colonel Santos with the DPD and with the USMC. Enforcer for the Tribunal of Paranormals."

Phelan would make a damned good poker player. Nothing about

his expression or the way he stood betrayed him. But his respirations and the sudden widening of his pupils did. Yes, he knew exactly who she was and he either knew or had a pretty good guess what she meant by listing her official roles.

But it was Oakley who caught Mac's attention. The woman inhaled sharply. Just a quick breath. Her right hand fisted at her side. From the way those fingers, once she relaxed her fist, twitched against her thigh, Mac suspected at one time she was used to wearing a gun there. Military maybe. Perhaps even a cop somewhere or a security guard. All Mac knew for sure was she wanted a better background check run on her. They definitely didn't know everything.

"I repeat, what the hell do you want?"

"Some answers." Mac leaned a hip against the chair at her side, gun still in hand. "Those answers will determine whether you remain free, at least for the immediate future or if I have you taken into custody and transported to the nearest jail."

"You can't," Oakley snarled.

Mac's smile was all predator as she let Cait stare out through my eyes.

"I can and I will. Try me," she said as Jael returned and reported the office was clear. "You heard what happened at police headquarters yesterday?"

"I doubt there's anyone in this part of the country who hasn't," Phelan sneered.

"Good. Then we can get down to business. You were both associated with the lycan pack that once lived in this area. Don't bother denying it. Not only does the Tribunal have proof of it but so do the local authorities."

"So what? It wasn't illegal then to associate with them and it isn't now." Oakley took a step forward and thought better of it when Mac arched a brow and shook her head.

"Actually, it is now, as you well know." Mac pushed away from the chair and holstered her gun. "When the Tribunal disbanded the pack, they made it illegal for any lycan to come through this territory without first getting permission from not only the local pride leader but from the Tribunal itself. So explain to me why three lycans have come to Dallas and why they were here within the last few hours."

"You're insane. We haven't seen a lycan since you and your kind either killed them or ran them out of town," Oakley said.

Mac smiled. she had Oakley pegged now. Phelan was the planner, the plotter. Oakley was the enforcer. But she wasn't a dispassionate one. She let her emotions rule her. While that suited Mac's purposes, it also made Oakley dangerous because it made her unpredictable.

"I hoped you'd be reasonable. Obviously, I was mistaken." Mac moved around the desk and checked it, pulling a gun from the top drawer. Holding it between two fingers, she looked at Phelan and tsk-tsked. "Naughty boy. Your partner there just admitted you know who and what I am. And still, you tried reaching for a gun. I must say, I'm disappointed."

"What do you want?" he asked for the third time, grinding out the words.

"It's really quite simple and exactly as I said. The two of you are known associates of the members of what used to be known as the Dallas pack. Some of that pack were identified and prosecuted as homegrown terrorists. The others were found to have been in violation of numerous of our laws and the pack was disbanded and the surviving members relocated under orders not to return. The Tribunal then issued an edict outlawing any lycan from entering this territory without getting permission from the local pride and from the Tribunal itself."

"Which they are well aware of, ma'am," Jael said, making a show of checking her tablet. "They both signed off on the order mandating them, as former followers of the pack, to notify the Tribunal of any lycans entering or staying in the area." Now she looked up, her smile as feral as Oakley's had been. "I can't say I'm impressed with their intelligence if they thought they could get away with hiding lycans from us."

"Now, now, Captain. They might not have known." Mac tilted her head to one side as if considering that possibility. "No, they knew. Otherwise, Phelan here wouldn't have been reaching for his gun."

AMANDA S. GREEN

"True." Now Jael studied them. "Your orders?"

"We'll give them one more chance to cooperate. If not." She shrugged, hoping at least one of them had a very active imagination.

"Bitch," Oakley spat.

"You have no idea." Mac tapped my fingers against her thigh as she considered her options. "Let's do this officially then." She recited their Miranda warnings before continuing. "As I said earlier, you are known associates of lycans, some of whom were identified, prosecuted and executed as homegrown terrorists. You were allowed to remain in Dallas and out of prison on the condition you never dealt with any lycans again and—please remember how important this part is—on the additional condition you notified the local pride leader, the Dallas Police Department and the Tribunal if any lycan crossed into this territory and came to your attention. Here's where it gets sticky for the two of you. There is more than ample evidence to prove you not only knew of the presence of at least three lycans in the area but that you failed to notify the proper authorities."

Phelan's expression tightened but he remained silent. Not that Mac expected anything different from him. He wasn't the sort to make a direct attack, at least not a physical one. He'd hire someone to do his dirty work. Oakley, on the other hand, looked ready to kill.

Trusting Jael to watch her and be ready to respond, Mac turned her attention to Phelan. As she did, the parallels between the two and Ferguson and Branson hit her. The lycan alpha, before his kidnapping, had been the planner, the one who knew the importance of taking the long view. Branson had been the muscle and the one more likely to strike out. What made Branson as effective as he'd been was he also knew how to clean up his messes. She doubted Oakley did.

"So here's the deal. Answer my questions, do so honestly and without holding anything back, and you'll be going home to your families tonight." Assuming they had families. Something else they needed to look into. "Lie to me, try hedge or just piss me off and you'll be heading to lockup."

"Su already told you. We haven't seen any lycans since your damned Tribunal held that sham of a trial." For the first time, Phelan showed some emotion. His eyes blazed and a muscle in his jaw tensed. "You murdered some good men and women in your quest for dominance and we won't play a hand in this new farce."

"I think he believes you a fool, ma'am," Jael mused.

"I think you're right." Mac shook her head, feigning disappointment. "Before you dig that hole you're standing in any deeper, let me be clear. I have scented the lycans. I scented them at the scene of the explosions. I scented them outside your building." She lifted my head, making a show of tasting the air in the room. "And I scent them in here. So tell me what I want to know, or you'll find yourselves sitting in a prison cell for the next decade or two, longer if I tie you to the bombing."

They tried to deny it. Mac expected that. She hadn't met a white-collar criminal—and that's basically what Phelan was. He laundered the money and gave them business advice, fronting for them on investments and the like—who wanted to admit to doing anything wrong. In the end, he'd be the easier of the two to break because he knew he couldn't survive prison. He valued his freedom and his comforts too much.

But that would take time. Time Mac had a feeling they didn't have. She needed something to force the issue and that was Oakley.

"You can't prove anything," Phelan said yet again. "Even if a lycan came in here, how would we know? You've admitted we're human. That means we can't scent them or whatever you call it. They certainly wouldn't announce themselves since those you so generously allowed to live from the pack think of us as traitors for signing that damned document. So get the hell out of my office and don't come back unless you have a warrant."

Mac looked at Jael and grinned. She really did love it when the bad guys started sweating and making mistakes.

"There is one way to prove what you say, Phelan."

He didn't respond but from the way he pursed his lips tightly together, she knew he wanted to say something else but stopped himself. Oakley flashed him a look that spoke volumes. She was pissed. She recognized the mistake he'd made, whether he had or not.

"How?" Oakley asked.

"You've got an excellent security system in here. That system includes cameras inside and out." Mac pointed to the carefully concealed cameras in the office, noting again Phelan's surprise. Until that moment, he hadn't realized they knew about the cameras, proving that like most criminals, he thought himself smarter than the rest of the world. "I have a feeling you run those cameras 24/7 outside and in the outer office. Hand over the video for the last twenty-four hours."

"Warrant," Oakley said, emphasizing each syllable of the word.

"Captain?"

Mac didn't look away from the two. She simply extended her right hand. A moment later, Jael placed a sheaf of papers in it. Once she had, Mac stepped forward and brandished them under Oakley's nose. It was a risk, one she figured Jael would ream her about later.

Take the bait, little fishy.

Human not fish, Cait reminded me.

I chuckled silently. *No, not fish but prey.*

Oakley snarled, her only warning before she struck out. The pages flew from Mac's hand and pain shot through her arm from wrist to elbow. Mac had to give it to Oakley. She at least knew how to hit the pressure points. Not that it would do her any good.

Mac's eyes narrowed. She lifted her left arm, blocking Oakley's right jab. The thrill of the fight raced through her as Oakley bladed her body. The blonde balanced on her toes, her hands up, her eyes alert. Everything about her screamed "fighter!". Good. That suited Mac just fine.

Mac ducked a left hook. Oakley's breath exploded as Mac followed up with a right jab to the kidney. Oakley danced away. Or tried to. Unlike a trained fighter, she forgot to take into consideration her surroundings. With the wall at her back, Jael blocking her exit, she had two choices: give up or try to fight her way past Mac.

Foolishly, Oakley chose the latter.

Oakley proved to be a brawler. Trained but not efficient. Between her own training, her greater strength and speed thanks to her shifter genes, Mac could make quick work of her. But Oakley needed to learn how foolish it was to plot against the Tribunal. Still, as enticing as it was to wipe the floor with her, Mac needed her conscious and able to answer questions.

She ducked under a poorly executed spinning backfist. Using Oakley's own momentum, Mac grabbed her by the arm and shoulder, spinning her into the wall. She hit with a thud strong enough to rattle the pictures hanging nearby. The hand at Oakley's shoulder slid over until Mac's forearm rested across the back of her neck. Mac leaned in, using her weight and greater strength to pin her there.

"Stand still," she growled in Oakley's ear.

Oakley cursed and continued to fight against Mac's hold. God, if she didn't know better, she would swear Oakley was a lycan. She was just as stubborn and just as foolish as her wolfish friends.

So Mac would treat her like one.

Mac shifted holds again, grabbing a handful of hair. Oakley grunted as Mac tightened her grip, using the blonde's hair to control her. A moment later, Mac slammed Oakley's face into the wall. The response was instant. Stunned by the blow, Oakley went limp. Mac pulled her cuffs and secured her hands behind her. By the time she recovered, mac had Oakley on her knees, forehead pressed to the wall, gun pressed to the back of her head.

"That just bought you a trip to lockup." And not the lockup Oakley expected. "Not only did you assault an officer, you assaulted a member of the military and a member of the Tribunal. So many charges with so many serious repercussions."

"You bitch," Phelan rasped.

Mac glanced at him, realizing for the first time that Jael had cuffed him as well.

"Ma'am, do we really have to transport them?" Jael asked.

She sounded almost sad at the prospect. But Mac saw the twinkle in her eyes and knew she was up to something. Might as well see how it played out.

"Do you have something else in mind, Captain?"

"Well, ma'am, you can be pretty damned scary when you're in this mood. Besides, they are human. It's possible they didn't know they had a couple of lycans come to see them. They might not know they were being used. Hell, it's possible they're being set up as the fall guys for what happened yesterday. I bet they'd be more than happy to help us if you'd reconsider bringing them in and charging them."

Phelan quickly looked at Oakley, his expression warning her not to try anything else. Then he looked at Mac, nodding so fast he reminded her of one of those bobbleheads sports teams hand out at games. Still, she made a show of considering Jael's suggestion. No need to let them know she didn't want to take them in—yet. She wanted to see what she could learn from them when they thought they were in the clear.

"You get one chance." Mac ground the words out, making it clear she would much prefer taking them into custody. "Did you know lycans were in the area?"

"No." Now Phelan shook his head.

"You had three men in here earlier today. Who were they?"

"Potential clients. Said they wanted to rent out warehouse space. We didn't have anything that fit their needs and they left. We can get you their names."

Which would be phony, but the aliases might still help. Not that she believed him for a moment.

"Oakley?" Mac looked at her where she now sat, her back to the wall, wrists still cuffed behind her back.

"I wasn't part of the discussion. Can't help you." She turned her head and spat blood onto the floor.

"Now, about those security feeds."

Mac waited, watching Phelan struggle to find a reason not to turn them over. Interesting. Was he worried whatever they showed would prove he lied? But he was also smart enough—or scared enough—to know he couldn't withhold them. The only question was how he'd try to stall handing the files over.

"I can't."

Mac arched one brow and reached down, ready to haul Oakley to her feet. As she did, she contacted Dispatch.

"No!" Phelan backed away from Jael until he stood against the wall. "I can't give them to you because the video files are stored off-site. I have to ask the security company for them."

Mac nodded to Jael who pulled her cellphone. "Their number?"

"I-I don't know. It's in our files."

She removed his cuffs and told him to get the number. Then she followed him, letting him know he couldn't do anything foolish like try to run.

"Okay, they'll prepare a copy of the files. But it's going to take time."

Mac pulled Oakley to her feet and turned her so she could remove the cuffs. Then she shoved the blonde away, knowing better to give her another chance to do something foolish.

"You have two hours to get the files. At the end of that time, I'll have someone here to pick them up. If you don't have the files, you'll be taken into custody." Mac said nothing else for a moment. "Look at me."

With Cait so close to the surface, her eyes glowed a deeper green than usual. Their experience with the lycans would tell them what that meant. Judging by the scent of fear coming from Phelan, he understood how high the stakes were.

"This is your only chance to prove you are no longer loyal to the lycans. Fail and you will pay the price, one that very well might be fatal."

Mac turned on her heel and left the office. Jael and Murray fell into step behind her. Without a word, they made their way to the SUV. Once inside, Mac motioned for them to hold their reports. She needed to check in. Now wasn't the time to get careless.

"Lee, I want eyes and ears to stay on the building. They have a two hour deadline to get copies of their security feeds. At that time, I want you and—" She thought for a moment. "Norwood to pay them a visit. If they don't have the files, take them into custody and transport them to Central. If they do have the files, do a bit of intimidating. Let them know what the Old Lady will do if I think the files have been tampered with or are incomplete in any way. Then leave. Make sure they hear the two of you talking about how I've ordered surveillance withdrawn if they cooperate. I want them scared and off-balance but not worrying we have eyes on them."

"Understood, ma'am."

"In the meantime, let me know if the situation changes here."

She ended the call and slid the key into the ignition. A moment later, she pulled away from the curb, knowing she needed to hear Jael's and Murray's impression about what just happened but wanting a moment to gather her own thoughts.

And boy did she have a lot of thoughts.

It seemed not just possible but probable Phelan and Oakley were involved with the bombing. To say that added a complication she didn't want or need was putting it mildly. It also pointed out a problem the Tribunal should have anticipated when it acted against the Dallas pack, not to mention the other packs involved in the attempted coup that led to the revelation of our existence to the public-at-large. They dealt with the lycans but not with the humans who weren't directly tied to what happened. The Tribunal took the easy way out and Mac worried that had finally come back to bite all of them on the proverbial ass.

14

"Mama!"

Mac smiled wearily and stepped inside. The moment she did, Xander raced across the room and launched himself at her. She caught him, relishing the feel of his arms and legs wrapping around her. After the last two days, this was exactly the sort of greeting she needed. She hugged him and placed a kiss on the top of his head.

"Missed you, Mama."

"Missed you too."

She nuzzled his neck, making him laugh before putting him down. As she straightened, she yawned wide enough to crack her jaw. She felt every hour she'd been up, every bump and bruise she suffered trying to get to her loved ones the day before. Her jaw ached where Oakley got in a lucky shot earlier. But at least she managed to avoid attending the press conference. That had to count for something, right? Now all she wanted was to make sure her family and friends were recovering. After that, some time with Jackson and the kids sounded very, very good.

Mac straightened and looked around. Jackson stood at the far side of the room, softly talking on his phone. Xander ran back to the sofa and grabbed up his father's iPad before plopping down in one of the two recliners. But it was the sight of Cam, carefully helping her grandmother eat some soup that brought tears to Mac's eyes. Smiling a little shakily, Mac did her best to fix a reassuring expression on her face before moving to join her daughter and mother.

"Hey, Mom."

She bent and lightly kissed Elizabeth's cheek. As she did, she reminded herself it was a good sign to find the woman sitting up some in bed, conscious and able to eat, even if it was only hospital soup. Maybe she'd be able to convince the doctors to let Elizabeth have something from the Irish Rose tomorrow.

"Mackenzie."

Elizabeth reached for her daughter's hand. As she did, Mac hooked a foot around a stool and dragged it closer to the bed. Then she blinked back those damnable tears that still burned her eyes. Face swollen, her nose and eyes bruised and her left cheek abraded from the airbag, Elizabeth looked like she'd lost the fight. But she'd never looked better to her daughter. She survived and she was going to make a full recovery. Nothing else mattered.

Nothing except the fact Ellen still lay unconscious on the second bed. Swallowing had, Mac moved almost silently to her bedside. Ellen looked so small and fragile as she lay there. A thick bandage wrapped around her right thigh. That leg was immobilized to prevent her from moving and causing further damage until she healed some. Her left ankle and lower leg were now casted and hung in traction. An IV snaked down, terminating in her right hand. Machines kept track of her breathing, pulse, blood pressure and who knew what else.

But she lived. Mac knew she needed to remember that. She still lived and the family owed Lolo Murray a debt they would never be able to repay. Mac knew, even if she hadn't said anything yet, that the witch had saved her grandmother.

"Mac?"

She turned at the sound of Elizabeth's voice. Doing her best to smile in reassurance, she returned to her mother's bedside. Then she looked to where Cam stood. Worry darkened her daughter's eyes. She wanted to reassure the girl but couldn't, not yet.

"Hey, Mom." She rested her hand on Elizabeth's, curling her fingers around to feel her mother's pulse. "Is Cam taking good care of you?"

"She is." Elizabeth smiled painfully at the twelve-year-old.

Mac grinned to see the blush coloring her daughter's cheeks.

"Me too!" Xander said as he ran across the room to join them.

Mac bent to once again lift him, barely managing to hold back her groan. God, she needed a shower to loosen her stiff and sore muscles.

Either that or a good, stiff drink.

"You too." Elizabeth reached out to rest a hand on the boy's foot. "You look tired, Mac."

"I am." No sense denying it. "How do you feel?"

"High." She nodded to the analgesia pump near the head of her bed.

"She refused to use it until the doctor said the pain would keep her from healing as fast as she would otherwise." Jackson took Xander from her.

"Mom," Mac scolded.

"Don't." Tears pooled in her eyes as she glanced in Ellen's direction.

Understanding, Mac reclaimed her hand and held it. "She's going to be all right. You have to believe that."

"I told her to stay in the car."

"I know. The kids told me." She brushed a lock of hair off her mother's forehead. "And you'll get your chance to tell her you told 'I told you so' soon. I promise." She surreptitiously reached for the pump's controller and pressed it. "I promise we'll wake you if anything happens. Rest now," she added as the door opened and Abby and Danny entered.

"So tired." Her words started to slur.

"Shhh. Sleep."

Elizabeth's eyes grew heavy and finally closed. Mac watched her, making sure she was all right. They'd come so close to losing her.

Unshed tears burned in her eyes as she turned and reached for Jackson. His arms slid around her, holding her close. She clung to him, trying not to break down in front of the kids. But it was hard, so very hard.

"Moira's next door," Abby said softly. "She brought dinner for everyone."

Even though food sounded really good, Mac didn't want to leave.

"Mac, don't," her younger sister said firmly. Mac recognized the tone. It was a mix of Elizabeth's Mom voice and Abby the doctor. "You need to eat. I doubt you've had anything of substance since before the blast."

Mac nodded. Food had been the last thing she wanted.

"Go eat. Freshen up and get some rest. Danny and I will sit with them."

"And we'll send for you if there's any change with either of them," her twin said.

Looking between them to her children, Mac nodded. As much as she wanted to stay, Cami and Xander needed her and she needed their father.

"She is going to be all right," Abby said softly when Mac bent to kiss their mother's cheek. "I promise."

Mac sniffled, ran a hand under her nose and nodded. Then she glanced at their grandmother, unable to ask the question foremost on her mind and praying Abby understood.

"She's getting better. They're keeping her sedated to give her body time to heal."

Mac inhaled once and then nodded. "Truth?"

"Truth."

She wanted to believe Abby. She needed to believe her.

"C'mon, Mom." Cam took Mac's hand and gently led her toward the door.

Mac smiled down at her, pushing back her own fear. "You two try to get some rest," she told her siblings and stepped into the corridor, waiting as Jackson followed, Xander in his arms.

"The hospital said we can use this suite." Jackson stopped at the door to the right of where they'd been.

Can pushed open the door and led her mother inside. As the door shut behind them, Mac shook her head. Someone, and she had no doubt it was hospital staff, tried to make it look less like a hospital room and more like a generic hotel room. There was even a round table masquerading as a dining table in the center of the room, marking the divide between sleeping area and sitting area. Several bags she recognized as coming from the Irish Rose, as well as two thermal carafes and a large thermal bag sat in the middle of the table. The enticing aromas of freshly baked bread, Irish stew and more filled the air.

"Kids, why don't you set the table?" Jackson suggested. "Leave the food in the bag to stay warm. We'll lay it out after your mom's had a chance to freshen up."

"That sounds like a great idea. I won't be long." Mac looked around and quickly spotted the bathroom door.

Jackson followed as she moved in its direction. Hearing her soft gasp as she opened the door, he chuckled softly, understanding. Instead of the cramped room barely large enough for a commode, sink and what they euphemistically called a shower, this one sported all the usual accoutrements as well as a small dressing table and a bathtub/shower combination.

"I ran by the house earlier and picked up clothes and other things we'll need," he said, closing the door after him.

It was crowded but not impossibly so.

"Thanks." She walked into his waiting embrace. "For everything."

"Mac."

He pressed his lips to her forehead and then stepped back, his hands resting on her shoulder. His eyes narrowed and he cocked his head to one side. Then, before she could react, he reached down and gripped the hem of her tee shirt. A moment later, he pulled it over her head.

"What happened?" he ground out at the sight of the bandage on her shoulder. A moment later, he grabbed her chin between thumb and forefinger and tilted her head so he could examine the bruise along her jaw. "And don't you dare tell me nothing or that you have it under control."

Pushing down her own anger, Mac cursed silently. She'd screwed up and she knew it. She should have told him sooner. Hell, she figured someone would have told on her. Obviously, they hadn't and now she had to diffuse the situation before he lost his temper.

Not that she could blame him.

She reached over and turned on the shower, as much to give herself a moment to consider how to explain as to cover their conversation. The kids did not need to hear this.

"Before you say anything else, I am fine. I would have let you know if I wasn't." She held his gaze, waiting until he nodded. "But something did happen, something I didn't anticipate. Culver is dealing with it and we're going to let him, at least for now." Her tone brooked no disagreement.

Jackson's jaw tightened but he nodded again.

She quickly told him about her run-in with Lagina outside the parking garage. His expression tightened and she scented his anger but he said nothing. Instead, he listened as she described returning to the SUV so she could shift. As she leaned against the edge of the dressing table, she told him how she once again scented the lycans and, worried, how she left the garage ahead of Jael and Murray.

Jackson growled low in his throat and his eyes danced with anger as she described what happened next. Not that she blamed him.

"Jack, you need to trust me on this. Culver is dealing with that asshole. I have the Ghostwalkers looking into him. He's clearly one of those who believes our kind should be separated from the rest of society and either caged or killed. It's possible, he's involved in what happened. Either way, he will pay for his attitude and for what he did."

"How badly were you hurt?" He reached out to gently touch the bandage.

"Not bad. It will heal in a few days." She flexed her arm to prove she told the truth.

"And this?" He ran a finger along her bruised jaw.

"I'll give you a full report after the kids go to sleep. But Jael, Murray and I paid a visit to the humans who took over Ferguson's business. They're involved. I'm convinced of it. I scented three lycans not only outside the building but inside the private office area. Probably came in through the rear door."

"And?" He crossed his arms and waited.

"They denied knowing any lycans had come to them. Denied pretty much everything. And I pushed them, knowing they were lying. One of them, a Suzanne Oakley, didn't take kindly to being threatened with prison—or worse. She got in a lucky shot." One Mac let her land, if she was being honest. "Again, it's nothing and it gave me one more thing to use as leverage against them."

"Please tell me they're both sitting in a cell."

She shook her head and then held up a hand to stop him from interrupting. "They know something, Jackson. I need to find out what. So they remain free and they are going through the motions of cooperating with us. Lee and Norwood confirmed when I was on my way here that they'd turned over their security feeds. Now we've got eyes and ears on them and on all their electronics. Hopefully, we'll get lucky and they'll lead us to the lycans before anything else happens."

"You should have told me you were going there."

He wasn't happy. She knew it. But he needed to understand her job as a cop, not to mention as the Tribunal's local representative—and that brought up something else they needed to discuss later—meant she needed to be the one to talk to the humans. They might fear him but she had the power behind her two roles to force them to cooperate or pay the price for their silence.

"I'm telling you now." She wouldn't argue with him. She didn't have the energy. "Jackson, I needed you here, protecting our family."

He sighed and nodded. Still, she knew he'd have more to say later.

"Get your shower. I'll make sure the kids leave you alone long enough to. Then you need to eat." He ran a gentle hand over her hair. "But you need to keep me in the loop, Mac. I don't like being ambushed by this sort of thing." He nodded to her bandaged shoulder.

"I promise." She unzipped her pants and shimmied out of them. "And I promise to answer your questions later, love. All of them."

He nodded and slipped out of the room, closing the door behind him. With a sigh, she finished undressing and stepped under the water, sighing in relief as it beat down on her.

Later, dressed in sweats, barefoot, her hair damp from the shower, she moved toward the table. Jackson stood and held her chair and she smiled up at him. Then she grinned as Cami and Xander hurried to sit to her right and left. Just like if they were home.

"I called Moira and thanked her for all this," Jackson said as they helped themselves to stew or shepherd's pie and fresh bread.

"Thanks. I'll touch base with her tomorrow."

"No need. She said she'd bring breakfast by. Said she and Annie had something special planned."

Mac grinned, not about to argue. The Irishwoman was an excellent cook, her eldest daughter even better. The only thing missing from this meal was a mug of freshly poured Guinness.

"Mama, what happened to you?" Xander asked as he studied her face.

"Someone I talked to today didn't like some of the questions I was asking, son."

"She hit you?"

"She did, Cam, and she learned how foolish it is to hit a cop." Hopefully, that would satisfy them because she didn't want to explain it further. She sat back and looked from her daughter to her son. "I know yesterday and today have been scary. They have been for your dad and me too. But you need to believe that Grandma and Gran are getting better."

"Why's Gran still asleep?" Xander wanted to know.

"Aunt Abby can answer it better than I can, Xander, but Gran needs to sleep right now to heal. When she's strong enough, the doctors will wake her up."

"Is she going to be okay, Mom?"

"I think so, Cam. But she's going to need a lot of help from all of us. Just like Grandma does right now."

"We'll help her, Mom. Promise," she said and Xander nodded in agreement, his mouth full.

"I know you will." Mac smiled at them and then dipped a piece of bread into her stew. "Is there anything else your dad and I can tell you?"

"How long are we going to have to stay here?" Cam asked. She waved her own piece of bread around the room.

"Cami." Jackson arched a brow, his expression telling Mac they'd already had this discussion.

"It's not that I don't want to be here for Gran and Grandma. I do."

"But?" Mac prompted gently.

"It was hard to sleep last night. The nurses kept coming in to check on them and kept waking Xander and me up."

The little boy nodded, supporting his sister.

"I know. I had a hard time sleeping too." Mac sat back, her dinner forgotten for the moment. "I understand you want to go home. I do too. But it's safer for you here right now and that makes my job easier. I don't have to worry about something maybe happening to you or to your father if you're here."

"And that's why the hospital is letting us use this room," Jackson took up. "You and Xander can sleep in the beds over there. Mom and I will sleep in the recliners. This way, we're close to Gran and Grandma and the others and Mom knows we're all safe."

Cami nodded. Then she looked at her mother, her eyes narrowing as she considered what her parents said. "Mom, why are you worried about us?"

Mac sighed and silently cursed her loose tongue. Then, seeing Jackson dip his chin, she knew it was time. Xander wouldn't understand much of it, but Cam needed to know. By shifting, she proved she was old enough to learn a harsh lesson about being a Pure.

"You already know part of it, Cam." She reached for her daughter's hand. "You warned me. Those two men you saw in the parking garage —well, the man and the wolf. You were right about them. They weren't normals. They were lycans."

The girl frowned, anger flashing in her eyes. Seeing it, Mac recognized it for what it was. Cam's panther was very close to the surface just then.

"Dad, did you tell any lycans they could be here?"

Mac grinned, proud of her daughter. Cam had obviously paid attention to the lessons they'd given her.

"No, love, I didn't."

"So they aren't supposed to be here."

"That's right, Cam." Mac waited until her daughter looked at her. "But there is more. I learned today there is at least one more lycan in the area. The fact they haven't let your father know they're here and the fact two of them were coming toward the car until you shifted to protect the others worries me. So, you guys staying here where you are safe and well-guarded helps me do my job."

"Okay, Mom." She leaned over and gave her mother a hug. "But you have to be careful too."

Jackson choked as Mac promised she would be.

"Daddy, what about Aunt Abby and Uncle Danny? Where they gonna sleep?" Xander asked.

"They're going to stay with Gran and Grandma tonight, son. Then they'll sleep in here while we go next door in the morning," Jackson said.

"Okay." Apparently satisfied, Xander turned his attention back to his dinner.

"Cam, are you okay?" Mac asked, worried about her daughter.

"Yeah, Mom. Just trying to figure some stuff out."

Since Mac had a pretty good idea what that "stuff" might be, Mac let the subject drop. It wasn't something she wanted to discuss with Xander there, not yet at any rate. The little boy was still upset his big sister could turn furry and he couldn't.

"Hey, little man, how about the two of us go check on Aunt Marie, Aunt Pat and Mike?" Jackson suggested later as Cami and Mac cleared the table.

"That sounds like a good idea." Before Cami could object, Mac continued. "Then Cam and I can check on them in the morning."

"Can we go to the cafeteria and get some ice cream?" the little boy asked.

Jackson laughed, ruffled his hair and said they could.

"You guys be sure to give them our love." Mac watched as Jackson collected his wallet from the small coffee table next to one of the recliners.

He moved to her and lightly kissed her. "We'll be a while."

His message was clear. He wanted her to take the time to talk with Cami. Nodding, she waved at Xander and watched as they left the room. Then she turned to her daughter. She had no doubt Cami had a million or more questions about this sudden change in her life and they might as well start discussing them.

"They left so we could talk, didn't they?" Cami asked as she handed her mother the last of the paper plates.

"They did." She dropped it into a plastic bag and then tied the top of bag before tossing it into the trashcan near the door. "Do you want to talk about what's bothering you?"

Cami gave a lopsided smile and nodded. Seeing it, Mac draped an arm around her shoulders and led her to the sofa. With the girl snuggled against her side, she waited. She wouldn't force Cami to talk, but it was hard to just sit there, knowing the girl was bothered by something.

"Mom, you and Dad explained a lot yesterday. I get that I probably shifted because I was so scared and I knew I was the only one who could protect the others because Gran was hurt."

Mac nodded. "Yeah. Kind of like how I started shifting after the lycan attacked me so long ago." They hadn't hidden what happened to her from their children.

"I even sort of understand why I didn't shift into a jaguar like you two. I didn't at first and then I talked to Aunt Abby. She told me it was kind of like how I have green eyes like you but Xander has brown eyes like Grandma. She talked a lot of science stuff I didn't understand, but I think it all comes down to how genes work in each of us."

"That's right, Cam." Mac smiled down at her, proud she understood that much. "It's like how your friend Rosie is tall, almost as tall as me already, and yet her parents are short. Genetics did that."

"I get it. I think." She gave a shrug.

"Is there something else bothering you, love?"

For a long moment, Cami didn't answer. Then she nodded. Mac

AMANDA S. GREEN

waited, wondering what other bombshells her daughter might be about to drop on her.

"Mama, when I started to shift yesterday, it was like someone was in my head telling me it would be okay, that I needed to trust her, that she'd take care of me and we'd protect the others together."

Mac blew out a breath. That most definitely wasn't what she'd expected Cami to ask about. Still, it made sense. Sort of. Sitting there, trying to figure out what to say, she wished her grandmother could help her. Ellen would know what to say. All Mac could do was play it by ear and pray she didn't screw up too badly.

"What specifically do you want to know, sweetheart?"

"Is it real? Is the voice real or did I imagine it?"

"Cam." She smiled when the twelve-year-old looked up at her. She knew using her daughter's preferred name signaled she was treating her as an adult. "I can't tell you for certain. But here's what your great-grandmother told me not all that long after I started shifting.

"Not every Pure *hears* their animal-self. That doesn't mean they aren't there. The fact they can shift proves the animal is there. But some of us, for whatever reason, actually hear our other selves.

"I've learned over the years to pay attention to what Cait says, especially if I'm in a situation that could get dangerous. Other times, well, let's just say she has a rather interesting sense of humor and she doesn't mind making me the butt of her jokes."

Like shifting back to human outside instead of safely in the house where no one can see us, Mac thought humorlessly.

At least she didn't seem to do that as much once the children were born.

"Does that mean my panther is a different person from me?"

Mac shook her head. It had taken her a long time to work her head around that very same question.

"Sweetie, you know something?"

Cami shook her head.

"I asked Gran that very same question. Here's how she explained it to me." She thought for a moment, recalling her grandmother's words. "It's confusing I know, to suddenly have another voice in your

168

head, talking to you, telling you what you need to do. Add to that the fact you are shifting into something other than human. But you are no different than you've ever been. That voice is simply another part of you. Think of it as that part that prevents you from running out into the middle of a street when a car's coming or that warns you something is about to happen if you keep doing what you've been doing."

"So why does she suddenly talk to me?"

"Because she knows you are worried and scared and she's trying to help you."

Mackenzie should remember this, Cait teased.

Or maybe you should, she countered.

"Did your Cait talk to you before you started shifting, Mom?"

Mac shook her head. "Cam, before I answer, you need to remember I didn't know shapeshifters were real back then. It wasn't until after the lycan attacked me and tried to turn me that I learned our kind really existed."

"Okay."

Mac knew she didn't understand, not really. That wasn't important. The fact Cami wanted her to explain was.

"That said, I always had what your grandma called my imaginary friend. Except she wasn't like the imaginary friends other girls my age talked about. I didn't realize until later, after I started shifting and Gran helped me make the connection with her, that it was Cait. She's always been with me." Mac changed positions so she could look more closely at her daughter. "Why? Does your panther talk to you?"

The twelve-year-old nodded.

Mac grinned and pulled her close. "That's good, Cam. Really good." She ruffled the girl's hair. "Has she told you her name yet?"

Cami ducked her head but not before Mac saw the sparkle in her eyes. "Yes, ma'am." When she looked up, her green eyes, so much like her mother's, glowed a deeper green. "Her name's Freydís."

Mac arched one brow and pulled out her phone. She quickly typed in the name and then inhaled sharply. Historically, Freydís was the daughter of Erik the Red. In legend, she was a famed Viking shield maiden. Reading that, Mac didn't know whether to be proud or scared to death.

Silly Mackenzie. Be proud. Is a good name, a strong name, one that fore-tells greatness for our daughter.

And that was what worried Mac. She knew what her own life was like. She didn't want to think about Cami having to do anything that came close to what she had since she started shifting. But that was the mother talking, not the alpha and certainly not the member of the Tribunal, something Cami or Xander would one day become.

"That makes you very special, Cam." She ran a hand over her daughter's head, pride filling her. "Not that you weren't before all this happened."

"Then there's nothing wrong with me?"

"Not one little thing."

"Cool." The twelve-year-old grinned and Mac marveled at the resilience of youth.

"I'd like to ask a favor of you, though, sweetheart. Would you shift for me, right here and right now?"

"Will you shift with me, Mama?"

Hearing the note of fear in the girl's voice, Mac nodded. As she did, she remembered how much it helped in those early days for Pat to be with her, shifting and teaching her what it meant to be a Pure.

"Of course, sweetheart."

She stood and moved to the door, making sure no one was around. The last thing she wanted was someone coming in while Cam was in the middle of a shift and scaring her. Then she pulled out her phone and texted Jackson, letting him know what they were about to do. With that done, she turned her attention back to her daughter.

"Okay, sweetie. Dad knows that he and you brother need to stay away for a bit while we do this." She motioned for Cami to stand and move into the center of the room. "Do you want me to talk you through it?"

Cami nodded, nervously chewing her lower lip as she did.

"I know it's scary at first, but it's really easy. First things first, Let's get undressed." As she said it, Mac grimaced. She hadn't told the kids about being shot. Cami was sure to ask about the bandage at her shoulder. "Before we do, I need to tell you one more thing. You're old enough to know this but your brother isn't. Okay?"

Cam nodded, her expression serious.

"There are people who believe our kind shouldn't be allowed to exist. They think we are monsters like in the movies. One of them saw me today while I was shifted and took a shot at me. He hit me, but he didn't hurt me badly. In fact, shifting will help me heal faster."

Cami's face screwed up in anger and then she glanced over her shoulder in the direction of the hospital room where their kinswomen lay.

"Can Gran shift and be better?"

Mac shook her head. "Not yet, love. She's hurt too badly. But just as soon as the doctors say she can, we'll help her do just that. I promise."

"Okay." She kicked out of her sneakers and then pulled off her clothes, placing them on the sofa. Then she watched as her mother followed suit. "Now what? I just shifted yesterday. I didn't think about it. It just happened."

"Let's sit on the floor." Mac gracefully did just that and waited until Cam joined her. "Now, close your eyes and think about your Freydís. Talk to her. Tell her you need to shift. Ask her to help you."

"Okay." Cami closed her eyes, and a look of concentration crossed her expression.

"Easy, baby," Mac soothed. "It's going to hurt. The more you fight against the change, the more it will hurt and the longer it will take to shift." She thought for a moment. Then she reached out and touched the back of Cami's hand, waiting until the girl opened her eyes and looked at her. "Do you want me to show you?"

Cami nodded once.

"Okay." She climbed to her knees and smiled at Cami in reassurance. "Ready?"

Another nod from the twelve-year-old.

Okay, Cait. Let's do this. Remember, this is to help Cami and Freydís.

Pain rolled over her and Mac gave in to it. Dropping to hands and knees, she pictured her jaguar form. Every pore burned as fur sprouted. Every muscle screamed in pain as bones broke and reformed. Panting, she reached for her jaguar-self. Whining softly as the shift progressed, all she could do was wait for it to pass and pray it didn't take too long or scare her daughter too much.

"That was really fast, Mama." Cami threw her arms around Cait's neck a few minutes later and the jaguar purred loudly. Then Cait gently butted her with her head. "My turn?"

The jaguar nodded.

It took longer for Cami to shift. Cait sat close to her, Mac watching through the jaguar's eyes as the girl closed her eyes. A look of concentration crossed Cam's expression before her features softened. Mac recognized the look and its cause. Cam was talking with her Freydís. The girl's features blurred and she cried out. Before long, a black panther lay panting on the tile floor. She lifted her head when Cait began grooming her. Then the jaguar curled around her, her message clear. They were to rest, to sleep. They could shift back later.

Half an hour later, the door opened almost silently. Cait lifted her head. Other than that, she didn't move as she recognized Jackson's scent. He stepped inside and smiled slightly. Then he carried a sleeping Xander to one of the two twin beds against the far wall. By the time he returned, Cait carefully stood and moved away from their daughter's shifted form. He watched as the jaguar shifted back, draping a robe around Mac's nude form.

"She okay?" he asked softly.

Mac nodded, smiling at the panther. "Her name's Freydís."

Jackson's brows winged upward. "She already knows her panther's name?"

"Yeah. Seems Freydís has been with her for some time now."

"We are so screwed, Mac," he chuckled.

"Tell me about it." She grinned and then studied the young panther. "Think we can get her into bed without waking her?"

He shrugged. "You go get ready for bed. I'll carry her over. If she wakes, I'll help her shift back."

"Thanks."

She reached up to lightly kiss him. Then she disappeared into the bathroom. As she did, she pulled back the collar of her robe to check her injured shoulder. Just as she told Cami, her wound already looked better. Hopefully, that meant the world would soon look better as well.

Not that she was going to be holding her breath.

15

"All right, Houston. What have you got?" Mac stood behind him, bleary eyed, clutching her to-go cup of coffee like a lifeline.

Whatever it was, it had better be damned good to excuse dragging her out of bed before four in the morning.

"I think we hit the jackpot, ma'am." His fingers flew over his keyboard. "Or at least we've got enough to make that jackpot a hell of a lot easier to find."

"Tell me before you show me."

"Yes, ma'am."

He waited as the two other tech specialists assigned to the unit came in and settled in chairs on either side of him. Lance Corporal Yvonne "Cloud" Osbourne glanced at Houston's keyboard and shook her head. Then she did something Mac didn't catch. A moment later, a virtual keyboard appeared on the tabletop in front of her. Mac chuckled softly at the blonde muttered something about being too old-school to Houston. It wasn't new and she waited to see what Chief Warrant Officer Hudson Bailey added.

"Children, behave yourselves in front of the Old Lady. Don't make me separate you," Bailey, call sign Badger, said.

"Such respect I get." Mac grinned and sipped her coffee. "Tell me why you thought it a good idea to drag me out of bed this early. Or do the three of you want to be transferred to the motor pool?"

"Not that, ma'am." Houston shot her a look of mock horror as he held his hands up in surrender.

"Then talk to me, Astro."

"We've been running through the videos, both from police head-quarters and the parking garage as well as around Phelan's office," Houston said. "It's a slow go because of the number of cameras involved, especially around the HQ. Cloud and Badger have focused on them while I took Phelan's office."

"So Tech Services got you the videos from HQ?"

"Finally, ma'am." No doubt about it, he didn't appreciate the delay any more than did Mac. "While we waited, we pulled the exterior videos from traffic cams, nearby buildings and even checked what had been posted on social media."

Osbourne nodded and quickly entered a command, activating several of the screens in front of her. "You wouldn't believe the number of videos that hit social media within an hour of the blasts. Most don't show anything of import, but a few might help piece together what happened. I've pulled those, copied them and sent word to Lt. Tanaka requesting DPD ask for warrants for the originals."

"Good. We'll get to them in a minute." Mac gave the young woman's shoulder a pat before continuing. "What else?"

"We've got video of a vehicle spotted outside the parking garage an hour or so before the first blast departing shortly before the blast. That vehicle showed up at Phelan's office ten minutes later."

Mac's mouth stretched into feral smile. Maybe getting up this early was worth it after all.

"Show me."

"Before we do, there's one more piece you need to know about, ma'am," Bailey said.

Frowning, she motioned for him to continue.

"We have video from inside HQ that may explain how the bomb was placed there."

She closed her eyes and counted to ten. Even though she wanted to start with that clip, she had a feeling she needed to see it through in chronological order. That would give her a better feel for what happened and, hopefully, why.

"Can you pull it all up, give me the different feeds in chronological order?"

"Yes, ma'am. We're already working on it," Houston said.

"Good. How long?"

"Another fifteen and we should be ready to begin."

"Get on it. Let me know when you're ready. I'm going to touch base with Tanaka and make sure she's on those warrants. Then I'm calling in part of the DPD team investigating what happened. They need to see this as well."

With that, she thanked the three and left their work area. As she did, she signaled for Jael to come with her. She wanted the woman's take on what they knew so far and then she needed to get her end of things rolling. Damn, but she hated these cases when she had to balance being a cop with being a member of Flynn's command.

"Well?" She took her place behind her desk and motioned for Jael to close the door.

"They've seen something they don't like."

Mac nodded, her expression worried. "Call Shelley and make sure she's seen Houston's request. Tell her what you can. Ask her to tap Lolo and Nate. I want the three of them here along with Deluca and Halstead."

"On it." She pulled her cellphone and started to place the first call before pausing. "You don't usually delegate this sort of thing, Mac. What's going on?"

"I'm going to contact my cousin." She gave a soft chuckle. Having Mateo as her immediate commanding officer helped—usually. She hoped this was one of those times and he could cut some of the red tape for her. "My gut tells me there is more to what's going on than we know. If I'm right, he needs know so he can take certain precautions."

"You think Flynn's holding out on us?" Now Jael's brow creased with concern.

"No, not really." She stopped Jael before she could say anything else. "Look, you know how things go when it comes to the chain of command. Things will be told to someone closer in the chain than to those who sit at the top of that chain. I want to make sure some of the other teams haven't seen something similar but have kept it out of the official chain and off the chatter."

Jael didn't like it, not that Mac blamed her. But she didn't object or deny what the younger woman said.

"I'll make a couple of calls as well, see if I can dig anything up." She paused by the door. "More coffee?" She nodded to Mac's now empty to-go cup.

Mac checked her watch before answering. "Give Tanaka time to contact Lolo. Then call Lolo and ask if she minds raiding her aunt's café for coffee and food for all of us. Tell her I'll call Drea with my credit card as soon as the shop opens."

Jael nodded and slipped out of the office, closing the door behind her. Mac leaned back, gathering her thoughts. Then she pulled her cellphone from her pocket and placed her first of what she knew would be several calls.

"This had better be good, Mackenzie," Brigadier General Mateo Santos groaned a few moments later.

She grinned, picturing him in bed, dark hair tousled, scrubbing one hand over his face. Then she heard another voice asking if everything was all right. Her grin turned into a wide smile and she couldn't wait to tease him about his latest conquest. But later, after they talked business. Good, clean—well, maybe not that clean—family fun could wait.

"It is. And sorry to wake you. But at least it's an hour later there than here."

She waited, listening to the sounds of him sitting up and getting out of bed. He softly told his companion to go back to sleep. A moment later, the sound of a door softly closing warned her he was ready to hear more.

"Talk to me, cuz. You wouldn't be calling at this ungodly hour if it wasn't important."

She quickly updated him on her conversation with Phelan and Oakley. His curse to hear her confirm the presence of at least three lycans in the area had her nodding even though he couldn't see her. Then she sobered, knowing that was only the tip of the proverbial iceberg she was dealing with.

"Mateo, my tech team is pulling together a compilation of videos from the different scenes. They think they've found something. I'll let you know when I've had a chance to review it all. But I need to know if you've heard any whisperings of something similar happening elsewhere."

For a moment, he didn't say anything. Worried, she waited, praying her gut was wrong in this instance.

"I haven't heard about any overt attacks like what you've had." The sound of him pacing said he didn't like where this was going. Too bad. She didn't like it either. "But I have heard rumblings of lycans 'straying.'" She pictured him making air quotes around the word. "There are rumors, if you can call them that, of lycans wandering into territories claimed by pures or witches, territories approved by the Tribunal."

"And?"

And why hadn't he or Flynn said something to her?

Or to the Tribunal for that matter. If they had, she'd know it.

Damn it, if someone playing politics kept that information from them and it led to her mother and grandmother being hurt, there'd be hell to pay.

"Reports only without confirmation." He paused and she could almost see him shake his head as the implications dawned on him. "And I should have followed up."

She didn't say anything. That was a discussion they'd have when they were together again.

"Follow up now and let me know what you find out. My gut tells me there's more going on than we know."

"Consider it done. Now, what else do you need officially?"

"If you haven't done it already, put everyone on alert. If the lycans are making a move, it needs to be met quickly and definitively." Now it was her turn to pause. "Mateo, this next is from me in my role not only as a member of the Tribunal but as its newly appointed Enforcer. The Tribunal's laws concerning lycans will be enforced. If any are found in territories where they shouldn't be, they are to be taken into custody and brought before the Tribunal. If any have violated human law, the authorities are to be informed. We don't want a war, but we will do everything possible to insure not only our own safety but the safety of the humans as well."

"Understood." Then he chuckled. "Does it get confusing with all the hats you're wearing, cuz?"

"You have no idea," she groaned. "Keep me in the loop, Mateo." She ended the call and motioned for Jael to enter when the woman knocked and cracked the door enough to look inside.

"I spoke to Tanaka and Murray." She placed a mug of fresh coffee on the desk in front of Mac. "Tanaka's notifying those you tapped. Murray said she'd call ahead to the café to have everything ready. Once she's picked it up, she'll roll here."

"Thanks." She indicated the chair in front of her desk. "Mateo said there have been unconfirmed reports of lycans wandering into protected areas. He's going to follow up and let me know what he finds."

"I made a couple of calls as well. Got pretty much the same information. No one's seen anything as overt as what happened here. A couple don't think it's related, but the others said they'd dig deeper in their territories to find out what they can."

"Let me know what you hear."

Jael nodded. "Now, how do you feel and how's your family?"

Mac leaned back, her mug cradled between her hands. "Mom's better. Cam was helping her with some soup when I got in last night."

"Cam?" Jael arched one brow in question.

"I told her if she's old enough to shift—and heaven help me. I still can't get my mind around that—she's old enough to choose what we call her. She likes Cam, thinks it sounds more grown up."

Jael chuckled softly. "She's growing up, Mac."

"Too fast for my liking." And that was putting it mildly. "Anyway,

Mom's hurting and it's going to be at least another few days before the doctors consider releasing her."

"And your grandmother?"

All Mac could do was shake her head. The longer Ellen remained unconscious, the lower her chances of ever waking up. Mac knew it but she couldn't bring herself to say it. Saying it made it real and she wasn't ready to face that possibility. Not yet and, hopefully, not for a very long time.

"The doctors are doing all they can right now." She gave a shrug. "The hospital gave us the suite next door. Abby and Danny are there right now getting some rest. Jackson and the kids are with Mom and Gran."

"And you?" She lifted her mug and used it to indicate Mac's injured shoulder.

"Better. Cam and I had a long talk last night. The others gave us some time alone. So we talked some more about what happened and about her shifting." She shook her head and one corner of her mouth quirked up. "Before we both shifted, she wanted to know if the voice in her head was her panther. Seems the cat's been talking to her for some time now." She rubbed her face with her left hand, wishing this was a dream she'd soon wake up from.

"And?"

"The panther's name is Freydís."

Jael blew out a long, low whistle. She understood what it meant for Cam to not only know her panther's name but to know it this soon.

"What does Cait say?"

Mac looked at her and growled. "She thinks it's funny. Said it's a good name, a strong name for Cam. Says it means she's destined for great things."

Jael laughed, waving a hand in an apology Mac knew she didn't mean.

"Sorry, but the two of you are so much alike. I have a feeling if you'd known your family history all along like Cami does, your Cait would be just like her Freydís."

"You just wait. I'm going to send her to you when she starts turning into a hormonal shifter. We'll see if you think it's funny then."

Before anything more could be said, a knock sounded at the door. Mac called out for the newcomer to enter. A moment later, Houston reported they were ready and the first of those she'd sent for were arriving. Mac thanked him and said they'd be there shortly.

"Depending on what we see, you and I may need to split up," she told Jael as they climbed to their feet. "I'm not going to cut DPD out of the case. But that means we need to coordinate closely between them and our Marines."

"As long as you have Norwood or Lolo with you if I can't be."

Mac nodded. Then she motioned for Jael to come with her. Time to find out what Houston and his people could tell them.

Ten minutes later, everyone Mac sent for had arrived. At her nod, the three tech specialists moved to the front of the room. A large video screen deployed from the ceiling as Osbourne sat down and opened her laptop. As she did, Bailey joined her. He opened a laptop and then set two tablets on the table between them.

"Colonel Santos asked us to put together a timeline of videos we've managed to go through so far." Houston nodded and a moment later, the image of the parking garage from before the first blast filled the screen. "The first series of videos will focus on the parking garage. The first begins sixty-eight minutes before the first blast. It consists of a series of videos taken from exterior and interior cameras and ends ten minutes prior to the explosion."

"A question before we start," Shelly Tanaka said.

Houston glanced at Mac and then nodded to Tanaka to continue.

"How confident are you about what the videos show?"

"Very, as I think you'll understand once you see them, ma'am."

Tanaka seemed satisfied and sat back. Mac inclined her head slightly, indicating Houston should continue. Without a word, he dimmed the lights and the video started playing.

Nothing looked out of the ordinary. Cars and trucks drove by, occasionally turning into the drive leading to the parking garage. Houston paused the video when a white panel van, the sort so many companies used, pulled up to the automatic arm and waited for a ticket to go inside. He zoomed in on the rear license plate. A moment later, a still image of the plate appeared in the upper right corner of a second screen. Then the angle changed, indicating a new video feed, this one from inside the garage. The image didn't show much beyond a male in a baseball cap and what looked like a generic work shirt. The man reached out the driver's side window and took a ticket. A moment later, the parking arm across the drive lifted and the van pulled inside the garage.

"Unfortunately, the cameras inside the garage don't show us the van's entire progress. But as you can see, it is captured briefly on several more levels. Our last video capture of it is on UL-2. There's no video of it leaving the garage and, as you can see from this still, it never left." He waited until the image of what had once been a white panel van but now looked like a pile of twisted, scorched metal, joined the other two on the second screen.

"Registered owner?" Tanaka asked as she flipped through her own notes.

"You probably know as much as we do, ma'am," Houston said. "The van was rented a week ago. The ID and address were bogus. We haven't turned anything up on facial rec yet, but we're still working on it."

"What else?" Mac asked from where she leaned against the wall at the back of the room.

A new video started, again showing the parking garage's exterior. Much like the last set of videos, they watched cars coming and going. A time check showed less than half an hour before the first blast would happen. Mac stood straighter as Houston paused the video when a grey Toyota Prius pulled into the drive. Once again, license plate and driver's image joined the growing collection of stills on the second screen.

And, as with the van, they watched the different camera feeds as the Prius drove through the garage to the same level where the van was later found. Coincidence? Possibly, but Mac doubted it. She learned long ago there was rarely anything that was simply "coincidence". More often than not, it was something planned by one or more actors.

This, she knew, had been planned. But why and what did it have to do with the blasts?

"Watch as the Prius leaves the garage," Houston said as the video changed feeds once again.

Mac's expression hardened as the Prius stopped at the exit gate. "Freeze it right there!"

As Osbourne did as she ordered, Mac stalked toward the front of the room. No said anything. They didn't need to. She felt their attention on the image on the screen. She stopped a few feet from it. As she did, she hissed out a breath.

"Blow it up and give me a side-by-side with the van driver."

Almost instantly, the two images appeared next to one another. Several curses came from behind her as the baseball cap wearing image from the first image matched the passenger in the Prius. Before she could order the techs to run a comparison, Houston assured her they'd already done so and he was confident they were the same people.

"Who's that damned Prius registered to?" she demanded.

"Unknown, Colonel," Houston said. "According to police reports, the plate was stolen a week ago. It's registered to a three-year-old Honda."

"Give me the information you've already gotten on it and I'll have someone run down the Honda and its owner," Tanaka said.

Mac nodded and Houston signaled Osbourne to do as the detective asked.

"We have video of that same Prius arriving at Phelan's office less than fifteen minutes later, Colonel. It parked in the rear of the building, so we don't have a feed of who got out."

Mac arched a brow. "Say again."

"We don't have video showing them once the car went around back."

"Tanaka, I want two detectives to pay a visit to Phelan's security company. I'll make sure they have search warrants. They were supposed to turn over all security feeds from the building. If we don't have video from the rear, they failed to give it to us. I want that video and I want to know why they withheld it." She waited while Tanaka instructed Norwood and his partner to see to it. "Houston, do we have any video from the interior of the building?"

"Negative, ma'am."

"Norwood, I want every video feed for the last week from that location. If the security company argues, contact Zee and have arrest warrants drawn up. If they say Phelan and/or Oakley told them not to hand over any of the feeds we requested, I want statements—sworn statements—to that effect from them."

"Understood, ma'am."

"Go. Your LT will brief you when you get back to Central." She waited for him to leave. Then she turned back to the others. "Shelly, have someone pull the video from the car rental location." She looked at Houston.

"Love Field."

At least it was in DPD's jurisdiction. "Pull the feed, get copies of all the paperwork and the ID he used to rent the van. The van would have had GPS. Get their okay for us to pull the GPS data. Let's see where the van went from the time it left the airport until it was left at HQ."

"If you'll excuse me, ma'am, I'll get together with Zee or someone else from the DA's Office and get the ball rolling on a warrant," Tanaka said as she climbed to her feet.

"Go. Keep me in the loop." She turned her attention back to Houston. "What else?"

"We're still pulling together the video from HQ, ma'am, but we may have gotten lucky."

Something in his voice told her she wasn't going to like whatever they'd found.

"Let's see it."

He glanced at Bailey and dipped his chin. Then he stepped away from the screen. Watching him, Mac wondered if he was doing his best to put as much distance between them as he could without actually leaving the room. That wasn't good. Not good at all.

Then the video started and it was worse than she could have imagined. Cursing, she watched it play through once. Then she ordered it stopped.

"Captain Lindsey, contact Chief Culver and tell him information's been uncovered regarding the case that he needs to be apprised of. Ask if he will join us here. If not, tell him we will come to him. Go!"

Without waiting, she turned to the rest of those gathered.

"This is not to be discussed with anyone not in this room. Hell, it's not to be discussed outside of this room until we've had a chance to brief the chief. Murray, as soon as we find out where Culver wants to meet, let Tanaka know. Then contact Zee and ask him to standby. I think he needs to be at the briefing as well. DeLuca, Halstead, full reports are to be readied for the chief."

She looked at each of them, some Marines, some cops, a few both. All dedicated to making sure those responsible for what happened were brought to justice. But she wasn't a fool. She knew what they saw on the video complicated things in ways none of them anticipated.

"Make your calls. We'll reconvene once we know what Chief Culver wants to do."

With that, she turned on her heel and left the room. She had her own to make, starting with her husband. He needed to send word to the pride and other shifters in the area to watch themselves. With lycans in the area, there was no telling what danger any of them might be in.

1 6

An hour later, Mac returned to the briefing room. Stepping inside, she nodded slightly. Everyone except Norwood and his partner had returned. Culver arrived a few minutes earlier and stood near the front of the room with Jael, Nguyen and Tanaka. None looked happy, not that she blamed them. She was anything but happy herself.

"Chief, do you wish to address the team?" she asked as she joined them.

"It's your briefing, Colonel."

"Thank you, sir."

She moved to the front of the room. For a moment, she studied those present. These were some of the best cops and best Marines she'd had the pleasure to serve with. Now she needed their help not only to close the case but to prevent war from breaking out between the lycan's and the rest of the world.

"All right, everyone, listen up!"

Instantly, the room fell silent as conversations ended and all eyes focused on her.

"Chief, I assume Jael's briefed you."

"She has."

Good. That made it easier.

"Then let's get started. Sgt. Lee, I want arrangements made to move the following patients from the hospital and to a safe location. The patients and their families to be moved are my own, Captain King and her son, Marie Duncan and her daughter- and son-in-law, I've already spoken with their doctors and they know we will have teams coming to the hospital today to assist with the move. I want you to coordinate the move with Jael."

"Understood, Colonel."

"Get your team on it as soon as we finish here. I want a plan in place within an hour of meeting's end." She turned her attention to the others in the room.

"This next piece of information is not to go beyond the DPD task-force working on the case and the Marines under my command. If it gets out before you are given authorization from either Chief Culver or me, I will make sure you lose your badge or your place in this unit. This is not just a situation where Texas laws have been broken. This is a matter of national security. If you have a problem with that, then you are free to go now. Just know that anything you have seen or heard up until now is not to be discussed with anyone." She waited, unsurprised when no one stood to leave. "Thank you." She smiled and nodded once.

"These two men." She tapped a finger on the image of the two inside the Prius. God, how was she supposed to say this? "When I entered the parking garage after the explosion, I caught the scent of two lycans. My husband confirmed it as did other members of this team. It is possible these two are those lycans.

"That is worrisome enough. However, when Captain Lindsay, Detective Murray and I went to question Davis Phelan to see if he knew any lycans were in the area, I scented the same two lycans around and in the office building. But they weren't the only ones. I scented one other lycan. None of them asked permission of the local pride leader to be in this territory nor did they ask permission from the Tribunal. That puts them, at the very least, in violation of Tribunal law. I have been authorized by the Tribunal to locate and take them into custody.

"I want both the DPD taskforce and my unit here to work together to identify these two and locate where they are staying. We are moving forward under the assumption they are involved in the bombing but, until we have enough evidence to link them to the bombing, we will use the violation of Tribunal law to arrest them." Heads nodded and she began to relax a little.

"That brings me to something some of you won't like. Because there is reason to suspect these two," once again, she tapped a finger against their picture, "of being lycans, any takedown team will consist of Pures. Backup teams will be human and witches. I will not risk any of you being injured—and possibly turned—in an attempt to arrest them."

"Ma'am, we can take care of ourselves," Tanaka all but growled.

"Shelly, in any other situation, I wouldn't hesitate to send you in. But I've tangled with lycans before." More than she wanted to admit. "I've seen what they are capable of when cornered. They aren't like the Pures. When they shift, they don't give a damn about playing fair. Human or shifted, they see the rest of us as prey and normals are nothing to them except something to hunt and kill. Or turn. One of my duties as your commanding officer is not to put you or any of the other cops under my command in jeopardy unnecessarily. This would be unnecessary."

"Colonel Santos is correct," Culver said. "And I not only agree with her plan, but I am making it an order. When these sons of bitches are located, a team selected by her will go in first. I'd like that to include members of DPD but understand if you feel your Marines are better prepared for such an arrest."

"No, sir." Her immediate reaction might be to use only Marines, but she knew the cops under her command needed to be part of this. "I want it to be a mix of both teams. Shelly, Lolo, we'll meet to discuss primary and secondary team makeups after the briefing."

Since they both seemed to be satisfied with that, she continued. "Houston, run the last video again. Chief Culver needs to see it."

With that, she moved to lean against the far wall. They might not have all the answers yet, far from it. But they were getting there.

Hopefully, they'd be one step closer before end of day.

More than that, she prayed they had the lycans in custody by then. As a cop, she didn't want to think about what they could do to her city. She'd seen it before, long before the world learned shapeshifters were real. The last thing she wanted was for any of them to decide Dallas was now their personal hunting ground.

That thought brought another and, with it, a spike of fear. "Shelly, check with the ME's Office. Make sure they haven't had any bodies come in over the last two to three weeks that show the signs of an animal attack."

For a moment, no one said anything. Then, as the implications sank in, more than one person began to curse. Tanaka's expression hardened and she quickly left the room, pulling her phone and programming in a number as she did.

"All right, Houston. Let's run the video. Chief Culver needs to see it."

Once again, the lights in the room dimmed. Houston explained the video came from cameras within police headquarters. The first focused on one of the two side doors DPD employees could use instead of going through the main entrance. They watched for several minutes as uniformed and plain clothes officers entered the building and moved through metal detectors. All very orderly and nothing out of place.

Then the door opened again and yet another uniformed officer entered. He stopped just inside the door and looked around. Even with the grainy quality of the feed, Mac saw his nerves. He shifted from foot to foot as he waited for the two detectives in front of him to finish going through the checkpoint and move out of sight. Then, with no one else waiting, he stepped forward.

For not the first time, Mac wished the video feed included sound. Unfortunately, it didn't. So they couldn't hear what the officer said to the screening officer when the man motioned for him to put his backpack through the scanner. Whatever it was, the screening officer smiled, slapped him on his arm and shook hands. Then the officer handed him the backpack and stepped through the scanner before retrieving his backpack. The same backpack that had not been checked or scanned.

"Their names?" Culver asked, his voice deceptively gentle.

"One moment, Chief." Lt. Halstead swiped a finger across her tablet's screen and then began typing. She looked up briefly and then back down, typing some more. Then she stood and moved to where Culver stood. "Chief, Colonel, the officer manning the screening station is Officer David Heritage. Two years on the job. Fairly clean rookie record but he got himself this assignment after several complaints from citizens concerning excessive force. IAB didn't find enough to warrant more than one three-day rip and an official 'counseling' entry. But that was enough for his CO to assign him to door duty as a result."

"Shelly, have someone ready to pick him up when they get the signal." Mac considered for a moment. Then, seeing Culver looking at her, she knew she needed to explain. "Sir, if we pick him up right now, it will tip our hand. You'll see in a minute." With that, she motioned for Houston to continue with the next bit of video.

They watched the backpack carrying officer enter an elevator and press a button on the control panel before stepping back. Even though he cleared the check point without problem, he still looked nervous. In fact, if anything, he appeared even more nervous. He shifted from foot to foot as the elevator slowly climbed toward its destination. He kept his head down to avoid making eye contact with any of the others in the car with him. Then, when the controls dinged, letting him know they'd reached the second floor, he all but jumped out—of the car and out of his skin.

The screen went black for a moment before another video started. They watched in silence as the officer walked down the hall, ignoring those he passed. A few looked at him strangely, as if his behavior wasn't normal. Mac made a note to get their IDs and have someone talk with them. If they knew the man, she wanted them interviewed.

The officer disappeared inside the men's room at the end of the hallway. Mac waited, even though she knew what happened next. For not the first time, she cursed the privacy concerns that prevented the department from putting cameras in the bathrooms. Because of that, they couldn't see what the man did inside. Not that there was any doubt about his actions, not in her mind.

Less than three minutes later, the bathroom door opened. The officer stepped out and started back down the hallway. Hearing Culver's hiss, Mac glanced at him and nodded. Then she signaled Houston to pause the video and bring the lights back up.

"Deluca, your thoughts?" she asked instead of commenting directly on the obvious elephant in the room.

"I have to preface this with reminding everyone that our investigation is still in its early days." He paused, his mouth firming. "Hell, that's legal speak and I'm not going to insult any of you with it. The evidence so far shows that the second blast originated in that bathroom. Our reconstruction is leaning toward the bomb having been planted in the air vent at the southwest corner of the room. The duct is secured, or it should have been. But all you'd need to access it is a screwdriver or something similar. If you have a battery-operated screwdriver, it would take only a few seconds to open it up, plant something inside the duct and then secure it back in place."

"What else can you tell us?" Culver asked.

"That explosive charge had the same signature as what we found in the garage. We got lucky because there are certain safeguards in the building's construction that don't show on the plans most people can access. One of those is how the support beams are reinforced. That is one of the main reasons the parking garage and building didn't suffer catastrophic damage."

"Who is that bastard, ma'am?" one of the Marines asked.

Mac smiled humorlessly. "That is the SOB who decided it was a good idea to try to shoot me while I was shifted yesterday." Without thinking, she reached up and gently rubbed her injured shoulder.

"He did what?" Tanaka ground out, her eyes flashing dangerously.

Mac quickly explained. "Chief, we need to bring him in."

"Agreed."

Mac shoved away from the wall and returned to the front of the room. This was her show again.

"From this point until further notice, the investigation has three prongs that must be followed. The first is the obvious: the explosives. Deluca, that's your baby. I want your team to continue focusing on the explosives used, the duds that were found and finding out if the signature on both match anyone in our database or elsewhere. Reports morning, noon and night to both Chief Culver and myself."

"Understood, Colonel." He began gathering up his notes.

"You're dismissed, Captain. I know you'd rather be working than sitting in a briefing." She smiled as he grinned in response.

"Soon as I know anything, you will," he promised before leaving the room.

"Now, as for the rest of it, here's how we're going to proceed. . . ."

Half an hour later, Mac ended the briefing. She watched as everyone went their separate ways. Cops and Marines hurried to gear up or return to their offices. Lt. Halstead sat with Houston and the other tech specialists and compared notes. Jael walked out with Tanaka, their heads together as they discussed their part of the upcoming operation. Then, seeing Culver's signal, she motioned for him to come with her. She knew this was a conversation best held in private.

"Are you sure about this, Mac?" he asked as she closed the door and motioned for him to take one of the seats in front of her desk.

"I am, sir. I don't see any other way to do it." She leaned against the edge of her desk, thinking for a moment. "Chief, I admit that none of this makes sense. If the lycans were involved with the bombing, then why would Lagina take part? He made it very clear yesterday what he thinks about our kind. The obvious answer is he didn't know what the lycans were." Which was extremely possible since he couldn't *scent* them. "But we have to be prepared for other explanations as well."

"How do you want to handle their interrogations?"

"What I'd like to do is scare the shit out of them and force them to cooperate, but I can't." Not if they wanted anything Lagina or Heritage said admissible in court. "But they will be treated like any

193

other suspect. I want them brought in and put in the cage. They are to be kept separated. Preferably, they aren't to know the other has been brought in. Once they're in-house, I'll figure out who does the interrogation. I want to see what the team leaders say about how they reacted when they were picked up before making that decision."

"And the lycans?"

She tilted her head back and blew out a breath. There were some things she could tell him but more she could not. He didn't need to know everything the Tribunal had decided. Not yet, at any rate.

"Sir, I'm walking a very tight rope here." She remembered Mateo asking her if she ever had trouble juggling all the hats she wore. The answer was a resounding "yes!" and this was one of those times. "There is no doubt the two, perhaps three, of them have broken Tribunal law. As the pride's female alpha and enforcer, I am duty-bound to enforce that law. As a member of the Tribunal and its appointed enforcer, I have the authority to do just that. So they will be taken into custody and held until a final determination of their fates is made."

"Mac."

"Chief, I know and I'm going to do everything I can to make sure they answer for the bombing if they were involved." She straightened and looked at him. "That's the tightrope. If we find enough evidence to link them to the bombing, they will answer for it as well. But you know as well as I do that they will not see the inside of a human jail. Because of what they are, they will have to be held at Black Crow."

He nodded. He understood but she knew he didn't like it.

"Phelan and Oakley?"

"We move on them as soon as we have a location on the lycans."

As if that was his cue, Houston knocked on the door. At Mac's command, he opened it and a moment later, he and Lt. Halstead stood just inside the office.

"Ma'am, we've got a possible location on the lycans," he reported.

One corner of her mouth lifted and her eyes gleamed as she motioned for him to continue.

"My team got the GPS report on the van used in the bombing and

Houston here got the report on the Prius," Halstead said.

"Really?"

"Bailey noticed the rental decal on the car's back bumper, ma'am," Houston said. "He did his magic and got us the readout. Lt. Halstead and I compared locations between the two reports and discovered there was one point they both shared at the same time, a location where the Prius is currently located."

"Do tell."

"Yes, ma'am. It is currently parked near Love Field at one of the motels just outside the airport. It arrived there last night and hasn't moved."

"All right. Alpha Team is to move out. I want them to take up positions around the hotel. Get eyes on the car and find out which unit the suspects are occupying. Two members of the team are to go in in soft clothes." She considered the options. "Walters and Keo. Tell them I want them looking like they aren't the kind used to staying at the Holiday Inn or better hotels. Let me know when they move out. The main team will move out to join them once they confirm the suspects are still on-site."

"Yes, ma'am."

"Lt. Halstead, excellent work. I'd appreciate it if you would continue working with Houston and his team. See what you can pull out of cyberspace about Phelan and Oakley."

"On it, Colonel." The woman stopped and grinned a bit impudently. "You do realize how confusing all this is, don't you? I don't know whether I'm talking to the cop or the Marine or what."

Mac chuckled. "If you think it's confusing, you should be in my shoes.

"Get me a location on both Oakley and Phelan. Once you do, let me know." Mac dismissed them and turned her attention back to Culver. "It looks like things are starting to come together, sir."

"It does and that means I need to get back to Central. Keep me in the loop, Mac."

"No doubt about it, sir."

Now to get ready for what looked to be a very long day.

17

"Status?"

Mac entered the observation room. The far wall was lined with half a dozen monitors. Three of them currently displayed three different interrogation rooms. Each room was identical when it came to furnishings. A cheap chair in front of a heavy table bolted into the floor. A second chair on the far side of the table. Each of those second chairs were occupied, the suspects handcuffed to a steel bar running along the top of the table.

"Lagina was home and tried to act as if he didn't hear the team outside. They finally broke down the door and made entry. They found him trying to climb out the bathroom window," Jael said, motioning to the center monitor.

Mac shook her head. Why did they always think it was a good idea to try to climb out of the bathroom window, usually when either naked or almost naked? Lagina sat at the table, his wrists cuffed, the cuffs secured to the steel bar, wearing nothing but a pair of boxers. The bruise starting to blacken one eye told her he'd been foolish enough to fight—or at least try to—when the team took him into custody.

"Did you have a medic look at him?" No sense in giving his defense attorney reason to scream "police brutality!".

"As soon as we got here. Nothing more than a couple of superficial bruises he got trying to break free of the arresting officer."

"Who was?"

Jael turned her head and grinned. "Brenda Vacha."

Mac chuckled appreciatively. Anyone foolish enough to try to pen a brutality rap on Vacha was in for a surprise. The jury would find it very difficult to believe the five-foot nothing brunette who weighed less than one hundred pounds fully clothed and dripping wet could hurt anyone, much less someone the size of Lagina. Except she was anything but helpless. She'd trained most of her life in various forms of martial arts, not the sort that looked good on film, but the sort that really did teach you how to fight and protect yourself. Add to that her shapeshifter genes and there was a great deal packed into her small body.

"Has he asked for his rep or for an attorney?"

"Not yet. Of course, we didn't exactly tell him why he was being brought in. He assumes it has to do with you."

Another grin. "Well, in a way, it does."

Jael nodded, turning her attention back to the screens.

"And the others?"

"Officer David Heritage there was manning his station when his CO, along with members of our team, relieved him of duty. He was Mirandized and brought up here. He's scared but he hasn't asked anything more than if he should contact his rep. Sanchez said he could if he wanted but reminded him it would just draw things out. He's giving the idiot some time to think."

"What about Oakley?" Mac jutted her chin at the monitor for the final interrogation room and the woman sitting at that table.

"She was picked up at the office. She's said only one word: lawyer. So she's getting to cool her heels. We didn't know if you'd want to go through that particular song and dance or if you wanted to play the domestic terrorist card, especially since you put it into play yesterday."

"Let's keep her waiting a bit, see if her nerves start to get to her." Not that Mac expected them to. "Start with Heritage. You and Murray. Push him on his relationship with Lagina. Remind him of the consequences of letting someone through the security point without checking their bags, like Lagina's backpack, or making them go through the metal detectors. Go with your gut. But don't promise him anything."

"And what are you going to be doing?"

"Monitoring here until I get word one way or the other about our lycan trespassers." She left it at that, knowing Jael would object if she knew Mac's plans.

Not that it fooled the woman. Her eyes narrowed and her mouth firmed. Then, with a jerk of her head, she led Mac away from the bank of monitors.

"You will not leave here without an escort. Promise or I will issue the order to both your commands."

Mac didn't sigh, but it was a close call. Instead, she nodded once. As she did, she mentally groused at the restriction. She was a cop, damn it, and an alpha in her own right. She didn't need someone babysitting her, much less protecting her. Just because she was brass didn't change the fact she was more than capable of taking care of herself.

"Go have your chat with Heritage."

Mac waited until the door closed behind Jael before reaching for her cellphone. Her fingers—well, her thumbs—flew over the screen as she sent a quick text. She waited, watching as Jael entered the interrogation room and read Heritage his rights. She didn't need the sound turned up to see how that rocked the officer. His eyes went wide. Then, cursing, he shoved back his chair and started to stand. Instantly, Jael switched from police captain to Marine gunny. Heritage dropped back onto his chair like a puppet that's strings had been cut. Mac chuckled softly and wondered for not the first time if somewhere down the bloodlines, Jael didn't have a shapeshifter ancestor. That sort of command was something she saw from alphas—*and*, she amended silently, *the best gunnies out there.*

Have confirmation. Two men checked in. Housekeeping reports a third has stayed there off and on. Been here for almost a month. Orders?

She considered for a moment before responding.

Hold position. Eyes on all possible exits. Do NOT let them slip out. Do NOT tip them off to your presence. Find out if the office has a record of phone calls. Not that she expected them to have been foolish enough to have used the phone in the room to set up anything she could pin on them. **Contact Zee if necessary for warrant for those records.** She checked her watch. **I'll be there in 30. Do not move in until I arrive unless they try to leave or you feel exigent circumstances.**

Roger that. Holding position. Eyes and ears. Stay out of sight but don't let them slip away.

Seeing the icon showing Norwood was still typing, Mac rolled her eyes and made a bet with herself about what he was about to say.

Do not leave Central without backup, ma'am.

She won the bet and owed herself five.

"Shelly, let me know if they give you anything of import." She paused at the door, thinking. "Since Oakley has asked for an attorney, return her to holding. Don't put her in the cage upstairs. I want her in with the dregs patrol brings in. Have someone from the team monitoring. Who knows, we might get lucky and she'll do or say something we can use as leverage."

"Understood, ma'am." The woman glanced at her, frowning. "Where will you be?"

"I'm heading out to the motel. We've got confirmation at least two of our suspects are there." She reached for the door. "And I'll take Murray here with me." She opened the door, revealing the detective waiting for her.

Tanaka chuckled and shook her head, not asking how Mac knew Murray waited in the corridor outside the room. "Lolo, don't let her do anything foolish." She held a hand up when Mac opened her mouth to protest. "No disrespect, Mac, but you're not just brass now but big brass. You need to remember that."

This time Mac didn't try to hide the fact she rolled her eyes. Then she nodded and, with Murray on her heels, left the room.

Half an hour later, Mac climbed into the non-descript van down the street from the motel. Murray stayed outside, putting the van between her and the motel, keeping out of sight. Inside, Houston worked the various monitors mounted on the van's far wall. He glanced over his shoulder and nodded to Mac before turning his attention back to what he was doing.

"Status?"

She rested a hand on the back of his chair and looked over his shoulder, One monitor showed the exterior of the room their suspects occupied. A second monitor showed video feeds from the body cams of each team member as they moved into position. A third screen was split in two; one half showing an overhead scene she assumed came from a drone and the second an infrared view of the room.

Houston adjusted the exterior feed, panning out to show more of the parking lot. "Prius is parked three doors down from the room, ma'am. Could be they were trying to be a bit less obvious about where they're staying. But my guess is the lot was full and that was the closest spot they could get."

"Any movement from inside?"

"Not much. My guess is they're waiting until night to move out."

Mac nodded. That made sense. Still, it would be nice to know exactly who was inside and what they were up to.

"What about their IDs?"

Houston reached for his tablet and scrolled through several screens before handing it to Mac. "IDs are fake but the images fit the men the night manager has seen coming and going. I'm running facial rec on them now."

"Good work." She studied the infrared feed. "I only see two."

"That's all I've been able to locate. Could be the third left before we got here."

That meant the two inside might be the two from the parking

garage or only one of them. Hell, it might mean there were more lycans in the area than they knew.

And the only way to find out was to move in and take these two into custody.

She reached for one of the earbuds sitting on the table and slid it into her left ear. Then she tapped it, waiting for the telltale beep indicating she'd been linked into the team's network.

"Striker's on-site," she said. "Status?"

"Team's in place," Norwood answered. "Ready to move in on your order."

"Roger that. Warrants from state, federal and Tribunal are in hand." Mac paused and thought for a moment. Much as she wanted to lead this part of the op, her place was where she was. "You're a go. Move in."

Mac stood there, watching the bodycam feeds as each team member moved closer to their target. Two members slipped inside the office at one end of the building. Mac nodded slightly, trusting them to make sure no one there warned the suspects. The rest of the team split, two members staying in front while two more moved around the building to help cover the rear. That left two more members of the team unaccounted for. A quick check of the different feeds revealed their position on top of the building across the street, sniper rifles focused on the target motel room.

Mac once again tapped her earbud, opening the mic. "Ace, Beady, you will hold fire unless they get past our people or I give the green light."

"Roger that, Striker."

She nodded even though they couldn't see her. She wanted to take the lycans alive. Dead, they couldn't tell her why they'd chosen to come to Dallas at this particular time and what they expected to accomplish with the bombings. But she wouldn't put her team or the public in danger. She would not hesitate to give the order to shoot if necessary.

"We're in position," Norwood said a few moments later.

"You're a go."

The man nodded and held up his right fist, three fingers extended. Mac watched the silent countdown.

Three.

Two.

One.

Go!

Norwood darted out from behind a car parked across from the target room. Behind him, keeping low to the ground were two other members of the team. The first, Cpl. Katrina Parnell, ran on four paws. With her black colored snout and ears with her fawn-colored body, she resembled a large German shepherd. Running next to her, Private Pasqual Warren shouldered his assault rifle, aiming for the door.

After one final check with the rest of the team, Norwood banged twice on the door. Mac winced slightly as the sound carried over her earbud.

"Police, open up!" His glove fist pounded against the door once again. "We have a warrant to enter. Open up or we'll break the door down."

Without waiting for a response, he stepped back. A moment later, his booted foot connected with the door. The frame by the doorknob shattered and the door flew open. Norwood dove inside, rolling to his feet, gun in hand. Across the room, a man rolled off the far side of the bed, using it for cover. A second man appeared from what Mac assumed was the bathroom, a towel wrapped around his waist, gun in hand. A brown and tan streak raced across the motel room, hitting the second man in the chest, a snarling mass of teeth and claws.

Barely daring to breathe, Mac watched the different feeds as her team moved in. Before either man had time to register what happened, Norwood and Warren had them cuffed and on their knees. Parnell sat in front of them, still snarling and sounding like she wanted to take a very large and painful bite out of one or both of them.

"Talk to me, Nate," Mac said.

"One lycan and one human," he replied.

"Administer the inhibitor and make sure they're read their rights."

"Understood."

"Move the rest of the team in to secure the area and begin searching their room and vehicle."

Mac stepped out of the van and nodded to the waiting Murray. With the younger woman on her heels, she crossed the street. As she updated Murray, she glanced around the parking lot. Part of her wondered at the absence of looky-loos. Another part shrugged it off. The folks who stayed in places like this usually wanted as little to do with cops as possible. She didn't doubt for a moment, at least a dozen sets of eyes watched them from behind drawn drapes, making sure they didn't come near. How many of them had flushed their stashes when they heard Norwood announce he had a warrant? A slight smile touched Mac's lips at the thought. Then she sobered as she neared the open door.

Game time.

"Ma'am." Norwood nodded in her direction.

Her lips twitched slightly. The coyote shifter took the easy way out addressing her that way. It gave her a moment to decide if she met the two suspects in her cop persona, her military persona or her Tribunal persona. Damn, she had way too many hats to wear these days but, this once, she planned on wearing them all.

"Names?" She glanced at the two men, still kneeling on the floor, hands cuffed behind their backs, ankles secured with flex-cuffs.

"This one." Norwood indicated the man in the towel. "Is Dominic Turner. The other is Victor Koray."

She nodded and then stepped closer. As she did, she scented the air, identifying the lycan—Koray. Not that she needed his scent to make the identification. The hatred burning in his eyes as he watched her, the anger she could taste in the air, told her all she needed to know. Still, it wouldn't hurt to get him to confirm it on video.

And she knew exactly the way to do it.

"Down!"

Her power as an alpha wash over the room. Instantly, everyone except Murray and Turner dropped to hands and knees or, in Koray's case, to their belly. Satisfied, Mac released her team from the order but kept Koray where he lay, whimpering in frustration. She considered for a moment before turning her attention back to Norwood.

"Have Turner removed to one of your vehicles. Read him his rights again." Better to be safe than sorry. "And hold position until I give the order to move out."

Norwood nodded and motioned to Warren. Without a word, Private Warren pulled Turner to his feet. As he did, the towel began to slip from Turner's waist. Mac frowned and told Turner to get him into some pants before taking him outside. Then she turned her attention back to the second suspect. He was the one she wanted to have a talk with.

"In case you haven't figured out who I am, my name's Mackenzie Santos Caine." She reached over and grabbed him by the collar and hauled him back to his knees. "Colonel Mackenzie Santos with the Dallas Police Department as well as with the Marines and attached to Homeland Security. But, more importantly, at least where you're concerned, Mackenzie Santos, a member of the Tribunal and its appointed Enforcer."

Koray's anger gave way to fear. She bared her teeth, her eyes going a deeper green as he did. She let him see her disdain. She wanted him to know she wouldn't hesitate to carry out the Tribunal's orders.

"Where is your companion?" she asked.

He struggled against Norwood's grip on his shoulders and snarled. When he looked back at Mac, his eyes burned with hatred. His wolf rippled across his features, trapped and unable to escape. Realizing it, he threw his head back and howled in protest. Mac waited, cat to his mouse.

"The inhibitor will prevent you from shifting for the next twenty-four hours. We will dose you again if necessary. You have two choices. Cooperate and tell us what we want to know or don't. If you do, I will inform the authorities, including the Tribunal, that you cooperated. It might save you from a death sentence. Refuse and I will have you transported to a secure facility where you will be held until time to appear before the Tribunal."

"Go to hell." He spat in her direction.

"Perhaps I'll meet you there." She gave a jerk of her head and Norwood hauled him to his feet. "Gag him, hood him and transport him. He can cool his heels while I arrange transport to the Tribunal."

"Wait!" He struggled against Norwood's grip. "You haven't asked me anything yet."

Mac grinned and leaned against the wall near the door, arms crossed, head slightly tilted to the side. Could it really be this easy?

"Where's your friend?"

"What friend? You've already arrested him."

She smelled the lie.

"Wrong answer. That's strike one." She straightened. "Care to try for strike two?"

He growled deep in his throat and once again tried to pull away from Norwood. Not that it would do him any good with his ankles still bound by the flex-cuffs.

"What the hell do you want to know?"

"The name and location of the other lycans you've been with since coming to Dallas."

Now he smiled almost confidently. Even as her stomach did a slow roll, Mac knew she wasn't going to get anything out of him. Not without rolling him.

Or without finding something to use as a lever.

Hopefully, she'd have that by the time they had him transported.

"Move him out. I'll meet you there." She turned to Murray as Norwood easily lifted the lycan over one shoulder and carried him outside. "Make sure this room is thoroughly searched. Check with the office and find out if anyone he's been seen with is on the books here. If so, let me know. I'll get warrants for those rooms as well. When you're done here, maintain surveillance in case anyone returns."

"And you?"

"I'm heading back to Central."

Murray stopped and cocked her head to one side. Sighing, Mac waited. It didn't take a mind reader to know the detective's next question.

"You aren't trying to ditch me, are you?"

Since that's exactly what she planned, Mac shrugged, a slight smile on her lips.

"That's not going to happen, ma'am." The look in Murray's eyes warned her not to argue. "We've enough people here to get the search done."

"I need a cop supervising."

Murray nodded. "Which is why I'll make sure Parnell shifts and stays here. She might be currently assigned to Robbery, but you know she's good."

"All right. You have five minutes. If you're not in the SUV by then, I'm leaving."

With that, Mac turned on her heel and left. She had too much to do to waste time here. But Murray's point was valid. Under her own orders, as a member of the Tribunal, she was supposed to have a personal guard. Obviously, since Jael couldn't be there, she'd tapped Murray to take her place.

And that was something they'd be discussing as soon as they closed this case down.

Four minutes later, Murray slid into the passenger side of the SUV. As she buckled in, she glanced at Mac, as if judging her mood. Realizing she let her frustration show, Mac sighed softly and smiled.

"Sorry. I'm having a hard time balancing all the different ways this case is tugging at me."

"I don't blame you, Mac." Murray paused long enough to radio Dispatch and report they were leaving the scene. "I'd probably have run to the hills screaming—or more likely cursing—long before now."

Mac chuckled, picturing the scene. Then she realized how much she wanted to do just that. "How about we do it together?" Devilment danced in her eyes.

"Sounds good."

Mac pulled out of the parking lot. "So, what did Jael tell you?"

"Make sure the old lady doesn't do anything foolish." Murray's imitation of the woman had Mac laughing in appreciation. "Mac, she knows the cop in you will follow the books. She has no doubt the

Marine in you will march into Hell before you break regs. But she also knows that as the Tribunal's enforcer, you may find yourself in a position where you have to toss the rest to the side. She also knows what that will cost you."

Mac nodded, her expression grim. Jael knew her too well. Thankfully.

"She's right. Just as I'm sure she told you I will do whatever's necessary to enforce our laws—shifter and normal."

"She did, not that she needed to." Murray paused, her expression betraying her thoughts. "Mac, we all know that. It's what makes you a commanding officer, whether cop or Marine, we'll follow into Hell. We also know you do everything you can to protect each of us, often to your own possible detriment. It's Jael's duty—and mine—to make sure you don't do so."

Instead of getting angry, Mac grinned. While she had to worry about the paras in town as well as her duties as a cop, Jael had to worry about keeping one of the local alphas as well as a member of the Tribunal safe. Obviously, she'd tapped Murray as backup when she couldn't be with Mac. All things considered, Mac liked her job better.

"No worries. I'll be good."

Murray made no attempt to hide her amusement. "For now."

Mac lifted her right shoulder in a half-shrug. "Contact Halstead. Tell her I want the suspects' electronics checked as soon as the evidence from the motel is transported to Central. I want to know every call and text they made. If she can use the GPS in the phones to track their movements, do it. Not only for while they've been in town but before. I want as complete a picture of those two as possible before their interrogations begin."

Murray relayed her orders. As she did, Mac forced herself to simply focus on traffic. She could do nothing more at the moment. She trusted her people, cops and military alike, to tie up all the loose ends at the motel. For now, she'd enjoy the lull in her day. Once she reached Central, she needed to update the powers-that-be in all aspects of her life.

18

Mac paused in the doorway and looked around. Most of those assigned to the investigation crowded into the much too small conference room. She tried not to sigh, but it was difficult. After the facilities at headquarters, this felt like a comedown for all of them. But at least they had somewhere to work. More importantly, none of her people had been killed in the blast. Those who had been injured, including Pat and Marie, would recover. The buildings would be repaired or rebuilt. Until then, they'd make do.

They had to. Not that she like it one little bit.

Nor, to judge from the grumblings of her team, did they.

At the far end of the room, Murray, Tanaka and Officer Holzer added information to a smart board, a white board and an old-fashioned chalk board. Nguyen and Halstead had their heads together in front of what looked like three laptops and several tablets. Detectives talked with forensic techs and representatives from the DA's Office moved between the small groups.

Taking advantage of the moment before someone realized she was there, she gauged the mood of the room. Anger still, as expected, but determination and a hint of satisfaction mixed with it. Good. That meant they were making progress. She only hoped it was enough.

She took a bracing breath and stepped inside. The moment she did, a uniformed officer she didn't recognize called the room to attention. Chairs scraped against the yellowing linoleum and feet shuffled. Normally, she'd tell them to continue what they were doing. But not now. Not when she needed to impress upon them all just how serious the situation was.

"Eyes front," she ordered as she strode across the room in the direction of the smart board. "As you know, we've brought in five suspects. As much as it pains me to say it, two of them are fellow police officers. Preliminary interviews have been conducted with only one of those arrested. The others have either just finished being processed into the system or have invoked their right to an attorney. Each will have one chance to revoke and give a statement. If they do not, they will be turned over to the Tribunal and held until a joint trial on charges of violating Tribunal, federal and state law can be held."

She turned to the smart board and studied the images currently displayed. When she turned back, she looked around the room, making eye contact with everyone present.

"I know this isn't what you want to hear, especially with regard to the officers—and I use that term loosely—involved. However, it is necessary. One of the latest arrests made is a lycan. You are each familiar with the rules concerning incarceration of their kind. They can't be housed long-term with human prisoners, not without risking them turning the humans they're housed with. That is why Black Crow Prison was established."

She motioned for them to find seats.

"Captain Lindsay, did Heritage have anything to say?"

Jael stood and moved to the front of the room. As she did, she glanced at her notes, as if refreshing her memory. Not that it fooled Mac. She knew the woman well enough to know Jael used the motion to give herself a moment to gather her thoughts.

"Heritage is a lot of things, but mainly stupid." Disgust roughened her voice. "It didn't take long to get it out of him. He and Lagina went to high school together. Got into a couple of scrapes then and during college that someone—and I plan to find out who—

managed to keep out of their official records, both criminal and school. Things that would have prevented them from becoming cops. They went their separate ways their second year in college but hooked up again in the Academy. Lagina was a year ahead of Heritage."

"What did he have to say about letting Lagina through without checking him?"

"This is why I say he's mainly stupid. Says Lagina told him he'd *accidentally* made off with something that should have been booked into evidence. Lagina had a change of heart and wanted to get it logged in before someone realized it wasn't there. So he didn't want a record of it coming through one of the security points."

"What was he supposedly slipping into Evidence?" Tanaka sounded as disgusted as Mac felt.

"Heritage swears he doesn't know. Not that I believe him." Jael thumbed through her notes before looking up again. "The man's stupid. I want to take a close look at his Academy record. He might have managed to actually fool his instructors, but something's off there and I want to find out what." She made a throwaway motion with her left hand. "I recommend he be turned over to IAB after Lagina is dealt with. My gut tells me he didn't have anything to do with what happened except for making it easier for Lagina to get the bomb inside. But he's going to clam up the moment he thinks he won't be charged with the bombing. Right now, the threat of sending him to prison is making him talk."

"Get with me after Colonel Santos finishes her briefing and we'll get the ball rolling," Zee Logan, the DA's representative on the task force, said.

"Thanks, Zee." Mac nodded once. "Tanaka, what about Lagina?"

"He shut me down pretty quickly. Lawyered up."

"Has he seen his lawyer yet?"

Tanaka shook her head.

"All right. Pull together everything you have on him and get it to me. If his attorney shows up, delay them. I want ten minutes with him first."

And if she couldn't get him to revoke in less than that, she didn't deserve her bars.

"Check your inbox, ma'am."

"Thanks." Another glance around the room followed by a nod. "The rest of you, be prepared to update your reports in half an hour."

With that, Mac started out of the room. She stopped long enough to instruct Murray to brief the others about what they found at the hotel. By the time Mac reached the door, Jael joined her. Together they walked down the corridor before taking the stairs down a level to the interrogation rooms.

A uniformed officer stood outside the center room. "Colonel."

"Officer Holmes, call down to holding and have Koray brought up."

"Yes, ma'am. Any special orders?"

She considered for a moment. Her smile was more her jaguar than human. "You're what? Six-four, two-ten?"

His brows knit even as he nodded once. "Yes, ma'am."

"Excellent." Another smile, one that sent shivers down his spine. "Grab another uniform, one at least as big and muscular as you are. Bring Koray down here, but without normal lycan precautions." She waved aside his questions before he opened his mouth. "The inhibitor's been applied and is active. I want him brought down like a normal perp with one difference. Take him into Interrogation and then leave him. Don't cuff him to the table."

"Colonel?"

"Don't worry. I'll make sure I document my order. There's a method to my madness, Holmes."

"Yes, ma'am." He didn't look convinced, but he nodded.

"Go on." Jael jerked her head in the direction of the elevator.

Holmes didn't waste any time arguing. He gave a half-salute and hurried off.

"Care to tell me what you have in mind, Mac?" Jael's expression left no doubt she didn't approve.

"You'll see." She gave another cat-and-mouse smile before opening the door to the interrogation room where Lagina waited for his attorney.

"What the hell do you want?" His eyes flashed as he tugged at the cuff securing his wrists to the table in front of him. "Lawyer."

"That's fine. I'm not here to ask you any questions."

Mac settled in the chair on the opposite side of the table. She sat back, crossing her legs at the ankles, and looked at him. She didn't say anything. Instead, she waited, aware of each of breath he took, every beat of his heart. When a single bead of sweat ran down the side of his face, she glanced at her watch and grinned. Ninety seconds. Not as long as she expected. Now to see if he was ready to talk.

"As I said, I'm not going to ask you anything, Lagina. I will, however, tell you exactly what you're looking at. That way, you'll be able to tell your attorney when he gets here." She reached for her tablet where it rested on the tablet top and slid her finger across the screen. "There is sufficient evidence to charge you with illegal possession of an explosive device, multiple counts of attempted capital murder, three counts of capital murder, terroristic threat, felony criminal mischief and more. The feds have given notice they will be charging your with making a terroristic threat, use of a weapon of mass destruction, conspiracy to use a weapon of mass destruction as well as other charges."

The single bead of sweat turned into several and his Adam's apple bobbed nervously as he swallowed.

"Then there are the charges the Tribunal of Paranormals will be filing against you, charges recognized under US and state law."

His nostrils flared as he inhaled sharply.

"You have been identified as having cooperated with known lycans in an attack against other paranormals and humans. You failed to notify local, state and federal authorities, including but not limited to Chief Culver and Alpha Jackson Caine, of the presence and identity of said lycans, not to mention their location. Your cooperation with these same lycans led to the deaths of three humans, a capital offense under Tribunal law."

She closed the cover on her tablet and looked at him, her expression betraying nothing. His, on the other hand, spoke volumes as did the strong scent of fear coming off him.

"If that isn't enough, Chief Culver has informed IAB about your actions and requested they take immediate action. Captain Owen Carlisle from IAB has asked that I relieve you of your badge, ID and service weapon. Since they are already in evidence, I will take possession of them long enough to transfer them to the captain's possession. As of this moment, per Chief Culver's agreement with IAB's recommendation, you are no longer a member of the Dallas Police Department."

She pushed back her chair and climbed to her feet.

"By the way, since you're no longer a member of DPD, you'll be placed in a regular holding cell until your attorney gets here." Her expression turned hard, leaving no doubt what she thought of dirty cops.

"You can't!"

His chair skittered across the tile as he quickly stood. The short chain connecting his cuffs to the table rattled as he tugged against it. Mac's jaguar stirred at the scent of blood as he rubbed his wrists raw. She pushed it down. If she let Cait out now, she might ruin everything she worked for—at least where Lagina was concerned.

"I don't have any choice. There are other suspects in this case I need to interview. You've asked for your attorney and I am honoring that request." She took a step toward the door and then stopped, looking over her shoulder. "Unless you want to talk to me now." It wasn't a question.

He didn't say anything. Not at first. Mac shrugged and once again reached for the door. As she did, Lagina dropped heavily onto his chair.

"All right."

Mac turned, her head cocked to one side. "All right what?"

"I'll talk."

She nodded to Jael and returned to the second chair. "You know the drill, Lagina. You need to waive your right to an attorney on the record."

"You're a bitch."

"I've been called worse." She leaned back. "The ball's in your court. What are you going to do?"

He closed his eyes, as if steeling himself for what came next. Then, he nodded once. Even so, his hands fisted on the table in front of him. Mac scented the anger and fear coming off him. This was that moment when he'd either agree to cooperate or clam up for good. She waited, patient, alert.

"I waive my right to counsel. I revoke my earlier demand to speak to my lawyer." He all but spat out the words. "Satisfied?"

"Almost." She gave a little smile. Then she opened the file she brought with her and tossed a photo onto the table, watching as it slid across the top before stopping just within his reach. "Tell me something, Lagina. Why in the world did you agree to work with lycans when it's obvious you hate paras?"

He sucked in a breath as his eyes went wide. Then they narrowed and he looked at her in suspicion. Interesting.

She leaned back and laughed, shaking her head. "You didn't know."

"You're lying." The words hissed out.

"Not at all. We've already arrested two linked to the blast besides yourself. One of them is most definitely a lycan. The other was working with him. So what is it, Lagina? Do you hate all paras or just me?"

"I'd never work with your kind."

She tsked him. "Trust me, lycans are most definitely *not* my kind."

He didn't say anything but she knew she'd shaken him. Good. Time to move in for the figurative kill.

"Tell me about that."

'That' was a split-screen picture of him going into the bathroom with the backpack and then coming out without it.

"What about it? I forgot my backpack." He tried to shrug but failed.

"I really thought you'd be smarter than this." Mac looked disappointed as she climbed to her feet. "You can't say I didn't try. Captain Lindsay will return you to Holding. We'll let you know when your attorney gets here."

"Wait!"

Mac arched one brow in question.

"All right. Tell me what you want to know."

Mac nodded and glanced at her watch. Nine minutes thirty-one seconds. Not bad. Not bad at all.

19

"You haven't lost your touch, kid." Jael leaned against the wall outside the interrogation room and grinned proudly.

"I learned from the best."

Mac lifted her arms over her head and stretched. As she did, she allowed herself a moment of satisfaction. Lagina presented no challenge. Not that she'd expected him to. After all, he knew the system and knew what happened to cops put into a prison's general population. More importantly, he knew her reputation. She played it straight and she didn't have any use for dirty cops. The best thing he could do was answer her questions and pray someone in the DA's Office or on his jury when the case went to trial believed as he did. Not that it would help him in the long run.

Idiot.

"Have they brought up Koray?"

"Two rooms down." Now Jael frowned. "Care to tell me what you have in mind?"

"It's simple, really. You saw part of it in the last interview."

Jael said nothing, simply waited for her to continue.

"I knew going in the best way to deal with Lagina was to play to his fear. The last thing he wants is to be dropped into gen pop somewhere."

Jael nodded.

"I plan to do the same thing with Koray. Except this time I'm going to play to his ego and hatred of the Pures."

Jael's eyes narrowed. "If you're planning what I think, you need to know I think you're playing a very dangerous game."

Mac nodded once, her expression serious.

"And I will pull you out and put that bastard down if he so much as looks at you wrong."

Now she shook her head. "Jael, you'll let it play out." She held up a hand before her friend could interrupt. "The inhibitor is working. He'd have shifted long before now otherwise. There is nothing he can do I'm not prepared for."

"So you think." Jael ground her teeth together and stalked down the corridor. Mac waited, giving her time to consider the various options and their possible consequences.

"Jael, you know more about what the lycans are capable of than almost everyone on the force. Koray may have received the inhibitor but that doesn't mean he's still human. His wolf will become more and more frantic as it tries for release. That means it will take over the longer he goes without being able to shift. He is losing his humanity even as we speak." Not that is going to be controlling him. That makes him much more dangerous."

"Which is my point." Now it was her turn to lift a hand, stopping Mac from interrupting. "You may think you're prepared, but he's going to react like a cornered animal. He'll be unpredictable and he knows he's got nothing to lose. Short of shifting, you are putting yourself in unnecessary danger."

"All of which makes him much more susceptible to what I have in mind."

Jael opened her mouth to say something and then snapped it shut. Speculation lit her blue eyes. Then she nodded. It might have been reluctant, but Mac would take it.

"All right. But fair warning. I'm not going to let him get close enough to lay a hand on you."

"He won't have the chance."

With that, Mac moved to the interrogation room where Victor Koray waited. She paused outside the door. Inhaling, she closed her eyes and reached for Cait. The jaguar padded to the front of her brain. Her senses expanded as the jungle cat pushed for release. She knew what waited beyond the door and looked forward to the encounter.

Mac wished she felt the same way.

Play with prey now?

Yes, but not the way you want.

Not the way Mac wanted either. She'd much prefer simply turning the lycan over to the Tribunal to deal with. But she needed information from him. Information that might prevent others from being hurt or killed—or worse.

But we are going to show him who the apex predator is.

With that, she reached down and opened the door. As the door closed, she checked it, making sure it locked behind her. Then she turned. Her smile, as she looked Victor Koray up and then down, was all predator. Her features blurred momentarily, revealing just how close to the surface her jaguar happened to be.

"You."

The lycan's voice as he recognized Mac dropped in pitch from what she remembered, raspy, almost gravelly. His eyes glowed as his wolf fought for release. His fists opened and closed, the muscles of his forearms tensing with each movement. When she didn't respond, he bared his teeth and growled. His head twisted on his neck, tilting this way and then that, as if by doing so he could shed the last shreds of his humanity so his wolf could come out.

Then, as if realizing they were alone in the room, a bitter smile twisted his lips. He took a step forward. Then another. As he took a third step, one corner of Mac's mouth lifted in a smile and he faltered. It wasn't supposed to go like this.

"Sit." Mac pointed to the chair near the far wall, the only furniture in the room.

"No."

He took another step and then and planted his feet. Posturing, striving for intimidation and failing. Not that he knew—yet.

"I said sit." Mac waited, watching. When he didn't comply, she inclined her head, her smile widening. "Very well. My orders from the Tribunal are clear. Your failure to cooperate leaves me with no choice. When I leave this room, I'll arrange for your immediate transport to a secure location of the Tribunal's choosing. You will be held there until you appear before them to answer for your crimes. I really hope you have your affairs in order because you've seen your last day of freedom and, unless I miss my guess, one of your last alive."

With that, she turned and reached for the door. It was a calculated risk. Turning her back on a lycan was the ultimate insult. It showed a lack of respect and, more importantly, a lack of fear. His wolf would demand he respond, no matter how foolish such action might be.

Which was exactly what she wanted him to do.

She began a mental count as her fingers closed around the doorknob. At one, the sound of Koray's rubber shower shoes scraping against the discolored tile floor as he took a step blended with the sounds of the cotton of the legs of his orange jumpsuit rubbing together.

Come on, little wolf.

At two, he stepped out of the shower shoes. The soles of his feet stuck briefly to the tile, sweat forming a bond with the floor she doubted he recognized. Just as she doubted he knew how much his scent gave away.

That's it, little wolf. You think you're the alpha but you're about to learn the ways of the world.

At three, she turned. As she bared her teeth, he stopped and paled. Her low growl sounded unnaturally loud in the small room. Hearing it, he swallowed hard and backed up a step, recognizing the true apex predator in the room.

Then his features blurred. He threw his head back and howled. Outraged, angry, needing release, his wolf fought for control. Muscles tensed and trembled. His breathing turned ragged. Mac waited, her gaze never leaving him.

"What did you do to me?" If possible, his voice was deeper, raspier than it had been earlier, a sure indication his wolf was close to the surface.

Without warning, he leapt. Cait chuffed in Mac's mind. Then Mac simply slid one foot to the side and sidestepped. Koray moved past her, unable to stop his forward momentum. Chuckling softly, she stuck out her leg. He tripped and hit the floor with a thud. He lay there for a moment before he shook his head and leapt to his feet. More slowly this time, he moved in Mac's direction.

"I'd think twice about it before you do."

His lips pulled back and he rushed toward her, arms outstretched.

"Down!"

He slid to a halt. Eyes wide, shook his head, as if denying what just happened. His muscles gathered. His right foot flexed, as if in preparation of taking a step. But nothing else happened. Hissing, fought to do something, anything.

"I said down." Mac's voice brooked no disobedience.

The lycan's fear filled the air. As it did, he slowly dropped to his knees. Mac waited, watching as his body tried to fight her command. Foolish. Such a foolish wolf to think he could best her. She was an alpha. She was a member of the Tribunal. She was so much more.

"Victor Koray, formerly of the Northern Alpine pack, you were kicked out by your pack leader for refusing to agree to the rule of the Tribunal. Other packs have refused to allow you to join them because of that refusal. Each of them have made sure to document not only their interactions with you but also how they have done everything possible to insure you know the rules pertaining to your kind.

"You are illegally within the boundaries of the Dallas pride. You are in violation of the Tribunal's laws about notifying it as well as the local pride or pard alpha of your presence. You are suspected of being a willing participant in the bombing at Dallas Police Headquarters, of killing three humans and injuring a number of others, not to mention the paras you injured as well. These are just the beginning of the charges against you. What say you in your defense?"

"Go to hell."

She tsk-tsked and shook her head.

"Very well." She smiled as she moved to stand in front of him. To add insult to injury, she reached out and lightly patted his bent head, much like an adult patting the head of a recalcitrant child. "Of course, the Tribunal may tell me to go ahead and carry out the order of execution they issued. That would make life much easier for all of us." She stepped back, waiting for his response.

"W-who are you?" He tried looking up from where he stared at the floor but failed. "I thought you were a cop."

One corner of her mouth quirked up. With thumb and forefinger, she lifted his chin. She wanted him to see her, to recognize the predator in her for this next part.

"I am Mackenzie Santos Caine, daughter of Elizabeth Santos and granddaughter of Elena Alexandra Ramirez–Saenz Graham Santos, direct descendant of Arturo Ramirez and Anna Saenz. I am also the granddaughter of Robert Alejandro Mackenzie Santos, direct descendant of Seamus Mackenzie. I hold a seat on the Tribunal and am its duly appointed enforcer."

He whimpered, fear licking at his expression. If not still held under the control of her order, he would have jerked his chin from her grip. Instead, he looked at her, sweat beading at his temples and rolling down his spine. Her nose twitched slightly as the smell of urine filled the room.

"You will answer my questions completely and honestly. Failure to do so will result in your immediate death as authorized by the Tribunal. Do you understand?"

"Y-yes."

"Good." Now she smiled and ran an almost gentle hand down his cheek. "Go sit in that chair and stay there until I tell you to move."

She stepped back as he crawled on hands and knees to the chair. Watching as he pulled himself up and sat, she shook her head. She knew before the interview he was no alpha. What she hadn't suspected was how far down the proverbial chain he'd be in a normal pack. Why would anyone use someone like him in something like the bombing?

Unless they wanted him caught or, more likely, killed in the explosions. Now that she thought about it, he made an excellent scapegoat.

And somehow she needed to find out who was behind what happened and what their ultimate plan might be.

Hopefully, Koray had some answers for her.

"Please." He all but whined the word. "Tell me what you want from me?"

She leaned against the wall and looked at him, studying him like she might some insignificant bug.

"It is quite simple." And yet so much hung on his answers, more than he would ever know. "You are going to tell me why you came to Dallas and who came with you. You'll tell me how long you've been here and who has helped you since your arrival. Then you're going to tell me exactly what your part in the bombing of police headquarters was and what you planned to do when you and your friend neared my family's SUV after the blast."

There were other questions, but she'd get to them in good time.

"We'll start with the easiest questions first. When did you first get to town?"

"Last month."

"When?" she pressed.

He pressed his lips together, fighting the need to respond. Finally, he blew out a breath and answered. "The fourth."

"See, that wasn't so hard, was it?"

He growled but, other than that, made no attempt to respond.

"What did you do upon your arrival?"

"We followed instructions and checked into the motel. Then we made contact with that bastard Phelan and his bitch Oakley."

One piece of the puzzle confirmed. "I take it then they were expecting you."

"Not us but someone."

"You're doing very well, Victor. I suggest you continue doing so."

He gulped and nodded.

"When you contacted them, what happened?"

"We were told to wait at the motel. We weren't to leave. One of them would come to us."

"Tell me."

It didn't take long for him to set the stage for her. He and his companions checked into the motel and waited. Except when the others sent him out for food and beer, they didn't leave their room. Three days passed before Oakley showed up. In the intervening time, all they did was watch TV, keep track of the news and weather and wait. It was boring but he knew better than to complain. This was his chance to prove himself and finally have a new pack to join.

"All very interesting, but it doesn't tell me what I need to know." Mac sounded almost bored. "What are your companions' names?"

He shut his mouth, struggling against the need to answer. Mac waited. She didn't want to completely roll him. Too many questions would be asked by those watching, those who didn't know the full extent of an alpha's powers, especially not an alpha from the older bloodlines. The last thing she wanted was for them start looking at her earlier investigations and the confessions she'd gotten out of suspects and wondering if she'd used her gifts as an alpha to force a suspect to confess.

More than that, she didn't want them fearing her because of what she could do.

"You've been doing so well, Koray. Don't stop now." She pushed away from the wall she'd been leaning against and took one step in his direction. "Tell me what I want to know and I will let the Tribunal know you cooperated."

At least to a certain extent.

He shook his head, his lips so firmly clamped together it reminded her of Xander when she wanted him to eat something he didn't like. Unfortunately for Koray, her little boy had more sense than he did.

"All right. Let's try this another way. You came into town with two other men. I don't need your confirmation to know one was lycan and one was human. The human, Dominic Turner, was arrested at the same time we took you into custody. Tell me the name of the lycan or I'll leave and go talk to Turner. I have no doubts he'll gladly answer my questions. Who knows, he might even say everything that happened—including the bombing—was your idea."

Koray's eyes widened. When they did, Mac fought the urge to smile. That one reaction told her something she hadn't known before. Something she wouldn't have believed possible. Koray was not only a beta but was so far down the chain even some of the pack's humans outranked him.

So why include him in this?

Whatever "this" might be.

Without warning, Koray blew a breath out through his nose and dipped his chin in resignation. "Kellan Lam."

"See, that wasn't too difficult, was it?"

He groaned and didn't lift his head to meet her eyes.

"Now tell me about Lam. Start with where he's from and how you met him."

This time it took longer to get the information she wanted. Koray gave it to her in bits and pieces. After leaving the Northern Alpine pack, Koray wandered for a couple of years. Finally, he found a pack he felt comfortable with, one that didn't bow down to the Tribunal. At least not according to him. That's where he met Lam. The man had been with the pack several years by then and took Koray under his wing, teaching him the ways of his new pack and his place in it.

Mac's stomach turned as she listened to Koray. Lycans truly were animals. No, they were worse than animals. Those not strong enough to defeat the pack alpha or become one of his inner circle became victims. They served at the alpha's whim—or the whim of whoever "took them under their wing". Koray, like others, was a victim.

But that didn't make him less culpable or less responsible for what happened. He could have gone to the local pride or pard—not to mention the Tribunal—at any time. He chose not to. Because of that, he would pay a high price, quite possibly his life, for violating Tribunal law.

"Where is Lam now?"

"Who knows?" Now the lycan looked at her, something close to satisfaction or possibly anticipation reflected in his eyes. "Your people blew it by moving in when they did. You missed him and now he can finish what we started."

"Which is?"

"Figure it out for yourself, bitch."

Remembering where she was, Mac fought the urge to roll him. Instead, she crossed to where he sat. He watched her near, his eyes growing wider the closer she came. She didn't stop until she stood behind him. When she rested her hands on his shoulders, he flinched. Then he sat still, except for the trembling of his muscles under her hands. Looking much like the mouse knowing the cat's about to pounce, he began hyperventilating as she bent and whispered in his ear.

"I'm offering you a chance to live." Not much of one, but the Tribunal could always take pity on him. Not that she expected it to. "Or I can carry out their warrant and execute you now. The choice is yours."

She patted his shoulder. To anyone watching the video feed, she'd simply been reassuring him about something. Even if they enhanced the audio enough to hear what she said, she crossed no lines. She did have an order for his execution from the Tribunal. His refusal to accept the Tribunal's power over him violated the various treaties it had with the United States. His failure to let Jackson—not to mention the Tribunal—know he was in town carried an immediate prison sentence absent mitigating circumstances. His part in the bombing carried an immediate death sentence because of the loss of human lives.

"Let's see if I can make this a little easier for you, Koray. We've got video of the van that carried the explosives used in the bombing of the police garage. That video shows you behind the wheel. Additional video follows the van—and you—to the floor where you parked the van and left it. Then we have video of a Prius leaving the garage a few minutes later. You are in the passenger seat. That Prius is the same one we found at your motel. My guess is the driver seen on the video was Kellan Lam."

She ticked each point off on a finger as she spoke.

"So let me lay it all out so you understand." Voice hard, expression cold, the Tribunal's enforcer now stood before him. "You will finish answering my questions. If you don't, I'll report to the various agencies and governing bodies wanting a piece of you that you are no longer cooperating." Now she smiled without humor. "Perhaps the Tribunal will decide to let the local authorities deal with you first. I know they've been wondering what the long-term effects of the use of the inhibitor will have on someone like you. There's speculation it will not only prevent you from shifting but kill your wolf if you take it long enough. Others speculate the wolf will take over but, being unable to shift, it will result in your going mad. There are others yet who think it might lead to your death because your body will begin working against itself as your wolf aspect fights the human aspect."

He threw his head back and howled. Gone was the anger from before. Fear filled his voice. His eyes all but whirled with it. The stink of it rose from him as sweat covered his face and stained his shirt. Not that she blamed him. The thought of never being able to shift again, never being able to talk with Cait, terrified her.

"I don't know where he is." Koray almost sobbed as he spoke. "B-but I know where he's going to be."

"Tell me."

"He and the others are going to finish what we started."

Fear grabbed at Mac and she forced it down.

"What do you mean?"

Koray looked up at her. His expression sent a chill down her spine. Not because he presented any danger but because he knew something she didn't, something important.

Something he didn't want to tell her.

"Mac, ask him who the others are." Jael's voice came over her earbud and Mac reached up, removing it and dropping it into her pocket.

For a moment, she considered what she should do. If she followed her gut, she'd violate the line in the sand she drew when she first started shifting. The line that prevented her from using her gifts as an alpha in a state criminal case. But this was more than that, so much more. If revealing this part of her abilities as an alpha saved lives, it was worth any price she had to pay.

Or so she told herself.

"Koray, I'm going to ask you just one more time. Tell me what you know about Lam's plans, where he might be and who the third lycan was that came to town with you or face Tribunal justice."

She shrugged out of her jacket, tossing it into the corner of the room. Without looking away from him, she unbuttoned her cuffs and rolled them above her elbows. It was a stalling tactic, something to give her time to decide her next move. But, judging from the way he watched her, from the way his tongue moistened his lips and how he swallowed almost convulsively, she made her point.

"I can't. He'll kill me."

"Who?"

She doubted he meant Lam.

"Who?" she repeated, easing her control on her jaguar and putting a hint of power in that one word.

He shook his head.

"Answer me!"

"D-derek R-reed."

Mac hissed in a breath. As she did, Cait pushed against her control. This was what she and the other members of the Tribunal had worried about for years. Reed somehow managed to avoid capture since they disbanded the Conclave and dealt with Cassandra and Alexander Wilkinson. Her grandmother and several others on the Tribunal warned he presented more of a danger than either of the Wilkinsons had.

She shoved her hands inside her pants pockets, fighting the urge to grab Koray by the throat and squeeze until he either answered her questions or didn't breathe again.

"Where's Reed?"

"Gone. Left the day of the bombing, before it happened."

"Where did he go?"

"I don't know."

"Tell me!"

Her power, no longer held back, rolled over him. He whimpered and fell to his hands and knees. He crouched like the dog he was. She knew his wolf crouched in his mind, ears flat, eyes darting as it looked for an escape. But there was no escape. Not now and not at any time in this bastard's future.

"I said tell me."

Her power lashed at him and he dropped to his belly. "I don't know. He told Lam he'd be in contact. Then he left."

"And Lam?" She cursed when he didn't answer right away. "Look at me, wolf." She waited until he tilted his head so he looked up at her. "Tell me where Lam is and who is with him. Now."

She didn't raise her voice. She didn't need to when the room all but vibrated with her power as an alpha.

Five minutes later, she left the room. Every instinct screamed for her to run, but she forced herself to walk. Before the door closed behind her, she reached for her phone. At the same time, she ordered the uniformed officer stationed outside the door to remain on post. The suspect wasn't going anywhere. Get him a clean jumpsuit and then hold for further orders. She didn't wait for the young man to respond. With her phone to her ear, she walked purposefully down the corridor toward the stairs.

"Mac, what the hell is going on?" Jael grabbed her arm as the stairwell door slammed shut behind them.

"Contact Mateo. Tell him to activate all units under his command. Reed is making his move. I'll explain in the car. Then contact our team. They are to converge on the hospital immediately. Secure the floor where our people are. Guards, armed and armored, on all entrances. They are cleared to use all means necessary to protect not only our people but everyone there. And get guards on Flynn as well as Culver. They may be targets."

With that, she raced down the stairs, taking them two and three at a time. As she did, she prayed they weren't already too late.

20

"What the hell is going on?" Jael reached for the grab bar as the SUV screamed out of the parking lot.

Mac hit the sirens and sped down the street. Her hands gripped the steering wheel so tightly her knuckles turned white. The string of curses she'd uttered since entering the vehicle became more inventive with each passing moment.

"Mac, you're scaring me. Tell me what's going on."

The younger woman drew a deep breath and held it for a long moment before exhaling. She took another corner, slowing enough to keep the SUV from tipping over before accelerating again. Then she reached up and tapped her earbud, using voice commands to call her husband.

"Mac, what's going on?" Worry thickened Jackson's voice and she put the call on speaker.

"Jack, I don't have time to go into detail. We fucked up. All of us. Reed's behind what's happened and he's not done. There's a group of lycans heading for the hospital. I've got reinforcements heading in but you need to take precautions until they get there."

God, her babies were at the hospital.

She forced down her fear and focused on the task at hand which, at the moment, was not killing herself and Jael.

"How many?"

Thank God, Jackson didn't demand an explanation. He knew her well enough to trust her.

"Don't know." And that scared the shit out of her. "Contact the pride. Call in the twins as well as Evan and Frankie. And let both Moira and Adrienne know. They may be targets as well."

"Where are you?"

"On my way." She braked and then jerked the wheel to the side, cursing as a driver refused to yield to her. "Be careful and make sure those bastards don't get to our people."

She ended the call and shot across two lanes of traffic to make her next turn.

"Koray not only named but ID'd Reed as the third lycan. According to him, Reed's gone. He doesn't know where. Not sure I believe him. But it's what he said about the other lycan, Lam, that matters. He's supposed to 'finish' the job."

"Mac, you've got to tell me more than that," Jael said.

"The bombing was meant to start a war between paras and normals. It is the first of a coordinated series of attacks, all being carried out by Reed's followers. Koray thinks Lam's next target is the hospital, knowing the Tribunal won't sit back if my grandmother and the others are killed."

"The other targets?"

"Didn't know. He overheard enough between Lam and Reed to know they had a bigger plan in play."

Neither said anything for a moment.

"Koray was their patsy." Jael spoke softly, not that it hid her anger. "As was Lagina."

"That's my guess."

And it made sense. A weak lycan who would carry out orders without question and a cop with an agenda. It was a ready-made distraction from the real culprit, one that would keep them chasing down leads that took them further and further away from the real person responsible for what happened—Derek Reed.

Mac turned her attention to traffic as they neared the hospital. Her head pounded. Cait pressed against her control, wanting to go faster. Her stomach churned. Why hadn't she insisted their people be moved sooner? Too many innocents, human and para alike, could get caught in the crossfire at the hospital.

She silenced the siren but kept the lights flashing as she pulled onto Junius Street. People ran out of her way, a few stopping to curse her. There'd be at least one complaint filed because of how she drove but she didn't care. The Malinowski Building, the tallest of the buildings comprising Henderson Medical Center, rose ahead of them.

Mac slammed on the brakes and bailed out of the SUV the moment it came to a full stop. Hospital security met her as she ran inside. With hands on their guns, they tensed until she shoved her badge in their faces.

"Secure all exits. Close down the security floor," she ordered as she moved toward the elevator banks. "Police and military reinforcements will be arriving shortly. No one in or out until they arrive." She jabbed at the button, cursing when the doors didn't immediately open. "Jael, brief them."

She looked around, trying to remember where the stairs were.

"Ma'am," one of the guards began, "we can't do that."

She closed her eyes and counted to two. She didn't have time to count to ten.

"Listen very carefully." She dropped her voice, not wanting to panic anyone who might overhead. "I'm not only DPD but I'm fucking USMC on assignment with Homeland Security. I have reason to believe one or more person or persons are heading here with the intent of killing the patients on the security floor. Unless you want to explain to hospital administration and then the DPD and the DA's Office why you not only failed to take reasonable steps to protect your patients and staff but allowed them to be killed, you will do as I say. Close the ER and shut down the elevators. Now where the hell are the damned stairs?"

Leaving Jael to deal with hospital security, Mac started off, finally having spotted a sign indicating the stairwell. As she pushed through the door, she pulled out her phone. A moment later, she waited for Murray to answer.

"I'm heading to HMC now," the younger woman said without preamble.

"Have Culver contact them. They need to close ER and reroute incoming patients." Her boots pounded against the steps as she raced upward. "Touch base with Lee and brief him. When you get here, full gear, Lolo. No exceptions. We're dealing with lycans."

"On it."

Mac shoved her phone into her pocket and slowed. Outside the door leading to the fifteenth floor, she paused and caught her breath. As she did, she considered the security strengths and weaknesses of the floor. Several years ago, after a very generous donation from the Tribunal through one of its corporate holdings, the medical center agreed to transform the floor into a secure floor. Normally, it was used for paras coming to the hospital for treatment. But, as in cases like this, when a para or first responder needed to be kept safely away from the public or the media, this floor was used.

Unfortunately, too many people knew about it. The fact it was the next to the top floor meant it was more easily defendable than if it were lower. However, someone could still get to it by going to the top floor and then coming down or simply coming up from the lobby. Six public elevators, two for patient and equipment transfer, four stairwells. Too many possible entrances.

"Damn it, Mac, wait!" Jael hissed from a flight below. "I'm getting too damned old to keep up with you."

Mac bit back a smile. Then she pressed an ear to the door. What she wouldn't give to have eyes on the floor. She needed to know if everyone was safe.

You have eyes, Mackenzie. Mate is there, Cait reminded her.

She pulled her phone and slid a finger across the screen to unlock it. Thumbs poised to begin typing, she paused. Something wasn't right. What?

She held her left hand up, signaling Jael to stop. Then she reached for the door. The bar gave way under her touch. The *snick* as the lock disengaged sounded unnaturally loud in the silence of the stairwell. Slowly, oh so slowly, she pushed the heavy door open. At first, just enough to peek through. Seeing nothing out of the unusual, she glanced over her shoulder, signaling Jael to stand ready.

Steadying her nerves, Mac once again lifted her left fist. Without saying a word, she looked at Jael and nodded once. Then she turned her attention back to the door. Slowly, listening for anything to warn of danger, she lifted one finger.

Then a second.

Before she lifted her third finger, a scream ripped through the air, challenging, angry. A second one followed. Mac's hand tightened around the silver door lever as she fought the urge to shift. No human screamed like that.

"Go!"

Jael put action to her order and elbowed past Mac, shoving the door open. That broke through Mac's paralysis. She burst into the outer corridor, her gun somehow finding its way into her hand. Cait tried taking over, only to be pushed back. Not that it prevented the jaguar from giving Mac an additional burst of speed.

A nurse appeared and Mac grabber her arm, hauling her into the nearest room. For a moment, she looked around, realizing they were in an office of some sort. Then, with Jael guarding the door, she lifted a finger to her lips. With her other hand, Mac tapped the badge at her belt. The nurse, eyes wide, nodded once.

"You need to get out of here."

The blonde shook her head. "I'm not leaving my patients."

Mac understood. She didn't like it, but she understood. "How many employees are on the floor?"

For a moment, the nurse didn't respond. Judging from her expression, she was taking a mental count. "A dozen, maybe fifteen."

Too many to get out without questions being raised. Besides, there was no way they could move the injured out.

Mac stiffened as a jaguar cried out, challenging someone or something. She was running out of time.

"Stay here. I've got help coming."

"Our patients--"

"We're going to do everything we can to protect them," Jael said, motioning for Mac to go ahead. "The best thing you can do right now is stay out here."

Mac left them, barely listening as Jael told the woman to lock herself in the office and wait until the police arrived. As she neared the double doors leading to the patient rooms, Mac stopped. She quickly slid out of her jacket, dropping it to the floor. Jael joined her as she pulled her spare clips from her shoulder holster and slid them into her hip pocket. Then she dropped her shoulder holster to the floor next to her jacket. Cait told her to strip and shift but she couldn't. Not yet. Not here, no matter how tempting it might be.

"Stay behind me."

Mac spoke softly as she used the key card the hospital gave her when her mother and grandmother were moved there. The lock snicked softly as she reached out and opened the door a crack. As she looked down the corridor, she cursed silently. Then she eased the door closed and stepped back, motioning Jael to come with her.

"At least one inside. He's at the nursing station. It looks like he's trying to get line of sight for a shot."

"How do you want to play it?"

Mac chuckled humorlessly. "Other than shifting and killing the bastard?"

Jael nodded.

"The only way we can. Try to make entry without him realizing it and maneuver behind him. If we can, we take him alive. But protecting the civilians is more important." She tried telling herself it didn't matter those civilians were family and friends, but she knew better.

"Let me take point."

Mac shook her head. As she did, she toed off her boots. She could move almost silently without them and that might be the difference between capturing the suspect or burying one or more of her family.

"Stay behind me."

She returned to the double doors and slowly, carefully pushed one side open. She slipped inside, gun held at the ready. She glanced around, taking in the scene before her. The corridor was empty, most of the doors on either side closed. The man knelt, his back to her, his gun aimed in the direction of one of the few open doors.

Mac's nostrils flared as she took a step forward. The moment she did, the man's head swung in her direction. The hand holding his gun followed, leveling it at her chest.

"Down!" Mac yelled, shoving Jael to the side.

Everything happened fast, fast, fast. Cait screamed a challenge in her head, one she echoed. The man threw his head back and howled. Then his eyes locked with hers. Eyes that glowed yellow, much as she'd seen other lycans' glow before they shifted. But how? She should have scented him before now.

Damn it!

"Drop the gun!" she ordered, running in his direction.

A roar from down the corridor startled her. She stumbled before quickly righting herself. Fortunately, the roar surprised the gunman as much as it had her. His curse was lost in the sound of a second roar, this one higher pitched. Desperately, Mac searched for the source, sliding to a halt and plastering herself in the all too small cover offered by one of the closed doors.

A jaguar stood in the doorway to the suite where her mother and grandmother lay. It stepped into the corridor, snarling, eyes blazing. Teeth bared, its head swung in Mac's direction. She didn't need to shift to know Jackson wanted her to leave.

Her breath caught as a young panther stepped to the jaguar's side. Jackson swung his head in the panther's direction and snarled. The message was clear. He wanted their daughter to get her shifted ass back inside the safety of the suite. Not that Cam obeyed. She snarled back at him and padded forward. As she watched her husband's shifted form grab their daughter by the scruff of her neck and force her back, Mac knew she'd find it funny in a decade or two. But, for now, both of them were a distraction she didn't need.

She couldn't stay where she was. When the man turned back to her, she'd be a sitting target. She needed to make her move while he was still distracted.

Cait, we can't shift but I need everything you can give me.

We protect mate and kit?

And mother and elder.

Mac glanced around quickly, locating Jael. She nodded once and then left the doorway. Her bare feet slapped against the tile as she raced at the gunman. He spun in her direction. His lips peeled back and his features blurred. Cursing, she leapt, her gun forgotten. She needed to stop him before he shifted.

Her shoulder struck the man in the midsection. His breath exploded as they went down in a tangle of arms and legs. Mac grunted, stars dancing in front of her eyes, when her head slammed against the corner of the nursing station desk. She struggled to hands and knees, shaking her head to clear away the cobwebs.

Jackson's roar echoed off the walls.

"No!" she shouted, climbing to her feet. "Protect the others."

Seeing the lycan tearing at his clothes, Mac cursed again. Then the corridor suddenly seemed to fill with people from both of the entrances. Cop and Marines—human, shifter and witch—raced forward. Several of them had already found their animal forms.

"Protect the others!" she ordered.

She didn't wait to see if they obeyed. She didn't have time to. The change was already on the lycan. It wouldn't be long before he completed his shift.

Buttons flew as she ripped open her shirt. She unbuttoned and then unzipped her pants. Then she released her hold on Cait, telling the jaguar they needed to shift *now!* This needed to be their fasted shift ever. They couldn't risk being caught by the lycan mid-shift.

Pain ripped through her and she did her best not to fight it. Bones broke and reformed. Muscles twisted and knotted. Fire washed over her as her pelt burst from her pores. Cait lifted her head and roared, challenging the lycan, keeping it focused on her rather than on the others.

"Mac, down!"

A shot drowned out Jael's shout. Pain lanced down the jaguar's side. Mac/Cait roared in pain, too far into their shift to do anything else. She smelled blood and felt it running down her side. Mac whimpered once before Cait took over and shoved down the pain.

Lycan will die!

No! Mac panted in the back of the jaguar's mind. *We need him alive. We need to know what he can tell us.*

Cait snarled, part disagreement and part frustration as she shook free of Mac's clothes. Finally, standing in front of the lycan, she bared her teeth, snarling. Looking out through Cait's eyes, Mac willed Jackson and Cami to stay back. She needed to know they were safe, that they would protect their family. This was her fight, and she would teach the lycan the foolishness of trying to hurt those she loved.

Cait screamed a challenge as the lycan finished his shift. His howl sounded hollow compared to the anger and determination in hers. She would not let him near the others. He would not hurt the children or any of the others they loved.

"Nate, Lolo, go!" Jael ordered as the jaguar slowly circled the lycan. "There are others in the hospital. Security is trying to contain them, but they need help."

Cait roared as Mac cursed.

"Do whatever it takes to protect the humans. Shift, magic, I don't care. Lethal force has been authorized." As Jael spoke, she slapped cuffs on the man who shot Mac and then tased him, muttering that she'd deal with him later.

Cait roared again, approving. This was an attack that went against not only human law but also Tribunal law. It bought an immediate death sentence to any para involved in the attack. Jael dealt with the human. Now she would deal with the lycan.

Jackson roared as they ran from the area, going to assist the others. Before Cait/Mac could react, an Irish wolfhound raced after them.

Moira. John followed her, a gun in each hand. Good. They had backup. Now to deal with this wolf.

Cait raced forward. One paw slashed out, claws extended. The wolf yelped as blood and fur flew into the air. Growling, it danced back, favoring its left flank. Cait watched, looking for an opening. Wounded, the wolf was more dangerous than ever.

Want to kill wolf.

We can't. We need him to find the one who ordered the bombing that hurt the others, Mac said.

Crouching, Cait let the wolf creep forward. Suddenly, she leapt. She landed on the wolf's back. Her claws raked down his spine and sides. Her mouth closed around the back of his neck and she bit down. Blood flooded into her mouth, warm and reminding the jaguar it had been too long since they'd hunted.

No, Cait! Let him go! Mac ordered.

Cait gave the lycan a brutal shake and flung him away. Whining, the wolf struggled to his feet. Cait growled in warning as the lycan took a step in her direction. Then the wolf yipped in surprise. A moment later, it collapsed where it stood.

Sides heaving as she gasped for breath, Cait backed away. She eyed the fallen lycan suspiciously, waiting for him to try to take her by surprise. Then Tanaka stepped forward, an odd-looking gun in hand.

"If one of you would shift back and talk to me, I'd appreciate it," she said as she toed the lycan. It didn't respond. "Jael, I assume your Marines have something we can use to secure him until he regains consciousness and shifts back."

Cait limped forward, whimpering softly in pain. She stopped at Tanaka's side and head butted her. When she did it again, Tanaka looked down. The jaguar nodded, a very human nod. Tanaka dipped her chin and briefly rested a hand on the jungle cat's head. Then she watched as Jael ordered two of the Marines to bring a cage.

"Mac." Tanaka knelt in front of Cait, looking her in her eyes.

Cait bared her teeth, reminding her Mac was not in charge just then.

"I have reports of his kind on premises." She nodded at the unconscious lycan. "Two additional floors confirmed. Ground and second."

Mac cursed inventively, unable to issue orders in her shifted form. Then, seeing Jackson and Cami moving toward them, she growled and hurried to intercept them. Hurt or not, she would not let them, and certainly not her daughter, put themselves in danger. Once next to her daughter, she repeated what Jackson's jaguar did earlier. She grabbed the panther by the scruff of her neck and did the animal version of marching her back to the suite. She released the panther and then batted her back in the room when Cam tried to move past her. The message was clear. The girl, whether human or panther, was to stay there.

Cait/Mac rubbed her head against Jackson's and started down the corridor. As she neared the double doors, she turned, her message clear. She couldn't open the doors with paws. She needed someone to do it for her.

"I'll stay with her," Jael told Jackson. "Shelly, we need additional security up here until they can be relieved."

"Unser, Rodriguez, stay here," Tanaka ordered two uniforms as they appeared through the double doors at the end of the corridor.

"Lieutenant," Unser began.

"Officer Unser, I believe my orders were clear. You and your partner will stay here. You will protect Colonel Santos' family, not to mention Captain King and her son and the others on this floor. Is that clear enough for you?" Tanaka pinned the officer with a look that had him withering before he nodded. "Good. Hold your post until you are relieved."

With that, she jogged down the corridor after Jael and Cait. The moment Jael opened the double doors, the jaguar took off at a limping run, the two women hurrying after her.

21

"Where the hell is she?"

Jackson pulled on his jeans and reached for his shirt. As he did, he growled, frustrated because no one answered him. Then he heard Abby at the door, talking to someone. Even though she they spoke softly, Jackson recognized the newcomer's voice. John O'Hara. The only question was if his appearance meant everything was all right or if things had truly gone to Hell in a handbasket.

The last time Jackson saw the man, he'd been racing out of the unit, a gun in hand. Ahead of him, his wife's shifted form, an Irish wolfhound, bounded down the corridor. She barked once at the doors before John opened them. A moment later the doors closed. That had been before Mac and the others arrived.

Carrying his shirt in one hand, Jackson stepped out of the small bathroom. As he did, he automatically checked his wife's mother and grandmother. Elizabeth sat up in bed, Xander nestled against her. Eyes dark with concern, she looked from her son-in-law to her youngest daughter. As she did, Jackson frowned, knowing he couldn't leave without at least trying to reassure her. Otherwise, she might try something foolish like getting out of bed to find answers for herself.

But of more concern was seeing Ellen still unconscious. A battle had raged just outside the room and it hadn't disturbed her. He wanted to believe it was because of the drugs the doctors gave her. He needed to believe it right now. The last thing any of them needed was for her to succumb to her injuries.

A furry head nudged his hand and he looked down. Cami, still in her panther form, stood next to him. He smiled and scratched between her ears. Equal parts pride and fear had gripped him when she appeared by his side just moments after he shifted and moved to the doorway to protect their kinswomen and little Xander.

And that was something they needed to have a serious discussion about later. She was too young and most definitely too new to her abilities as a shapeshifter to put herself in danger like she had. But she was her mother's daughter and it's exactly what Mac would have done.

He dropped to one knee and gently turned the panther's head until they looked eye to eye.

"Cami, I want you to stay here." He shook his head when she bared her teeth. It was as close as she could get to disagreeing with him. "I know you want to go find your mother. So do I. But I need to know your brother and the others are safe. I'm trusting you to protect them. Can you do that for me? For your mother?"

The panther dipped its head.

"Good girl." He gave the dark fur a rub and stood. "Abby, where's your brother?"

"He just texted. He was in the cafeteria when the hospital went into lockdown. He's on his way back here now."

Jackson nodded. A moment later, he moved to stand next to his mother-in-law's bed. His hand was gentle as he cupped Elizabeth's cheek. Then he bent and placed a kiss on Xander's head.

"I've got to make sure things are under control, Liz. You're safe here. Mac's people are guarding the corridor and Cami's going to stay with you." As he spoke, the panther very carefully climbed onto Ellen's bed and stretched out next to her. "Abby will let me know if you need me."

"What's going on?" She reached for his hand, her grip still weak but her eyes ablaze with worry.

"I don't know everything yet." And, by God, someone had better fill him in soon or there would be hell to pay. "But several lycans and humans tried to get in here. Cami and I kept them out until Mac and her people arrived. I need to go now to see that the lycans are dealt with. The cops can deal with the humans."

"Mac?" Fear roughened her voice.

"She went after the others once the ones up here were subdued." He couldn't tell her the rest. Not yet. "I promise to be back as soon as I can." He gave her hand a reassuring squeeze and looked at Cami. "Keep them safe. When I get back, we'll talk about everything that's happened."

With that, he crossed the room to where John O'Hara stood by the door. John arched one brow and glanced down at Jackson's feet. Frowning, Jackson followed his gaze. Then he blew out a breath and returned to the bathroom and his discarded running shoes. Less than a minute later, he was back at the door.

"Let's go."

In the corridor, John moved to Jackson's side. Without a word, John handed him a gun. Jackson nodded, his expression grim. Then he checked the .45, making sure a round was in the chamber. One of the first lessons Mac taught him a lifetime ago was to always have a round in the chamber if he thought danger was near.

"What's the situation?" he asked as they jogged down the corridor toward the double doors.

Before John could answer, the doors opened. Jackson stopped, the gun in his hand rising into the ready position. In his head, his jaguar screamed a challenge. They would kill anyone trying to get past them. Usually, Jackson would tell the jungle cat to wait. After all, they weren't as bloodthirsty as his wife and mate. But not today. Not after seeing the lycans and others trying to get to his family and loved ones and not after seeing one of them shoot at Mac.

He blew out a relieved breath as Murray stepped inside. The witch quickly sized up the situation and kept her hands visible. She waited until both Jackson and John relaxed and lowered their weapons. Then she hurried toward them even as they moved in her direction.

"What's going on?" Jackson tried not to show how worried he was as they left the unit and hurried down the corridor toward the elevators.

"The situation is in hand now. At least I think it is. Tanaka and Jael have teams continuing to search the hospital. But we have prisoners secured downstairs, waiting for transport."

"And Mac?"

"She's down there with them."

Something about Murray's response worried him. As he jabbed the down button with one finger, he made a decision. "John, would you go back to the unit and keep an eye on my family? At least until I can send someone from the pride up to relieve you?"

The man didn't hesitate. He nodded once. Then he reached out and rested a reassuring hand on Jackson's arm. They stood that way for a moment before John turned back to the secured area. As he did, the elevator *dinged* and the doors slid open.

"Lolo, what aren't you telling me?" he asked as the doors closed behind them.

"Best if you see for yourself, Alpha."

The fact she addressed him by a title worried him. Instead of asking all the questions that raced through his mind, he nodded once. As he did, she programmed the car for the ground floor.

The moment the elevator doors opened, sights, sounds and smells assailed them.

The lobby to the right of the elevators was filled with people. Some stood, weapons at hand, guarding the area. A number of people, some human and others shifted, sat or lay on the floor. Painfilled moans came from some of them. The scents of blood, sweat and over-powering fear and anger filled the air.

"Alpha." Jael moved in his direction. Her expression grim, anger burning in her eyes, she escorted him to the near side of the lobby. "So far, we have more than a dozen lycans and humans in custody." She nodded to the center of the lobby.

Jackson's lips peeled back and his jaguar once again demanded release. The need to avenge their people, to punish those who tried to hurt even more, ran through him. He shoved it back. Worry for his wife and the others overrode it. He was the alpha. This was his territory, and he would see the Tribunal's laws enforced.

Almost two dozen Pures, witches and humans circled fallen or captured lycans and humans. Several shifted lycans lay there, bleeding out, too badly injured to shift back and heal. Others were secured, inhibitors already applied. The humans, those not being treated for injuries, were cuffed, much like their lycan counterparts.

Jackson looked around, worried because he didn't see Mac. Then he saw his wife's jaguar form standing over a wounded Pure. The jaguar dipped her head and gently nosed the Irish setter. Her tongue flicked out, lathing a deep laceration on her flank. Annie O'Hara knelt next to her mother's shifted form, telling her it was going to hurt. Then she began treating Moira's injuries.

Jackson closed his eyes and fought for calm. A moment later, he glanced around the lobby once again. It looked like a war zone. Which, if he was honest, it had been. Pushing the thought aside, he reached for his phone. Much as he hated doing it, he sent word to John that he needed to get to the lobby. He'd wait to tell him about Moira until he could do so in person.

"Captain Lindsey." He stepped further into the lobby, his face a mask hiding his emotions. "Are these all the intruders?"

"No, sir." She didn't make any attempt to hide her anger or her disgust. "Two others, both human, are dead. Their bodies were left in situ until we receive further orders. I have teams guarding those scenes. Lt. Tanaka and I have additional teams, a mix of para and human, searching the hospital and its grounds to make sure none of the suspects slipped away in the confusion."

He nodded. Then he turned his attention to the prisoners, at least those conscious.

"I am Jackson Caine, alpha of the Dallas pride. You are trespassing in my territory. You have violated Tribunal laws not only by trespassing in my territory but by attacking this hospital. You have put humans and paras alike in danger. You face prison on the state charges I am sure will be filed against you. I will be bringing charges against you to the Tribunal where you will face death."

His voice, cold and hard, had more than one of the prisoners whimpering in fear.

"The lycans have been administered the inhibitor, Alpha," Jael said.

He nodded once. Then he looked down, smiling in relief to see his wife's jaguar-self leaning against his leg. Forgetting the others for a moment, he knelt and ran a hand down the jaguar's flank, frowning at her whimper of pain.

"You need to shift back now, Mac," he said softly. "You need to take command of the situation."

He looked up at Jael who seemed to understand what he wanted. She reached down and lightly rested a hand on the jaguar's ears. Then she told the jungle cat to come with her. As they walked off, the jaguar definitely favoring her right side, Jackson once more stood.

"Until they get back, keep doing what you've been doing, lieutenant. And make sure your people know how important it is that we make sure no lycan escapes."

"Consider it done, Alpha."

22

Mac lay on the bathroom floor, panting in pain. She couldn't remember the last time shifting back to human hurt so badly. All she wanted to do was lay there and whimper. But cold from the tile seeped into her bones and blood pooled beneath her. gritting her teeth, she opened her eyes and looked around, praying someone had something to help stop the pain.

"Easy, kid." Jael knelt next to her and lightly rested a hand on her upper arm. "Can you sit up?"

"Maybe," she rasped.

Jael gently slid an arm under her and helped. Teeth chattering, Mac leaned against the wall. She watched as Jael pulled a backpack close and rummaged inside. A moment later, the woman produced a medical kit. Instead of protesting as she normally would, Mac tilted her head back against the tiles and closed her eyes. She'd seen enough to know she needed the help. Her injuries might not be serious, but they were painful.

And she'd been shot again, damn it!

Silently, Jael worked. She cleaned and bandaged what she could. Mac hissed out a breath as her mentor worked on the wound along her side. Then, as the topical anesthetic started working, she sighed in relief.

"Clothes?" The word came out in a croak.

Jael pressed a bottle of water into her hand and watched as Mac twisted off the top and downed most of the bottle before setting it asked. Then she reached for the second backpack.

"Murray grabbed your go-bag when she was upstairs." She pulled out underwear, a pair of black cargo pants and a DPD tee shirt. "Let me help you."

Mac shook her head. Then she reconsidered and held out a hand to her friend, letting Jael pull her to her feet.

"Thanks." She padded across the tile to study her reflection in the mirror. "Status?" She dressed as quickly as she could, grimacing as pain grabbed at her when she moved wrong.

"Still clearing the hospital and grounds. Prisoners contained in the lobby. That includes the bastard who shot you." Jael paused and listened to something coming in over her earbud. "And hospital administration is hyperventilating about what happened and how the public will view it."

Mac closed her eyes and sighed heavily. "All right. Let's go see if we can unruffle some feathers." She looked around for shoes and frowned.

"Flops will have to do until we find both shoes, kid. You kicked them off before shifting and one got lost in the fray." Jael fought her smile and failed.

Mac rolled her eyes and accepted the flops the woman handed her. Not exactly the most professional or the best if she needed to move fast, but they'd do for the moment.

"Injuries?" She accepted her phone and earbud from Jael. After sliding the phone into her pocket, she slid the earbud into place in her left ear.

"A few on our side, including Moira. But the docs say everyone will be all right."

"But?" She knew that look on Jael's face and it didn't bode well.

"Three hospital employees were attacked by the lycans before we could get to them. Their injuries have been treated and they're being transported to a safehouse as we speak. A medical team is already waiting for them. That's something else hospital administration is having a fit about."

"Let's go deal with this then." She started out of the bathroom and then stopped. She considered their options for a moment. "Jael, report what's happened to Flynn. Tell him I'll be in touch as soon as I have things under control here. Same with my cousin. Request additional support here until we know exactly what we're facing."

"Done and done."

Mac smiled. Of course, Jael had already done so. That's part of what made them a good team. They knew how the other thought, as Jael's anticipation of her orders proved.

Ignoring her pain and the exhaustion dragging at every muscle, Mac slowly made her way out of the bathroom. Jael took up a position behind and slightly to her right. To anyone looking at them, Jael merely deferred to a senior officer. But Mac knew better. Her friend was there to help her if she needed it.

"Are you all right?" Jackson asked softly as he moved to her side.

She nodded. Much as she wanted to lean against him, let him give her the support she knew he wanted to, she couldn't. Not until this mess was handled.

"Lt. Tanaka, have the humans been evaluated and treated for their injuries?" she asked, ignoring the prisoners for the moment.

"They have, ma'am."

"Detective Murray, have the paras in the group been checked and, where applicable, given the inhibitor?"

"Yes, ma'am."

Mac nodded. She knew the answers already but, seeing the very nervous hospital administrators and members of hospital security, she wanted them to hear not only that but what came next.

She stepped forward, her gaze sweeping the prisoners, her expression leaving no doubt what she thought about them.

"My name is Mackenzie Santos Caine, daughter of Elizabeth Santos and granddaughter of Elena Alexandra Ramirez–Saenz

Graham Santos, direct descendant of Arturo Ramirez and Anna Saenz. I am also the granddaughter of Robert Alejandro Mackenzie Santos, direct descendant of Seamus Mackenzie. I am one of two alphas for the Dallas pride and a member of the Tribunal."

Someone gasped. Mac guessed it was one of the lycans. The litany of names and titles would mean little to a normal. But to a para, it meant she had the authority to call for their immediate execution without worry of repercussions.

"Those of you who are human will be transported to jail where you will be given the chance to speak with an attorney if you so choose. You will be held there as charges are drawn up against you by the District Attorney's Office. If, during our investigation, it is found you are a para and have not revealed it to us, you will be immediately transferred to Tribunal custody and all charges against you will be heard by the Tribunal and all punishment meted out by that august body."

She nodded to Tanaka who, in turn, motioned for uniformed officers and detectives to take the humans into custody and transport them.

"Put them into individual interrogation rooms. Make sure they can't talk with one another on the way over. Go ahead and start the interrogations once they've been read their rights. I'll be along shortly."

"Understood, Colonel." Tanaka briefly braced to attention before turning to supervise the transport of her prisoners.

"As for the rest of you, you'll be transported to a secure facility where you will be held until arrangements are made to transfer you to Tribunal custody." She paused, making sure each of them got a good look at her and knew she wasn't kidding. "Try to escape and you will be put down. This is by order of the Tribunal. You have violated multiple laws for our kind and you knew the penalty before doing so. As the Tribunal's appointed enforcer, I have the right—no, the duty—to carry out your executions if you fail to comply with their orders."

She looked around until she spotted Lee and Norwood. "Get them out of here. Medical teams will be standing by to treat the wounded as needed."

Lee motioned for the Marines to get the lycans out of there. Mac watched as they were marched outside and loaded into waiting vans. Then, as they drove off, she inhaled deeply before turning to face the hospital administrators.

"Dr. Brown, Ms. Collier, I want to thank you for you assistance and for that of hospital security. I assure you the search continues to make sure no other lycans or their accomplices remain on hospital property. Detective Murray is running point on that and will keep you apprised of the progress of the search."

Murray stepped forward and nodded.

"I also want to assure you that the Tribunal, as well as DPD and the Dallas pride, will help pay for any damages caused this day. Henderson Medical Center has been a good friend to all of us. You haven't differentiated between human and para. Because of that, you and yours came under attack today. We will help make everything right."

"Thank you, Colonel Santos," Dr. Paul Brown, medical chief of staff, said. "Several of our people were injured by the lycans. What about them?"

Mac nodded, her expression softening. She understood his worry.

"We'll take very good care of them over the course of the next few weeks. Even though the danger of them turning is very slim given the lack of seriousness of their wounds, we don't want to run the risk. I'm sure you understand."

Both Brown and Collier nodded.

"The safe house where they'll be staying is very comfortable. They will be able to contact their families and, according to what their doctors say, perhaps even visit with them in person. You or your representatives will be able to see them as well. This is merely a precaution for their safety as well as yours."

"And if they do become infected?" Lisa Collier, chief executive officer for the medical center, asked.

"As I said, the chances of that happening are very slim considering their injuries." Mac simply arched one brow when Collier opened her mouth to say something. The slightly overweight brunette closed her mouth and waited for Mac to continue. "If, however, one of them does turn, they will be informed of the laws pertaining to paras and to lycans in particular. Laws passed not only by the Tribunal but by Congress as well. If they agree to follow those laws, they will be registered with the Tribunal and with the governments."

And that was something Mac still had a personal problem with. She understood the necessity on the public safety level, but it still smacked of the government keeping track of "undesirables" and history had a long list of such efforts, none of them good. At least not in the long run.

"If, however, they refuse to follow the rules, there are steps the government will take. These steps will include making sure they are not allowed to return to their work here." Several heads bobbed up and down and Mac nodded grimly. Even so, she knew she needed to speak with the other members of the Tribunal about it. The actions this day would negatively impact all of them, at least in the short term.

"With your permission, I'll arrange for several of the cleaning crews the Tribunal uses to come in and deal with the areas we know the lycans accessed."

Both Brown and Collier seemed to almost wilt in relief.

Leaving Jackson and the others to finish soothing their ruffled feathers, Mac made her way across the lobby. As she dropped to her knees next to the wounded Irish setter, she looked at Annie O'Hara in question. The young woman smiled and that was enough to reassure her.

At least a little.

"Moira." Her voice broke as her hand gently stroked the "dog's" neck. "You and I are going to have a serious discussion when you're better."

The shifter whimpered softly and then moved her head enough to let her lick Mac's hand.

"Do you know what happened, Mac?" Annie asked softly.

Mac nodded, guilt filling her. "She tried taking on a normal who slipped in behind me while I was dealing with a couple of his lycan friends."

Annie soothed her mother and then smiled at Mac, understanding reflected in her eyes. "That's part of her duty to the pride and the Tribunal, Mac. You need to remember that."

Mac shook her head. She was supposed to be the protector, not the one needing protection.

"Let's get a gurney for her. Take her upstairs to the security wing. Then she can shift and her injuries can be treated." Mac looked around. Seeing a uniformed officer nearby, she signaled him, telling him to find a gurney. "No arguments from you either." She affectionately ran a hand over the setter's head. "I'll be up to check you just as soon as I can."

"I'll take her up," Jackson said softly as he joined them. "You need to have another word with them." He jerked his head in the direction of Brown and Collier.

"About?"

"About letting the injured return to work if they haven't been turned."

Mac considered hitting her head against the tile floor and decided against it. She already had a headache and didn't want to add to it.

"All right." She climbed to her feet, groaning as she did.

"I'm sorry, I'm not sure what to call you right now," Ms. Collier said as Mac joined them.

Mac chuckled, hoping this helped diffuse the situation. "I know. It gets confusing even for me, especially when more than one of the hats I wear are in play at the same time. How about calling me by my rank?"

"That works." Collier smiled a little uneasily. "We're already getting concerned calls from donors and employees about what happened."

Here they go. Before long, they'd be talking optics and donations and the sort of political games Mac detested.

"I understand. This could have been a disaster. But it wasn't, thanks to the quick action of your own security team as well as members of both the DPD and the Marines." Mac smiled even as she signaled she wasn't through. "You might point out to those who are concerned about what happened that HMC wasn't the only institution attacked today."

She'd been listening to various reports coming in over her earbud from her tech specialists. At least three more facilities, two police stations and one school, had been attacked. Fortunately, those attacks met with as little success as had this one.

"The government and the Tribunal know who is behind the attacks and are making every effort to locate and apprehend him and any other followers he might have."

"So it wasn't just here?"

"No, Dr. Brown, it wasn't. In fact, I feel certain the evidence will prove the same paras and their associates who attacked here were behind the bombing of police headquarters."

Both administrators sucked in a breath. Mac nodded again.

"As for your employees the lycans attacked, I know I don't have to remind you of the law. If they have not been turned by the attack, their jobs will be waiting for them once their injuries have healed. They won't face any punishment or retribution for what happened or for the time off they had to take." Now she pinned each of them with a look that spoke volumes. She planned on making it her business to insure no one was further injured out of fear of what might happen.

"Of course, Colonel."

Collier's strained smile confirmed Mac's suspicions. She didn't want the injured to return to work. Well, too fucking bad.

"Good, because I'd hate for it to get out that HMC showed prejudice against innocents in this situation."

Collier opened her mouth only to snap it closed when Brown lightly touched her arm. Instead of saying whatever she wanted, the woman dipped her chin once in curt agreement.

"Good." She smiled and motioned for Murray to join them. "Detective Murray is one of DPD's best. She's handling part of the investigation into the bombing and is lead investigator on today's events. She's going to stay here and keep you up-to-date on the status of the search of the buildings and grounds. Detective, report to me when you've finished."

Leaving them in Murray's capable hands, Mac looked around and spotted not only Jael but Jackson as well. Her brow knitted in concern as she slowly crossed the lobby to join them. She reached out and gently touched her husband's hand. Then she continued in the direction of the elevators. If she could just make it inside one of the cars, she'd be fine. She'd be away from prying eyes and could give in to the pain and exhaustion, at least for a few moments.

"Jack?"

She didn't say anything else as they joined her. She didn't need to. At least she hoped not.

"John was in the elevator when we were ready to take Moira up. Since he was with them, I stayed here."

She nodded and almost sobbed in relief as the elevator dinged and the doors slid open.

Mac stepped inside, Jackson and Jael on her heels. The moment the doors slid shut, Mac leaned against Jackson. She welcomed the supporting arm he slid around her waist. With a sigh, she closed her eyes and rested her head against his shoulder. She needed to find her shoes and head out. But to where? The jail to interview the humans taken into custody or the warehouse where the lycans were being held until they could be transferred to the Black Crow site?

God, what she wouldn't give to get some food and rest.

At least the media hadn't been around for what happened.

Unfortunately, social media was a very different matter.

"Shit!" She straightened and then gasped in pain.

"Mac?" Jackson looked down at her in concern.

"Cameras," she hissed, sounding very much like a pissed off cat.

"What cameras?" Jael asked.

"Security cameras. Cell phones." She beat a fist against her forehead, trying to clear away the cobwebs. "They'll have caught everything."

Including her shift and possibly Jackson's and Cam's as well. Then there were the encounters with the lycans. It wouldn't take long before someone leaked the security footage or sold cellphone video taken during the fight.

Damn it! This was going to be a PR nightmare.

"We'll deal with it later," Jackson told her. "We've dealt with worse before and you know it."

He was right. Not that it made this any easier. Still, maybe she could say it was all above her pay grade and let Culver and Flynn deal with any fallout that might happen. It sounded like a good plan. Now to figure out a way to make it work.

For now, she would happily let it be someone else's headache. She wanted—no, she needed—to see for herself that her family was all right. Then she wanted to check on the others injured in the blast. After that came the phone calls she needed to make. The Tribunal, Flynn, Mateo, and Culver, just to name a few. Maybe she could even find something to eat and grab a nap somewhere in all that.

But before any of that happened, she wanted to make sure Cami was all right. In the last couple of days, the girl had shown more bravery than many did in their entire lives.

God, let's hope she doesn't make a habit of it. At least not until she's older.

23

Half an hour later, Mac sat on the edge of the narrow bed. She gritted her teeth as Dr. Patek poked and prodded the various cuts and scrapes and worse she'd sustained over the last few days. He muttered something about "damned fools" before finally admitting Jael had done a good job cleaning the worse of Mac's injuries.

"If I didn't know you better, Mackenzie, I'd swear you did this sort of thing on purpose." He finished stitching the wound down her side and carefully situated a bandage over it.

"I promise you, Doc, I don't."

Hell, she'd be happy to never have to use his services again.

"I know, but it's hard to accept when you've been shot twice in basically one day." He stepped back and looked at her closely. "If you were a normal, you'd be in this hospital bed instead of sitting on it. One more injury and I'm going to sedate you until you're healed."

"Doc," she growled.

"I mean it, Mackenzie." Now he gave her a look so much like one of her mother's she hunched her shoulders and looked at the floor tile. Then he rested a gentle hand on her shoulder, waiting until she looked up at him. "Mac, I know you don't go out trying to get yourself hurt. But it is my job as your physician to make sure you don't cause yourself further injury because you won't take time to heal."

Much as she wanted to object, she couldn't. He was right. Not because she was one of the pride's alphas. Not because she was a cop or even because of her role in General Flynn's command. No, this was because of her place on the Tribunal. She didn't doubt for a moment the other members gave him orders to make sure he did everything possible to not only keep her alive but to insure she was in the best health possible.

Damn it. When had life gotten so complicated?

"I'll be good, Doc. Promise."

He tilted his head to one side and smiled slightly. "You'll try," he corrected.

She laughed and held her hands up in surrender. "Your point." She reached for her shirt and pulled it on, doing her best not to wince as she did. "I know you'll be giving Jackson a full report. Will you at least tell him I didn't fight you on any of this?"

Maybe that would help ease her mate's worry.

And maybe pigs could fly.

"I will." He helped her to her feet and steadied her as she stepped into her cargo pants. "You need food and rest and not necessarily in that order."

"Soon."

Hopefully, very soon. She didn't know how much longer she could go without falling flat on her face. But it had to wait at least another couple of hours. She still hadn't checked on her family and friends. Nor did she know if the final preparations had been made to move them to the safehouse. As much as hospital administration wanted them out, she wanted it more.

"I mean it, Mackenzie."

"I know, Doc, and I actually agree with you. Unfortunately, there are a few things I need to do first." She tucked in her shirt and buckled her belt. "And you can help me there. If the safehouse is ready, can the others still be moved today?"

He thought for a moment. She waited, giving him time to consider her question and how to answer.

"It will do most of them good to get out of here, especially after today," he said finally. "That's especially true where Pat and Marie are concerned. From what their nurses have said, it's been everything they can do to keep them in bed."

"Hand me my phone?"

He nodded and reached for the cellphone where it rested on the bedside table. Mac thanked him and quickly programmed in a number. As she waited for her call to be answered, she looked around for her shoes. Jackson brought them in earlier, slipping in and out of the room without a word.

"Lee, is everything set for the wounded?" she asked when he answered the call.

"Yes, ma'am. I just got word from the medics that the last equipment has been set up and tested."

She nodded to Patek. "Send vehicles to transport them along with escorts. I'll make sure the staff here has everyone ready." She paused when Patek lifted a hand to catch her attention.

"Your grandmother is going to have to be kept flat and her leg stationary," he said softly.

She nodded and relayed the information to Lee.

"Understood, Colonel. I'll make sure the transport teams know. Estimate arrival in thirty. I'll update you when they are ready to roll out."

She thanked him and ended the call.

"I'll make sure they're all prepped, Mac. I'll be riding with your grandmother."

She smiled, relieved. "Thanks, Doc."

He patted her shoulder and said he'd check in with her later. Then he left the room, closing the door behind him. As he did, she blew out a breath. It would be easier to protect the others at the safehouse. She knew that from past experience. But, more importantly, he wouldn't have agreed to move her grandmother if he believed it detrimental to

AMANDA S. GREEN

Ellen's recovery. She chose to look at it as an indication the woman was getting better. She had to look at it that way.

A soft knock sounded at the door. It opened a moment later and Jackson slipped inside. He smiled and crossed the room. When he pulled her close , she wrapped her arms around him. For a long moment, she held on, needing the love and support he offered. Then she pulled back enough to lift her head and kiss him. He framed her face with his hands and kissed her again. Then he rested his forehead against hers.

"Can you get some rest yet?"

She shook her head. "I need to report in and then I want to make sure everyone's settled at the safehouse."

"Why don't you relax while we wait for the transport teams?"

She started to refuse but something about him made her stop. "Jack, what's wrong?"

Dear God, she couldn't take much more.

"Easy, sweetheart. Nothing's wrong." He pulled her close once again. "I'm sorry. I didn't mean to worry you. It's just that your daughter is refusing to shift back."

Mac stepped back and frowned. "My daughter?"

"Most definitely your daughter. My daughter would never be so willful." His lips twitched as he tried not to smile.

"I'll remember this when your son starts shifting."

Jackson muttered something about how he wasn't ready to even think about that possibility. Then he grinned at Mac. "Seriously, she's stretched out on Ellen's bed, doing her best to ignore all of us."

"Jackson." Mac chuckled and reached for his hand. "You're her father and her alpha. You don't need me to make her shift back."

"Mac."

She couldn't believe it. He whined. He actually whined.

"Jackson." She shook her head. "Come on. I'll show you how it's done." Or not. It would serve him right if she let Cam stay shifted until they reached the safehouse.

Hand-in-hand they walked next door. As she stepped inside, Mac chuckled almost evilly. Her mother sat up in bed, carefully sipping a

262

mug of coffee. Abby stood next to her bed, checking her vitals. Danny and Xander sat across the room. Her younger brother held her son on his lap and read to him. But it was the sight of Cam, dressed in jeans and tee shirt, sitting next to her great-grandmother's bed that left Mac grinning proudly and Jackson shaking his head.

Of course, the oh-so-innocent look the girl gave them told Mac that Cam had played them both.

What in the world were they going to do when she wanted to start dating?

"Transport teams will be here shortly to take everyone to the safehouse." Mac crossed to her mother's bed and bent to gently kiss Elizabeth's cheek.

"Mom?" The woman looked at Ellen, worry writ large on her face.

"Her too." Mac gave her hand a reassuring squeeze.

"You coming with us, Mom?" Cam asked.

"I am. I want to make sure everyone gets settled all right." And she needed to figure out a way to tell her daughter to stop trying to drive Jackson crazy. "Abby, Dr. Patek is going to ride over with Gran. Will you right with Mom?"

"Of course." She cocked her head and looked closely at Mac. "You need to get some rest, big sister."

"I will soon. Promise."

"What can we do to help get them ready?" Danny stood and settled Xander on the sofa.

"Make sure your things are out of the other room and collect what you brought from home for Mom and Gran."

"We'll take care of it." Abby motioned for her twin to come with her. "You sit and rest until we have to leave."

"How about sit and make some phone calls?"

"If you have to." The look she gave her older sister warned of dire consequences if Mac did anything else. "We'll be back in a few minutes, Mom." She kissed Elizabeth's cheek and waited as Danny did the same. "We'll pack for everyone," she added before leaving the room.

"Mackenzie, are you all right?" Elizabeth gripped her hand and looked at her in concern.

"I am." Seeing her mother's disbelief, she smiled a little guiltily. "I promise. I'm going to be fine. Right now, the main thing wrong is I'm exhausted. I need to report in, check in with my people and then I'm going to fall face first into bed for a couple of hours."

"Promise me you will." Elizabeth pressed the back of Mac's hand to her lips. "Please."

Not wanting her mother to worry, Mac promised. Then she moved across the room to the sofa. She dropped onto it with a weary sigh. It was so tempting to put her feet up and lay her head down. But she couldn't, not yet.

"Cam, come here." She pulled out her phone and sent a quick text to her cousin, telling him she needed to report in. By the time she sent the text, her daughter joined her, curling up at her side. "Two things and I promise we will discuss them further. And, no, you aren't in trouble. However, when there's danger, you have to promise you will obey your father or me, whoever is there. You were very brave shifting to help Dad protect the others. But, once I got here, you became a distraction for both of us. You'll learn to recognize what he means when you're both shifted. It's something we'll both work with you on."

She nodded and promised to do as Mac said.

"One more thing. When one of us tells you to shift, it doesn't matter if it is to shift into your panther or back to human. You shift. That's especially true where your dad's concerned. He's always going to be your dad, but he is also your pride leader. You need to remember that."

"I was just kidding." Cam spoke softly, almost tearfully.

"We know that, sweetheart. And we aren't mad at you. I've been known to stay in my shifted form after your dad's told me to shift back. It's not too big of a deal when it's just family. But you can't ignore his instructions when there are others around, especially if they are members of the pride."

"Duh, Mom." She rolled her eyes and Mac chuckled before ruffling the girl's hair.

"Duh, yourself." She kissed Cam's cheek and checked her phone as it signaled an incoming text. "In this case, however, you didn't know if there might be more trouble."

Cam didn't say anything for a moment. "I think I understand." She climbed to her feet and hurried to where her father stood. She threw her arms around him, hugging him tightly. "Sorry, Dad."

"That's okay, kiddo. This is new to all of us." He slid an arm around her. "Let's let your mom make her calls."

Mac silently thanked him and read her cousin's message. As she did, she relaxed a little. Jael's report had given both him and Flynn enough information to get started on. She was to call in after the move to the safehouse. Until then, make sure things were buttoned down at the hospital and report to the Tribunal.

Hopefully, by the time she had, the transport teams would be there. She could worry about everything else after that.

24

Two hours later, Mac sat on the sofa in the "apartment" she'd be sharing with her family until it was safe for everyone to return to their homes. Leaning back, she allowed her sore, aching muscles to relax for the first time in what seemed an eternity. The peace wouldn't last, at least not for her. But she'd accept it while she could. Work would demand her presence all too soon.

In the next room, her mother and grandmother slept, their hospital beds side-by-side. Abby and Danny had the rooms next door. The safehouse, another warehouse not too far from the hospital, was crowded with the injured and their families, not to mention the medical teams and security personnel. That meant doubling up some, but no one objected. Everyone understood the danger still existed. They weren't out of the woods yet just because a few arrests had been made. They wouldn't be until Derek Reed was found and taken into custody. Until then, Mac swore to do all she could to not only keep the others safe but to uncover the full extent of Reed's plans for Dallas.

But not now. Now she needed rest and she needed this time with her family.

A smile touched her lips as her fingers combed through Cam's hair. The girl lay on the sofa, her head in Mac's lap. Jackson sat in a recliner, Xander on his lap. Danny and Abby were in the next room with Elizabeth and Ellen. Except for the injured women, it felt like a family night together.

"Annie just texted. She said her mother's demanding to go to the pub." Jackson slid his phone into his pocket. "She also said not to worry about Moira making a break for it. Her father's standing guard at the door and Declan is on his way over with dinner for everyone."

Mac's mouth watered at the thought of food. At the same time, her stomach growled. Cam giggled and then sat up. Her green eyes sparkled as she grinned at her mother.

"You need to eat, Mom."

"Gee, what makes you think that?" She threw her arm around the girl's shoulders and hugged her close. "Until Declan gets here, why don't you see if there's not some juice in the fridge. If there is, would you bring me a glass?"

"Sure, Mom." Cam climbed to her feet. "C'mon, Xander. Let's see if we can't find Mom and Dad something to drink."

Jackson watched as they ran into the small kitchenette. When he looked back at Mac, he grinned proudly. Then he moved to join her on the sofa. Once seated, he pulled her close. She relaxed against him. Resting her head on his shoulder, she closed her eyes. She was so tired. If luck was on her side, dinner would get there soon and then she could get some much needed rest.

God, she hoped so. Not that she had much choice. When she reported to Culver, his parting comment was to order her not to report for duty until morning. He didn't care if the city was being hit by meteors. She wasn't going to do anyone any good if she fell on her face in the middle of the investigation.

Nor had he been the only one. General Flynn had been even more direct. He not only told her to get some rest, but he issued orders to her command not to bother her before morning. If something came up before then, Jael was to be notified.

If that hadn't been enough, Jackson took her phone from her after she finished reporting to the Tribunal and told her she'd get it back come morning. For a moment, she considered arguing. Then she took a good look at him. He looked as tired as she felt. Strain etched lines from the bridge of his nose to the corners of his mouth. They both needed to rest and, more than that, he needed at least a few hours when he didn't have to worry about her.

Besides, her earlier prediction proved all too true. The first videos of what happened at the hospital hit the internet before the prisoners were booked into jail. By the time those wounded in the bombing were settled at the safehouse, reporters were doing everything they could to chase the story down. Not only was DPD's public information officer inundated with calls and emails asking for a statement, so was the hospital. Much to her surprise, the hospital set the record straight about what happened. They thanked the members of the DPD as well as representatives from Homeland Security for their quick action. They, along with the hospital's security force, protected patients and employees alike. Yes, lycans had been part of the group that invaded the hospital. No, they still had no explanation why but they trusted the police to keep them informed.

That's when Dr. Brown stepped up to the mic and made it very clear the only paras involved in the attack were lycans. Pures and witches, along with normals, protected the hospital and everyone inside. Their actions only confirmed what everyone already knew: paras, with the exception of the lycans, were not a danger to normal humans.

Mac hoped Brown and the other administrators maintained that attitude as the investigation moved forward.

So, for now at least, one disaster averted.

"What are you thinking about, love?" Jackson shifted slightly and pulled her onto his lap.

She snuggled up against him, smiling as she heard the kids talking in the kitchenette. "Everything that happened today and how we managed to dodge one very big bullet."

"The videos?"

She nodded.

"What did Culver tell you?"

"Not to worry about it. He asked me to write up my report and send it to him before I crashed for the night. Otherwise, I'm off duty until morning."

He seemed to relax a little and she looked up at him. Smiling gently, she cupped his cheek with one hand and brushed her lips against his.

"Jack, I'm fine. Truly. Just a little battered around the edges."

"More than a little, love." His arms tightened around her and she hissed softly as pain radiated from her injured side. "Sorry." He tried to pull away, but she held his arms around her.

"I'm fine," she repeated. "Look, I promise as soon as we've eaten and I've sent my report to Culver that I'll go to bed. I'm going to shift for a couple of hours. That will help."

With that, she slid off his lap and started toward the kitchenette to see what was keeping the kids. Halfway there, she paused. Head cocked to one side, she listened. Something, she wasn't sure what, caught her attention. There it was again. A soft moan.

Worried, she hurried toward one of the three bedrooms attached to their "suite". Slowly, carefully, she opened the door. Light from the room behind her illuminated the two beds across the room. Elizabeth slept in the first.

Praying, Mac stepped further into the room. As she did, she looked at the second bed. When she did, Ellen's head turned in her direction.

A sob that felt like it tore through her ribcage escaped Mac's lips. Without thinking, she hurried to her grandmother's bed. She lightly cupped the woman's cheek with one hand while she pressed the call button with the other. That signaled the medical team down the hall.

"Gran." Tears ran down her cheeks. "Lie still." She scrubbed the back of her hand under her nose. "You're safe."

"W-what happened?"

"Lots and I'll tell you everything after the doctor's seen you and you've gotten some more rest. I promise."

Hearing someone behind her, she waved them inside. She didn't need to turn to recognize Jackson's scent. He moved almost silently to stand behind her. He rested a hand on her shoulder and softly said he'd sent for the doctor as well as Abby and Danny. Then he slipped out again, giving her the time she so desperately needed with her grandmother.

"Mackenzie, please."

"Shh, Gran. Everything's going to be fine." She cleared her throat, swallowing against the emotion threatening to choke her. "I promise."

Seeing Ellen conscious and aware, she could finally believe it.

Ellen looked around, eyes dull with pain. Mac saw the moment her grandmother recognized what sort of room they were in.

"W-where? Not hospital."

Mac nodded. Part of her reveled in the knowledge her grandmother realized all that but another part worried about it. She didn't want to explain all that happened the last few days, not until Ellen was stronger.

"We're at a safehouse, Gran." She refused to lie. "And we are safe. I promise."

"Need to know." Ellen's grip on Mac's hand tightened. "W-what happened?"

"Gran." Mac didn't groan but it was close. "What's the last thing you remember?"

A hint of a smile touched the old woman's lips. "You looking like you were going to kill Flynn."

Mac chuckled. "Actually, I was thinking about trying to make a run for it."

Ellen's brow furrowed as she tried to remember. "Did I fall?" Her gaze traveled down the bed to her injured leg.

"No." She tried to decide how much to tell without upsetting her grandmother. "There was an accident in the parking garage and you were hurt."

Ellen inhaled deeply and moaned in pain. Then she turned her head on her pillow "Liz."

Mac instantly reached out to stop Ellen before the woman tried to

271

sit up. She recognized the tensing of muscles and the mother's need to check on her child. Cursing because none of them anticipated that particular response, Mac gently sat on the edge of the bed. With one hand, she turned Ellen's face so her grandmother looked at her and not Elizabeth.

"Mom's well on her way to recovery, Gran. I promise."

As if that was her cue, Elizabeth woke. Mac smiled, relieved, as her mother immediately looked in their direction. Seeing Mac and, more importantly, seeing Ellen awake, she fumbled for the bed controls and raised the head so she sat up. Tears sparkled in her eyes and she pressed the fingers of one hand to her lips before "throwing" her mother a kiss.

"How bad?" Ellen asked.

"Are you hurt?"

The woman shook her head. "Liz."

"I promise she's going to be just fine. You both are." She hoped.

"Mac's right, Mom." Elizabeth shifted carefully on the bed. "The doctor said I can get out of bed later today if I'm careful."

"Truth?"

"Truth. We wouldn't lie to you about this, Gran."

"What else?" Ellen's voice betrayed her growing exhaustion.

"Lots and I'll tell you everything after you've gotten some more rest." She glanced over her shoulder as the door opened. A smile touched her lips to see her younger sister dressed in flannel sleep pants and a spaghetti strap tank, medical bag in hand. "Let Abby take a look at you. We'll talk some more when she's done." She kissed Ellen's cheek and stepped aside, giving her sister room.

Abby softly reassured Ellen everything was going to be all right. As she did, she checked the woman's vitals. At the same time, Mac moved to their mother's bed. Elizabeth reached for her hand. Together, they watched as Abby worked. Mac's respect for her little sister grew as they did. Gone was the headstrong teen who leaped, repeatedly, before looking. A compassionate, extremely competent adult replaced her. As much as she sometimes missed the girl her sister had been—

even though she'd driven Mac insane on more than one occasion—she couldn't be prouder of her.

"Shh, Mama." Mac gently wiped away the tears rolling down Elizabeth's cheeks. "She's going to be all right." Something she finally believed.

"Mac's right, Mom." Abby glanced at them over her shoulder. "Gran, I know you have a lot of questions, but you need to rest. We'll tell you everything after you have. But, I know there is one bit of news Mac wants to share with you."

Mac's eyes went wide before she narrowed them in suspicion. What the hell was her sister up to?

"Which I will do after you rest some more, Gran." Mac smiled at her grandmother before glaring at her sister. "You and Mom both need to try to get some more sleep."

She stood and kissed Elizabeth's cheek. A moment later, she stood next to Ellen's bed and repeated the action with her. When she straightened, she realized Ellen already slept. Before she could say anything, Abby assured her their grandmother was all right. She'd be dropping off like that for some time. It was her body's way of making sure she healed.

"Go eat and then get some rest, Mac. I'll sit with them. Danny's going to join me as soon as he finishes talking with Brooke."

"Let me know if she wakes again?"

"I will. But only if you promise to get some rest now."

Mac smiled and hugged her. "I do and thanks."

She took one more look at their grandmother, reassuring herself Ellen truly was getting better, Then she left the room, quietly closing the door behind her.

"Mama?" Fear filled Cam's voice as she hurried to Mac, throwing her arms around the woman.

"Shh, baby. Gran's going to be all right." She stroked Cam's hair and looked across the room. Jackson stood at the entrance to the kitchenette, Xander in his arms. "She woke up and she knew where she was." Well, kind of. "Aunt Abby's going to sit with her and Grandma. She'll let us know when Gran wakes again."

"She's really going to be all right?"

"That's what Aunt Abby said."

"Good." Cam nodded emphatically, as if the matter was now settled. Then she stepped back and reached for her mother's hand. "Come on. Declan brought dinner and we're hungry."

Laughing, Mac let her daughter drag her to the small dining table. Food sounded good, almost as good as bed.

An hour later, Mac lounged in one of the recliners, banished there by Jackson and the kids while they dealt with their dinner dishes and the leftovers. Their cheerful banter mixed with her relief to know Ellen would be all right. For the first time since the explosion, one layer of tension after another seemed to melt away. The case wasn't closed and wouldn't be, at least not for her, until Reed was in custody. But, for now, it looked like the immediate threat was over. She could pause and rest, catch her breath and gather her thoughts.

Her eyes grew heavy. She pushed the recliner back further, trusting Jackson to wake her to go to bed later. For now, she'd nap, knowing her family was safe.

"W-what?"

She sat up, reaching for the phone she didn't have. Rubbing her eyes, she tried to remember where she'd left it. She knew the ringtone as it repeated. The ringtone that awakened her. Before she gained her feet, Jackson turned to her. He pointed a finger at the recliner, his message clear. She was to sit down and stay there.

Rebellion rose only to be pushed back. She needed to trust him. If the call was important, he'd let her know. If it was just someone ignoring the order to not disturb her until morning, she didn't need to speak with them. Even so, she couldn't relax until she knew for sure who called and why.

"It's Norwood. He has a report." Jackson's displeasure was evident from his tone of voice to his expression as he handed her the phone.

"Talk to me, Nate."

"Sorry to bother you, Mac, but Jael agreed I should call."

Mac hissed in a breath and climbed to her feet. When Jackson opened his mouth to protest, she shook her head. Then she nodded to the kids working at the sink. He nodded, his expression speaking volumes. Hoping they both jumped to the wrong conclusion, Mac crossed to the small bedroom she and Jackson would share as long as they stayed at the safehouse. "What happened?" She leaned against the closed door, steeling herself for more bad news.

"We've finished interrogating the lycans."

"Really?"

Part of her was surprised they hadn't needed to bring her or Jackson in for the interrogation. Lycans usually didn't give up anything without having an alpha roll them. Of course, there were exceptions as Koray proved.

"Let's just say they had some incentive." Norwood chuckled almost evilly, spiking Mac's curiosity.

"Who did what?"

She knew her people. They didn't resort to torture—ever. So what sort of incentive could they have used to get such quick results?

Norwood chuckled again. "Let's say Jael in full gunny mode mixed with Lolo standing nearby, juggling fireballs and occasionally shooting one past the head of whoever they were questioning did the trick."

Mac couldn't help it. She giggled and the giggle turned into a laugh as she pictured the scene. Jael on her own when she was in full gunny mode, as Norwood said, was more than intimidating. Add in Lolo and her fireballs and Mac made a mental note to remember that combination.

"Those two should never be left together unsupervised." She struggled to stop laughing. "What did they find out?"

"They came from various packs around the country. Each had either left their packs or had been kicked out after the Tribunal issued the edict about territorial rights and registration with the local prides or pards if moving in or through a claimed territory."

She thought for a moment. "Nate, that many lone lycans coming together my accident or fate or whatever doesn't make sense. They're pack animals."

"And they have a pack. Koray tipped us to it as you know."

She nodded even though he couldn't see as another piece fell into place. "Reed."

"Bingo, boss.

"Keep going."

"Each of them are part of this new pack. We're still working to get a territory location for it. But they're all terrified of Reed."

That didn't surprise her. Hell, she'd be scared of him if she let go of her anger.

"Each of them confirmed he sent them here. They came singly or in groups of two or three. Initially, there were a dozen of them. But the others left with Reed. Those who remained were tasked with finishing the job the bombing started."

Mac considered for a moment. It made sense but something was missing. Something important.

"Nate, they haven't told you everything."

"Ma'am?"

"Think about it, Nate. You have a group of lycans and they crumbled when faced by a human woman and a witch. That means none of them are strong enough to lead. I doubt Reed would leave them to carry out his orders without making sure someone was around to supervise and make sure they didn't fuck it up."

He cursed inventively and she smiled slightly. He hated missing something and this was a very big something.

"Suggestions?" he asked.

"Identify the weakest of the prisoners and push him. If I need to come in or if I need to send Jackson, let me know. We need to know who Reed left in charge and we need to know everything they do about this person and about Reed."

"I'll get with Jael and Lolo now." He sighed before continuing. "Sorry for disturbing you, boss. Get some rest now. We'll have a report ready once we finish the interrogations."

After telling him to update both Flynn and Norwood, she ended the call. Then she tossed her phone across the room. She watched as it slid over the mattress, stopping just short of the pillows. Enough work. Now she needed family time and sleep. Hopefully, nothing would interfere until morning.

Later, after putting the kids to bed and checking on her mother and grandmother one last time, Mac returned to the bedroom. Every muscle ached. Exhaustion dragged at her. She didn't have the energy to completely undress. Instead, she kicked off her running shoes and stepped out of her pants. Then she fell face first across the bed.

Jackson found her that way when he entered the bedroom a few minutes later. Before he could do anything, she told him she wasn't asleep—yet. He grinned and moved to her side. His hands were gentle as he helped her finish undressing. She tried to reassure him when his face grew tight at the sight of the bandages she sported. He didn't say anything. Instead, he helped her under the sheet and then undressed.

When he joined her a few minutes later, she moved to rest with her head on his shoulder, one leg over his. His hand stroked her back and his lips brushed the top of her head. Then he listened as she told him everything she hadn't earlier, things he needed to know as pride leader.

"Shh, baby." He lightly kissed the top of her head. "Rest now."

"Tired."

"You've pushed yourself so hard. You need to sleep." His hand traced gentle patterns across her back. She sighed and snuggled closer to him. "Trust your team, love. You trained them well. They'll tie up the loose ends and then we can focus on finding Reed. But you're not going to be able to do anything if you work yourself into exhaustion or worse."

She nodded again.

"Besides, there's the little complication of your daughter to deal with."

She chuckled and leaned up on one elbow so she could look at him. "I do believe you had a little something to do with Cami's conception."

"A little something?" he repeated. "I'd show you my little something if you weren't so tired."

She leaned over and nipped his lower lip. "Maybe I'm not that tired."

"Sleep first. Then I'll show you just how little I'm not." He pulled her down and settled her against him. "I've been worried about you, love."

"Sorry." She pressed her lips against his jaw.

"Sleep now."

She sighed and settled her head against his chest. With his arms around her waist, she cleared her mind. Sleep wasn't long in coming.

25

The next morning, Mac smiled and leaned against the doorframe of the bedroom where her mother and grandmother lay on their hospital beds. Liz sat up, enjoying her first cup of decent coffee since being injured. She looked battered and bruised, but her eyes were bright, and she listened closely as Dr. Patek talked. He reassured them both that she and Ellen would be all right. But it would take time. For Liz because she was human and for Ellen because of the seriousness of her injuries.

"Make sure they do as I said." He pinned Mac with a firm glance before leaving the room.

Mac hurried to Ellen's bedside. Her hands gentle, she helped her grandmother sit up some. Then she adjusted the bed and pillows, watching Ellen's face to make sure she wasn't hurting too badly. Once satisfied, she kissed her grandmother's cheek.

"Feel up to trying some broth?"

Ellen nodded. When Mac turned to leave, the woman reached for her hand, stopping her.

"Please."

Mac turned. One look at her grandmother's face told her the woman wasn't saying please for the broth. She wanted information.

Since Mac would want the same thing if their positions were reversed, she nodded once. Then, as she gently settled on the edge of the mattress, she looked down at their joined hands. The question became how much to tell her. Dr. Patek had been very clear. Ellen was not to be upset by anyone or anything.

"There was an explosion in the parking garage, Gran. You and the others were caught in some of the fallout from it. Mom was trapped behind the steering wheel. You'd gotten out and debris hit you. That's how your leg was injured."

"The children?" Fear lit her eyes.

"They're fine." Now Mac smiled proudly. "Cam did exactly what we'd expect. She protected her brother and she did what she could to help you and Mom until we could get to you."

"Good girl."

"She's a very good girl."

"What else?"

Here came the tricky part. Mac quickly made a decision, hoping it didn't come back to bite her on the ass.

"Gran, before I say anything else, know I've been in almost constant contact with the Tribunal as well as with Flynn."

Ellen's eyes narrowed but she didn't say anything.

"There was more than one explosion. IEDs had been planted in both the parking garage and in HQ. Fortunately, all those cameras I kept warning everyone about before we went public did their job. We got images of the bastards who placed the bomb in the garage. Another conspirator tripped up and revealed his role without meaning to. They're all in custody."

"Safe?"

"Yes, we're safe."

Ellen closed her eyes and Mac waited, fully expecting her to fall asleep again. Instead, her grandmother opened her eyes a moment later. The moment she did, Mac knew that despite all the drugs currently being pumped into her, she'd put it together. Damn it!

"Then why here?" She motioned to the room.

"Because there's more." Mac gently pulled her hand from her

grandmother's and got to her feet. She needed to pace. Hell, she'd like to run, anything to keep from having to tell her grandmother the rest of it before she was fully healed.

"You have to promise you will leave this to me, Gran." She pinned the woman with a firm look, the one Cam called her "mom look". "Several things have come out in the course of the investigation. First, a group of lycans has been in town close to a month. They Tribunal has been notified and you know what that means."

Ellen nodded, her expression grim.

"We also have proof that some of Ferguson's former associates, human ones, knew of their arrival and have helped them since they got here. One has already been taken into custody and we are looking for the other."

"There's more."

Mac ground her teeth. For not the first time, she wished Ellen didn't know her as well as she did. The last thing she wanted was to tell the woman about Reed. Not yet at any rate.

Before she explained, the door opened. Cami stepped inside. She carried a tray and the smells of broth and tea entered with her. Seeing both her grandmother and great-grandmother awake, the girl grinned and hurried forward. She placed the tray on the table between the two beds before kissing Elizabeth's cheek. Then she turned to Ellen, tears in her eyes.

"I'm so glad you're better, Gran." She held Ellen's hand in hers and leaned forward to kiss her cheek.

Ellen smiled and ran her hand over the girl's cheek. Then she stopped, her eyes going wide. Mac chuckled softly at the look the woman gave Cam. It was priceless and Mac had a feeling it matched her own when she first came upon her daughter in her shifted form.

"Mackenzie?"

"It seems your great-granddaughter is living up to the family name, Gran." She draped an arm around Cam's shoulders and smiled down at her daughter. "The last thing Mom told Cam before losing consciousness was to take care of her brother."

"You shifted?"

Cam nodded and then buried her face against her mother's chest.

Ellen smiled and held a hand out to the girl. Mac nudged Cam and nodded to Ellen. Cami grinned and took the woman's hand. Mac kept a grip on her shoulder, wanting to make sure she didn't forget and jump onto the best to hug Ellen.

"I'd like to see."

Cami looked up at her mother. Mac nodded. Then she laughed as the girl hurried to the adjoining bathroom. She should probably warn her grandmother about Cami's shifted form but decided not to. Hopefully, Ellen's excitement about this new aspect of her great-granddaughter's life would distract her long enough for her to fall asleep, giving Mac a reprieve from telling her about Reed.

"Gran, meet Freydís," Mac said as the young panther padded across the floor in their direction.

Ellen gasped. Worried, Mac looked at her. Instead of the pain she expected to see reflected on her grandmother's expression, Mac saw only surprise and pride. Ellen watched Freydís as she neared. Before the panther could climb into bed with her, Mac stopped her.

"Go to your grandmother. I'll help Gran with her broth. When she's done, if you're very careful, you can rest in bed with her."

Freydís dipped her head in a very human-like nod. Ellen's gaze remained on her as she climbed into bed with Elizabeth. The woman's fingers caressed the panther's ears before moving to scratch under her chin. Freydís purred loudly and her eyes closed until only slits remained.

"She knows her name?"

Mac nodded. "Cam told me Freydís has been with her for a long time. Much like your Xiomara."

"And you didn't suspect anything?"

Mac barked out a laugh. Then she shook her head and reached for the bowl of broth and a spoon.

"Trust me, neither Jackson nor I had a clue." She watched as her grandmother took several spoonfuls of the broth. "And let me tell you, Xander is not happy. He's tried and tried and tried to shift like his sister and he can't. It's not fair."

Both Ellen and Elizabeth laughed at her impression of her youngest child.

"That sounds like your brother and sister after they learned you could shift and they couldn't." Elizabeth said, her eyes twinkling in amusement. "Trust me, a five-year-old is much easier to take in that situation than teenagers."

"Mackenzie, are you all right?"

Mac's heart skipped a beat as she wondered how Ellen knew she'd been injured. Then she realized her grandmother meant Cam. Smiling, she spooned more broth into Ellen's mouth and nodded. She might be at a loss as to what to do about having a pre-teen daughter who could finally shift, but she was all right. At least where that was concerned.

"I am." She glanced across at her daughter's panther-self and smiled proudly. "Although, I'll admit to being more than a little surprised to see she shifts into a panther and not a jaguar."

Ellen smiled and nodded. "We'll talk about it later."

"Thanks." She set the bowl back onto the tray on the table. "Ready to rest some before the doctor comes check on you?"

"Yes."

Mac squeezed her hand. A moment later, she motioned to the panther. Freydís carefully climbed off of Elizabeth's bed. She moved with barely a sound around the bed until she stood next to Mac.

"Very careful now, love."

Mac watched, ready to react as needed, as the panther climbed onto the narrow bed. As she settled gently, protectively on the mattress next to her, Ellen's hand absently rubbed Freydís' ears. Then she smiled in a way Mac hadn't seen in a very long time.

"Sleep now, Gran. Freydís will stay with you."

The panther looked up and nodded once.

"Mom, do you need anything?"

Elizabeth shook her head, smiling as she watched her mother and granddaughter. Then she lowered the head of her bed some and settled back. Leaving the three to rest, Mac retrieved the tray with its contents and left the room. One hurdle avoided. But how long could she continue to avoid her grandmother's questions?

As long as necessary to protect the elder, Cait told her.

"How are they?" Jackson asked as she entered the kitchenette.

He sat at the small dining table. Abby and Danny sat on either side of him. Danny quickly climbed to his feet. Before Mac could protest, he took the tray from her and told her to sit down. Abby poured her a mug of coffee and pushed a basket of fresh pastries in her direction. Thanking her sister, Mac grabbed a scone. Then she leaned back and smiled.

"They're better." She quickly recounted her conversation with Ellen. "I didn't say anything about what happened yesterday or about Reed." She lowered her voice in hopes Ellen wouldn't overhear.

"Good." Abby nodded emphatically.

"What now?" Danny asked as he returned to the table.

"Gran realized something changed with Cam." She chuckled at the memory of the look on her grandmother's face as she put it all together. "She wanted to see Cam after she shifted. Right now, the two of them are curled up in bed."

"And?" Jackson prompted.

"She didn't seem surprised to discover Cam shifts into a panther." And that was something else they needed to discuss once Ellen was stronger.

"You are going to be so screwed as she gets older, big sister." Abby grinned as her groaned.

"Maybe we'll send her to live with you for a year or two." Now it was Mac's turn to grin as her sister paled at the thought. She knew Abby loved her niece and nephew. But the thought of dealing with a hormonal teenaged shapeshifter was enough to terrify anyone with an ounce of sense.

"Mama!" Xander appeared from the bedroom he shared with his sister and all but launched himself at his mother.

Laughing, she caught him and kissed his cheek. He threw his arms around her and gave her a wet kiss on the cheek before wriggling out of her grasp. "Breakfast?"

Jackson ruffled his hair and reached for his hand. Mac watched, a smile on her lips, as father and son debated what the boy would have to eat. Then, as she finished her coffee and the last bite of her scone, she looked at the time. Much as she'd like to stay where she was, Derek Reed remained on the loose and, as long as he was, he presented a danger to those she loved.

"I need to get going." She stood and stretched. "Let me know if anything changes with them or the others?" She nodded to the first bedroom where Ellen and Elizabeth rested.

"We will," Abby assured her. "But you be careful, sis."

"I will." She carried her dishes to the sink. "My phone?" she asked Jackson.

He smiled and pulled it from his hip pocket. She checked and relaxed to see no new messages. Then she reached up to kiss him.

"I'll keep you in the loop. Promise."

"You'd better." He cupped her chin and kissed her again, laughing when Danny suggested the get a room.

Wishing they could, Mac sent a text to Jael, telling her she'd be ready to leave in half an hour. She needed to head into Central to check on things there Once that was done, they'd be in the field. It was time to find Reed once and for all.

26

"We have a location, Colonel."

Mac grinned and all but rubbed her hands together. For two days, cops and Marines worked side-by-side as they followed every lead in their hunt for Phelan and Lam, who had not been one of those arrested at the hospital. Sleep had been in short supply for all of them as they worked. Each member of the team understood the dangers the two presented, not just to the people of Dallas but to everyone.

"Who and where?"

"Phelan," Lt. Halstead replied without looking up from her screens. "His cellphone came on and pinged off of a tower in the Lakewood area. It was on long enough for us to get a location."

"Excellent." Now she did rub her hands together. "Show me what you have."

It didn't take long. Unless he moved after his cellphone deactivated, he was holed up in a rental house. It hadn't taken the techs long to dig through real estate records to tie the house with Phelan's company.

Mac considered for a moment. She'd prefer knowing for sure he was there, but she didn't want to run the risk of him getting away before they received confirmation.

"Captain Lindsay." She grinned as Jael entered the room. "We have a target. Three teams. Alpha is to be paras only. That will be the lead strike team. Gamma will be human or a mix of human and para. Omega will be our tech team. Houston, Halstead, decide who you want to go. All teams are to be ready for briefing in half an hour."

Ten minutes later, Mac stood in front of her locker in the women's locker room. She stripped out of her slacks and DPD polo shirt. For a moment, standing there in her underwear, she considered. A few moments later, she stepped into black cargo pants with reinforced knees. Then she pulled on a black, long sleeved tee shirt. Black tactical boots followed. Finally, she settled her tactical vest over it, frowning at the weight.

It didn't take long to finish. Knives with quick release sheaths were fastened to forearms. More were slid into sheaths in her boots. She strapped a kukri to her left thigh and attached a combat axe to her vest. Her M4 hung from a quick release sling. An M1911 rested in a holster on the front of her vest. Another was strapped to her right thigh. Additional ammo, as well as two tasers, several flashbangs and zip-cuffs hung from her vest or rested inside its pouches.

She lightly punched Jael on the shoulder. If their intel was good, they would soon be one step closer to finding Reed.

God, their intel had to be good.

"Ready?" she asked as Tanaka joined them.

Both women nodded, their expressions grim.

"Then let's do this."

The plan was simple. She learned long ago to keep it that way. The more complicated the plan, the more things that could go wrong—and she most definitely did not want anything going wrong today.

"Alpha team is the contact team," Mac said as a member of Houston's team displayed a satellite image of target and the nearby houses. "Once on-site, take up positions here, here and here." She indicated points at the front and rear of the home.

"Gamma, you will be here and here." She marked locations down the block from the target. "Uniforms will block the streets in front and behind the target address. They will be far enough down the road so he shouldn't be able to see them. Alpha and Gamma will approach on foot."

"How do you want us to make entry?" Norwood asked.

"You'll hit the entries at the same time. On my count, Ace and Tweety will put tear gas through front and back windows." She nodded to two of the team's snipers. "Entry teams will go in, announcing yourselves when you do."

She paused and looked around that room, making eye contact with each person gathered. "Full gear. We don't know what we're going to be walking in on. Phelan may be alone or there may be lycans with him."

"Once Alpha team has secured the scene, any prisoners are to be transported. The determination of where will be made by me on-scene. Then Gamma team will move in and help search the scene and interview neighbors." She held up a hand before anyone could interrupt. "Gamma, you are the last line of defense during the entry. I cannot and will not risk you being attacked and turned if lycans are present. However, I am not going to leave you out of this. I promise."

Mac finished the briefing, telling everyone to watch their sixes. Then she followed them out of the room. It didn't take long for everyone to climb into cars, armored SUVs and vans. Only one SUV remained unoccupied. Mac walked to it, reaching for the driver's door handle before Jael could get there.

"Ma'am?" the woman asked.

"I'm driving."

She didn't give Jael time to object. Instead, she climbed in behind the steering wheel and closed the door. A moment later, Jael climbed into the front passenger seat. Tanaka and Murray took the back seat."

"You're not planning on going in with the entry teams, are you?" Jael asked as they drove off.

"I am and, before you try to argue, I have to. The Tribunal was very specific when I reported in." Not that Mac disagreed. She only hoped it kept Jael and the others from arguing too much.

And she hoped this didn't blow up in her face.

To her surprise, they didn't argue. But what Jael said next was, in Mac's mind at least, worse.

"I have my own orders from the Tribunal."

"As do I, ma'am," Murray added.

Mac didn't know whether to roll her eyes or close them. Since closing them while driving didn't seem like a very good idea, she rolled them. Then she waited to hear what they had to say.

"You go in after the breech team and after Murray and me."

"How about we go in together?"

"No, ma'am. Our orders were very clear. You aren't to go in until after we do," Murray said.

"All right." She smiled when they stared at her in disbelief. "Nothing from you, Shelly?" She glanced at the woman's reflection in the rearview mirror.

"No, ma'am." Tanaka grinned. "I know better than to get into a pissing contest between the three of you."

Mac chuckled softly. "Wise woman."

Two hours later, Mac stepped out of the rear of a van parked a block down the street from their target. As she did, she sighed softly. She'd spent more time in the rear of vans and planning takedowns in the last week than she had in the last several years. Part of her reveled in it. She'd missed this part of the job. But another part knew it was time to let others do it.

But that would come after she closed down the hunt for Reed and this was one more chance to do so.

She reached up and tapped her earbud.

"Striker here. Alpha team, be ready to move out on my signal. I'm on my way in." She nodded as Jael and Murray joined her, one on each side. "Gamma leader, are your teams in place?"

"Roger that, Striker," Tanaka replied.

"Good. All teams, here's our status. Omega confirms two people inside the house. They are in the middle of the structure, what appears to be the family room. Multiple egresses from there. The most direct is out the back door. Next most direct is down a short hallway and out the front door. Alternatives require moving to different parts of the house and bailing through windows. Gas to go in through the front window and back sliding glass doors. Follow up with flashbangs. Questions?"

She jogged down the block, making her way to where the rest of Alpha team waited.

"All right, team leaders. Move your people into place." She nodded to the other members of Alpha team. "Lee, you've got the back. Take three with you. Two stay outside to cover the back."

"Roger that." He jabbed a finger at two of the team and then took off at a jog, cutting through the neighbor's yard until they could jump the back fence. "The rest of you are with me. You two." She motioned to Keo and Walters." You have the front. Make sure no one tries to climb out a window. Vincent, you'll kick the door. Parnell, the moment he does, lob a flashbang as far into the center of the house as you can. As soon as it goes off, we go in."

"Yes, ma'am."

No one spoke as they fanned out, keeping low to the ground. Mac crouched behind a brick planter, Jael at her side. She waited as each member of the breaching team reported in. Then she signaled her snipers, Ace and Tweety. This time, instead of being in perches high above their heads, the two raced across the lawn, Tweety heading to the back of the house. The moment he reported he was in place, Mac signaled Ace. The count was his.

"On three," he radioed. "One... two... three."

Glass shattered as he fired through the front window. The moment he did, Vincent kicked in the front door. Mac listened as Lee ordered the back door breached. A moment later, two loud bangs filled the air as the flashbangs detonated. Trusting them to have disoriented anyone inside, Mac pulled her rebreather mask into place and rushed inside.

"Police! Stop!" she yelled as she entered the front hall and saw someone racing up the stairs to her left.

Before she could order pursuit, Norwood and Parnell ran after him. She continued toward the center of the house. Lee's initial report confirmed a second person there, hiding behind a locked door. As if that would stop her now.

The sound of a gunshot came from upstairs. Two more shots followed. Mac stopped, listening. Without a word, she turned and motioned for Jael to find out what happened. The woman told Murray to stick with Mac before bounding up the stairs. Trusting Jael to make sure the situation was under control, Mac continued on her way.

"What have you got?" she asked Lee as she entered the family room.

He stood before a door on the far side of the room. From beyond it came the sounds of someone rustling about. Those on watch in the backyard reported a man appeared to be trying to escape through a window before he saw them and ducked back inside.

Good. The rat was trapped. Now to get him out of his hole.

"Phelan is down," Jael reported over Mac's earbud. "We're coming back down."

Mac nodded even though the woman couldn't see. Apparently, Phelan had been more foolish than she thought. Well, pulling a gun on any of her people was a mistake he'd never make again. At least not on this plane of existence. Dead is dead and was he very, very dead.

Mac pulled a flashbang from the pouch on her tactical vest. For a moment she considered it. Then she approached the door. Using hand signals—after all, there was no sense warning whoever hid in the room beyond—she ordered Lee to be ready to kick in the door. Then she held up three fingers.

Two.

One.

None.

The master sergeant leaned back and kicked, splintering the wood around the latch. The door flew open, the doorknob lodging deep in the wall behind it. As it did, Mac lobbed the flashbang inside. She ducked, covering her ears and shielding her eyes. Then she rushed inside, gun in hand, sweeping the room.

A roar to her right warned her. She turned, sidestepping. A grin touched her lips as a man moved toward her.

Foolish, so foolish.

Eyes red, watering almost uncontrollably and swollen from the tear gas. Disoriented from the flashbangs. Desperation drove him but it also made him careless. Mac waited for him to close in. Then she stepped once more to the side. Her right leg flashed out, tripping him. Her left fist smashed against his temple, further disorienting him. He grunted and went down. Before he could recover, Lee and Murray were on him. Murray jabbed a needle into his neck, releasing the inhibitor into his system. Lee hit him with a charge from a stun gun, incapacitating him until they had him secured.

Mac watched, listening as the rest of the team checked the house, making sure no other unpleasant surprises awaited them.

"Shelly, take control outside," she radioed. "One of his neighbors will have heard the shots and reported them."

"Already on it, Colonel. Dispatch has been notified."

"Excellent. Tag me if you need me." Leaving Lee and Murray to finish with their prisoner, she returned to the family room. "Someone open the doors and let's get this place aired out." She pulled off her rebreather, hissing as her eyes started burning.

Damn, there was still too much tear gas in the air to be comfortable.

She pulled the rebreather back on, cursing her foolishness.

"Tear this place apart. You know what we're looking for. Get Cloud and Halstead in here. Any electronics go with them."

"What about him, ma'am?" Lee asked as he dragged their prisoner out by his collar.

"Standard security measures for transport and then get him out of here. I'll meet you there."

She couldn't wait to see what he had to say.

Mac entered the interrogation room two hours later, Master Sergeant Lee behind her. At her signal, he took up his position next to the door. Trusting Lee to have her back, not that the prisoner could do much restrained as he was, Mac took her place at the table opposite him.

She sat silently studying him. How had she missed it? When she saw the photos of him earlier, she hadn't recognized him. But now, being so close to him, she realized her mistake. She not only recognized him, she knew without a doubt he was the connection they'd been looking for. The connection between Cassandra Wilkinson, Bahram Yazhari and Derek Reed. The evil triumvirate that damn near started a war between Pures and lycans.

"Kellan Lam, you have exactly one chance to save your life. Tell me where Derek Reed is and you'll live to leave this room. Then you can plead your case before the Tribunal. You have sixty seconds to decide."

"Go to hell."

She leaned back and smiled almost gently. She'd expected as much. Well, he was about to learn how foolish it was to come after her family. This time, she didn't need to worry about non-paras seeing what she could do. He wasn't at the county jail. He was at the holding facility set up by the Ghostwalkers to hold prisoners until they could be transported elsewhere. As soon as she finished with him, Lam would be transported to Black Crow Prison.

If he didn't force her to kill him out of hand.

"Consider your response very carefully, Lam. It would be smart to start by considering who I am."

"You're nothing but a Pure bitch."

She laughed, startling him.

"Technically, that's exactly what I am. However, just to do this properly, I am Mackenzie Santos Caine, daughter of Elizabeth Santos and granddaughter of Elena Alexandra Ramirez–Saenz Graham Santos, direct descendant of Arturo Ramirez and Anna Saenz. I am also the granddaughter of Robert Alejandro Mackenzie Santos, direct descendant of Seamus Mackenzie. I am the mate and wife of Jackson Caine, alpha of the Dallas pride and an alpha in my own right. I am the enforcer for the pride. I sit on the Tribunal, representing the Mackenzie bloodline. I am also the Tribunal's Enforcer, tasked with carrying out their orders when our laws are broken. That means it is my duty to deal with you. How I do so depends on you."

He howled, fighting against the chains holding him in place.

Mac shook her head. Lycans were so predictable. He knew he couldn't escape his bonds any more than he could shift now that the inhibitor had taken effect. But that didn't stop him from trying.

She waited, letting him tire as he continued to fight for freedom. Finally, he sat still, panting, sweat darkening his shirt and running down his face.

Without a word, she laid out row after row of pictures. Photos of the bombing, the various people—human and lycan—they'd captured. The lycans killed in the attack on the hospital. Even of the house he and Phelan sheltered in before their discovery. The final photos were of the various pieces of evidence they seized there and in a storage unit they shouldn't have been able to trace to him.

Then she laid out a photo of Derek Reed.

"You have no rights, Lam. The government of the United States recognizes there are times when the Tribunal must deal with those under our jurisdiction without having to worry about the rights a human criminal enjoys. This is one of those times. You conspired with others, said conspiracy leading to the deaths of humans and paras. Your actions are part of a larger, coordinated effort to create discord between paras and humans. You have hunted humans as if they were no better than animals. Your life is forfeit unless you convince me otherwise."

She placed a hard copy of the Tribunal's death warrant on the table in front of him. Then she pulled her gun. His eyes went wide as she checked to make sure a round was chambered.

"I'll see you in Hell, bitch."

"You could have saved yourself." She slid the gun back into the Kydex holster at her waist. "I guess you forgot the part about me being an alpha. So let me remind you."

She stood and placed her hands palm down on the table. Her eyes bored into him. If he could, he would move away from her. But he couldn't.

"You will answer my questions. You will do so fully and honestly." She spoke softly even as her power as an alpha rolled over him.

He whimpered and shook his head.

Mac straightened and walked around the table. Lam's eyes all but whirled in his head as he watched her. When she stopped behind him and placed her hands on his shoulders, he yelped like a dog being whipped. She ran a gentle hand over his head, soothing him.

"Tell me." She put more power into those two simple words.

His muscles trembled under her hands as he fought the compulsion.

"Tell me where I can find Derek Reed."

He couldn't talk fast enough.

27

Six weeks later, Mac sat at a table at a local coffee shop, sipping a café mocha. The morning paper rested on the table in front of her. Her attention wasn't on it, however. It was on a Lexus and the apartment entrance across the street.

She reached up and wiped her mouth. "Status?" she asked into the mic hidden under the cuff of her leather jacket.

"We've got movement. Someone's coming out," Murray reported.

Mac grinned as she spotted the younger woman. She sat at the bus stop, looking like a bored college student. Other members of the Ghostwalkers manned positions nearby, ready to move in on her order.

"Remember, we do this fast and clean. If it looks like any civilians are in the line of fire, we fall back and follow him."

She'd prefer taking him now but she wouldn't put others at risk.

Across the street, the doors opened and several people walked outside. Mac watched, barely daring to breathe. Their intel was good. She knew it. But what if it was wrong? What if this was another dead end?

She smiled and pumped her fist under the table as the doors opened once again. This time, a tall, slender man stepped outside. To the casual observer, he looked like a successful businessman. His suit was most definitely not off the rack and his shoes cost more than she made in a year as a cop.

She stood, her coffee and paper forgotten, and moved toward the coffee shop entrance. As she did, she kept her gaze on the man. After all this time, after all he had done, she'd never mistake him for anything but what he was: a lycan needing to be put down.

And soon, Derek Reed would face the Tribunal's judgment.

She saw the moment he caught the first scent of one of her people. She knew it was a risk using Pures. But it was a risk she was willing to take. Besides, she had safeguards in place, starting with Murray.

"Move in!" She burst outside the coffee shop and sprinted across the road.

Instantly, a dozen men and women converged on Reed. He froze, his eyes going wide. Then he looked around. It wasn't fear Mac saw in his eyes but calculation. He weighed his options, looking for something, anything he could use against his pursuers. Then he smiled and her blood ran cold as she spotted what he'd seen.

"Someone get them out of here!"

She pointed to a young mother pushing a stroller down the street in Reed's attention. Instantly, Murray ran in their direction. As she did, the young woman stopped, her mouth forming an "O" of surprise. Then, before she could object, Murray scooped the baby up out of the stroller and into one arm. With the other, she grabbed the mother and all but dragged her down the street to safety.

Reed howled to realize he'd been denied a victim. He tugged at his tie, dragging it over his head. Mac cursed, realizing what he planned.

"Take him down!"

Reed turned, his eyes locking on hers. Even as his features blurred as he started shifting, he smiled. He knew her. Good. Then he'd know who finally defeated him.

"Now!" she yelled.

Three Ghostwalkers fired. Reed's head snapped around. Before he could react, the barbs from three stun guns hit. His system lit up like the proverbial Christmas tree. That was all it took. Before the effects of the charges wore off, Norwood and Lee had him down on the sidewalk. His hands were cuffed and zip-cuffs were secured around his ankles. Lee administered the inhibitor. Then the men pulled Reed to his knees, holding him between them as Mac neared.

Mac stepped onto the sidewalk and walked almost casually toward the three men. Reed knelt on the concrete, struggling against his bonds. He had no chance of escaping. Not with both Lee and Norwood holding an arm.

And especially not with the little accessory placed around his neck.

"Listen closely, wolf," the big man growled in Reed's ear. "This collar is very special. We had it made just for you. Try to fight us and the witch over there." He pointed to where Murray now stood, a small controller that looked like a key fob in one hand, a bouncing ball of fire in the other. "She'll happily activate it. The first shock will take you down. Try again and she'll up the stakes. The second shock will have you pissing your pants. You might even shit them. Please be foolish enough to try a third time. That shock will fry your brain, saving all of us a lot of trouble." He locked the collar in place. Then, as if just realizing Mac neared, Lee grabbed Reed by the hair and forced him to look at her.

"You bitch! I'll kill you." Reed struggled against Lee's grip.

Mac stopped. Without looking at Murray, she lifted her right hand and held up one finger. A moment later, the lycan stiffened. His jaw clenched and his body shook as the collar activated. At the count of five, Mac nodded. Murray lowered her hand. Reed's reaction resembled that of a puppet that had its strings suddenly cut. He pitched forward. The only thing that prevented him from faceplanting on the concrete sidewalk was Norwood catching him. He held Reed as the man's chest rose and fell in quick, shallow breaths. Sweat pricked out on Reed's face. His earlier howls of outrage turned into pain filled whimpers.

"Enforcer?" Norwood looked at me in question.

Mac nodded and stepped forward. There was one more thing she needed to do before handing him off for transport.

"Hold him."

She didn't need to say anything else. Norwood grabbed a handful of Reed's hair and forced the man's head up. As he did, Mac smiled slightly. She wanted him to see her for this next bit when he learned, just as Wilkinson and Yazhari had, how foolish it was to mess with her family and friends.

"Reed, I'll assume from your earlier reaction that you know who I am. But let's make it clear for the record."

"Go to hell!"

"You'll be there long before I am."

His eyes widened in disbelief and he renewed his struggles against Lee and Norwood. Not that it helped him. He wasn't going to get up from the pavement until Mac said he could.

"Derek Reed, we've met before, but let me remind you who I am." Her voice turned cold, hard. "My name is Mackenzie Santos Caine. I am the daughter of Elizabeth Santos and granddaughter of Elena Alexandra Ramirez–Saenz Graham Santos, direct descendant of Arturo Ramirez and Anna Saenz. I am also the granddaughter of Robert Alejandro Mackenzie Santos, direct descendant of Seamus Mackenzie. I am the mate and wife of Jackson Caine, alpha of the Dallas pride and an alpha in my own right. I am the enforcer for the pride. I sit on the Tribunal, representing the Mackenzie bloodline. The other members of the Tribunal have appointed me as its Enforcer and my first task as such has been to track you down and bring you to stand before the Tribunal to answer for your crimes."

"No!" He threw his head back and howled.

Disgust filled her. He knew he was caught but refused to accept it. Well, too bad. The Tribunal possessed more than enough evidence to convict him for his crimes. Hopefully, by the time they finished searching his apartment, they would have even more.

But, for now, she knew people watched, cameras out as they streamed what happened.

"Look at me!" She eased her control on her jaguar, letting her features blur and her eyes turn an even darker green. "I said look at me." Her voice deepened and power rolled over him. She might not be as strong an alpha as her grandmother, but she didn't need to be, not with Reed.

He whimpered and did as instructed. When he did, his eyes went wide, almost dilating with fear, as he finally took in her appearance. Good. she had very carefully dressed for this moment, putting as much care into her appearance as most women put into preparing for an important date. But instead of an expensive dress and shoes, she wore all black. Not the black cargo pants and long-sleeved tees her team wore. No, she wore black leather slacks, boots and a black turtleneck. Over that she wore a black leather duster. She was danger walking and, judging by Reed's expression, he knew it.

"Reed, it is my duty to inform you that you are being taken into custody to answer multiple charges leveled against you by the State of Texas, the United States and the Tribunal. Among the charges you face is the charge of engaging in acts of domestic terrorism. You will therefore be treated as an enemy combatant until we have transported you to a secure location."

With that, she looked at Lee and dipped her chin. He nodded in response. A moment later, he and Norwood pulled Reed to his feet. Mac waited, standing a few feet away, to see how Reed responded.

The lycan didn't disappoint. Even secured as he was, even with the threat of the collar, he struggled against the men's hold on his arms. Mac watched, a bitter smile on her lips. When he realized he couldn't shift, his howl of fear and outrage echoed off the buildings lining the street. In that moment, Mac knew she made the right decision to administer the inhibitor immediately. Clearly, his wolf was a large part of the man. It controlled so much of him, even when Reed was in human form, she was surprised he retained any humanity. Now that wolf was helpless, just as Reed's victims had been.

"The state and federal charges against you include capital murder, attempted capital murder, multiple violations of the federal Terrorism Act, and more," she continued. "They will be explained in detail once you reach your destination. You have also violated laws set forth by the Tribunal, including but not limited to violating the territory of the Dallas pride, violating the territory of the Central Texas pride and pard, causing injury to Pures to be named, causing injury to humans, inciting violence against humans, witches and Pures. If convicted by the Tribunal on any of these charges, you face not only banishment but death. Consider yourself lucky the Tribunal values your rights more than you do those of anyone else. Otherwise, it would have already signed your death warrant."

Angry murmurs sounded around them as the growing crowd began putting together why he was being taken into custody. Someone from behind Mac offered to help "teach him the error of his ways". She smiled slightly. Her grandmother had been right. This very public takedown of the man would help to restore some of the faith the normals lost in paras after the bombing.

Hopefully, that change of heart would continue.

"Get him ready for transport," she ordered.

Lee and Norwood reached down and hauled Reed to his feet. As they did, he proved how much of a coward he really was. His pissed himself. As he did, some of the onlookers laughed and pointed, adding to the lycan's humiliation.

How quickly the big bad wolf became a laughingstock.

Thank God.

"Consider this as you are transported to the location where you'll be held until you face judgment. We have those you used in Dallas in custody. They have detailed what you ordered them to do and what you promised in return for their obedience. We have their electronics as well. We used them to find your communications with the others, communications that inexorably link you to the bombing that cost six people, all humans, their lives and injured a number of others—human, Pure and witch.

"We know you promised to turn humans in return for their cooperation. You promised the lycans you lured into the Dallas territory that they would be free to hunt humans once war broke out between our kind and the humans. We know you helped plan the attack on the medical center where Elena Alexandra Ramirez–Saenz Graham Santos and others injured in the blast were being treated and that you gave the lycans involved your 'permission' to kill or turn any humans they encountered in that attack."

She nodded to Lee who once again forced Reed to his knees.

"Derek Reed, you will now be transported to a secure location. Any attempt to escape will be met with lethal force. The inhibitor will be given to you on a daily basis until your fate has been decided. Do you have anything you wish to say before you I turn you over for transport?"

"This isn't over," he snarled, struggling against Lee as the burly Marine held him on his knees. "We will win this war. We will!"

"You lost long ago. You're just too foolish to realize it." She pointedly turned her back on him, the ultimate insult for thier kind. "Get him out of here." She walked away, knowing what would happen next.

"Don't you turn your back on me, you bitch!"

At the edge of the street, she turned back. When she did, she felt a moment of pity for him. Then she remembered all he had done and wanted to do. He was worse than anyone she had dealt with for the Tribunal save Cassandra Wilkinson. He deserved whatever fate the rest of the Tribunal chose for him.

Mac jerked her head toward a waiting van. When she did, Norwood and Lee hauled Reed upright. Then they dragged across the sidewalk, the tips of his expensive shoes leaving a trail of polish and leather behind. She watched as he was lifted inside the rear of the van. A moment later, the doors slid shut and the van sped off.

"Captain Lindsay, take a team and search his apartment. Nothing gets overlooked."

"Understood, ma'am." She turned and issued orders to others of the team before sending them inside the building.

Mac drew in a deep breath. They'd gotten lucky and she knew it. So much could have gone wrong, especially when she glanced around the crowd that gathered as she dealt with Reed. Now, seeing cellphones out and knowing they were still livestreaming, she steeled herself. Where was the public information officer when she needed him?

"Hey, what's going on? Did he really do all those things you said?" a young man who couldn't be more than eighteen asked. When he tried to move closer, Murray hurried to intercept him.

"He did." Mac shoved her hands into her pockets.

"Are you really a shifter?" a little girl asked.

Mac looked around, trying to locate her. Finally, she saw the girl who couldn't be much older than Xander, hiding behind her mother. Smiling, Mac pulled her hands out of her pockets, letting mother and daughter see she was unarmed and doing her best to look friendly and reassuring.

"I really am." She knelt on a knee several feet in front of them, well aware of how others gathered around, wanting to hear their conversation.

"That is so cool," the girl gushed, stepping out from behind her mom. "What do you turn into?"

Mac grinned. "What do you think I turn into?"

For a moment, the girl studied her. "I think you turn into a really big cat because you're a hunter and cats are hunters."

Mac nodded and her eyes twinkled. In the back of her mind, Cait chuffed with laughter.

"You're right." She held her hand out. "My name's Mac. What's yours?"

The little girl looked up at her mother who nodded. Once she did, the girl stepped forward and reached for Mac's hand, shaking it.

"My name is Sophia Grace Caras."

"Well, Sophia Grace Caras, my name's Mackenzie Santos Caine. I'm very pleased to meet you."

The dark-haired little girl looked up at her mother and grinned. Then she looked back at Mac. "Are you a police officer?"

"I sure am." Among other things.

"I want to be a police officer when I grow up," Sofia told her. "My grampy was one."

"Then your grampy was a hero." Mac stood and dug into her pocket. A moment later, she pulled out two business cards. "Sophia, I would be honored if you'd let me show you around police headquarters some time." She handed one of the cards to the girl. Then she turned her attention to the girl's mother. "With your permission, of course."

"We'd both like that, Colonel Santos." The young woman tucked the business card into the front pocket of her jeans. "Ava Caras, ma'am. I believe you know my father-in-law, Sophia's grampy." She grinned down at her daughter.

"Really?"

"Yes, ma'am. Assistant Chief George Caras. He retired a couple of years ago."

Mac grinned. She not only knew Caras but respected him. He'd been in charge of Cyber Crimes for the Department for years.

"Please tell him I said hello."

"I will." She reached down and lifted Sophia, settling the girl on her hip. "I'm sure you have more important things to do than talk with us right now, Colonel. But thank you for taking time to reassure my daughter."

"It was my pleasure." Mac shook Ava's hand before grinning at Sophia. "We'll talk later, kiddo. Promise."

She turned and started off, smiling as Ava told those still gathered the show was over. When she slid inside her SUV, she chuckled. Of all everything that could have happened, that was the absolute last on her list of things to expect.

"You do realize that's going to be all over the news and social media by nightfall, don't you?" Murray asked as she slid in on the passenger side.

Mac nodded.

"You've been so careful since your people came out of the closet not to advertise what you are. Why now?"

Mac turned the key in the ignition and carefully eased into traffic.

"It's time."

And probably past time.

"I don't understand."

Mac glanced at her and smiled. "I didn't either until I was talking with Gran the other day. We got lucky when we made our existence known, Lolo. You know that. The lycans played into our hands. Their actions let Flynn and the President cast Pures as the good guys, the protectors, and the lycans as the monsters. It worked—for a while.

"What we didn't anticipate was how continuing to blend with the normals would breed distrust among so many. It was like we were trying to hide. Sure, there are some of my kind who went public with what they are. But most of us who are in positions where public trust is so important haven't. So when these latest attacks happened, all the public knew was that paras had attacked their kind."

"So you decided to appoint yourself the goodwill ambassador for shapeshifters?" Humor laced the younger woman's voice.

Mac lifted a shoulder in a half-shrug.

"Lolo, when I started thinking about it, I realized I don't want my children growing up in a world where they have to fear letting people know who or what they are. I know there will always be some who fear us—just as there are those of my kind and yours who fear humans. But it's time we quit hiding in the shadows."

Especially as long as folks like Reed were out there trying to cause trouble between paras and humans.

"Has the Tribunal discussed it?"

Mac nodded. "It has, including your aunt and the other witches who sit on it."

For a moment, Murray didn't say anything. Then she laughed softly.

"Life is never dull when you're around, Mac."

She grinned. "Where would the fun be if it was?"

Mac relaxed and slowed to a stop at a red light. As she did, she considered the last few months. Finally, after years of waiting for the proverbial shoe to drop, it had. They might not have been prepared but they had responded quickly and effectively. Derek Reed would no longer be the boogie man they feared, wondering when he'd suddenly appear and what sort of damage he'd do in the process. Hopefully, the Tribunal would soon close the book on this sad chapter of shifter history.

One thing was certain, however. A new chapter was starting for Mac. Between a tween who was already shifting—and Mac so did not look forward to having a hormonal teenaged shifter in the house—taking on more duties with the Tribunal, including being its Enforcer, and taking a very public step out of the shadows, life would never be the same.

And how the hell was she supposed to forget the biggest surprise of all?

It turned out she and Elizabeth were more alike than any of them realized. Mac started shifting after Samuel Wilcox attacked her and tried to turn her so long ago. Elizabeth shifted for the first time less than two weeks ago.

To say that was a surprise is putting it mildly.

And, like her granddaughter, Elizabeth shifted into a black panther.

Life continued to throw curveballs. Fortunately, Mac was getting better at fielding them.

She hoped.

But damn, she'd really love to have a decade or two without any more "little surprises".

AUTHOR'S NOTE

I want to thank you for coming on this journey with me. When I wrote Nocturnal Origins, the first of Mackenzie Santos' adventures, I had no idea it would turn into a series, much less one that has gone on this long. Over the years, Mac has faced hardships and triumphs. She's grown even as she's had to face losses that came close to breaking her. With Jaguar Rising, Mac's life is changing once again. It's going to be fun seeing where events take her.

Mac and company will be back later this year. Keep an eye out for an announcement of her next book.

Now I have a favor to ask each of you. If you would take a few minutes and leave a rating or a review on Amazon, I'd appreciate it. The best form of promotion any writer has is word-of-mouth. In today's digital age, that happens through reviews on Amazon as well as mentions on social media. It would mean a great deal if you'd help spread the word.

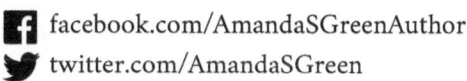

facebook.com/AmandaSGreenAuthor
twitter.com/AmandaSGreen

ALSO BY AMANDA S. GREEN

www.ingramcontent.com/pod-product-compliance
Lightning Source LLC
Chambersburg PA
CBHW020338180626
46812CB00001B/254